GROUPER'S LAWS

GROUPER'S LAWS

D. Philip Miller

Writer's Showcase
presented by *Writer's Digest*
San Jose New York Lincoln Shanghai

Grouper's Laws

All Rights Reserved © 2000 by D. Philip Miller

No part of this book may be reproduced or transmitted in any form or by any means, graphic, electronic, or mechanical, including photocopying, recording, taping, or by any information storage retrieval system, without the permission in writing from the publisher.

Writer's Showcase
presented by *Writer's Digest*
an imprint of iUniverse.com, Inc.

For information address:
iUniverse.com, Inc.
620 North 48th Street
Suite 201
Lincoln, NE 68504-3467
www.iuniverse.com

ISBN: 0-595-12902-1

Printed in the United States of America

For Penny the Pooh and the Cigar
for no particular reason.

Acknowledgements

"The Way You Look Tonight." Words and music by Jerome Kern and Dorothy Fields. ©Copyright 1936 Universal–Polygram International Publishing, Inc., a division of Universal Studios, Inc. (ASCAP) Copyright Renewed. International Copyright Secured. All Rights Reserved.

Chapter One

The singing of the tires was his executioner's song. In minutes, the faded yellow bus would disgorge him at his place of incarceration where, physically or spiritually (or both), he would suffer certain death from the unthinking actions of an unspeakable collection of geeks and goons. Blondie could envision no other outcome from his first day at Fenton High.

On rolled the bus, past copycat collections of brick ramblers and two-story colonials where runty trees and whiskers of grass fought for existence on burned over late-summer lawns. Look-alike homes for think-alike people, Blondie thought, most of them occupied by families fleeing Baltimore for a hoped-for taste of country living.

Blondie had begged his dad not to move to Fenton after he retired from the small Signal Corps base in Percy fifteen miles away. He'd stressed to him the importance of living someplace more sophisticated than Fenton—a place where people covered their mouths when they belched.

His dad hadn't found his comment amusing.

"People are the same everywhere," he'd said.

Maybe for adults. Not for kids. Every kid in Mayhew County knew Fenton's adolescents were the least civilized of all known teen rabble.

This morning, the evidence was indisputable. Stop after stop, they'd piled onto the bus—cretins of every form and in every costume imaginable. Long-necked boys in loose-fitting western shirts and blue jeans.

Pony-tailed girls in poodle skirts, with stick legs and braces on their teeth. Duck-tailed fatsos in stretched-out tee shirts. Aspiring harlots with pale lipstick and beehive hairdos.

The boys tripped each other getting onto the bus or shot each other the finger or farted or cleaned their ears with pencils. The girls giggled or gossiped or taunted the boys or stared out the window as if they weren't there at all. Could he possibly, Blondie considered with dismay, be genetically linked to creatures such as these?

Blondie sat by himself on the blood-red vinyl on one of the last seats toward the rear, staring at the graffiti scratched on the back of the seat in front of him. "J.S. LUVS R.L." "GO FLYERS" and the inevitable "FUCK YOU." For relief, he lowered his eyes, only to encounter on the rubber-grooved floor myriad deposits of chewing gum turned to stone, miniature hairballs, paper wads, pencil erasers and cigarette butts. And this was only the first day of school!

It was even more dismal than he'd contemplated. Again, Blondie felt his sense of betrayal well up inside. Why couldn't his parents have moved to Baltimore? At the very least, why couldn't his dad have bought a house near Percy so he could have finished high school with the kids he knew? So what if his dad had landed a job with the Fenton water district? There were other water districts, other jobs.

The day would get worse. He'd have to go to the office and meet the principal who would say something fatuous like, "It must be pretty difficult changing schools at the start of your senior year. But I suppose you're used to it, having grown up in the military."

Everyone always thought that. What did they know? Did they expect him to say, "Actually, it's pretty scary?" Did they expect him to give them that much of an edge?

The sun slanted through the dusty window onto his face, drawing him from his anxiety. Blondie loved the feel of sun on his face. Its rays were warm through the glass, though Blondie remembered the air's cold bite while he'd been waiting at his stop. He loved autumn: its crisp mornings, its turning leaves, its tinge of nostalgia. For a moment, he transported himself to another time, another place, where the coming of fall had been free from the threat of school.

An object flew to the front of the bus where it banged against the side of the driver's seat. The driver, a near dwarf of great girth, cast a malevolent glare to the back of the bus. He muttered something indecipherable and turned the wheel.

They entered a more established development where homes were constructed of sturdy fieldstone and lawns carpeted with a rich green shag. White-shuttered windows looked out upon summer zinnias and dahlias.

Spewing gravel, the bus rattled to a halt. Blondie's throat tightened. Each stop drew him nearer his doom. He'd never been able to think of anything beyond that first day in a new school, no matter how many times his family had moved—the awful staring of the students, the disgusting cooing of concerned teachers, his own overwhelming self-consciousness.

Blondie consoled himself with the thought that within eight hours he'd be back home again, eating dinner with his mom and dad. But it was a knowledge that held no emotional content and offered no solace. Emotionally, there was only that first moment, the first creeping caterpillar of a day in a new school when he was the magnetic pole for a thousand prying eyes.

This time, Blondie promised himself he would be ready. He would withdraw so far inside himself that faces would register no more than far-away clouds and voices no more than distant echoes.

Then *she* got on the bus. Into the midst of the riotous freak show walked a Madonna, the apotheosis of young womanhood. Her skin was pale as daybreak, her lips red as fire, her hair dark and shiny as a moonlit sea. She was slender, boyish—as he preferred—her movements lithe and unstudied.

Blondie's libido awakened with a fusillade of longing and lust, routing his first-day fears. He watched entranced as she approached him in a straight dark skirt, pink sweater, rolled-down socks and penny loafers, carrying a vinyl gym bag in the crimson-and-cream colors of Fenton High School.

As she drew near, he realized the seat next to him was vacant. My god, was she going to sit beside him! What would he say? He wasn't prepared. His face burst into flames. His tongue flopped once or twice inside his mouth as he tried to form words to cast her way, then turned as fat and lifeless as a dead fish. Blondie mustered all his will and forced his mouth into a rictus-like smile that was wasted on the angel's back as she seated herself two rows ahead. A homely girl with pigtails who'd followed her onto the bus plopped down beside her.

Blondie glanced around, expecting a stir from the young males on the bus, an echo of the tremor that had shaken him. They were as busily committing perverted acts upon each other as before. What was wrong with them? Didn't they realize a queen had just boarded the bus? No wonder they were so lost.

A raucous grinding of gears and a sudden jolt knocked Blondie from his reverie. He looked out the window and his skin froze. They were here: the Big House!

Blocking the horizon was an endless gray facade. It stared at him with a hundred eyes of glass. And behind each of those unblinking squares would be scores of smaller eyes ready to examine his every pore, his every move.

Blondie sat paralyzed as the unruly horde massed for the exit. He stared at the stainless steel letters that named his prison: F-E-N-T-O-N-H-I-G-H-S-C-H-O-O-L. His mind added the only possible subtext: *Nothing inspiring ever has—or ever will—happen here.*

When he glanced around again, his Venus was gone, swallowed by the multitude that had erupted from the massed army of buses. A fearball as cold and compact as a dead star settled in the bottom of Blondie's stomach. The moment of truth had arrived.

Chapter Two

Like toothpaste oozing from a tube, Blondie squeezed his lean body through the frenzied throng and off the bus, wishing all the while he were more nondescript. At six foot three, he towered over his new schoolmates, his corn-silk hair floating like a whitecap above waves of brown and black scalps. Why did he have to sport hair like an albino's? Why couldn't he ever gain any weight? Why did he have to look like a fucking Ichabod Crane?

He avoided looking at himself in the glass panes of the school entranceway. He didn't want to be confronted by the sight of his prominent ears, ready for lift-off, and his Adam's apple, ready to burst through his throat. For years, he'd pushed his ears closer to his skull and his larynx back into his neck. All he'd ever gained for his efforts were red ears and a sore throat.

Blondie kept his chin up and his eyes dead ahead as he bobbed through the stream of untouchables thrashing their way through the double doorway. He wasn't going in looking at the ground. He would maintain his dignity no matter what horrors the day offered up.

Remember to breathe. Pace yourself. Don't trip or you'll go under. Yet, within yards of the doorway, the milling crowd divided and dispersed like runoff from a spring shower. Soon, he was nearly alone, staring down long corridors of shiny black linoleum flanked by gunmetal lockers.

He was supposed to report to the principal's office, but which way was it? Every hallway looked the same. Blondie stopped to get his bearings and was launched from his spot by a sudden impact from behind.

"Kee-rist, don't just fucking stop in the middle of the hall," a voice growled.

Blondie turned to face a squint-eyed youth in an embroidered denim shirt. He was leaning toward Blondie and glaring at him as if ready for a fight.

"I'm sorry," Blondie said, immediately regretting it. What had he done wrong?

The boy was a good four inches shorter than Blondie and even thinner, his neck thin and crooked as a vulture's. But his reddish arms were hard, as were his angular face and colorless eyes.

"He's staring at you, Buford," said a nearby fat kid in coveralls.

The hard-faced boy ignored his companion and continued staring at Blondie. The boy's eyes bored into his self-confidence like augers. His legs began to liquefy.

"You know what he reminds me of, Buford?" the chubby one called to his friend. "A giraffe. A white giraffe." He started to giggle.

Buford's eyes never wavered. Blondie returned his gaze though his heart was racing. Seconds congealed into minutes, then eons, as the boy continued to stare. To break the unbearable tension, Blondie asked: "Did you know that monkeys stare at each other as a way of establishing dominance?"

Later, he thought maybe he'd meant it as a joke.

"I think the giraffe just called you a monkey," the fat kid said.

Buford's eyes narrowed even further and his body shifted as if he were going to strike out, but whatever his intention, it was cut short by a shout from down the hall.

"Is there a problem, Barnwell? Aren't you supposed to be in class?"

Blondie, who'd been suffering the dread thought that others were watching the mortifying confrontation, unlocked his eyes from Buford's and looked around. The hallway was empty except for a man approaching in a rumpled brown suit.

He was a big man with a big face and a powerful ambling gait.

"It's the Bear," the fat boy whispered to his friend.

"Why aren't you ever where you're supposed to be, Barnwell?" the man demanded of Blondie's tormentor. His eyes looked like they'd just been stropped.

"This jerk ran into me."

The big man ignored the boy's challenging tone.

"It's amazing how many people run into you," he said to Buford with an air of tedium. "Now, get on to class."

"I'll remember this," the hothead whispered to Blondie as he passed.

The man now turned to Blondie. He was as tall as Blondie, but much heavier. Although his anger seemed to have passed, Blondie found him intimidating.

"Why aren't you in class?" he asked in a surprisingly soft voice.

"This is my first day. I'm supposed to see the principal."

"Well, you're going the wrong way." The man's annoyance returned.

Blondie wanted to turn and head right back out the door. His classmates at Percy had been right. Kids at Fenton were animals—and so were the staff. What had the skinny kid called this hulk? The Bear?

"Follow me," the man ordered.

Resisting his impulse to flee, Blondie followed him down a series of corridors to a door bearing, in gilt letters, the word "Office." Once inside, the big man delivered Blondie to a frail gray-haired man with baggy eyes and strolled away.

"Thank you, Mr. Bearzinsky," the tired-eyed man mumbled after him. "Name?"

"Reimer," he stammered.

"Mrs. Spritz, can you find a file for a Reimer?" the man wheezed.

Blondie looked at the hand-lettered wood sign on his desk: Jacob Clapper. Blondie assumed he was the principal, although he seemed much less powerful than the man who'd brought him here.

Genie-like, a slender frizzy-haired woman appeared, carrying a beige paperboard file in her hand. She flitted about the small room like a hummingbird until Clapper held out his hand. Then she dropped the file into his palm and zipped away.

Clapper opened the folder and took out a single sheet of paper. He looked at it for several minutes before murmuring, "Bernard Reimer."

Blondie twisted in his chair. God, he hated that name. It had to be the all-time nerd name. Luckily, since seventh grade, everyone but his parents and his teachers had called him Blondie.

Clapper cleared his throat and gave him what Blondie supposed he intended as a fatherly look.

"It must be difficult changing schools between your junior and senior years," Clapper said, mustering a heavy-lidded look of concern, while failing to suppress a yawn.

Blondie set his jaw and fixed his gaze on the balding crown of Clapper's head.

Clapper coughed. A faint line of spittle appeared between his lips.

Don't choke on me, Blondie silently begged.

Clapper began reciting a litany of school rules. As he went on, his voice wound down like an unplugged phonograph.

"...dressed appropriately and on time," Clapper intoned as he ground to a halt. His head slumped forward and his eyelids drooped to half-mast. Just when Blondie feared the old man had expired, he drew one more breath and exhaled the name of his assistant.

The bird-lady appeared instantly as if she'd been counting down to Clapper's finale. She towed Blondie from the office and escorted him down the hall. Ahead was a windowed green door. A muffled pandemonium emanated from it. To Blondie, the sound was a composite of all the fierce epithets and indignant protests of sinners cast into hell. *Don't open that door, lady.* He was sure a geyser of gremlins and goblins would explode from the room.

As they drew nearer, however, the sound from the room began to diminish and the harsh tapping from Mrs. Spritz' wooden-heeled shoes grew louder and louder. By the time she opened the door, shoving Blondie forward by the small of his back, the room was hushed and every eye was upon him.

Blondie's throat constricted and his stomach rumbled so loudly he was sure it was audible to all. His eyes scanned the room looking for danger, each new face contending for his attention. One arrested his gaze.

It was a face such as he'd never seen on a head such as he'd never seen—the face of a boy-man on a head squeezed from his collarbone, growing larger as it progressed upward. Except for his thick lips and protruding eyes, the boy's face would have been smooth as a balloon. His nose was almost nonexistent, his ears small and flat, his dark hair parted in the middle and plastered onto his head. His face was pinkish-purple, as if from the pressure of whatever filled his head.

This boy-man looked at him. There was no threat to his gaze, no curiosity, no surprise. It was as if he were looking at someone he'd seen many times before.

"Take a seat," the teacher ordered. Blondie looked her way and was astounded to see a woman as tall as he, an Amazon with equine features. He figured she must have escaped from one of the horse farms that surrounded Fenton.

The woman arched her brows and Blondie realized he hadn't moved. He followed the angle of her inclined head and began making his way toward the back of the room. He felt the eyes of at least two dozen onlookers scraping his face and setting it ablaze.

He banged his knee into the sharp edge of one of the metal desks as he pinched his way down the narrow aisle. He winced, but uttered no sound. To cry out would surely call his classmates down upon him. He fell into an empty seat at the back of the room.

A small fellow in the next desk looked his way. His face was broad and concave as if a giant had pressed his thumb into it. Hair the color and texture of straw spiked at all angles from the flat crown of his head like pick-up sticks. Just Blondie's luck—he'd been seated beside a fucking troll!

For a long while, Blondie stared down at his lap, willing the teacher to speak, to break the awful stillness his arrival had caused. Finally, she did, and Blondie felt safe enough to open his beige spiral notebook and write at the top of the first page: "Fenton High (ugh!). Trigonometry. September 6, 1961. Miss Spalding."

The boy next to him leaned over.

"She's a real c-cunt," he said in a high voice that carried.

Nervous titters erupted nearby. Blondie plastered his eyes to the blank page in front of him.

"Caldane!" Miss Spalding's voice was sharp and sudden like a rifle shot. "Shut your yap."

Blondie became aware of a deep rasping sound a few desks away. It came from the bigheaded boy. He was trying to stifle his mirth.

The teacher glared at him for a moment and then her face split into a gap-toothed grin. Blondie was astounded. The witch seemed amused by the bigheaded boy. No, more than that...there was a trace of affection in her face. The bigheaded boy never changed expression, though. He just sat Buddha-like, motionless except for a faint quivering in his large torso.

Miss Spalding began discussing an arcane principle of trigonometry and the class returned to the buzzing anarchy Blondie had heard from the hall. Being an outsider and not privy to the undercurrent of excited chatter, Blondie did his best to follow her convoluted logic. Big-boned as she was, Miss Spalding now and then tossed her head in a way that was almost coquettish.

Just before the bell, Caldane leaned toward Blondie again and whispered, "Her l-lover was k-killed in a motorcycle accident."

Civics class proved a welcome contrast. The kids seemed normal and the teacher, Miss Darlington, was an attractive, auburn-haired young woman with a confident and cheery manner and freckles across the bridge of her nose. A couple times, she directed a warm smile at Blondie as if trying to put him at ease. He relaxed his guard a smidgen. Perhaps not everyone at Fenton High ate their young.

It wasn't until fourth-period English that Blondie saw either the straw-haired kid or the bigheaded boy again. In the meantime, he'd forced some coagulated spaghetti and wilted lettuce into his stomach in the school's correctional-style cafeteria. He was still choking back indigestion as he recorded the date and "English…Mrs. Buckley."

When the latter, a large-rumped lady with buckteeth, entered the room, a ferocious belch erupted from the rear of the room. Blondie turned quickly, but saw only the bigheaded boy gazing serenely toward the blackboard.

Mrs. Buckley shook with suppressed rage.

"It's you, Whipple. I know it's you," she hissed at him.

So that was the strange fellow's name, Blondie thought. He waited to see what he would do. Whipple didn't acknowledge her words with even a shift of his eyes. Unable to evoke any response from him, Buckley stomped to her desk, where she began furiously arranging papers and pencils.

As the class proceeded, Blondie perceived that Whipple had a kind of retinue. To his left sat a handsome young man with a fluid body and longish dark hair. His face was etched into the delicate features of a Byron—high cheekbones, aquiline nose, cupid's-bow lips. He seemed familiar. Blondie recalled that he'd glimpsed him in the rear of his third-period chemistry class.

To the boy-man's right was a compact little fellow with a mop of hair shaped like an inverted bowl. Beside him was a muscular kid with a flat top, and behind him was Caldane from first period. Blondie could tell they were a group, although they seemed to have nothing in common.

Throughout the period—as Buckley droned on about the importance of Chaucer to the development of modern English literature—a slight hum periodically arose from their midst. Other students occasionally glanced toward them as if expecting something to happen. Blondie caught their sense of anticipation. But what did they do? What were they known for?

The bigheaded boy maintained his stoic pose until the bell rang. His comrades had done no more than mutter to each other under their breaths from time to time, leaving Blondie's undefined expectation unfulfilled.

As he left class, Blondie realized he felt drained. He was glad only P.E. and study hall remained. Phys-ed brought no more than the slight discomfort of being new, since they engaged in no physical activity and hence Blondie could postpone until another day the embarrassment of a group shower. Study hall was a snap, with no teacher at all. An occasional visit by the Bear was sufficient to keep the peace.

When the last bell of the day rang, the promise of life outside Fenton High revived him and Blondie hurried to his bus. Halfway home, he remembered the dark-haired girl he'd seen that morning. He looked around and spied the homely girl with pigtails sitting by herself. His angel was nowhere in sight.

Chapter Three

The bus deposited Blondie at the end of Friar Lane, just across the street from the dirt embankment that marked the edge of Heritage Acres, the new development where they lived. Blondie flew across the road and clambered up the bank to his back yard, still more dirt than grass, then cut across a corner of Mr. Grafton's yard to their house—a colonial-style tri-level, the bottom half brick, the top aluminum siding. Six smallish square columns—the "colonial" part, Blondie guessed—supported the portico above the front porch. In his estimate, their house lacked originality and grandeur, either unforgivable in his pantheon of values.

Blondie hurried through the living room, vaguely noting the burl coffee table with its sprout of dried flowers, the hutch peopled with Hummel figurines, his mother's paintings on the wall. He was in a panic to reach the sanctity of his upstairs room and relieve himself of the almost unbearable tension he felt inside. It had been a hard day, he told himself, but he knew that wasn't the cause. It was the same insistent force that had driven him since he was thirteen: *sperm pressure.*

Blondie sprinted up the gray-carpeted stairs to his bedroom. He smiled in anticipation as he reached down and pulled out the bottom drawer of his dresser. There, hidden between two sweaters was the secret treasure of his life: a 1959 calendar of nude pinups he'd managed to smuggle out of France.

His favorite was a frontal shot of a young lady on a red satin sheet. She had her legs squeezed together so you couldn't see her pubic hair—or maybe it had been airbrushed away. All in all, it was a photo a guy could get off with. And he had. But just as he wrapped his eager fingers around the calendar, Blondie heard a car door slam. His mother, a first-grade teacher, must have returned from school early!

Blondie stuffed the calendar back beneath the sweaters, skinning his knuckles against the top of the drawer. His heart was knocking against his ribcage like a blind bird.

Blondie waited for his mom to barge into the house the way she usually did. The house remained silent. Blondie walked over to his window. A dark car sat in the carport of the house next door. The noise must have been caused by their new neighbors, the ones they'd yet to meet...or even see.

His passion routed, Blondie tramped back down the stairs and out the back door to the utility shed. Lurking inside were his "thunder sticks," the two-year-old set of golf clubs his parents had won at bingo, and a garbage sack full of shag balls. Blondie grabbed a pitching wedge and the sack and headed for one of the few patches of grass in the back yard.

He dribbled the balls out of the bag, isolating one with the club head. Taking careful aim at a fledgling ash tree, Blondie imagined himself Arnold Palmer at Cherry Hills in the summer of 1960, charging from behind. He just needed to flip the ball up near the flag and victory was his.

Blondie chunked the ball about three feet, digging a divot in their just-seeded lawn.

Damn!

His next shot plopped into the ground halfway to the ash. Pathetic. Blondie pulled another ball from the cluster.

"Head down, nice smooth swing," he told himself.

B-z-z-zing. The club caught the ball on the hosel, shanking it low to the right and long. It skittered across the string that marked their property line into the next yard. Blondie stared at the rebellious sphere for a moment before marching after it. He looked down to avoid tripping over the string and, when he raised his eyes, he saw that a large black boot settling over the ball. Blondie's gaze slowly rose from the boot to a heavy thigh, then upward to the huge torso and head of a Minotaur! It had to be. No human could be so menacing.

A scowl etched the beast's boxlike face, while his serpent eyes scoured Blondie face. Blondie's stomach flipped. He remembered the name he'd seen on the mailbox next door: Potter.

Mustering all his nerve, Blondie started to ask for his ball back, but no sound came from his throat. He decided it was just as well. The man didn't seem the type to grant favors.

"Sorry," Blondie managed to mumble. As he turned away, he imagined he saw the beginning of a smile crease the ogre's taut mouth. Bearing the dead weight of the man's gaze upon his back, Blondie gathered up his wedge and sack of balls and put them back in the shed.

"What a wimp," he thought as he entered the house. "I should have kicked his ass." Then he visualized the man again. "No way. No fucking way."

Blondie just got back to his room when he heard a loud bang and felt the wall shake. His mom had arrived. He wished she weren't always so boisterous. Being big was no excuse. She called to make sure he was home and he answered, but he remained in his room. He wasn't ready to face her yet.

Shortly, Blondie heard his dad come in. How much more softly he entered, almost as if he were sneaking in. He briefly considered telling his dad about the man next door. But what good would it do? His dad wouldn't do anything. He'd just tell Blondie he shouldn't have hit his ball in the guy's yard—"turn the other cheek" and all that crap.

Blondie wondered how he could ever have been a soldier—not that he'd been a real soldier. Only a telecommunications engineer. The only thing he'd commanded had been a brigade of blueprints. Blondie thought of his father and how he trimmed his nails and nose hair every day, of the pomade he used to keep his hair down, of his overall prissiness. No, his dad would never confront a man like Potter.

He was reading the newspaper at the kitchen table when Blondie answered his mom's call to dinner. He noted the thinning brown hair on his dad's egg-shaped pate, the faint moustache above his thin lips, and the wisps of hair poking from his pinched nose. Blondie had trouble accepting him as his father—he was too small, too old…too *insignificant*.

Then again, maybe he wasn't his father. Maybe he'd been adopted. After all, his parents both had brown hair and his was snow white. How could they explain that?

"That Maris, he sure is something," his dad said to him. "I think he's going to do it."

"I don't think so. No one will ever beat the Babe."

"How did things go today, Bernard?" his mom asked, as she placed a roast on the table.

"Just fine," he lied. How could he tell her about the angel on the bus, the jerk in the hallway, the bigheaded boy? If he said anything, he'd spend the next half hour explaining what he meant.

"No problems?" his dad asked as he sat down.

"I said fine, didn't I?"

"You don't have to be testy, Bernard," his mom scolded.

"It was my first day of school, that's all."

"Well, it was my first day at school too, but I'm not being grouchy."

His mother carved the meat, her heavy arms wielding the knife with authority, her eyes intent, dark as the seared skin of the roast. Flecks of gray sprinkled her chestnut hair. His mom was growing old. The thought made Blondie nervous.

"What should we watch tonight, Francis?" she asked his dad.

"Whatever you want, dear," he answered. He kept reading his paper.

Was this the way marriages were? If so, Blondie decided, he would never get married. What he wanted from a woman was passion. He thought again of the girl on the bus. Was she the passionate type? He was sure she could be with the right guy, someone who would be sensitive to her needs. Someone like him.

"Did you hear me, Bernard?"

"What?"

"I asked if you wanted more meat," his mom repeated.

"No, no, I'm fine."

After dinner, he watched *Cheyenne* and *The Rifleman* and later *The Andy Griffith Show* with his folks. His dad loved all that small town stuff—Mayberry and Aunt Bea—probably because he'd grown up in a small town in South Carolina, a place where everyone knew everyone else. The kind of place where everyone counted, where everyone developed roots. Not like his own childhood, being jerked somewhere new every time his dad had been reassigned.

When Blondie returned to his room, moonlight was streaming in the window, turning the gauzy curtain into a silver veil. Blondie undressed in the dark, leaving only his skivvies. Then, feeling his way in the faint light, he placed a worn record on his small phonograph. Soon, he was listening to the soft, lilting strains of "Theme from a Summer Place."

For a moment, his parents' voices broke through his musical cocoon. Their tones were sharp, cutting. Blondie feared they were going to get into an argument. They'd been doing that a lot lately. His dad had told him it was because his mom was going through "the change of life," but the only thing new about their quarreling was the frequency.

Blondie was relieved when the house fell silent again. He started the phonograph one more time, curled under his covers and envisioned Sandra Dee and Troy Donahue, the two young lovers from the movie, fighting to be together against their parents and society. Yes, that was how it should be.

He thought again of the dark-haired beauty from the bus. He imagined kissing her and then removing her clothes. He could picture her lying naked on the bed, shy and modest. She would be a virgin, of course.

"It's all right," he'd say to her. "I'll be gentle."

He felt a stirring in his loins, then a tugging at his underpants. He found himself reaching for his one constant friend.

"Forgive me, please forgive me," Blondie whispered to his angel's phantom image as he transported himself into a spasm of bliss.

Chapter Four

After four days at Fenton High, Blondie had found no evidence of higher life forms within the student body. His schoolmates' predilections lay in horsing around in the halls, acting up in class, and, except for occasional rude stares, ignoring him. A notable exception was the rawboned storm trooper he'd encountered his first day. Barnwell had passed Blondie a couple times in the corridor, thankfully always when it was crowded, and although he'd said nothing, his look had told Blondie he hadn't forgotten. The only one who actually talked to him was the runt with the stutter—the Caldane kid—and Blondie was pretty sure he didn't want to be identified with him.

The school day's only relief was an occasional glimpse of *her*, the nameless dark-haired girl. Several times, he'd seen her walking with the pigtailed girl who rode his bus. She was usually wearing a solid-colored sweater with a straight skirt and bobby socks. Nothing fancy—your basic female high schooler's outfit. But that didn't matter. She was beautiful. At a certain angle, her eyes were almost violet. In a certain light, her skin was almost translucent. In a certain mood, her cheeks revealed the tiniest of dimples.

Blondie wondered about the other girl, too. He couldn't say she was totally ugly, but she was close enough to be in danger. What could she possibly have in common with his Madonna? Was it what his mom had told him once—that pretty girls always surrounded themselves with plain ones so they'd stand out even more?

Once, he'd passed close by her in the hall. He'd managed to fire off a smile, a wasted expression left hanging like a holograph in the air behind her retreating form. He told himself she probably hadn't seen him. He knew it didn't matter. Even if he weren't painfully awkward around girls, even if she'd been in one of his classes where he might have had a pretext for speaking to her, he'd still be an out-of-towner, a newcomer. In the harsh world of high school society, she was as remote from him as the farthest star.

His isolation added to his despair. He needed to connect with someone, *anyone*. Thus, he was secretly grateful when Jerry Caldane approached him at Friday lunch holding a tray of the cafeteria's strange-looking offerings.

"M-mind if I j-join you?"

"Why not?"

Blondie shrugged.

"You're n-new here."

Blondie contemplated a smart retort, but nodded instead.

"Sometimes it's h-hard to be accepted even wh-when you're not n-new."

It was the first personal comment anyone had made to him. Blondie looked at Jerry and appraised him coolly. He detected a faint strawberry mark under his left eye, like the remains of a welt. He hadn't noticed it before.

Jerry's face reddened under Blondie's gaze.

"What're you trying to say?" Blondie asked, keeping his expression neutral.

"B-being in a group. If y-you're n-not in one of the groups here, y-you're n-nobody."

"I don't want to be in a group," Blondie said. "I don't need any group."

He must've spoken more forcefully than he'd intended, because Jerry clammed up. He caught him looking toward a table full of guys halfway across the room. It was the group that sat together in fourth-period

English. Whipple's bulbous head protruded from the mass like a polyp. Except for him, Blondie knew none of their names, except he'd once heard the muscular one with the flat top called "Brick."

"Real shit," Blondie said.

"Wh-what?"

"This..." Blondie held out his fork, "what they call food."

"Oh yeah," Jerry quickly agreed. "R-real shit."

"Who're they?" Blondie asked, inclining his head toward the table Jerry had been watching.

"A b-bunch of assholes."

"That's what I thought."

"Hey, you better w-watch what you say."

Blondie was surprised at Jerry's sudden shift of sentiment. He could be a fierce little mouse.

"I thought you didn't like them."

"They're okay."

"Are you one of them?"

"S-sorta."

What did Caldane mean by that? Blondie didn't want to set him off again by asking.

"Is that big guy their leader?"

"Who? Gr-grouper?"

"Grouper? I thought his name was Whipple."

Caldane snickered.

"Why do they call him Grouper?"

Caldane looked at Blondie as if he were an idiot.

"After the fish?" Blondie realized he was losing face. "So who are they?"

"They're the B and F Club."

"What the hell is that?"

"Just a b-bunch of assholes," Jerry replied, returning to his earlier refrain. "Stuck up, too. They think th-their sh-shit doesn't smell."

"B and F?"

"Brick and F-feller. Feller's that g-guy with the long c-curly hair. H-he started the Club."

Blondie scrutinized the young man with the Byronic air. He did appear to be the leader, talking and gesturing and drawing smiles in return. Blondie found his manner—graceful and self-assured—highly appealing.

"What does this B and F Club do?"

"Raises h-hell," Jerry answered proudly.

"How do you get into this club?"

"Gr-grouper says it's a matter of class. H-he says if you have any you c-can't belong."

"There must be more to it than that."

"W-well, you c-can't be a b-billy."

"A billy?"

"You know…a hillbilly."

"You mean like the Hatfields and McCoys?" Blondie was mystified.

"Gr-grouper says they've come d-down from the h-hills and th-threaten all of Western c-civilization."

What was Caldane talking about?

"Gr-grouper says that you can t-tell billies by a three part test. F-first, do they like triple f-feature Elvis Presley m-movies? S-second, do they think g-getting into a f-fistfight in a tavern is the b-best way to spend a Friday n-night? And m-most important, do they hang things f-from their dashboard mirrors?"

"What kind of things?"

"F-fuzzy dice. G-girls g-garter belts. You know."

Suddenly, what Caldane was saying began to make sense.

"These people—the ones you call billies—do they like to pick on people for no reason?"

"Y-you b-bet. B-billies are b-bullies."

Caldane smiled at his cleverness.

"Have you heard of a kid named Buford?" Blondie asked, trying to sound as casual as possible.

"B-buford B-barnwell? That t-turdbag. Are you k-kidding? Grouper calls him the k-king of the b-billies. Why?"

"I heard he was a tough guy, that's all."

"M-maybe h-he thinks h-he is," Jerry said defiantly.

"You wouldn't be afraid of him then?" Blondie asked. He noted how thin Caldane's arms were—not much thicker than hockey sticks—and how his head barely reached Blondie's shoulders.

"N-no way."

"Good, next time I see Barnwell, I'm going to let him know there's one guy here who isn't afraid of him."

"H-hey. Wh-what are you trying to d-do? N-nobody s-said anything about t-telling B-barnwell anything."

Blondie chided himself for yanking Jerry's chain.

"How about the big fellow?" Blondie asked, nodding toward Whipple. "Could he take Barnwell?"

"The Gr-grouper? Grouper's not a f-fighter. He wouldn't f-fight anyone."

Blondie was disappointed. The guy was big enough.

"B-brick could whip Buford's ass, though," Caldane said.

Blondie scoped him out. His physique was neo-fireplug—no neck, just square head on square shoulders.

"Would he, though?" Blondie asked.

"Probably n-not. B-brick mostly d-doesn't get involved in d-disputes. H-he doesn't like to be b-bothered."

Blondie was disappointed. He wanted revenge—and, he realized a trifle shamefully, he wanted someone else to get it for him.

There was only one guy left, the mop-haired fellow next to Brick. He appeared disinterested in the furor around him, scanning the lunchroom from beneath his thick bangs. Though short, his body seemed solid.

"How about the guy with the funny haircut?" Blondie asked.

"D-dispatch? I d-doubt it. He can be shitty s-sometimes, though."

"Why do they call him Dispatch?"

"F-feller says it's b-because h-he can n-never get a second date with any girl."

Blondie gave him a quizzical look.

"H-he always g-goes for all the c-cookies on the f-first date. He d-dispatches them, g-get it?"

Blondie thought it was a stretch.

"Do all of them have nicknames?" he asked Jerry.

"All except F-feller. He says h-he's too c-cool to need one."

Blondie looked at Feller again. He could imagine him saying that.

"How about you?"

A sour look crossed Caldane's face. His jaws clenched. Blondie could tell he'd hit a nerve, so he eased off.

"This Barnwell guy. How come I don't see him in any of our classes? Isn't he a senior?"

"H-he's a senior all right, b-but he's not r-real bright. H-he's vocational. You kn-know, shop and auto mechanics…courses like that."

"Are there many billies here?" Blondie asked, returning to their previous topic.

"Y-yes."

"Are they one of the groups you mentioned?"

"Th-they're not a gr-group. At least, n-not l-like the others. Gr-grouper says th-they're a subspecies of Homo Sapiens and n-not to be c-confused with real p-people."

According to Jerry, the "real" groups were the jocks (athletes), the pols (student leaders), the brains (intellectuals), and the chops (cheerleaders).

"Where does this B and F Club fit into the scheme of things."

"Feller says w-we're the f-free spirits, the unconventional ones. The Grouper says w-we're just misfits."

Blondie laughed, while noting Jerry's inclusion of himself in the club.

"At least there's one honest man among the group."

"Br-brick doesn't like him to s-say that. He t-told him to c-cut it out."

"So why are you so pissed off? You seem proud to be associated with them."

Caldane's face reddened.

"F-feller says I'm j-just a pledge. That's wh-why I don't have a nickname. F-feller's the club p-poet, the n-namer of n-names. H-he says I haven't d-done anything n-noteworthy enough to qualify for full membership."

"Like what?"

"W-well, D-d-dispatch got in for g-getting caught w-with his hand up a g-girl's skirt in church. By the priest. And Br-brick got in for p-pissing in the f-football c-coach's shoes."

"Noteworthy accomplishments, to be sure," Blondie commented dryly. "What did Grouper do?"

"Gr-grouper never h-had to do anything. F-feller says h-he's a c-curiosity the Club n-needs."

The bell rang and the cafeteria erupted into a stampede of gangly adolescents. Caldane followed Blondie to fourth-period English and took the seat next to him, displacing a slight kid with glasses, braces and pimples.

Blondie was beginning to find Caldane's company tiresome, but he wasn't about to push him away. He viewed him as a potential link to the mysterious B & F Club, and, much as it sounded juvenile from Jerry's description, it sounded like one group he might stand a chance of joining.

This afternoon, Mrs. Buckley—Caldane called her "Bucky" because of her large front teeth—spent almost the whole period deploring the lack of recognition Alexander Pope had been accorded by literary historians.

"He's every bit as important as Shakespeare," she concluded, staring out at the class, daring someone to dispute her. She then assigned the class a chapter on Pope as homework for the weekend.

The only noteworthy occurrence in Buckley's class, in Blondie's view, was when the Grouper looked over at him just before the bell and gave him a wink. Blondie realized he'd been acknowledged and, even though he didn't know what he'd been acknowledged as or for, he took it as a good sign.

Again, Caldane followed him from class, seemingly intent on forging an alliance with him.

A familiar motion snagged Blondie's eye and his brain zoomed to red alert. Coming straight for them was his dark-haired idol and her pigtailed friend. A tremor pulsed through his body, wobbling his legs. He willed them to stop shaking and forced himself to hold his chin up. *Stand tall, walk proud, act as if you don't even see her.*

Blondie remembered Caldane. How could he be cool with Caldane by his side? He moved a step away, so she might think he was walking alone.

"Wh-what are you d-doing?" Caldane asked.

That ruined it. She must have seen Caldane talking to him. She'd think they were buddies. Oh God!

As soon as they'd passed, Blondie asked Caldane as casually as he could who she was.

"W-which one?"

"That dark-haired girl." Blondie gestured with his head.

"T-tammy H-hollander?"

So that was her name.

"Who was she with?"

"Ph-phyllis Scarff. Why?"

"I don't remember seeing them around."

"They're j-just j-juniors. That's why."

Caldane gave him a suspicious look.

"You're n-not interested in th-them, are y-you?"

Them? Certainly not *them*. Was Caldane brain-dead?

"No, just curious. The Hollander girl is kinda cute."

Caldane looked back.

"Y-yeah, I g-guess. But she's pretty flat ch-chested."

Blondie barely managed to stifle his outrage. Where did this twerp get the nerve to judge his queen? So what if she didn't have big tits? He didn't like big-breasted girls. They were too mature or motherly or female or something.

The day slid to its end, with only the humiliation of his first group shower in P.E.—what could be worse than a bunch of naked guys all standing around subtly comparing peckers?—to interrupt its otherwise unremarkable course.

It was incredible! He'd done it. He'd survived a whole week at Fenton High. Of course, there were thirty-eight left. But he wasn't going to dwell on that. He'd been sprung for the weekend.

Chapter Five

By eight, Blondie paced his room like a caged tiger, periodically pressing his face against the windowpane. Now and then, cars passed beyond the streetlights at the end of their cul-de-sac, stealing from the development like panthers. He imagined them filled with guys and girls his age, off to evenings of pleasure beyond description.

It was Friday night. The whole weekend loomed before him like a promise and he had nowhere to go. He had no friends. He had no hangout. He had no girl.

He'd *never* had a girlfriend. He'd made out with a couple girls, but he had never gone with any. It was his looks. He knew it was. He was too boyish, too wholesome, too clean. He craved a rugged jaw and cleft chin like Kirk Douglas. Or a dark shadow of whiskers like Humphrey Bogart. Any mark or feature that would say he'd been around, that he was a man of substance, that he wasn't to be trifled with. Instead, his face was as smooth and white as an egg, his hair fine as swan's down, his eyes as powder-blue as a spring sky.

"He who blooms last blooms best," his mom had told him once. In Blondie's experience, it was just the opposite. The guys who grew muscles first, whose voices changed first, who shaved first, got the girls. Girls wanted a guy who was *mature*. It didn't matter if he had mattress ticking between his ears or if he sweated like a fat man at a free dance.

Blondie turned off the light and lay back on his bed in despair. He wanted—he needed—someone to love. He caressed the pillow beside his head. He could be loving. He could be gentle. He knew it. All he needed was someone worthy of what he had to offer. Someone beautiful.

"Bernard, what have you been doing up there?" his mom asked him when he went back downstairs. She was across the living room rearranging the figurines in her hutch.

"Just thinking," he said, as he walked over to her.

"Thinking about what?"

"You know…just stuff."

Christ, why was she quizzing him?

"I think something's bothering you. Tell me what it is."

She sat down on the divan and patted the seat next to her.

He wasn't about to sit down next to her. He wasn't a little boy. But he could use some consolation.

"I'm bored," he said.

"Well then, why don't you go down and watch television with your dad."

"That's not what I need."

His mom's large mouth rounded into a sympathetic pout.

"I know. It's difficult starting over, making new friends."

"It's not about friends," he blurted, before he could stop himself.

"What then?"

Her dark eyes warmed with concern.

"Is it a girl?" she queried.

He couldn't tell her, could he? That would be just too dumb.

"More like the lack of one," he admitted.

His mom chuckled.

"Your day will come," she said.

"Yeah, like when? I'm already a senior and I've never had a girlfriend."

"How about that Susan Feldman you dated last year?"

Blondie groaned. He'd taken the little pest to the movies twice because he'd been desperate for company. All she'd done was talk about clothes and makeup and stuff like that.

"I'm just too weird-looking."

"Why Bernard, you're a nice-looking boy." Although he knew mothers were duty-bound to say such things, he liked hearing it anyway. "You just need a little more confidence when it comes to girls."

O-o-o-h, why had she added that? What if it wasn't his looks? What if he just didn't have enough confidence? That would be even worse. It would make his loneliness his own fault.

"Francis told me there was a time when he thought he would never have a girlfriend either," his mom said. "And now look, we've been married almost 18 years."

She was comparing him with his dad? That was supposed to buck him up? His dad was so square he wore white socks to work. He couldn't imagine him ever romancing anyone, including his mom.

"Go on, Blondie, go down and watch TV with Francis. It'll cheer you up."

"Nah, I think I'll read."

Soon he found himself back on his bed, contemplating his sorry state. He bet no one in the B and F Club was lying around by himself on a Friday night. Even if they didn't all have girls, they had each other. That was more than he had.

* * * * * * * *

Schizzt...schizzt...schizzt. Jesus, what kind of nut was making so much noise so early on a Saturday morning? Blondie stomped to his window. The day was clear and the sun was already halfway up the sky. Blondie could see no one. *Schizzt...schizzt...schizzt.* There it was again, coming from the back of the house.

Blondie opened his door and strolled across the hall in his pajamas. His parents' room was empty, bed already made. What time was it?

From the rear window, Blondie saw Mr. Potter stabbing a shovel into the gravely earth. Behind him were small burlap sacks crowned with thorny branches. *Roses.* Potter was planting a rose hedge between their two yards. Just because he'd hit a golf ball into his yard? It was possible, of course, that Potter just liked roses, but he hardly seemed the type.

Blondie couldn't take his eyes off Potter's enormous back as he placed each rose bush into the ground, or the size of his forearms. What did he do for a living? Shoe horses?

Potter turned his head toward his house. Blondie followed his gaze past the 1959 black Buick Invicta parked in his carport to a woman standing on the back porch. She was cut from the same mold as Potter, but smaller and with white hair. What kind of guy would live with his mother at his age? Maybe a homicidal maniac like that fruitcake motel-keeper in *Psycho*. The thought gave Blondie a chill.

When he'd dressed and made his way downstairs, Blondie found his dad fixing an old radio on the kitchen table. He liked to do things like that. He hated to get rid of anything.

"Good morning, Bernard," he said.

Why did he always have to be so formal? Why couldn't he just be a regular guy?

"I left you some bacon."

Blondie thanked him, got some milk from the fridge, and sat down across from him. Blondie watched his father work as he chewed on the bacon.

"What are you going to do with that when you're done?"

"I don't know. Put it on the shelf in the utility room. We don't really need it right now."

Blondie tried to think of something else to say, something that might spark a genuine conversation between them. He didn't know what that might be.

Blondie waited until Potter finished his planting, then he got out his wedge and his golf balls and practiced his chipping. This time, he aimed away from Potter's yard.

After a can of tomato soup for lunch, Blondie retreated to his room to read. He reached under his bed and pulled out his mom's copy of *Lolita*. Blondie knew there was no reason to hide it from his mom—she didn't care what he read—but his dad had called it "trash."

Blondie thought it was pretty good, even though he found its premise a little screwy. He could almost understand why a twisted old fart like Humbert Humbert might be attracted to a teenaged nymphet like Lolita. After all, *he* was attracted to teenaged nymphets. But he couldn't see it the other way. Why would an attractive girl want to hang around with a middle-aged man? That was sick.

Blondie wondered what it would be like to be a well-known author like Earnest Hemingway or Mickey Spillane. He imagined he could write whenever he wanted and travel to exotic places to find scenes for his stories. That would be the life. Then again, Hemingway had shot himself to death that summer. Blondie promised himself he'd never get that intense.

The important thing was to become famous—and to attract beautiful women. He bet Tammy would be impressed. Girls were like that—attracted to guys who accomplished things. On the other hand, girls could get by on good looks alone. It didn't seem fair.

It seemed forever until it was time to watch the *Buddy Parker Show*. Couples were whirling and bopping to the song "Does Your Chewing Gum Lose its Flavor on the Bedpost Overnight?" when he turned on the set. Blondie hated the tune. It was a dumb song by a dumb Englishman. What could you expect? The English had never had any good rock-and-roll bands and they never would. They talked too funny.

He loved the next song, though—"Take Good Care of My Baby" by Bobby Vee. It made him think of Tammy. He wondered if she had a boyfriend and how he could find out without her knowing it. Maybe she'd had her heart broken recently. That could be an opportunity for a sensitive guy like him.

Blondie turned his attention back to the screen. Jesus, now that old fart Parker was cozying up to one of the girls. Gross! Parker had to be as old as his dad. The girl—her named was Tina—gave Vee's song an "8." Blondie thought it was worth at least a "9." With all the makeup she wore around her eyes, she looked like a vampire. She kept glancing at the camera and smiling like a chimpanzee. Baltimore girls sure were goofy.

All girls were goofy. On the one hand, they acted so innocent with their teddy bears and frilly Sunday clothes. On the other, they wore bikinis and lipstick and teased as if they wanted to be fucked. How was a guy supposed to know how to act around them?

Blondie knew what he wanted. He wanted his girl to be a virgin. That was important. Blondie couldn't imagine being romantic over a girl some other guy already had put his thing into. Yuck!

Chapter Six

Monday morning, a new kid was waiting at Blondie's stop. He looked to be about Blondie's age—medium height, small-boned and narrow-hipped, with square shoulders and short-cut hair. He had an earnest face with an upturned nose and freckles. Howdy Doody in a crew cut. When Blondie drew near, he held out his hand.

"Hi, I'm Rudy Tilly," he said. "I live in the house behind you."

Blondie was too surprised to speak. The guy was treating him like a real person.

"My dad took me to school last week," he said. "That's why I wasn't on the bus."

"I'm Blondie Reimer. I'm a senior."

Boy, that was an intelligent thing to say.

"Yeah, I know."

Blondie gave him a questioning look.

"Mr. Clapper told me," Tilly said, blushing. "I'm supposed to know these things. I'm president of the senior class."

Blondie couldn't help being impressed. The president of the FHS senior class—and he was talking to him. Blondie noted how nattily he was dressed—in a Madras shirt, navy sweater, and khaki pants, all crisp and wrinkle free. Was that what made him presidential?

"My folks moved to Fenton two years ago," Rudy said. "It takes a while to make friends here."

"You're telling me."

Rudy laughed.

"I saw you're in the academic program," he said. "Have you thought about college yet?"

"Only a little," Blondie replied. "You?"

"I want to go. To be honest, my grades aren't real sharp."

"Maybe I could help you. I do pretty well in school."

Blondie wondered if that was too arrogant.

"Would you? I stink at trig."

"Sure."

Blondie felt his spirits expand. He was having an intelligent conversation with somebody who was somebody. And he could even give him some help!

"Boy, I didn't think anyone was ever going to buy your house," Rudy said. "I guess your folks just aren't bothered by all that talk."

What talk? Blondie looked at Rudy, perplexed.

"You mean you haven't heard about Potter? They say he killed a man."

An ice-cold centipede ran up and down Blondie's spinal cord. The beast next door *was* a murderer.

"How?" he heard his voice squeak.

Not an axe. Don't let it be an axe.

"My dad said he beat a guy to death in a fight over some girl."

Blondie's Adam's apple clenched. He wanted to ask Rudy more, but his thoughts were disrupted by the rattle of gravel as the bus slid to a halt in front of him. Maybe Rudy would sit by him.

"Well, catch you later," Rudy said as he got on the bus.

Blondie's spirits slipped back a notch. Rudy took one of the bus's unoccupied bench seats. Blondie wondered if he should take a chance and sit beside him. He decided that would be too presumptuous. Don't push it, he advised himself.

Blondie was surprised when the ungainly pigtailed girl—Phyllis something Jerry had called her—got on the bus and sat down by Rudy.

He was even more surprised that Rudy didn't seem to mind. He even talked to her. That was probably how he got to be class president...being nice to everyone, even scags.

All through first period, Blondie found himself dwelling on Rudy's revelation about Potter. No wonder they'd gotten such a good deal on their house. They might as well have bought next door to the Bates Motel. Blondie flashed on nutso Norman Bates sticking the knife to Janet Leigh in *Psycho*. He shivered.

"B-boy, you're sure t-talkative t-today," Caldane said to him. Blondie had forgotten he was there.

"Sorry," he muttered. He didn't want to talk to Jerry right then. Life and death was on his mind. Death mostly.

His mood picked up in civics class. Miss Darlington was his favorite teacher, and not just because of her tomboy face and athletic body. She tried to make what she was teaching relevant to them. At the start of each class, she led a discussion about some event from the morning headlines. Blondie could tell she cared about what she was telling them. He liked that about her, too.

"Why do you think Dr. King and his followers are risking injury to sit at all-white lunch counters in the South?" she asked, placing her index finger against her nose and staring intently out at the class.

"Because they don't have good food at nigger restaurants," a wiseacre called out.

Miss Darlington recoiled. It took her a minute to regain her composure.

"We don't refer to Negroes that way," she scolded the respondent. "Let me ask it another way. Why does Dr. King believe that Negroes have a right to eat at white lunch counters?"

This time, she looked at Blondie and smiled.

"It's the law," Blondie said. "The fourteenth amendment to the Constitution guarantees blacks the same rights as whites."

Miss Darlington beamed at him and he felt his face start to glow.

"Exactly, it's the law. But isn't there an even more compelling reason?"

This time no one said anything. Blondie knew what she was getting at, but answering twice in a row would look like he was "kissing ass."

"Because it's right!" she declared.

Blondie was proud of her for saying that. But he wondered why there were no black kids in school. There were plenty of black people in Fenton—high-school age too. Where did they go to school? Why weren't there any at Fenton High? Wasn't integration the law of the land? He decided to ask Caldane when he saw him again.

Blondie's third-period chemistry teacher, Mr. Farber, was short and wiry, with butch-cut reddish hair and a raptor's features and intensity. His movements were so precise Blondie imagined he practiced them before each class. Today, he walked the class through the chart of the elements, from hydrogen all the way up through uranium and plutonium and all the other man-made atoms adults had created to blow the world up with. He talked as if chemistry was the most important thing in the world—like one of those kooky scientists from a sci-fi flick, the kind who'd create a giant spider without a second thought.

Just before class ended, Farber told them that they would soon begin doing experiments, and that he wanted them to work in pairs. He passed around a sheet of paper with the assigned teams. Blondie was surprised to see he'd been paired with Paul Feller. He turned around. Feller was leaning back in his chair, his hands clasped behind his head, grinning. What did that mean? Had Feller set it up for them to be partners? How? And why?

When the bell rang, Blondie headed for him to ask, but Feller managed to break through the throng and speed off down the hall toward the cafeteria before Blondie could catch up. By the time Blondie arrived at the lunchroom, Feller had already passed through the serving line and was heading toward a table with the rest of his group. Blondie wasn't about to crash their scene.

He saw Caldane sitting alone. After loading his tray, he joined him. He asked him where Fenton's black kids went to school.

"They g-go t-to the Negro h-high school," Jerry answered matter-of-factly.

"Why don't they go here?"

"I d-don't know. I n-never thought about it. B-but who'd w-want them?"

His attitude annoyed Blondie, but he chose not to rebuke him. Caldane was his only source of information about what went on in school.

Over time, Blondie confirmed what Jerry was telling him. Fenton High life revolved around its cliques. The "jocks," not all of them, but the real stars, tended to congregate outside the homeroom of Bobby Clements, the school's top athlete, doubly blessed with the looks of a Roman god. The "pols" hung around the school office first thing each morning where Martha Magister, the big-boned, open-faced student body president, announced the day's activities over the intercom. Blondie often saw Rudy there and he was always pleased when Rudy acknowledged him. That had to give him some status.

The "brains" collected around Mary Cherry, a senior with an alleged astronomical I.Q. who shared Mrs. Buckley's English class with him. The cheerleaders, or "chops" as Brick reportedly termed them (after "lamb chops"), sometimes gathered around Bobby Clements and his group, although more often they remained aloof. ("It doesn't matter," Caldane reported Feller had said, "because they're all fucking the jocks anyway.") They often could be found in the gym before classes started, practicing their routines in blue gym shorts and white turtlenecks. Blondie had been surprised and pleased to see Tammy among them.

There were plenty of kids who didn't fit any of these categories, Blondie realized, and not all of them appeared to be "billies" according to Grouper's definition. He supposed they were too unremarkable to merit any classification at all.

Blondie realized he was extremely curious about this Grouper character. Caldane spoke of him as if he were a legend in his own time. Whenever Blondie asked Jerry a question that was the least bit philosophical, he'd say, "Th-that's one for the Grouper." But so far as Blondie could tell, judging from the classes he shared with him, Grouper never *did* anything. He just sat in his chair and breathed heavily and looked bored.

Somehow, though, his presence in her English class seemed to infuriate Mrs. Buckley. She continually tried to catch him short by wheeling on him with difficult questions about literary figures, characters or quotations from their readings. Blondie was impressed when Grouper unfailingly wheezed out the correct answer. Invariably, after each of her defeats, Bucky would tighten her lips around her teeth and emit a faint whinnying sound.

It wasn't Grouper, though, but Caldane who caused the first big scene in Bucky's class. On Wednesday, she began to wax eloquent about the symbolism of various features of Hawthorne's *House of Seven Gables*. As she rambled on, she unearthed ever-deeper meanings in the shape of the house, the number of gables, even the furnishings in the rooms. Cheering on her every excess was her chief sycophant, Mary Cherry. Blondie was briefly sorry Mary was such a suck-up. She wasn't bad looking, with Dutch-girl features and golden hair cut pageboy style. However, as she continued egging Bucky on, in her mincing, supercilious way, murderous thoughts prevailed.

Brick ripped a piece of paper from his ring binder, scribbled something on it, folded it over, and wrote something more. He passed it to Grouper, who read it and gave a faint nod of approval. Grouper passed the paper on to Feller, who passed it on to Dispatch, who passed it on to Jerry, who doubled up when he read it. After a few spasms, Jerry passed the note to Blondie.

It was addressed "To Mary Cherry." Inside it read "I bet you'd suck Nathaniel Hawthorne's you-know-what." It was signed "An admirer." Blondie was impressed by Brick's creativity. He'd been assuming he was a complete zero.

The note passed through several more hands before it reached Mary. She took it in the same secretive manner in which it was offered and opened it, beaming as if she were about to receive a sonnet from a lover. Her eyes widened as she read the words and an anguished wail broke from her lips, causing Mrs. Buckley to break off her singsong literary analysis. She gaped at Mary, who sat before her with one hand raised and the other over her mouth.

"Yes, Mary dear, what is it?" Mrs. Buckley asked her sweetly.

Grouper groaned.

Mary handed Mrs. Buckley the note. Bucky blanched and then peered out at the class, as if expecting the guilty party to betray himself by cringing before her glare. No one moved or changed expression.

"Someone in this class has very little respect for literature," she finally said.

She maintained her sour look for several seconds, then a smile began to advanced upon her battle-zone face. Blondie flinched because he knew she was warming up to one of her impromptu literary quizzes. Her smile reached a toothy maturity as she said, "Today, we're going to learn about an English writer of the 18th Century. He's someone who's bequeathed us many famous quotations, but they're usually attributed to another, better known English writer. Now, who would like to take the first question?"

No one but Mary ever volunteered. When, as usual, no one raised a hand, Bucky looked her way. Mary was staring at the ceiling, a pout on her face. Her arms remained crossed.

Rebounding from this reverse, Bucky scanned the room for a suitable victim. There was a massive shifting of heads as the class members looked here and there to avoid making eye contact.

Brick placed his lips against his forearm and blew on it, making a loud, farting sound. Bucky jerked her head in his direction, but, by the time her eyes reached him, Brick's face was a mask of calm. Beneath the table, he pinched Jerry's thigh. He cried out in pain.

Bucky shifted her gaze to Caldane. He squirmed and lowered himself in his seat, as if trying to slide under the desk. He hated to be called on in class because of his stuttering.

"Jerry Caldane," Bucky called. "You seem to have lots of energy today. Let's hope that some of it has reached your cranial region."

He stared at her apprehensively, his eyes barely above the desktop.

"Jerry, please, you must learn to sit up straight. Posture like that can lead to curvature of the spine."

He maneuvered his weasel-like body upright.

"That's better. Now here's my first question: What famous 18th century writer said, 'To err is human, to forgive, divine?'"

Caldane looked around in panic, as if he'd never heard the expression before. Brick put his hand in front of his mouth as if he were about to cough and whispered: "Shakespeare."

"Sh-shakes..." Jerry began.

"No, not Shakespeare," Buckley interrupted. "Many people attribute that quote to Shakespeare, but it was another who said it. Does anyone know who that was?"

Giving into the temptation to display her knowledge, Mary Cherry's hand shot up.

"Who said it?" Brick called over to the Grouper.

"That most pernicious purveyor of Enlightenment pap—Alexander Pope—from his *Essay on Criticism*."

Mary overheard Grouper and shot him a nasty look.

"Yes, Mary?" Bucky said.

"Alexander Pope, from his *Essay on Criticism*."

"Very good, Mary," Bucky gushed. "Yes, that's quite correct. Alexander Pope. Quite often, his aphorisms are confused with those of Shakespeare."

She turned back toward Caldane and gave him the look of a forgiving mistress about to toss her dog a bone.

"Now, with that in mind, Jerry, if I were to ask you who said, 'Fools rush in where angels fear to tread,' what would you answer?"

Jerry, who'd been berating Brick for giving him the wrong answer, missed not only Mary Cherry's response, but Bucky's latest question. He looked at her with a vacant expression.

"Well?"

"Shakespeare," Brick whispered again.

"Sh-sh-shakes…Shakes…Shakes…."

Several students snickered. Jerry's face turned crimson.

Bucky stared at him in amazement.

"No, no, no. Don't you get the gist of my questions? Now, let's try another one. Who said, 'Hope springs eternal in the human breast'?"

Jerry's face was aflame. He was breathless with self-consciousness. Blondie feared he was going to suffocate.

"It's gotta be Shakespeare this time," Brick murmured to Jerry, "I'd bet all the money I have."

"Shakes…Shakes…Shakespeare!" Caldane cried out, triumphant at squeezing the treacherous name from his lips.

Bucky clapped her hand to her forehead in disbelief. Grouper groaned. The class roared. Jerry fell to his seat in uncomprehending disrepair.

"Why do I even try?" Bucky muttered.

"Dumb shit!" Dispatch hissed at Caldane from behind.

That set the class off again, even louder.

Bucky jumped up, knocking her desk askew. Fury pinched her face.

"Dismissed!" she shouted.

"But the bell hasn't rung, Mrs. Buckley," Mary Cherry reminded her.

"The hell with the bell!" Buckley hissed at her. "Dismissed," she repeated loudly to the milling class, "Go to gym class, go to study hall, go to h…."

"Mrs. Buckley!" Mary gasped.

"I don't care," Buckley's eyes were growing moist, "just get out."

The bell rang and students exploded into the hall, buzzing and clamoring. Caldane chased after Brick still berating him, a terrier snipping at the heels of a mastiff.

Grouper ambled slowly out of the class, wiping his nose with a handkerchief and sniffling as if to clear his sinuses. Blondie had been impressed by Grouper's knowledge of literature and wanted to tell him so, but he'd never spoken to him before and didn't want to come across as overly familiar. As if he'd read Blondie's mind, the Grouper cast his small eyes his way and, after putting his handkerchief into his back pants pocket, beckoned to him.

"To survive," Grouper said to him throatily when Blondie approached, "one must be aware of certain universal principles...shall we call them laws?"

Blondie gazed at him in anticipation of some revelation, but Grouper turned and waddled away. Blondie was disappointed. He felt he'd been on the brink of being taken into the Grouper's confidence. The incident in Bucky's class, however, gave Blondie an idea of how to score some points with the B and F Club.

The next time he saw Feller in the hallway, he called to him. Feller gave him a curious and appraising look.

"Do you remember Jerry Caldane's episode in Bucky's class?"

"Of course," Feller replied.

"Is that the kind of performance that might qualify him for full membership in your club?"

"What do you know of *our* club?" Feller asked sharply.

"Caldane has filled me in a little," Blondie answered defensively, before recovering and asking in an aggressive tone, "Why, is it a secret?"

"Not really." A small smile creased Feller's lips. "To answer your question, we would certainly give strong consideration to any situation in which someone makes a complete asshole of himself."

"I recognize that I'm not a member of your group," Blondie said more respectfully, "but I thought if Caldane was being considered for full membership, you might need a nickname for him."

"I'm in charge of names," Feller shot back at him.

"Yes, I know, and you're obviously quite good at it." Blondie hated the unctuous tone in his voice. "I had an idea, that's all, and I thought you might be interested."

His servile manned seemed to soften Feller.

"We've never solicited for names, of course, but I suppose we should be big enough to accept suggestions from outside. What is it?"

"Shakes," Blondie answered.

"Shakes? Hey, that's not bad. Of course, we'll have to consider the matter as a group."

"Of course."

The next morning, Jerry came up from behind and grabbed Blondie's shirtsleeve. His face was scarlet with anger.

"Sh-shakes, huh? You th-think that's a g-g-good name for me. Well, it st-stinks."

"I thought you wanted a nickname."

"S-something with d-dignity. Not Sh-shakes."

"So, tell them you don't like it."

"I d-did."

"Well?"

"It d-didn't matter. They g-gave me the n-name anyway."

Despite Jerry's ire, Blondie was pleased. They'd used the name he'd suggested.

Thursday was the day for experiments in chem. class. For the first time, Blondie would be engaged in a common enterprise with Feller. The task: heating sulfur to see how it changed states with the rise in temperature. Farber pranced around the room like a martinet, scolding those who hadn't properly lit their Bunsen burners or placed the proper amount of powder into the glass cylinders.

"Worse than a fart," Feller said as the odor escaped from the container.

"Yeah," was all Blondie could think to say.

Feller pushed a lock of hair out of his eyes and scrutinized him.

"You wouldn't be looking for a group to join, would you?"

"Not necessarily," Blondie quickly replied.

"Too bad."

Feller turned his attention back to the burner. He didn't say anything more. After they'd completed their experiments and cleaned up their equipment, Farber launched into a lengthy lecture on the many uses of sulfur and all its compounds.

Blondie felt he had to take a chance.

"You do seem to have an interesting collection of characters in your group," he whispered to Feller.

"That's exactly how I think about it." Feller rubbed his cheek and gave Blondie an appraising look. "You strike me as pretty perceptive…creative, too. 'Shakes'—that was good. And you've got a certain style."

A certain style? Blondie started to probe further, but thought better of it. He wasn't sure he'd like the answer.

Farber had moved on to the role of sulfur in military armaments.

"Without sulfur," he told the class enthusiastically, "World War II wouldn't have been possible."

"I mentioned you to the guys," Feller murmured toward the end of the hour. "They're not opposed."

"Opposed to what?"

"Why, picking up your contract, of course."

After the bell rang, Feller invited Blondie to join him and "the guys" for lunch. Blondie didn't attempt to hide his glee. He was being brought in. What else could it mean?

When Blondie exited the cafeteria line, he saw that Feller was sitting with all the B and F Club members. Caldane was with them; apparently, he'd been embraced back into the group. Blondie assumed a confident air and strolled over to the table. Feller had saved him a seat.

"Fellows, this is Bernard Reimer," Feller said. "His nickname is Blondie."

"It took me s-six months to get a n-nickname," Jerry protested.

"Would you jack down? He already has a nickname."

"H-he's not even a m-member."

"Well, we'll make him an apprentice member if he likes…"

Feller looked toward Blondie.

"Sure," Blondie said.

"Good. Then it's done." Feller looked around thoughtfully. "Okay now, let's see…. You know me and Caldane. How about the Grouper?"

Grouper nodded.

"And Brick?"

Blondie allowed as how he'd seen him around.

"This other fellow here is Dispatch."

Blondie looked into the round face beneath the mop of dark hair. Dispatch didn't appear to notice.

He stared straight ahead with a look of mild displeasure. Feller told Blondie his real name was Darrel

Kendall and that Brick's was Howard Brickowski.

"Why don't you have a nickname?" Blondie asked him.

"I'm the namer of names. I don't need a nickname."

Feller looked around as if to see whether his explanation would be accepted, then he continued.

"We especially wanted you to be here, Blondie, for the enunciation of a new law, since you were a witness to the events which led to its discovery—to be specific, Shakes' fiasco in Bucky's class."

Blondie nodded.

"One of our functions as a group is to uncover the true laws that govern human behavior," Feller added. He turned to Grouper.

Grouper looked solemnly toward Caldane.

"Obviously, there was a law at work in Bucky's class yesterday," he said. "I believe it's a new one. But how to properly phrase it…."

Grouper took out his handkerchief and wiped his nose, although it was dry.

Everyone looked toward him expectantly.

Finally, his deep voice boomed forth as if God himself had chosen to speak:

"Only an asshole takes advice from an asshole."

Chapter Seven

Rain strafed the windowpane in machine-gun bursts as Blondie stared out the window, forlorn. Another Fenton Saturday with nothing to do and rain to boot. He listened to Sarah Vaughn sing about another September in the rain. She almost made it sound romantic. Maybe it if he were ensconced in some mountain cabin with a fire going and a girl in his arms....

Blondie had hoped after his acceptance into the B and F Club that he'd be invited along with them this weekend. All day Friday, his antennae had been straining for any hint of an invitation. All Feller had said was, "Be ready to go on a sortie with us some time." Blondie hadn't known what to make of that. He'd only heard the word "sortie" before from his dad and then in the context of an attack of some kind.

"Blondie," his mother called.

He opened his door.

"I'm going into town to get my hair done. Do you want to come along?"

She had to be joking. Did his mom think he'd want to spend Saturday with her—or be seen with her? Cool guys didn't hang out with their mothers.

He declined. But when he heard the front door shut, he changed his mind and went running after her. The alternative was sitting around the house watching *Captain Kangaroo* or *Shari Lewis and Her Puppets*.

His mother gave him a knowing smile when he opened the car door.

"What?" he asked.

"Nothing."

Blondie hated that smile. Sometimes, she acted like she could read his mind. Well, one of these days he was going to surprise her.

The rain eased as they headed into town. Before they reached the rusty sign at the town limits, the sun broke through. Blondie perked up.

Fenton's main drag was Front Street, a gauntlet of ticky-tack two-storied structures, relieved only by a small park and the granite bulk of the Mayhew County Courthouse. The park's only feature was a tarnished copper statue of Fennimore Fenton, the town father. Honoring the founder of Fenton struck Blondie as equivalent to celebrating the discoverer of earwax.

The Hustler was playing at the Marylander Theater down the street. Blondie had seen it at the post theater in Percy just before they'd moved to Fenton. He wondered what it would be like to be Fast Eddie Felson, pool hustler…being so good you could win close against lesser talents without them even knowing they'd been taken…traveling from town to town, making money as you went, completely self-sufficient. But then, even Fast Eddie had needed a girl.

Blondie thought of Tammy. He wondered if she'd be attracted to someone like Fast Eddie. If so, he'd spend more time at the pool hall. He scanned the streets in case she was out and about.

"What are you looking for?" his mom asked.

He ignored her.

His mom turned left into an alleyway beside Maxine's Hair Salon, her destination.

"You're awfully quiet today, Bernard," she said after shutting off the motor. "Are you all right?"

"Of course I'm all right," he mumbled. "Why wouldn't I be all right?"

He appreciated her taking an interest in him, but not with *that look*…like he was about to drown.

"You were looking for someone back there, weren't you? A girl, I bet."

She *could* read his mind. It was spooky. Blondie pursed his lips. He wasn't going to bite. No way.

"It wouldn't be Susan Feldman, would it?"

Ugh!

"Susan doesn't even live in Fenton, for Pete's sake," Blondie snapped. "Anyway, this girl is much prettier than her."

Now he'd done it.

"Why don't you ask her out?"

"She'd never go out with me."

"Why not? You're a nice boy."

Nice? That was a synonym for "eunuch" to teenaged girls.

"Mom, she's beautiful," he said in exasperation. "She could have anyone."

"Then why not you?"

Blondie groaned.

"I'm no star."

"You are to me."

Why couldn't his mom ever get what he was saying? She'd been young once.

"Pretty girls get lonely, too. I know. I was pretty once myself."

How many times had she told him that? He'd seen the photos and, yes, she'd had been pretty once, long before she'd gained so much weight—but she hadn't been gorgeous. She hadn't been *perfect* like Tammy.

"Girls have the same feelings as boys, you know," she added.

Now, that was preposterous. Girls weren't even the same species as boys! They thought buying new shoes or changing hairstyles were major life events. They never ran, even when crossing the street. Besides, they didn't need *it* as much as guys—and that was major. How could his mother be so naive?

Blondie told his mom he had "things to do" and bolted from the car. He decided to check out the records at the Bonanza Variety Store. He found them in the dim recesses at the rear of the store. It was so dark he could barely make out the names. He was looking for the *Bristol Stomp* by the Dovells, but he couldn't find it, so he wandered over to the bookstand. His enthusiasm picked up when he found a copy of *The Carpetbaggers*. He'd heard there were some juicy parts in it. He skimmed page after page, looking for a key word that would tell him he was onto something—an expletive or a body part. But he couldn't come up with anything.

Vexed, Blondie crossed the street to Rexall's. Blondie looked around the store trying to find out where the rubbers were kept...just in case he ever got real lucky. He'd seen some of their names in a men's magazine a friend had shown him once—*Love's Glove, Ecstasy* and such. They almost sounded sexy, but Blondie couldn't imagine what a girl would find attractive about a guy wearing one of those. Of course, he couldn't imagine what a girl would find attractive about a pecker.

"Can I help you?" the pharmacist called to him.

Blondie shook his head and hurried out.

"Bernard!"

His mother was heading his way. What was she doing out of Maxine's so soon? His cover as a cool guy was under full parental attack.

"Are you sick?" she asked when she reached him.

"No. Why?"

"I saw you coming out of the pharmacy."

Oh yeah. What could he say he was doing in there?

"I thought I needed some toothpaste."

"Where is it?"

"I remembered I didn't need any after all."

"Well, no matter. Didn't you say you needed some underwear? Why don't we pop into Cunningham's and get you some."

Buy underwear with his mom in broad daylight? He'd rather get his nuts checked by a woman doctor.

"No way," Blondie said.

His mom grabbed his arm and began tugging him toward the store. Just as they reached the entrance, Feller came strolling out. There was nothing to do, nowhere to hide. The leader of the B and F Club had caught him red-handed with his mom. He saw his chances of being embraced into the group flying into oblivion like the last passenger pigeon.

"Hi, Paul," he said, feeling like a fool. "This is my mom."

His mom looked at Blondie and lifted her eyebrows.

"Mom, this is Paul Feller," he quickly added. "He's in my class."

"Mrs. Reimer, I'm pleased to meet you."

Blondie couldn't help admiring how smooth Feller was. Nothing seemed to shake him. He, on the other hand, felt his insides squirming like a sack full of snakes. As he began contemplating the mechanics of *seppuku*, he heard a high-pitched cry.

"Paulie! Yoo hoo, Paulie."

Paulie?

A petite dark-haired woman in a gray wool coat and high heels came racing toward them.

"Mrs. Reimer, Blondie, this is my mother," Feller said when she arrived.

Now it was Feller's turn to dance. Blondie was happy to see a flush appear on his face.

"I don't know why Paulie wanders off when we come to town together," she said.

Maybe this wasn't so bad, Blondie thought. They each had something on the other now. All the same, Blondie was pleased when Paul and his mom trundled on down the street. Jesus, parents were embarrassing.

Halfway home, his mother gave him a pensive look.

"You weren't in the pharmacy looking for something besides toothpaste, were you?"

"Like what?" he asked innocently.

"Has your dad ever talked to you about sex?"

Was she kidding? His dad hardly talked to him at all.

"It's best to wait," she said.

"Mom!"

It was absurd. He didn't even have a girl and his mother was warning him about sex. If only she had reason....

"Sex can be good, though," she continued after a long pause. "I've always wished your father was more passionate. I guess it's because of his religion."

She began to sniffle.

Blondie sighed and looked out the window. He didn't want to hear about her sex problems. The idea of his mom and dad having sex—anyone their age having sex—was both incomprehensible and distasteful. Sex was for young people with attractive bodies. People his age...like him.

"Thank God I have you, Blondie. You have feelings. Your father has never really loved me, you know," his mom said, her large mobile face beginning to quiver. "He's always put his family first."

Blondie knew she wanted him to comfort her. Why couldn't she understand it wasn't his place. Besides, he didn't know how to comfort a grown-up. He was only a kid.

When they returned to their cul-de-sac, Mr. Potter was puttering in his front yard in an old sweatshirt. Blondie tried to read the faded lettering on the back to see if it was prison issue. Potter didn't look their way as they shot up the driveway.

"That Mack Potter isn't very neighborly," his mom complained

Mack? The psychopath had a first name? How did his mom know? He wondered if he should tell her he was a killer. He decided it would only frighten her to no purpose. They weren't about to move.

Blondie expected to find his father parked in front of the television watching the college football game of the week, but the family room was quiet. Blondie followed his mom into the kitchen, where they found him banging away on a typewriter.

"Francis, what are you doing?" his mom asked.

He muttered something under his breath.

"You're not doing something for that silly military organization you joined, are you?"

His face got red.

"It's not silly. Besides, I'm the new secretary."

Blondie tried to remember the name. The military order of something or other. A bunch of ex-officers who met once a month to debate America's military strategy. Blondie thought it was pretty hokey, especially if the other members were like his dad—soldiers who'd never fired a gun in anger.

"So what *are* you doing," his mother repeated.

"Writing the president."

His mom rolled her eyes.

"And what are you telling him?"

"That we should get out of Vietnam."

Blondie'd never heard of the place. He could tell his mother hadn't either.

"Well, I'm sure President Kennedy has plenty of advisors already."

His dad kept typing without looking up.

Much later—after supper and after Blondie had nearly gnawed off his index finger from boredom—his mom opened his door to invite him to church the next day. He didn't know why she bothered. He hadn't gone to church for three years, ever since he'd been kicked out of Sunday School for supposedly questioning the virgin birth of the Christ child. All he'd said was, "Yeah, sure." That was the first time he'd realized there were other people as serious about religion as his dad.

But hey, he'd given God a chance. He'd prayed to him for years before giving up. When he'd asked for a train set one Christmas, he hadn't gotten one. When he'd prayed for snotty Marilyn Goetz's family to move and take her with them, they'd stayed put. He could think of plenty of other prayers that hadn't been answered, like ones for darker hair, bigger muscles, and a car of his own. One of his religious instructors had suggested he wasn't approaching God in the proper spirit. Another had told him God answered prayers in *mysterious* ways. He considered that a cop-out. Blondie wanted Him to reply in obvious and immediate ways.

He wasn't prepared to give up on God entirely, though. Everyone deserved a second chance. That was why, when the last light in the house had gone out, he clasped his hands together.

"God, there's this girl...." he began.

Chapter Eight

Spalding's gap-toothed grin arced across Blondie's consciousness like a rim view of the Grand Canyon as she droned on about sines and cosines, secants and tangents. So what if trigonometry had helped Renaissance sailors circumnavigate the globe. Were any of them going to set off in three-masters to find new lands? Why couldn't they study something useful, like how to act cool or how to get girls?

Blondie noticed Rudy Tilly across the room, his lips tracing every syllable, his brain cells struggling with her pretzel logic. Grouper, several desks away, showed no signs of listening to Spalding at all. His eyes were targeted a foot or two above her head. A serene smile hung from his nose.

Spalding twisted a strand of her coarse dishwater hair and grinned in his direction.

"Walter," she asked in an amiable tone, "would you please explain the sine of an angle in the context of a circle?"

His inner-tube lips barely moved as he replied.

"The sine of an angle increases to one from zero to 90 degrees, decreases to zero from 90 degrees to 180 degrees, decreases to minus one from 180 degrees to 270 degrees, then increases to zero from 270 degrees to 360 degrees."

Blondie was impressed. The guy was a human computer.

Spalding beamed at him for a moment. Just before she looked away, Grouper winked at her.

After class, Blondie invited Rudy to his house to review the day's trig lesson. He was pleased by Rudy's ready acceptance.

Miss Darlington was in the hall talking to Mr. Bearzinsky when he arrived at Civics class. As he passed, he heard the Bear refer to her as "Sandra." That startled him; he never thought of teachers as having first names. When she entered the classroom, Miss Darlington was smiling.

Sandra, huh, or was it Sandy to those who knew her better? Blondie found himself repeating her name. He wondered if he was developing a crush on her. Nah, he was in love with Tammy or whatever you called it when you felt like he did about someone you'd never even talked to.

Miss Darlington began the class by asking how many of them had heard of a place called Vietnam. Blondie jerked to attention. That was the place his dad had been writing about. Only one kid raised his hand.

"What do you know about it?" she asked him.

He told her his dad had mentioned it as a place threatened by the communists, that's all. She seemed impressed he knew that much.

"Our government has been keeping its involvement in Vietnam pretty much a secret," she said. "There are already hundreds of U.S. military personnel there as advisors. I'm afraid we're going to wind up in a war."

Blondie was sure she was wrong. Why would the United States fight about some place no one had ever heard of? Still, he knew America had to draw the line against communism where it made sense. The reds were a bunch of nuts willing to risk the destruction of the planet for their goofy ideas. For once, his classmates were in agreement. Freddy Benson summarized their mood: "We oughtta just nuke them all and get it over with."

At lunch, Blondie spied Shakes sitting with Feller and Brick. Blondie felt confident enough of his status to head their way. Shakes was sucking milk into his straw and blowing it into his mashed potatoes. Feller eyed him disdainfully while Brick stared at the wall. Blondie couldn't figure him at all, but then he'd always been mystified—and intimidated—by silent types, especially if they had muscles. Brick did. Nonetheless, he felt compelled to say something to him—weren't they part of the same gang?—so he asked him how he thought Fenton would fare in Friday night's football game.

"Fuck the game," Brick said.

"Brick used to be on the team," Feller explained. "That was before he pissed in the coach's shoes."

"Why'd he do that?" Blondie asked Feller, as if Brick weren't there.

"He didn't like him."

A thin smile creased Brick's face.

Blondie felt the cafeteria bench shift as Grouper's soft bulk settled next to him. Dispatch appeared on the opposite side of the table. He plopped down with a scowl on his face.

"What's the matter, Dispatch?" Feller asked him, "you get shot down again?"

"Girls are fucked up," he groused.

Blondie was gratified to know someone else suffered over females.

"Who this time?"

"Susan Conner."

"Didn't you go out with her last weekend?" Feller asked.

"My second time, too."

"Jesus, Dispatch, that's almost going steady for you."

"Yeah."

"So?"

"So she won't go out with me again."

Brick looked at Dispatch impatiently.

"The question is, 'Did you get any?'" he said to him.

"Almost."

Brick snorted.

"Fess up, Dispatch," Feller said, "What happened?"

"We were making out like crazy, but when I tried to get my hands in her pants, she got mad. She told me her priest said sex before marriage was wrong."

"Damned Catholics," Brick muttered, now sympathetic.

"F-fucking m-mackerel snappers," Shakes added.

"It's not that we're prejudiced," Feller said to Blondie. "As far as we're concerned, people can believe any stupid thing they want. It's just that Catholic girls won't put out."

"Why don't you try Protestant girls then?"

"Where's the challenge?"

Someone was nuts here, Blondie thought, and it wasn't him.

"Besides, most of the good-looking girls are Catholic," Feller added.

"I even bought her dinner," Dispatch continued to carp. "That should be worth something."

Grouper fastened his bulging eyes on him.

"Have you ever considered treating a girl with respect?" he asked.

Dispatch looked at Grouper as if he thought Grouper was putting him on.

"Na-a-ah."

They talked so casually about sex. Were they all getting it? That possibility made him uneasy. It also bothered him that they talked so crudely about girls. Where was the romance?

Blondie followed Grouper from the cafeteria.

"Can I ask you a question?"

Grouper nodded.

"What is it between you and Spalding? You seem to be the only one in class she likes."

"Perhaps that's because I'm the only one who treats her as the least bit attractive. Every woman likes a little flirtation."

Blondie stopped his next step in mid-stride. Coming straight toward them was Tammy. She was wearing a checked pink blouse and blue skirt and she was alone.

Grouper, off in his own world, ambled ahead. Now he was alone too.

"Hello," he surprised himself by saying to Tammy when she passed.

She seemed startled, then looked at him as if he'd materialized from the linoleum.

"Hello," she murmured.

"Yes," he whispered.

Then she was gone.

Yes? Had he said yes? Why had he said yes? That was stupid. She was going to think he was stupid. He *was* stupid. Had her voice sounded like wind chimes? Blondie was sure it had. Hadn't it?

Grouper leaned against the wall, waiting for him. A bemused smile was on his face.

Blondie was happy to see Rudy that evening. He seemed like a genuinely good guy. Besides, he had standing at school. However, helping him turned out to be more work than Blondie had anticipated. He was surprised at how dense Rudy was when it came to understanding basic concepts. He thought the class president would have more going for him in the smarts department.

The next day before class, Dispatch marched up to Blondie in his self-absorbed fashion and handed him a small envelope. Inside was a wedding announcement from the parents of a Mary Jo Flaherty announcing the imminent marriage of their daughter to a Paul Poindexter. Most of the announcement—dated April 13, 1957—had been crossed out and replaced with the following words: "You are formally invited to a B and F Club Sortie on the evening of Friday, September 29, 1961." There was no signature—only the words "Appointments Secretary."

When Blondie looked up, Dispatch was gone. *Sortie.* There was that word again.

"What does it mean?" Blondie asked Shakes a little later in the hallway. "What do you do on a sortie?"

"Well, there's n-no s-set thing," he answered. "But w-we almost always get dr-drunk."

"Is that all?" Blondie asked him.

"If th-things don't d-develop."

What things? Blondie felt his cool slipping.

"We're g-going to start at the g-game," Shakes said.

Oh yeah, the game. Blondie had forgotten. He hadn't been to a football game yet. At the least, he'd get to see Tammy strutting her stuff in front of the stand. He was still thinking of her when he took his seat in chemistry class.

A get-to-work glare from Farber focused Blondie's mind on the task at hand, which was the making of hydrochloric acid. He asked the class to form up in their assigned teams. Seconds later, Feller appeared at his side.

He poured salt into a beaker of sulfuric acid. The mixture steamed slightly.

"Did you get my invitation?" he asked Blondie.

"You're the club appointments secretary?"

"Sure. President and treasurer too."

"What does Brick do?"

"Brick doesn't do anything."

"Then why do you call it the B and F Club?"

"Brick said he wouldn't join unless I used his initial too."

"How'd this club get started?"

"It was sort of a revolutionary process. We all kind of revolved into each others' spheres of influence and then the gravity of our massed personalities pulled us into a synergistic bond."

"What?"

"That's physics. Grouper calls it the law of attraction of dis-synchronous bodies. You know, misfits."

Blondie was astounded.

"You openly admit you're misfits?"

"I don't admit I'm a misfit," Feller answered placidly. "I'll grant the others are."

"And the others agree?"

"Of course not. None of them has enough insight—or honesty—to realize he's a misfit—except Grouper, of course. But he doesn't consider the term derogatory. Of course, I wouldn't be telling you this if I didn't think you were an exception."

Blondie felt flattered.

"Well, gotta get back to my desk," Feller announced abruptly. He sauntered away.

"Wait, where are you going? The experiment's not over."

Blondie realized the class had gone silent. He looked around—right into Farber's face. His breath smelled bad.

"How are you doing, Mr. Reimer?"

Farber's breath began to smell even worse—like burning rubber.

"I think your experiment is going awry," Farber commented acidly.

When Blondie turned around, the beaker was smoking. Someone had dropped a cork into it. That explained the burning smell.

Feller winked at him from his seat in the back. He'd set him up! When the class ended, Blondie stormed angrily toward Feller.

"Why'd you do that?"

Feller graced him with an almost Christ-like smile.

"I didn't really want to. The other guys told me you had to pass some sort of initiation before we took you on a sortie. This one was pretty mild. We made Dispatch ride down Main Street with his head out the window and a Trojan on his nose."

Blondie felt somewhat mollified.

"Don't be sore," Feller continued. "I've got big plans for you."

What plans? Blondie was afraid to ask.

"Be in front of Rexall's at 7:30. We'll pick you up in the P-mobile."

Feller chuckled as he walked away.

P-mobile?

Chapter Nine

Like a mythic steel beast, the Pussymobile—a shark-finned, two-toned, purple-and-white 1958 Dodge Custom Royal Lancer—roared from the bright tunnel of Friday night Front Street and screeched to a stop in front of Rexall's. To Blondie, who waited shivering in a light sweater and Levis, its menacing chrome teeth and high-beam eyes served notice to the weak and faint-hearted to step aside. The B and F Club was on the prowl. And he was going to be with them!

Dispatch, the P-mobile's owner and keeper, held the steering wheel in a death grip, his eyes fixed straight ahead. Brick sat next to him with Feller riding shotgun. Shakes opened the back door for Blondie. As he got in, he could just distinguish Grouper sprawled like a beanbag chair in the shadows of the rear seat.

Feller explained to Blondie that Dispatch had named his car, first, from an excess of optimism, and second, because it had an electric reclining front seat to snare unsuspecting females.

"Most of us are of the opinion 'Pussymobile' is a misnomer," Feller went on. "We're not sure he's even fingered anyone in here."

Dispatch disputed Feller by embarking on a lengthy enumeration of his many conquests.

"Aw, shut up, Dispatch," Brick said. "You couldn't find your dick with both hands."

The first priority of a sortie, Feller told Blondie, was making a "run." Blondie understood from his words that a run consisted of finding a place to buy beer. Indeed, they soon wheeled in behind the Fenton Diner, an aluminum slug of a building. Their target was a dingy hole beneath the diner named the Suds Cellar. Blondie didn't understand how any of them could buy beer, since the drinking age was twenty-one and none of them were even eighteen. He asked Feller.

"Grouper could probably buy without any identification because he's ageless," Feller said, "but Grouper's a pussy, so Dispatch does it."

Blondie examined Dispatch's face in the skimpy light from the street. He looked to be no more than seventeen. Certainly not twenty-one.

"Dispatch has a fake ID," Feller explained. "Besides he's got balls."

He then asked each of them to pitch in a buck to buy a case of beer. Elementary math told Blondie that was four beers each. That was four more than he'd ever drunk in his life, his sole experience with beer to this point being a few sips a G.I. had offered him.

Feller told Blondie that Pabst Blue Ribbon had been selected as the official beer of the 1961-62 "season."

"Last year it was Carling's, but after a close vote, we decided it was panther piss."

"Yeah, p-panther p-piss," Shakes echoed.

"Don't fuck up," Brick instructed Dispatch as he got out of the car.

"One t-time, D-dispatch showed the b-bartender his student activity c-card," Shakes said.

"I thought he didn't get nervous," Blondie remarked.

"That d-doesn't mean he d-doesn't f-fuck up."

Dispatch reappeared shortly, wearing a smirk and carrying a brown cardboard box. He handed it through the window to Brick and then drove around town until he saw what he was looking for—an empty and secluded parking lot. It didn't seem to matter to any of them that it belonged to the First Methodist Church. Dispatch pulled in behind the chapel and killed the motor.

Grouper, who'd said nothing to this point, let out a long sigh and extended his huge paw over the front seat.

"Can you wait a minute?" Brick fussed at him as he ripped open the top of the case. He pulled a can opener from his jacket and began puncturing the hard steel tops one by one.

Blondie was amazed at the way they attacked their beers. They poured the golden liquid down their throats as if they'd just crossed the Sahara. Blondie wasn't about to tell the rest of them he could barely tolerate the stuff.

"One down, three to go," Brick announced with a loud belch. He offered everyone another can.

Blondie'd barely started on his first, but he wasn't about to betray his tardiness. He propped the can between his feet and reached for another. He began drinking it as fast as he could.

Every so often, Shakes would speak up and say something that everyone else ignored. Periodically, Brick would belch or fart and Feller would get on him for it. Otherwise, the P-mobile's cavernous interior was silent. Was this how a sortie went? It didn't seem very exciting.

Feller reached the same conclusion.

"What have we got here, a fucking graveyard? Blondie must think we're a bunch of corpses."

"Y-yeah, c-corpses," Shakes repeated as Grouper wrenched open another beer and Brick belched again.

"Ah, hell, why do I even bother with you jerk offs?" Feller muttered. "Come on, Dispatch, let's go to the game."

"Fuck the game," Brick said as Dispatch hit the ignition.

"Well, that should tide us over," Blondie said after he'd finished his beer. He was already a little woozy.

"Tide us over?" Feller asked. "Oh, you mean until after the game."

Blondie hadn't meant that at all. Was Feller suggesting the case they'd bought was only the *pre-game* refreshment? No way could he drink any more without getting tipsy...and he couldn't come home drunk. His parents would kill him.

As the P-mobile slid from its sanctuary, Blondie heard Grouper sigh again. When they passed under the next street light, Blondie saw that his eyes were closed. A beatific look illuminated his face.

"Grouper loves beer," Feller said.

Despite a warm tingling in his head, Blondie felt a chill between his shoulder blades when they arrived at the parking lot. He was heading into uncharted waters. All the goofballs and good-for-nothings from school would be at the game, but under less control.

Cars were crammed from curb to curb: cherry red Chevy Bel Airs with air scoops on the hoods, low-riding Ford pickups with mud flaps, long-nosed Edsels, classic Dodge hot rods—every kind of medium-priced to worthless vehicle Blondie could imagine. Most needed immediate first aid, their rusty scratches, bent fenders, and chipped chrome crying for the ministrations of a body-shop wizard.

Dispatch gunned the P-mobile through two wooden barricades labeled "Keep Off Grass" and parked on it anyway. A stream of students, plus a fair portion of adults, funneled through a gate in the cyclone fence behind FHS's bleacher section.

Mr. Farber guarded the gate, tickets in hand. He seemed as humorless and intense as ever, his short red hair aglow from the stadium lights. He scowled when he saw them.

"Fifty cents, boys," he said.

"Be careful, the Bear's watching," Feller whispered to Blondie, tilting his head.

Vice-principal Bearzinsky, a shadow beneath the bleacher, scrutinized the incoming crowd.

Shortly after they'd all paid, a surf-like growling began at the far end of the field and built into a roar. Through a break in the crowd, Blondie saw the home team run onto the field through a cordon of cheerleaders. They shook red-and-white pompoms as the player raced past. Blondie peered down the line of short skirts and bare legs to see if *she* was there. She was! That she seemed less boisterous than her comrades made her all the more appealing. He didn't want her to be a mindless Pollyanna.

The players huddled around Coach Warner in front of the bleachers as the cheerleaders executed a routine. At the end, they leapt into the air, kicking their legs outward, displaying dark blue panties.

"All r-right, sh-show us y-your privates," Shakes shouted.

Blondie sighed. Was it his fate to keep company with Philistines? He realized he and Shakes were alone.

"Where'd the others go?" he asked Shakes.

"L-looking for D-delores."

"Delores?"

"D-delores Clitoris."

Delores Clitoris? That couldn't be her real name.

"The guys always l-look for D-delores during a g-game. She's supposed to be a r-real nympho."

"Why?" Blondie asked.

"H-hormones, I g-guess."

"No, dummy," Blondie said. "I meant why are they looking for her?"

He hoped they weren't planning a gangbang. He hadn't signed up for anything like that. The thought of it tightened his stomach. If that was the kind of thing they did, they could include him out.

"D-dispatch always tries to t-talk D-delores into c-coming back to the c-car and g-giving everyone a hand j-job."

That was just as disgusting to Blondie—and just as unacceptable.

"Would she do that?"

"She never h-has."

Shakes giggled.

"Then why....?" Blondie started to ask, then quit.

"They'd h-have more l-luck with Flapping Fl-florence."

"Who?"

"Florence G-goldfarb," Shakes explained anyway. "Her f-father owns the h-hardware store. Brick c-calls her Flapping Fl-florence because she likes to s-sit between two g-guys and p-pull their p-puds. H-he says she l-looks like a b-bird taking off."

What kind of girl did things like that? And why? It seemed gross beyond measure to Blondie.

"This Florence did that with Brick?"

"N-no. H-he just heard about it."

"Isn't there anything you guys know from firsthand experience?" Blondie asked, exasperated.

"Wh-what are y-you sore about?"

"Nothing. I'm going to watch the game. Alone."

Blondie began climbing the bleacher so he could see the field better. At the top, he found the Grouper sitting by himself. Blondie was surprised. He'd assumed Grouper had gone off with the rest of them.

"What are you doing here?" he asked Grouper as he took a seat next to him.

"Watching the game, of course."

"I thought you'd be with the others."

"What? With that trollop?"

A look of contempt crossed his face.

Blondie felt relieved. They weren't all mad.

Grouper crossed his thick arms and legs and peered out at the field. Blondie followed his gaze. The sight was magical: the lime-green grass encased by the high dark walls of the night...the colorfully-dressed crowd tossing back and forth like exotic fish caught in the tide.

Brown scars in the earth marked where the two teams had battled. They were at the south end of the field, helmets down, facing each other for another ferocious charge. The cheerleaders were shouting, "Two, four, six, eight, who do we appreciate?" in spite of the fact the other team had the ball. But so what? All Blondie cared about was that Tammy was there. He imagined she was performing just for him.

"You like that one, don't you?" Grouper said.

Blondie felt like he'd been caught window peeping.

"Just enjoying the cheers. That's all."

Grouper grunted.

An eruption of noise snapped Blondie's mind back to the game. The opposition had fumbled the ball. Fenton High began to move. Unconnected as he felt to his new school, Blondie nonetheless felt a tremor of excitement as the Flyers made several first downs in a row.

Over and over, he heard the crowd murmur "Clements, Clements." Blondie guessed he was the nimble halfback who kept carrying the ball. He was tall for a running back, but he had shifty feet and a powerful glide. Blondie saw Tammy watching him. He felt jealous.

A hand grabbed his ankle.

"What the…?" Blondie looked down. Shakes had climbed up the back of the bleacher and was perched between two support beams.

"Are you nuts?" Blondie asked him. "You could kill yourself."

"Come on d-down," Shakes implored him. "I've g-got s-something to show y-you. G-grouper t-too."

Blondie glanced at Grouper. He was focused on the game.

"I'll pass," Grouper said.

Christ, Blondie grumbled to himself. He squeezed past knotty knees that pummeled his legs until he reached an aisle, then made his way to the underside of the bleacher.

"L-look," Shakes said, holding up a prophylactic. Blondie could tell it had been used. He gagged.

"You brought me down here to show me that?"

Shakes acted hurt.

"There's m-more," he said. He tugged at Blondie's sweater and pulled him further beneath the bleacher.

"L-look up," he said.

Blondie glanced up at the people standing above.

"So?"

"W-wait'll there's a b-big play."

A few minutes later, the crowd bellowed like a bull lanced by a picador. It rose in a wave.

"Now l-look. Y-you can see Mrs. Fogarty's snatch."

Blondie had no idea who Mrs. Fogarty was. He could make out several women overhead and he could see part way up their skirts, but then everything went dark. The furor ended and everyone sat down.

"D-did you s-see it?"

Blondie shook his head.

"I d-did. I'm sure I d-did."

"It was dark." Blondie said, not wanting to argue.

"She w-wasn't w-wearing any panties. It w-was a great squirrel sh-shot. I w-want to tell Brick."

"Then tell him."

"Y-you've got to b-back me up. He never b-believes me."

"How about if I say you might have seen it?"

"N-nobody ever b-backs me up," Shakes complained.

Blondie heard a low scraping noise behind him. He turned and saw two shadows mounting the fence. When he recognized their shapes, he stepped back into the shadows.

"Oh, sh-shit," Shakes said. "It's Barnwell and Purdy."

"I thought you weren't afraid of them."

"They'll k-kill me if they c-catch me alone," Shakes said.

In spite of his own trepidation, Blondie was annoyed by Shakes' comment.

"You're not alone," he said. "Now, why do you think they're out to get you?"

"Sh-sh-sh."

The figures dropped to the ground and briefly looked in their direction. Blondie felt his heart speed up. Then, soundlessly, they sneaked off. When they were out of sight, Shakes answered Blondie's question.

"I m-mooned them."

"What?"

"Y-yeah. I m-mooned them. Last weekend. They were p-parked down by the B-burger Palace and Brick m-made me m-moon them."

Blondie was growing wise enough not to ask why. He was also beginning to tire of Shakes' company. He went searching for the others.

Blondie found them in a semicircle on the far side of the gym. Leaning against the wall in their midst was a semi-cute girl in a black leather jacket and tight black skirt. She had to be Delores.

At first, Blondie thought she was seventeen or eighteen, but closer, in the pale reflection from the gym's windows, he could tell that, in spite of layers of makeup, she was no more than fifteen.

"How about just me, then?" Blondie heard Brick ask her.

For a moment, Blondie imagined something sinister in the tableau before him…a gang rape. But as he approached, he noticed that Delores was laughing. It was all an act. The guys were teasing her and she was teasing back.

"I wouldn't touch any of your things," Delores declared.

"Not even Goliath?" Brick asked her.

"Goliath? Is that what you call it?" She laughed. "I bet I'd need a microscope to find any of your little dickies. If I even wanted to, which I don't."

Feller began to chuckle. Blondie could tell he found the whole scene grand theater. Blondie heard footsteps behind him and turned to see Grouper and Shakes approaching.

"I wondered where you guys were," Feller said.

The rest of group turned toward them as well. While Shakes recounted how Buford and Purdy had jumped the fence, Delores walked away.

"Billies getting in for free?" Grouper said. "Unacceptable."

"Ah, this whole scene sucks," Brick said in disgust. "Let's get some more beer."

Grouper readily agreed: "Girls are okay, but **a beer is a man's best friend.**"

"Hey, isn't that a law?" Blondie asked Feller.

"You bet. It just isn't a new one."

With Grouper leading the way—his huge torso rocking forward with each stiff-legged step from his stilt-like legs—the Club made its way back to the P-mobile.

Just before they reached it, Blondie heard a rasping sound. Brick was dragging his can opener along the side of a red-and-white Ford Galaxie Skyliner.

"What are you doing, you moron?" Feller yelled at him.

"It's the Bear's car," Brick answered.

"I know, I know. Jesus. Get in the car."

Feller shoved Brick toward the P-mobile. Dispatch already had started the motor and as soon as they were all in, he gunned the motor, sending up a rooster tail of grass and dirt.

"Christ, can't any of you do anything right?" Feller screamed. "Dispatch, just give it a little gas."

The P-mobile lurched forward, tipping Blondie's leftover beer. He felt the cold liquid settle into the bottom of his shoes.

"What'd you do that for?" Feller yapped at Brick.

"Bearzinsky's an asshole," Brick replied.

"That's not good enough. We don't do things like that in this group."

"Ah, blow it out your ass, Feller," Brick mumbled.

Blondie was glad Feller was on Brick's case. He couldn't condone vandalism.

As they were leaving the parking lot, they saw another car speeding from a nearby exit. A black Mercury Meteor.

"Hold it!" Feller commanded.

Dispatch stomped on the brake.

"What's up?" Brick asked.

"That's Jump-em Johnson's car," Feller said. "And Susan Conner was in it."

"Not Susan Conner, Dispatch's steadfast virgin?" Grouper asked.

"The very same. Can Johnson succeed where Dispatch failed?"

"No way," Dispatch said.

"The question seems to be," Grouper said, "what happens when the unstoppable member meets the impenetrable hymen."

"Why don't we find out?" Feller said. "Hit it, Dispatch."

"Y-you m-mean a c-car chase?" Shakes asked.

"CAR CHASE!" the rest of them shouted.

Chapter Ten

Up Front Street and west on Home Street, south on Horace and east on First Street. The P-mobile's cat eyes lasered through the darkness—subjecting drunkards and derelicts to blinding light—while its rubber paws pulled them forward in gut-wrenching lunges. But their quarry eluded them. The black Meteor had been swallowed by the night.

"Way to go, Dispatch, you lost them," Brick sniped.

"Feller didn't even tell me to follow them until they were nearly out of sight," Dispatch defended.

"The true warrior never waits for orders," Feller declared.

"Ah, get fucked," Dispatch growled.

They were all nuts, Blondie decided. They were the Three Stooges, the Bowery Boys, the Marx Brothers. They barked and bit at each other like a pack of wild dogs. They cursed and blasphemed like candidates for hell. *They were his kind of guys.*

"What about the beer?" Brick demanded.

"B-beer, b-beer, b-beer…." Shakes began chanting.

Brick and Dispatch joined in…a group mantra. Grouper boomed out "beer" in final punctuation.

"All right," Feller agreed. "Back to the Suds Cellar."

Soon, another case of Pabst floated from the Suds Cellar astride Dispatch's chunky shoulders. Four more beers each, Blondie thought in dismay. He still felt a little unsteady from the can and a half he'd downed so far.

The group killed off another two beers each in the diner parking lot, Blondie struggling to keep pace. With each swig, the mood inside the P-mobile gravitated further toward the manic.

Dispatch flicked on the radio. Dion was belting out his new hit, "Runaround Sue."

"Hey, isn't that your girl Susan?" Brick taunted Dispatch.

"She's not my girl." Dispatch grumbled.

The song jazzed them even more. Soon, everyone was shouting the words.

"H-hey Blondie, h-have y-you ever heard Brick's f-first law of s-sexual dynamics?" Shakes shouted above the din.

Blondie shook his head. He thought Grouper was the only one who made laws.

"Brick, t-tell Blondie the f-first l-law of s-sexual dynamics."

"Eat me," Brick responded.

"Ah, go ahead, Brick," Feller urged. "This is a chance to show everyone that you're not a complete ignoramus."

Brick scowled at Feller.

"Okay," he grumbled. "The heat of the meat is directly proportional to the angle of the dangle multiplied by the mass of the ass, so long as the square of the hair remains constant."

Shakes giggled.

"What d-did I t-tell you?" Shakes said to Blondie, who had no idea what his point was.

"Oh Christ, here comes Turley," Dispatch said, turning the key in the ignition.

Blondie followed Dispatch's gaze and saw a police cruiser turn off Front Street and head their way. His stomach seized up. What if they got busted? He could already feel himself turning into a spineless noodle under their condemning eyes.

Dispatch kept the P-mobile idling until the bubbletop slowed and disappeared behind the front of the diner.

"He's circling," Feller said.

Dispatch eased the P-mobile out and around the diner. Just as it rounded one end, the taillights of the police car disappeared around the other.

Feller congratulated Dispatch as he turned south on Baltimore Pike.

"H-hey l-look..." Shakes shouted, pointing behind them.

The black Meteor was crossing the pike on Flynn street, a hundred yards behind.

"Where are they going?" Feller asked.

"They must be going to Susan's," Dispatch answered. "She lives just around the corner."

"It's not even ten-thirty," Brick said. "Johnson wouldn't be taking her home now."

"Maybe she's more resistant than we thought," Feller responded. "Let's find out."

Dispatch turned around at the first place he could. By the time they reached Flynn, the Mercury was already parked halfway down the block. It appeared deserted.

Dispatch eased the Dodge alongside the curb across the street and killed the motor.

"You dickhead," Brick said, "You stop right under a street light."

Dispatch reached for the key.

"Don't move now," Feller said. "You'll draw attention."

"There's no one in the car," Brick said. "This is a fucking wild duck hunt."

"Wild goose chase," Feller corrected.

"Whatever."

"GET DOWN!" Grouper ordered.

Two shadowy heads had surfaced from the Meteor's depths.

Everyone ducked but Grouper, who was in shadow and, with his bulk, had nowhere to go.

"What's happening?" Feller asked him from a crouch.

"They're apart. She appears to be talking to him. Or arguing with him."

"I told you she was tough," Dispatch said. "You'd need a backhoe to get into her snatch."

"Yeah, well, what were they doing a minute ago, when we couldn't see their heads?" Feller asked.

Dispatch didn't respond.

"Wait a minute," Grouper said portentously. "She's moving toward him. He's putting his arm around her. THEY'RE DOWN!"

Slowly, five heads rose in the P-mobile. All peered intently at the car across the street.

"God, they've been down five minutes," Feller said after a while. Blondie didn't think it had been anywhere near that long.

"Y-yeah. I w-wonder what they're doing," Shakes said.

"Maybe Johnson's playing hide-the-salami with her," Feller said.

"Or m-maybe h-he's m-muffdiving," Shakes giggled.

"Come on, you guys," Dispatch pleaded. "She isn't that kind of girl."

"At least not with you," Feller replied evenly.

What were they talking about, Blondie wondered. A guy putting his mouth between a girl's legs? Now, that was gross.

"THEY'RE UP," Grouper announced. His voice was like a klaxon sounding on a submarine...dive, dive! Everyone but Grouper slumped from sight again.

"They couldn't have done anything," Dispatch said. "They didn't have time."

"Give me a break, will you?" Brick responded. "He could've reamed her out good by now."

"THEY'RE DOWN," Grouper thundered.

"Give me another beer," Brick said as the group slowly inched up into sitting positions. Feller handed out another round. Blondie took another, although he already was having trouble making out the shapes in the car across the street.

Another beer went down before Grouper said, "THEY'RE UP!"

They slid down on curved spines.

"God, Johnson must've taken her around the world," Feller remarked. Blondie wondered what that meant.

"They're probably just snuggling," Dispatch said.

"Yeah, and Santa Claus lives in my basement," Brick retorted.

"Aw, shut up," Dispatch snarled at him.

"WHAT?"

"Forget it, Brick," Feller said. "You gotta remember that Dispatch has feelings."

"In a pig's ass he does."

Blondie briefly flashed on a pig's backside…pink and round with a corkscrew tail. The tail begin to spin, then his head began to spin. He leaned forward on the back of the front seat.

"Are you all right, Blondie?" Feller asked.

"Um-mm," Blondie replied through clenched lips. He felt a warm column of something soft pushing up into his throat.

"THEY'RE DOWN."

"They're up, they're down," Brick repeated sarcastically as he sat back up. "Push-ups in a cucumber patch. They're doing it, I tell you."

"You don't know that," Dispatch said, still resisting.

Someone stuck another beer in Blondie's hand.

"What do you think, Grouper?" Feller asked him.

Years cycled by in Blondie's mind before Grouper finally spoke.

"A woman's virtue is often a matter of circumstance."

Blondie didn't remember anything for a while after that. The guys must've grown tired of debating Johnson's and Susan's behavior, because the next thing Blondie saw was a large neon sign that said "Burger Palace." He was on his back with his head across Shakes' lap.

"He's gonna hold it," Blondie heard someone say.

"No, he's not," someone answered. "He's going to lose it."

"Please, n-not on m-me," Shakes begged.

"Well, now, look who's arrived."

Blondie recognized Brick's voice. Then he heard another voice that sounded familiar.... an unpleasant one.

The neon sign began to turn black and the night sky began to turn white. The world was turning into a photo negative. A buzzing in his head kept him from making out the words being spoken, but Blondie thought he detected angry tones.

Like a geyser of oatmeal, the warm column in his throat began pushing into his mouth. Blondie knew there was no holding it this time. With a surge of energy born of compassion for Shakes, Blondie flipped over on his stomach and opened the door. He just managed to push his body forward and get his mouth over the pavement before he blew.

The last thing he remembered as he lost his cookies were someone's feet beneath his erupting maw.

* * * * * * *

A muffled clanging echoed through the chambers of his skull—someone building a boiler deep within his brain. At first, Blondie could see nothing but black. Then, slowly, a pattern emerged...cross stitches of white, like sutures. As the clanging continued, he seemed to float upward in the void until the objects ratcheted into focus. He found himself face-to-face with a pair of black canvas sneakers.

His mother's voice calling him to breakfast yanked him from the last clutches of sleep. His head was pounding and the taste in his mouth was ferocious. Sand filled his eyes. The door eased open.

His mother peeked in and said, "Time to get up, dear. You're going to be late to school."

Blondie stumbled into his pajamas and felt his way to the kitchen. Everything—walls, stairs, furniture—was fuzzy and indistinct. Worse, things kept moving before his eyes..

His mom and dad were already dressed. His mom smiled pleasantly at him. His dad smiled pleasantly at him. They seemed to know something he didn't.

Blondie sat down and placed his elbows on the Formica tabletop. He dropped his head into his hands.

"Is everything okay, son?" his mom asked.

He looked up through half-opened eyes. She was staring at him.

"You don't look good, son," his dad said. He smirked at him in a malevolent way. "I think you're hung over."

His mom froze, mouth agape. Everything was too bright, but Blondie couldn't shut his eyes.

Then his dad winked at him and said, "The best thing for a hangover is a stiff belt."

He reached under the table and brought up a bottle of Kentucky Turkey. He poured three glasses. His mother licked her lips as she reached for one.

Blondie woke up in a sweat, his sheets stuck to him like flypaper. He looked over at the clock: 9:26. Why hadn't his mom come for him? He remembered. It was Saturday. His parents let him sleep as late as he wanted on Saturday.

Blondie forced himself to get up. While shaving, he rammed his big toe into the portable heater and cut it. Drops of blood spotted the cold tile as he searched for some bandages. He spilled them on the floor opening the box. He couldn't find one to fit his big toe. When he put shaving lather on his toothbrush, Blondie decided he wasn't ready to face the day. He went back to bed.

His folks were gone when he woke. A note taped to the refrigerator read, "Gone to buy groceries, lazy bones. Fend for yourself." Blondie poured some cereal into a bowl before he discovered the thought of milk made him sick. He scrounged around in the fridge until he found a couple small winter tomatoes from Florida. He ate them raw with salt.

He picked up the newspaper his dad had left on the dining table and turned to the sports page. Roger Maris hadn't hit a home run the night before. Good. He was still tied with the Babe. Blondie didn't want Maris to get the record. The Babe had been a Baltimore boy.

A large photograph of President Kennedy and the first lady graced the front of the next section. Blondie admired JFK. He was like a god—so handsome, so confident. He fantasized himself as a young Jack Kennedy. He bet Tammy would go for him then…probably all the way. In spite of his reverence for her, an image of her lying naked on a bed popped into his mind. Her dark triangle of femininity was aimed right at him. The thought of it made him shiver. Were other guys this nuts? No wonder girls had such immense control over them. Thinking of Tammy stirred a thought in his muzzy mind.

"This is the night of the CYO dance…." Blondie tried to trace the idea further by adding, "That means…" He couldn't remember what CYO stood for. After a few moments of concentration, it came to him—Catholic Youth Organization. The dance was in the basement of a church, Church of the Sacred Bleeding Heart or something like that. Shakes had told him the whole club was going.

"Big deal," Blondie'd replied.

Shakes had given him a sly look.

"T-tammy's usually there."

What a scumbag she'd think he was if she saw him now. He had to finish shaving, then shower and get dressed. Had to.

Blondie was proud of his transformation by the time his parents returned from their trip into town. Tight, appropriately faded jeans. White shirt with collar turned up. Sand-colored Hush Puppies. Except for roadmap eyes, he looked pretty good. He hid them behind a pair of sunglasses.

"Why are you wearing sunglasses in the house?" his dad asked.

"Really, Bernard. It's not good for your eyes," his mother added.

Blondie donned a sweater and went outside on the porch. Sharp light etched his retinas. He squinted and forced himself to focus on the sharp outline of a just-framed house on a far hill. He wanted to use it like a knife to whittle away the haziness inside his head. But staring at the house gave him a headache.

He went back into the house and joined his dad, who was watching a football game in the family room. He never said a word to Blondie, although he griped about a couple bad calls in a way that seemed to include him in his disaffection.

Dinner that evening was a struggle because his mother kept trying to get him to eat more, unaware that what he'd already eaten had driven him to the verge of nausea.

"Do you have plans for tonight, Bernard?" she asked.

"Going to a dance," he mumbled.

"A dance. How nice."

How could he tell her? He didn't want nice. He wanted action.

Chapter Eleven

By the time 8:00 p.m. rolled around, Blondie was going stir crazy. He'd started to watch *Perry Mason*, but he couldn't get into it. His mind kept jumping from one thing to the next. He felt there was something he should be remembering, but he couldn't get a fix on it. His heart leapt when he heard the hammering engine strokes of the P-mobile.

Dispatch's eyebrows were knotted together when Blondie got in the car. The corner of his mouth jerked when he put the car in gear. Blondie could tell he was agitated.

"Something bothering you?" he asked.

"Nearly got in Kathy Ricardo's bra last night," Dispatch said.

"Nearly?"

"She had on this fucking double hooker. I couldn't get it undone. When I asked her to help, she said her mood had passed."

"Tough luck," Blondie said.

"What's wrong with the people who make those things? I mean, they oughta put the hook in front."

Blondie couldn't suppress a grin. No wonder he liked this bunch. They were at least as fucked up as he was.

"Cheer up, Dispatch. Things could be worse."

"Yeah, I know. I could be you."

Blondie didn't like the sound of that.

"What are you talking about?" he asked.

"You threw up all over Buford's shoes."

A fault line opened in his consciousness.

"Barnwell?"

"Yeah, how many other Bufords do you know?"

"Those were his black sneakers?" Blondie blathered, fighting the truth of it.

"Well, they *were* black. Now they're all kinds of colors. If Brick hadn't been there…." Dispatch's voice trailed off.

"Was Buford real mad?"

Dispatch's jaw dropped. He stared at Blondie.

"He said you were dead meat."

DEAD MEAT. It sounded so ominous, so final. An image: a tangled mass of blood and hair on the highway…road kill. His fate.

"Why didn't he go after me last night?"

"Are you kidding? You had puke all over your shirt."

His shirt. What had he done with his shirt? Oh yeah, he'd dumped it in the laundry hamper—right where his mother would find it! Well, at least she wouldn't beat him to a pulp like Buford would.

"He still might have killed you if Brick hadn't have told him to lay off," Dispatch added.

"Buford's afraid of Brick?"

There was hope after all.

"Some, but Brick said he wouldn't want to tangle with Buford either."

"What was Buford doing beside the P-mobile?"

"Just giving us some gas. Nothing serious."

Dispatch headed south out of town, past the bowling alley and Shain's used car lot. Just past Shain's, Dispatch turned left onto a gravel road bounded on one side by a rickety fence. The homes were father apart than in town, but smaller and more run down. Some had rusting appliances on their porches.

Shakes' home was a ramshackle bungalow behind a stunted willow. A tire leaned against the front stoop, apparently a castoff from the aging

Studebaker in the drive. A pane in one of the front windows was missing, the glass replaced with a dark rag…a house with a black eye.

A light flared inside when Dispatch honked the horn. A few minutes later, Shakes shuffled out in a flimsy wool jacket and dark pants. He affected a jaunty walk as he approached the car, but his smile seemed feigned. A shadow fell across his left cheek. It failed to disappear when he opened the door and the light came on.

"What happened to you?" Blondie asked him.

"I r-ran into the dr-dresser."

"You aren't that short," Blondie said, attempting humor.

"I s-said I d-did, d-didn't I?"

"Hey, no need to be sore. I don't give a shit if you're clumsy."

Dispatch drove on, picking up the rest of the gang—Brick, Feller, and the Grouper. Blondie whistled softly when they arrived at the Whipples. Class: fieldstone with gables and wainscoting on the second floor, set back from the road in a grove of trees. A mansion by Fenton's standards. Blondie wondered what Grouper's dad did.

All aboard, Dispatch directed the P-mobile back toward the outskirts of town, where, on a small hill a block off the highway, they arrived at a gray stone structure with a white spire—the "Church of the Bleeding Martyr" according to the sign in front. Halfway down the hill was a parking lot full of cars no self-respecting adult would have owned. Dispatch added the P-mobile to the collection.

Music blared from an open door beneath the sanctuary. Guarding the entrance was a balding, mild-mannered-looking man in gray slacks and an argyle sweater. Behind him was a sign: "Alcoholic Beverages Forbidden." In longhand, someone had added "Ditto for Drunkenness."

Inside, kids were milling about like barnyard fowl seeking feed—fluttery, disordered. A turntable and records were stacked on a card table at the far end of the cavernous room. The deejay, a gangly youth with glasses and an unfortunate complexion, slapped a record on the turntable.

Elvis began belting out "Little Sister." A few girls looked hopefully around. Boys avoided their looks and talked with friends or leaned against the wall, smoking.

With a start, Blondie saw that one of the wall-bound smokers was Buford. Blondie ducked behind a support beam. He looked for Purdy, but didn't see him. He turned to find himself facing Bobby Clements, star halfback. Bobby appraised him in a non-threatening way.

"You're new here, aren't you?" he asked. He was wearing a burgundy sweater vest over a white shirt. Blondie noted his powerful, sloping shoulders and confident gaze. He was glad Bobby hadn't asked him why he was hiding behind the post.

"Yes, new," Blondie answered.

"You hang around with Feller and his group," Bobby said in such a neutral way Blondie couldn't tell if hanging around with them was good or bad.

"Sometimes," Blondie answered, hedging his bets.

Blondie turned his attention back to Buford. Peering around the post, he saw that Buford's sidekick Purdy had joined him. Now there were two of them.

"Is Buford giving you a hard time?" Bobby asked.

Blondie started to lie, then thought better of it.

"He doesn't like me."

"He's a jerk."

Blondie admired the casual way Bobby said it, as if he didn't care whether Buford heard him or not.

"Guess I better check things out," Bobby said, strolling away.

Alone, Blondie grew fearful. He edged his way toward Brick and Dispatch, who were standing in a corner, casting disdainful glances at a group of girls.

"What do you think of that one?" he heard Dispatch ask Brick.

Blondie followed Dispatch's glance and saw a plain, but nice-looking girl in a pink dress. Not bad, he thought.

"A dog," Brick said. "a real hound."

"How about her?"

This one was tall, with a hint of mustache.

"Another barker," Brick responded.

His expression suddenly changed. His eyes glazed over and his mouth fell open. Blondie followed his look. Coming through the entrance was a girl in a short black skirt so tight it seemed painted on. Her large breasts challenged the tensile strength of her bright red blouse. Her face bespoke sexual understanding.

Blondie looked to Dispatch for an explanation, but he was transfixed as well, apparently suffering a brain boner.

"Who's that?" Blondie asked.

"Linda Lapidus," he murmured, as if waking from a dream. "She's just a tenth-grader, but...." His voice trailed off.

"Does she go down?" Blondie whispered, hoping his question would make him sound knowledgeable about such things.

"Nobody knows."

"Why are you two so crazy then?"

"Just wait," Brick replied.

Feller walk over to the nerdy kid behind the turntable and said something to him. A few seconds later, the bouncy beat of "The Twist" filled the room.

"Ask her to dance," Brick said to Blondie.

"Me?"

"Go on, ask her."

Blondie wasn't about to do any such thing. She was too formidable. Without warning, he found himself tumbling forward until he was almost on top of her, propelled by a hard shove in his back. The girl brought her eyes up to his and raised her brows.

"Wanna dance?" Blondie asked huskily. His face felt like the inside of a boiler.

She shrugged.

Blondie led her toward two other couples who were dancing. As soon as he turned toward her, she began to dance. She didn't do the Twist. What she did had no name. With her legs rooted, she rocked her pelvis back and forth at him, at first slowly, then faster and faster. There was no mistaking the motion. She was *fucking* the space in front of her. Blondie was glad he hadn't stood too close. Her mons would be pounding his thigh like a jackhammer.

Everyone had to be watching. He bet his face was as red as baboon's backside. He felt like someone who'd taken a bitch in heat to a high-class dog show. He cast an angry glance Brick's way, but Brick was paying him no attention. His eyes were epoxied to Linda's hips. His head bobbed with every thrust. It was the same with all the guys. Even the girls were watching her, although with far less enthusiasm. He was foolish to feel self-conscious. Nobody was watching him at all.

Except Buford. Blondie picked him out of the crowd, staring at him with his cold cat's eyes and clenching and unclenching his fists. Purdy was watching him, too, a vengeful smile on his flabby face.

How would he ever get out of this, Blondie wondered. First, he was going to be embarrassed to near death, then pummeled the rest of the way. DEAD MEAT.

Still gyrating, Blondie scanned the room for a way out where he didn't have to pass by Buford. His eyes caught on a face in the crowd. Witnessing Linda's wild dance of love was his Venus—Tammy. She was wearing a white angora sweater over a blue skirt. She suddenly shifted her gaze to him. He tried to read the look she gave him. She probably thought he was some kind of Satyr, joined as he was in a frenetic mating dance with an out-of-control pelvis. How would he ever explain? He had to get off the floor.

The record ended just before he reached the point of despair. Buford began walking his way. His gait was both casual and purposeful, the swagger of the executioner.

"Thanks," Blondie mumbled at his exhausted partner. He ducked his head and edged away from the couples milling onto the dance floor at the first strains of "The Lion Sleeps Tonight." The lights began to dim.

Blondie circled away from Buford and Purdy. He came to a door marked "restrooms" and shoved his way through it. He darted into the men's room, surprising a youngster squeezing a zit. He bolted from the room.

Blondie opened a stall door and sat down on the john to catch his breath.

He heard the door open again, so he loosened his belt and dropped his pants to the floor to avoid suspicion. It was the wrong move.

"Well, well, look who's taking a shit," he heard Purdy say.

"No dummy. He isn't taking a shit. He *is* a shit." That was Buford.

Blondie was in for it now. How would he ever get out alive? In desperation, Blondie began making farting sounds by blowing on his arm with his mouth.

"Kee-rist!" Buford exclaimed. "I'm going to have to waste him while he's on the can."

Fingernails scraped against the metal.

"You're going to have to crawl under there and get him," Purdy said.

"Bullshit. I'm not crawling under a stall door even to kill this worthless turd."

Good, Blondie thought. Maybe they'll leave.

"You go under," Buford told Purdy.

"Me. I don't want to do that."

"Get your fat ass down on the floor and grab his fucking feet," Buford ordered.

Blondie heard some grunting, then a fleshy hand began reaching for his ankles. He brought his heel down on the back of Purdy's hand.

"Jesus!" Purdy shouted.

"You dumb fuck. Let me look under there."

Buford peered under the stall door, his face contorted with rage.

The door to the restroom opened again.

"What are you two doing?" a man inquired.

Grasping at a potential reprieve, Blondie shouted, "What's wrong with you guys? Why don't you go after girls?"

"You bastard," Buford yelled back. "I'm going to pull your nuts right out of their sack."

"Who are you talking to like that?" The man's voice rose. "I don't like your attitude. In fact, if you don't leave the premises right now, I'm calling the police."

A long silence followed the man's threat. Blondie could sense Buford's fury. It crackled the air like an approaching thunderstorm. Finally, he heard the door open and crash shut. They were gone.

"You in there. Come on out."

Blondie pulled his pants back up and fastened them. He opened the door.

Standing before him was the mild-mannered man who'd taken his money at the door.

"What's going on?" he demanded.

"Sir, I don't know. Those two boys came in while I was going to the bathroom and they began making remarks of a perverted nature, so I hid in the stall."

The man's eyes narrowed in skepticism.

"Sounds fishy to me. You better get back to the dance."

"Yes sir." Blondie detested the unctuous tone in his voice.

When he reentered the main room, it was dark except for a rotating mirrored ball on the ceiling, which cast shards of light onto the shadowy dancers below. When Blondie's eyes adjusted, he saw Brick and Dispatch with Feller and the Grouper. Tammy was standing nearby, talking to the homely girl who rode his bus.

"Let's blow this joint," Dispatch said as Blondie arrived. "It's scag's night out."

"Where's Shakes?" Feller asked.

"He's been following a dumpy little Jewish girl around all night," Brick answered.

"Janine Raznosky?"

"She looks like a woodpecker with that nose," Dispatch said.

"Yeah, and that's all I'd put in her too," Brick commented.

Feller sent Dispatch to collect Shakes. He reappeared shortly, dragging Shakes by the arm.

"I c-could've n-nailed her, I t-tell you...."

"No. You could've needled her," Brick said.

"It's time for some processed barley," Grouper announced to general acclaim.

They began trooping toward the exit, but Blondie didn't move.

"Aren't you coming?" Feller asked.

"I'm not ready yet."

Feller gave him an inquisitive look.

Sweat broke out on his forehead. How could he explain his paralysis to Feller? How could he make him understand that the evening would be a bust if he didn't dance with *her*? The idea scared him to death, but he had to do it—and it had to be a slow dance, so he could hold her tight.

"Blondie isn't ready to go yet," Feller called after the others. They turned and looked at him.

Blondie heard the strains of a new song, a slow song. It was now or never. Blondie told his wooden legs to move and, to his surprise, they did. He peg-legged himself across the dance floor, feeling condemned, knowing she'd turn him down...knowing also that he was a slave to his fate.

She was looking away when he reached her. The pigtailed girl looked at him in surprise. Tammy turned her head.

"Would you like to dance?" he asked her—too forcefully, he thought. Nerves.

"Okay."

Blondie was flustered by her acceptance. He'd been preparing himself for rejection. Still, he retained enough presence of mind to lead her into the swaying crowd.

When he took her in his arms, she rested her head on his chest as if he and she were steadies. Her hair was soft against his cheek and her smell was fresh like…like what? Like clean hair? He was flipping out.

The Lettermen were crooning.

> "Someday, when I'm awfully low and the world is cold,
> I will feel a glow just thinking of you
> and the way you look tonight.
> You're lovely, with your smile so warm
> and your cheeks so soft,
> there is nothing for me but to love you,
> just the way you look tonight."

Time slowed and the rest of the world disappeared behind the lacy curtain of his infatuation. He was suspended in sweet nectar, slowly revolving in perfect harmony with his angel. On and on the Lettermen sang as he floated with her above the world somewhere, lost in the place where the very idea of love begins.

Blondie didn't even notice when the song ended. He was startled when her arms fell away from him. She gave him a warm smile—what did it mean?—and walked off.

For a moment, he stood alone in the middle of the dance floor, disoriented. Had she been with him in that faraway place? Or had he been hallucinating?

The whole club was watching him, Grouper most intently. Dispatch signaled for Blondie to come along. While the others filed out, Grouper lagged behind. A melancholy expression gripped his face.

When the rest were too far away to hear, Grouper leaned toward Blondie and whispered: **"Only assholes fall in love."**

Chapter Twelve

His dad had planted an ash tree in the front yard in mid-September. "Best time to plant a tree," he'd said. A few dozen leaves had decked its limbs then. Now, a month later, only one remained. Blondie identified with the solitary leaf. He felt like he was just hanging on and any day a stiff breeze would blow him away.

Sunday. His parents already had left for church. Sunday. Two weeks and a day since he'd made an ass of himself in front of *Tammy's dad* at the CYO dance. Feller had given him that unwanted piece of news as soon as he'd arrived at school the following Monday. Since then, he'd been semi-depressed, passing through the halls of school as unobtrusively as a monk.

Not only was he afraid of encountering Tammy—her dad had surely told her about his bizarre behavior in the restroom—but he could tell from Buford's glares that the animosity he'd aroused by puking on his sneakers had been compounded enormously by his more-or-less calling him a homosexual.

"Billies are big-time into being he-men," Grouper'd told him. "You can call a billy a drunk, a wife-beater, even a child molester, and probably get away with it. But never call one a pansy. That's a challenge to his manhood."

Grouper had said it in a scornful way, but Blondie recognized the truth behind his words. There would be no forgiving. The only thing that was saving him from Buford's harsh knuckles so far, he was sure, was carefully planning his routes to and from class so he always was in as big a crowd as possible.

Blondie continued to stare out the window. The sky had clouded over in long gray ridges, like the underbelly of a whale. Perhaps it would snow. It could make him no more a prisoner.

Blondie heard the Pontiac whoosh up the driveway and soon the report of a door being shut. He heard his mother's heels smack across the front porch and shortly the sounds of her sobs inside the house. He heard his dad call his mom's name just before their bedroom door slammed shut. What was it this time? After a while, he heard a knock at his bedroom door and his mother slipped into the room.

She'd quit crying, though crimson blotched her face. Her expression was a mix of anger and hurt. Blondie immediately felt the weight of her need.

"Your father..." she began in a tone of outrage. She began to cry again. She plopped down on the bed, her body heaving. Blondie went to her and awkwardly placed put his arm around her.

After a while, she told him his dad had refused to skip the next meeting of his military group to attend an open house at her school.

"He's more concerned with those washed-up old sots than he is about me," she accused.

Was this the kind of thing other husbands and wives got upset about? If so, what was the point of being married?

"Don't you think you're overreacting, mom?"

"Sure, take his side," she said. "Men always stick together."

Blondie was flattered that she'd called him a man, but stupefied that she thought he and his dad shared some commonality of outlook. He was beginning to get a headache. But, he could tell his mom was beginning to calm down. Her wracking sobs had given way to sporadic tremors.

"Your dad makes me so damn mad!" Her anger flared again.

"I know, mom."

"You don't know everything about Francis and me," she said in a much softer voice.

"What do you mean?"

"Never you mind. When you're eighteen," she answered. She sighed deeply and trudged off.

Blondie knew her upset would be over by the time she finished cooking dinner, but now he was curious. What had she been talking about? A secret? He bet he knew what it was: he was adopted. That would explain his light coloring, why he felt so little in common with his dad. He was probably impotent. Blondie'd read about it in a booklet in the doctor's office.

Later, after dark, tiny snowflakes began to fall—nothing much, a half-hearted effort by the weather gods, but a harbinger of winter's approach.

When he awoke the next morning, Blondie felt a modicum of enthusiasm about going to school. Feller had offered to chauffeur him in his dad's aging black-and-white two-tone Fairlane. So it wasn't a Corvette or even a souped-up Chevy—how many kids got to go to school in any car at all? Besides, this would give him a chance to know Feller better. He was the only one of their group with any status at school.

Blondie waited a minute or two after Feller arrived so he wouldn't think he was too eager, then sauntered out.

"I don't get dad's car very often," Feller said after he got in. "Not much, is it?"

"One day away from the bus is not to be sneered at."

Feller laughed.

"You don't think much of the kids here in Fenton, do you?"

"Do you?" Blondie shot back.

"Ah, they're not so bad. A little rough around the edges maybe."

"They're all edges."

Feller laughed again. He didn't seem to mind what Blondie was saying.

"You don't identify with them, do you?"

Feller shrugged.

"I'm not planning to spend my whole life here anyway."
"What do you think you'll do?"
"I don't know. Take pictures maybe."
"You mean be a photographer?"
"Yeah, I like to do that. I'm in Photography Club, you know."

Blondie didn't know. He'd passed on joining any clubs first semester because he didn't know anyone.

"It could be great to travel the world, just taking pictures of new places and people and getting paid for it...." Feller stopped.

"Yeah, that could be great," Blondie agreed. He was impressed. Feller had dreams too.

"You?" Feller asked.
"Sometimes I write things."
"Like what?"
"Stories, poems."
"Yeah? Can I see some?"

Blondie felt threatened. What he wrote was personal. Feller might think he was a jerk if he read them.

"I guess."
"No big deal," Feller said. "If you want to, I'd be interested. If you don't, that's all right."

Blondie liked the way Feller never seemed to push. He was smooth in a way Blondie didn't think he ever would be. Everything was so important to him.

That was probably why he liked Miss Darlington so much. She was the same way. She was passionate this morning about what was going on in the South, where Martin Luther King and his followers were registering blacks to vote.

"No one's keeping them from voting now," one boy said.
"Actually, they are," Miss Darlington replied. "In most Southern states, Negroes have to pass tests to prove they're qualified to vote."

"What's wrong with that?" the boy shot back. "You should be smart enough to know the issues before you're allowed to vote."

"Perhaps," Miss Darlington conceded, a trace of a smile on her face. Blondie knew she loved it when she was able to capture the class's attention. Most of the time they just sat like lumps of coal or horsed around with each other. "But no one is making whites take any tests and many of them couldn't pass the tests either. Beyond that, most Negroes are intimidated from even taking the tests."

"Still, they're breaking the law," a girl named Alice said.

"True, but are the laws fair?"

"The people in the states passed them," Alice argued.

"Yes, but only some of them got to vote."

Blondie admired the calm way Miss Darlington listened to everything the class threw at her. He wouldn't have been so calm.

Some of the kids talked about Martin Luther King like he was a real threat to the American way of life. Blondie didn't understand that. Negroes just wanted to vote like anyone else. That *was* the American way of life, wasn't it?

He raised his hand and proclaimed his support for what the marchers were doing. Blondie noted the look of approval on Miss Darlington's face and felt a jolt of gratification. As he was leaving class, she stopped him and asked if he'd be willing to do a short report on the history of Negro voting in the South for extra credit. Blondie felt as if she'd asked him to take up the cause himself.

In contrast, Mrs. Buckley's class was as stultifying as ever. She was reading them *To Helen* by Edgar Allan Poe, a love poem that struck Blondie as overdone. He noted how Mary Cherry hung on every syllable as if Poe were praising *her* beauty. He wanted to gag.

Instead, struck by a sudden inspiration, he grabbed his pencil and began scribbling in his notebook. After a few cross-outs and erasures, he felt he'd engineered his own masterpiece of poesy.

Snot

Little green ball rolled to a clot,
heavenly creature though you're not,
nevertheless inhabited you are.
Fertile green planet, bacterion star!
Proboscian emerald oft hurled into space,
or speedily hid in some darker place,
there to remain forever and ever
or until someone not so clever
fondles you and your pinnacled mountain,
then washes you off at a water fountain.

It was perfect. He folded the page and passed it to Feller. He read it and nearly split a gut. His muffled cry caused Mary to turn and shoot him a fierce look of disapproval. Water filled Feller's eyes when he looked back at him. He gave Blondie the A-okay sign.

"What, what?" Bucky shouted. She glared around the room through her bifocals. Still gazing suspiciously at them, she moved on to another poem equally as offensive.

Feller slipped his poem to the Grouper. He remained as impassive and Buddha-like as ever. When he was through reading, though, he looked up at Blondie and gave him an appraising look. Blondie was sure he detected a hint of heightened respect in his eyes. He wanted it to be so.

"Boy, that was one great poem," Feller said on the way home. "You really should be a writer."

Blondie laughed.

"Do you think it could sell?" Blondie asked.

"I liked it a lot better than that stuff from Poe."

Blondie knew Feller was trying to be supportive. He also knew that he'd have to do a lot better than *Snot* to be a writer. It was just a knockoff. The hard thing was coming up with something of your own. And making it so good people would pay money for it.

He wondered if Tammy would be impressed if she read *Snot*. He suspected not. More likely, she'd be grossed out.

"You go out on dates, don't you?" Blondie asked Feller.

"Sometimes."

"Anyone special?"

"Nah."

"Not interested in anyone?"

Blondie couldn't imagine Feller being afraid to ask anyone out with his looks.

"I used to go with Ethel Philbin," Feller said after a while.

"Ethel Philbin? Bobby Clements' girl?"

Feller laughed. "She wasn't Bobby's girl then."

Blondie was thunderstruck. Ethel was a knockout, a supernova on the high school scene, head cheerleader and the most glamorous girl in school. He was sitting right in the car with someone who'd gone with her.

"When was that?"

"Ninth grade."

Well, that *had* been a long time ago. Still, Blondie was impressed.

"Did you get anywhere with her?" Blondie asked.

"Just making out. A little petting outside her clothes."

"Do you think Bobby…?"

"I'm sure he's getting all he wants," Feller said ruefully.

"Why do you say that?"

"Everyone's older now. Besides, I know Bobby."

A pensive look clouded Feller's features. Blondie wondered if he was feeling what Blondie suspected—the sadness of glory days gone by. If so, at least he'd known them once. Blondie wondered if he would ever see any "glory days."

"How about the other guys?" he asked. "Do they date?"

"Well, Dispatch is always in there pitching, I'll give him credit for that. No one else in the group, really."

"Grouper?"

"Who would date the Grouper?"

"There are ugly girls, too."

"He wouldn't want them."

"But if he's unattractive himself.... ?"

"That's not how it works," Feller said, ending the discussion.

Several weeks thereafter—somewhat in wonderment—Blondie realized his days were falling into an almost tolerable routine and that he was gradually shedding his new-kid-at-school feeling, the feeling that every day would throw insurmountable challenges at him. There were challenges all right, but even if they seemed insurmountable, they were avoidable. Like sticking to the crowd whenever he saw Barnwell. Like looking away every time he passed Tammy in the hall. Like never, ever making eye contact with Miss Spalding, Mr. Farber or Mrs. Buckley.

Friday nights were reserved for football games and beer. Even if the games were out of town, they were usually in the county, so they'd all pile into the P-mobile and take off for Percy or Babbington or Oakdale. The games were the same for Blondie whether Fenton won or lost. They were always about watching *her*.

Saturday nights were either spent at the bowling alley playing pool or playing the pinball machines or drinking beer in the P-mobile in some deserted lane, regaling each other with observations or stories about their schoolmates. Only one of them ever held back—the Grouper. He seemed happy enough to be with them, but he seldom offered more than a wry observation, or, on even rarer occasions, one of his laws. Blondie wondered what went on in his head.

Yet, the first time he was presented with a chance to find out, Blondie nearly passed it up. One week early in November, everyone but he and Grouper had managed to snare a date for Saturday night—even Shakes, who'd struck up a bit of a relationship with the Raznosky girl. Blondie's inclination was to scrap the evening and stay home. Grouper didn't shoot pool or play the pinball machines—he boasted of having no interest in, or skills at, any activity requiring the slightest coordination. Since the Grouper had never spoken to him for more than a few minutes, Blondie figured sharing a few beers with him in some out-of-the-way place would be uncomfortable at best.

"Well, I guess we should bag Saturday, huh?" Blondie said to Grouper after everyone else had revealed their plans.

Grouper cocked his head and gave Blondie an inscrutable look.

"Do you believe in fate?" Grouper asked when they were alone.

"What?"

"Pick me up at my house at 8:00 Saturday night," Grouper said as he shambled away.

The Whipples' mini-castle was lit up like an amusement park when Blondie pulled up in the Dart Saturday night. There were small lights under every shrub and tree, sconces on either side of the garage doors, and floodlights illuminating the front of the house. Their lawn seemed prepped for a championship match of lawn bowling, mowed to a uniform height and devoid of the crabgrass, dandelions, and clover that gave Blondie's lawn such character.

"Pretty impressive, huh?" Grouper commented as he eased his large frame onto the bench seat next to Blondie. He was wearing dark slacks and a white cable-knit sweater over a navy turtleneck. "My dad felt we were depriving our neighbors of an opportunity to admire our house at night."

His voice was perfectly even, but Blondie could taste the sarcasm.

"Why don't we go somewhere different tonight?" Grouper suggested.

He guided Blondie to a place he called his "overlook." It was at the top of a small bluff and at the edge of a pasture. Points of light sparkled below—Fenton at night.

There would be no drinking tonight. Nether of them had summoned the courage to make the buy.

"My dad's a lawyer," had been Grouper's excuse.

"I've got enough troubles already," had been his.

"I come here once in a while when I need to think," Grouper said to Blondie after a few moments. "No one else knows about it."

Blondie was surprised and pleased. Grouper was treating him as someone special.

"Why me?" he asked.

"You seem different from the others."

Blondie wasn't sure he liked that. For the past two months, he'd been working at being one of the gang, as much like the others as he could be.

"How so?"

"You're more sensitive..."

Sensitive? Blondie didn't want to be viewed that way. It was downright dangerous at Fenton High.

"I'm just like the others," Blondie protested.

Grouper snorted.

"Why do you think I'm sensitive? Because of my poem?"

"Hardly," Grouper answered dryly, "although it showed some talent. What it did show is that you're a thinker, someone who doesn't just swallow conventional notions of what's beautiful or true."

"Like what?" Blondie had no idea what he was talking about.

"I don't know. About the way we are, I suppose."

Grouper's voice faded into the darkness as if his thoughts had turned elsewhere.

"Like who is?" Blondie asked, frustrated at Grouper's opacity.

"No, I think you're sensitive because of *her*," Grouper responded, returning to Blondie's previous question. "You see more to her than she is. You've turned her into an ideal."

Blondie winced.

"I wouldn't go that far," he said, "It's more like...."

"You don't have to explain. I'm not making a judgment. I admire you for it." There was sadness in his voice.

"Have you ever felt that way about a girl?" Blondie asked. He hoped Grouper would share a similar feeling.

"Never. But I can imagine your feelings."

Blondie felt cheered by that. He looked up at the moon, almost blinding in its radiance. It was so clear, so remote. Sometimes, he wished he could be like the moon, observing what occurred on earth without needing to be a part of it or have any feelings about it.

"You think I'm wasting my time with Tammy, don't you?" Blondie asked him.

Grouper wheezed and coughed a few times, then shifted his body. His big head was now in the moonlight, his face pursed with thought.

"What I think isn't important. You have no choice in the matter."

"I suppose you're going to tell me there's a law at work."

Grouper chuckled.

"All right, what is it?" Blondie asked.

"**Nothing hooks the romantic soul like the unattainable**," he said.

Chapter Thirteen

His mother liked Rudy. She deemed him "clean, well-dressed and polite." Blondie suspected she was contrasting Rudy with him and his friends, although she'd only met Dispatch and Feller. She told Blondie that Dispatch was "surly" and needed a haircut. Her verdict on Feller was that he was "a little too sure of himself."

When Rudy came over for help on his trig, he made a point of saying hello to Blondie's parents and finding some compliment to pay them. That rated big with his mom. And Rudy always seemed genuinely appreciative of the help Blondie gave him. So why, Blondie wondered, did he always feel a trace of resentment toward him? Was it because Rudy was a luminary at Fenton High and he wasn't? Or because, so far as Blondie could tell, Rudy had done nothing to boost Blondie's standing there?

Then again, his reputation was hardly his biggest concern. That was *survival*. Everyone told him Buford had been laying for him ever since the CYO dance. Blondie feared one day Buford was going to find him alone and beat him to death.

Perhaps it was fitting that he should die, now that Tammy had receded even farther from his grasp, to that impregnable place beyond the known universe where dazzling girls insulated themselves from the unwanted affections of average guys like him. In his less pessimistic moments, however, Blondie believed there was a remote possibility his life might work out—if he could get out of his predicament with Barnwell.

He briefly considered the rational approach. Perhaps he could request a moment of Buford's time and explain to him that there was his hostility was unwarranted. On the other hand, Grouper had just about convinced him billies were impervious to rational debate. But what if he could offer Buford something he wanted? A trade for his life. Hm-m-m, what could it be? Grouper claimed that billies were particularly fond of bad-tasting beer. Club members considered a local beer, Hartz Green Label, the vilest of all brews. He could offer Buford a six-pack of that.

Blondie had no great confidence in his plan—Buford might punch him out before he had a chance to say anything—but he had no alternative. The hardest part was finding a safe way to present his proposal to Barnwell.

Opportunity soon presented itself in the Cro-Magnon form of Ralph Purdy. Mid-week, Blondie found him leaning against the lockers, licking his lips and cooing at passing girls. His attention propelled them down the hallway even faster. Blondie heard one whisper, "Gag me."

"Hey, Purdy," Blondie called to him.

"Up yours, dead man. You don't talk to me."

"You guys misunderstand me," Blondie said in the most amiable tone he could muster.

"Let's see. You were an asshole baby who grew up to be a complete shit. Did I get it right?"

Purdy stuck his jaw out in an aggressive manner.

This was going to be harder than he thought. Blondie felt a momentary gust of self-loathing for even speaking to Purdy. Nonetheless, he pressed on.

"I thought if I bought you and Buford a few beers, you'd realize I wasn't really your enemy. Maybe we could even be friends."

"Who'd want to be friends with you, skunk breath?" Purdy's moon face screwed into a look of disdain. He squinted his eyes. "What about beer?"

"Just thought a little beer could make you see things in a new light."

"A little beer?"

"Okay, a fair amount of beer."

"Like how much?"

Jesus, why was Purdy making him negotiate? The whole scene was growing more and more distasteful by the minute.

"Say a case."

Shit, he hadn't meant to go this far. A case cost money.

"H-m-m-m-ph. A peace offering, huh? I'll pass it along to Buford. You better hope I get to him before he sees you. He's got the sharpest goddamned knuckles I ever felt, I can tell you that."

Purdy waddled off.

On his way to English class, Blondie began to have second thoughts about what he'd done. What if the guys in the Club found out? They'd recognize him for the weenie he was. He was just going to have to hope they never found out. After all, survival was more important than saving face.

After his experience with Purdy, Blondie found the pre-class turmoil of fourth period English a welcome diversion. Shakes and Brick were arguing over something while other kids traded the latest gossip. Mary Cherry was writing Ernest Hemingway's name on the blackboard while rubber bands and paper airplanes flew through the air, many aimed her way. Only Grouper seemed immune to the uproar. He sat serenely in the back row, his hands folded over his abdomen.

The bell rang and, with a whoosh, Bucky appeared like a broomless witch. She was carrying a heavy book that said "Anthology" on the side. Bucky smiled at Mary, frowned at Shakes, nodded at Grouper, and gave Blondie a look of mild irritation. She immediately started discussing

The Old Man and the Sea, the book she'd assigned the class to read. She asked who'd like to give a critique of it.

Mary's hand shot up. Blondie was amazed when Bucky looked past her and dismayed when her eyes fastened on him.

"Bernard Reimer. It's been a while since we've heard from you."

"I didn't raise my hand," he objected.

"Well, have you read the book?"

"Sure."

Actually, he'd only read the cover notes.

"Then, give us a brief synopsis and tell us what you thought of it."

Blondie cleared his throat.

"It's about a fish."

Someone sniggered.

"I mean it's about a guy who catches a fish."

"Yes, that's right," Mrs. Buckley encouraged him. "Go on."

"This guy catches a big fish..." What else had been in the short summary? "...and on his way back to his village, a bunch of sharks eat it, leaving nothing but the skeleton."

Blondie was pretty sure that was right.

"I suppose that that's the bare bones of the matter," Bucky said, drawing a few titters from the class.

"How did you like it?" she asked him.

"Fine."

"Could you elaborate a little? What did you like about it?"

Actually, he hadn't liked it much at all.

"There aren't many big words in it," Blondie said.

Mary Cherry snorted.

"It is true that it's written in a simple style," Bucky agreed. "What do you think the moral of the story was?"

Why was she asking him all these questions? Blondie could feel dozens of eyes nibbling at his skin like feeding piranha.

"Don't go fishing where there are sharks?"

Bucky's clamped her lips around her huge front teeth and glared at him. "I don't think you really understood the book, Mr. Reimer."

She turned to Mary with a bountiful smile. "What did you get from the book, dear?"

"Oh, I just think it was full of powerful metaphors for how life is." She recited a litany of the book's virtues.

"Thank you, Mary. That was well done," Bucky said when Mary finished. She began to write some of Mary's points on the board.

A loud braying resounded across the room. Bucky wheeled around like a cape buffalo.

"All right, who did that?" she demanded.

The room was still.

Bucky turned back to the board. From out of the air, a mouse fell on Mary's desk. It lay stunned for a second, then began to stir. For an instant, Mary stared at the groggy creature in disbelief. Then, she began to scream. The mouse staggered to its feet and began running around the desk, seeking a way down.

"Get that filthy creature out of here!" Bucky shrieked when she saw it.

Blondie saw a chance to get back in Bucky's good graces. He strode to the front of the room and grabbed the frightened rodent around its waist. It bit him on the finger. A tiny drop of blood appeared. Blondie cursed and dropped it back on the desk.

"You're going to need a shot for that," Mary said.

This time, Blondie picked the mouse up by the tail. Bucky gave him a grateful look as he marched out of her class with it. He began second-guessing himself as soon as he reached the hallway. He had not idea what to do with the squirming beast, which was struggling to raise its head and bite him again. He decided the easiest thing would be to take it outside and let it go.

As he walked down the corridor, he happened to glance through the glass in a classroom door—and there *she* was! His Tammy. She was standing in front of the class, holding out her hands toward them. Blondie figured it had to be drama class.

Intrigued, he crept closer. She suddenly moved out of his view. He pressed his face against the glass to see where she'd gone. She reappeared and turned his way, raising her arms in the air as if appealing to the gods above. She stopped in mid-motion and stared straight at him, mouth open. Her classmates turned to see what she was looking at.

Blondie realized he was framed in the class's view, mouse in hand.

Peals of laughter rang out behind the door.

Blondie felt a tap on his shoulder. He turned to face Mr. Bearzinsky. He wore a crooked smile on his face.

"Having a little fun, Mr.....?"

"Reimer, sir. Bernard Reimer."

"Oh yes. The transfer student from Percy. Tell me, is this what students do down there?"

He was still smiling, but his eyes were flint.

"No sir. You don't understand. I was just taking this mouse outside."

"Is it time for its walk?"

"It's not my mouse."

"I'm glad. Now, just give it to me."

"Well, I don't..."

"Just do as I say, Reimer, and you may graduate one day."

"Yes sir."

Blondie handed Bearzinsky the mouse. It immediately bit him on the thumb, jumped to the floor and raced down the hall out of sight.

"You stupid...." Bearzinsky grabbed Blondie by the shirt collar and hustled him down the hall. "Now, I've got to get a tetanus shot."

"Me too." Blondie held up his finger.

"Good," Bearzinsky said.

Mrs. Shively, the school nurse, was unprepared for the double mouse mauling.

"All I can do is put some alcohol on it," she said to Mr. Bearzinsky apologetically.

"Why'd you have to bring a mouse to school, anyway?" she asked Blondie.

He didn't attempt to explain.

"I don't understand how it could bite both of you."

Mr. Bearzinsky glared at her.

"Well, you'll both have to go see a doctor as soon as you can. Who knows what diseases that mouse might have. You know they'll eat anything—old bacon grease, leftover melon rinds, coffee grounds, spoiled meat...."

"I get the picture, Mrs. Shively," Bear snapped.

"This should be good for a three-day suspension, mister wise guy," Bear told Blondie once they were back in the hall.

"I was just removing it from class. I don't know who brought it."

"A likely story."

"Ask Mrs. Buckley."

"That old...," the Bear began, before catching himself. "Yes, I suppose I should."

Blondie noted Shakes' look of alarm when Bear hustled him back into her class. He had a pathological fear of the Bear. Grouper kept his eyes straight ahead, although Blondie caught the hint of a smile.

Blondie was relieved when Bucky verified his story—reluctantly, it seemed to him. Bearzinsky seemed disappointed.

"I don't ever want to have to deal with you again," he threatened as he went out the door.

As Blondie sat back down, his relief turned to dismay as he remembered Tammy's astonished look. Why were events conspiring to make him a complete ass in her eyes?

After class, Blondie confronted Grouper and asked him who'd thrown the mouse at Mary's desk.

"Brick, of course. He detests her."

"He's ruining my love life," Blondie blurted out.

Grouper looked at Blondie quizzically. Blondie told him how Tammy'd caught him watching her with the mouse in his hand.

Grouper eyes twinkled.

"Don't you know the first rule of courting, my boy," he said, and Blondie knew he was about to receive another of Grouper's laws. "**Never go calling with mouse in hand.**"

Chapter Fourteen

Armageddon. Blondie could see it in his mind. A fireball big as Maryland. A mushroom cloud halfway to the moon. His parents incinerated. He, somehow surviving, deep in a cave beneath the earth, sick from radiation poisoning.

A couple weeks before, the Russians had exploded a 50-megaton bomb. Khrushchev said they had an even bigger one, a "doomsday device" that could end life on earth. It was horrible to contemplate. Nonetheless, Miss Darlington wanted to talk about it—and the scariest part was that most of the class acted as if the issue had no relevance to them. Had they been lobotomized? Didn't they understand that an arsenal of ballistic missiles was pointed their way?

Maybe it was him, though, who was out of step. Maybe he just worried too much. That's what his mom said—"There's no point worrying about things you can't change" was how she put it. Perhaps she was right, although he'd always believed that worrying about something helped ward it off—like a charm. He still felt unsettled when the lunch bell rang. He shared his dread about the big bomb with Feller.

"Cheer up, Blondie, you take things too seriously," Feller said. "Tell you what, why don't you spend the night at my house tonight and we can talk more about things?"

Blondie wasn't sure his mom would go for that, it being a school night and all. However, she seemed happy he'd made a friend. She even drove him over and came in to chat with Mrs. Feller for a few minutes.

After dinner, he and Feller watched television for a while with his folks, then went upstairs to Paul's attic quarters, a bathroom and a long bedroom crimped at the sides by the angle of the roof. It was furnished with two single beds across from each other, a chest of drawers, a bookcase, and a desk.

Neither he nor Paul made any pretense of opening the books they'd brought home. They'd come to talk. Blondie asked Feller what it was like growing up in Fenton. In response, he went to the bookcase, took a large scrapbook from it, and handed it to Blondie. It was filled with photographs of Feller's life—standard-issue baby pictures, pictures from birthday parties, family portraits from Sears. Blondie came upon some photos of Feller in a little league baseball uniform. He towered over most of his peers.

"Isn't that Bobby Clements?" he asked.

"Yeah."

"You're so much bigger."

"I was an early bloomer. It gave me an edge back then."

Another picture was from a teen party. Feller was standing next to a young Ethel Philbin. He showed it to Feller.

"Glory days," Feller said wistfully.

Blondie was envious. Feller had a history. There was a continuity to his life. When he put the scrapbook back on the shelf, he noticed a number of three-ring binders labeled "Paul's Photos."

"Mind if I look?" Blondie asked.

Feller looked a little sheepish, but told him to go ahead.

The binders were crammed with photographs of landscapes and buildings. Blondie could tell Feller had been aiming for artistic effect. But whether it was the limitations of the camera—a Brownie, Feller told him—or the photographer, Blondie found them uninspiring. They were nowhere near as good as the pictures in *Life* or *National Geographic*.

"They're good," Blondie said anyway. Why douse someone else's dream? Besides, what did he know about photography? "Have you shown them to anyone else?"

"In Fenton? Are you kidding?"

Feller put on his pajamas and went to the bathroom to brush his teeth.

"Please don't mention the photos to anyone," he asked Blondie as he crawled under the covers.

"No, I wouldn't."

"Have you taken your college boards yet?" Feller asked.

"No. Have you?"

"January. Got any idea where you might go?"

"I haven't given it much thought," Blondie said.

"Most of the guys are going to the University of Maryland. They don't have the grades to get into anywhere else. Brick might not even swing that."

"Is that where's Grouper's going?"

"I don't think so. He told me his dad wants him to go to some fancy school."

"How about you?" Blondie asked.

"There's a little school in Pennsylvania, in the Poconos. It's called Smith-Reid. It's got a good photography program. Co-ed, too. I'm thinking I might go there if I can get in."

Feller looked over at Blondie.

"Smith-Reid's pretty good in English, too. That's what you're interested in, isn't it?"

"Some kind of writing."

"So what do you say? Want to join me up there?"

Blondie had hardly given college a thought. But he was flattered by Feller's invitation.

"That could be fun. Let me think about it."

Feller turned out his bedside light, plunging the room into darkness.

"I saw the way you were dancing with Tammy," Feller said after a time.

Blondie didn't respond.

"I like her, too," Feller said.

Strangely, Feller's admission didn't cause Blondie any concern. He was glad someone else could understand his feelings.

"Have you ever told her?" Blondie asked him.

"No."

"Have you ever dated her?"

"No."

"Why?"

"Afraid to ask, I suppose."

Blondie was surprised. He thought Feller had nerve, at least a lot more than he did.

"You're not what you seem," Blondie's words floated across the darkness.

"What's that?"

"Devil-may-care. Super confident."

"Is anyone?"

"Super confident?"

"No. What they seem."

The room fell quiet. Only a faint glow of light from the small window on the far wall eased the gloom.

"Have you ever gone out with that Delores girl you were talking to at the game?" he asked Feller after a while.

"Yeah."

"Did you ever do it with her?"

"You mean screw her? No."

"Why not? I could tell by the way she looked at you that she'd let you do it."

"I've got to have some respect for Henry."

"Who's Henry?"

"My dick."

"Your dick?"

"Sure. Don't you have a name for your dick?"

Feller made it sound abnormal not to. Blondie wracked his brain for a response.

"Nessie," he blurted out.

"Nessie? That sounds like a girl's name."

"You haven't heard of the Loch Ness monster?" Blondie challenged, hoping to mask his discomfort by taking the offensive.

"Oh yeah," Feller answered, with a sudden note of respect.

"When my dad was stationed in France, we went up to Scotland on a trip...." Tired as he was, Blondie could feel his mind going into overdrive. "...and it was kind of hot, so I snuck off from my family and went for a skinny dip. There I was floating on my back in this little cove when a boatload of tourists came by and...well, the rest is history."

Feller chuckled appreciatively.

"They say it's about sixty feet long and has six or seven humps," Blondie went on. "Really, it doesn't have any humps. I'd put some water wings on it to keep it from sinking into the cold depths of the lake. As far as being sixty feet long...of course, they didn't see it when it was hard."

Feller began to roar. He put his pillow over his face to keep from waking the house. Blondie knew he'd scored big with him.

"Nessie, huh?" Feller said after a while. "Wait'll I tell the guys this."

Blondie lay back on his bed and smiled at the ceiling. He began to think about Tammy. He wondered what it would be like to make love to her—or for that matter any girl. Suddenly, he felt an urgent need to know. He wondered if there was a way to wheedle it out of Feller without giving away the fact that he was a virgin. Perhaps there was a way....

"How many times have you done it?" he whispered into the darkness.

He congratulated himself on his cleverness. Next, he could probe for a couple names and ask how they were in bed. If he was lucky, he could get the information he wanted without volunteering anything himself.

There was a long stillness and Blondie feared that Feller had fallen asleep.

"I've never done it," Feller finally answered.

"You've never done it? But what about all the things you've said? You seemed to know all about it."

"I never said I did it, did I?"

Blondie eased up on him.

"What about the others?" he asked.

"I don't know. Who'd admit he was a virgin?"

"Yeah. I know what you mean."

"Are you?" Feller asked.

"What?"

"A virgin?"

Blondie didn't see any point in hiding it now that Feller had come clean.

"Yeah," he admitted.

"Why are you a virgin?" Feller asked.

"I don't know. Lack of opportunity, I guess. How about you?"

"Not lack of opportunity. Delores asked me to do it with her once. It may be hard for you to understand, but it's what I said before. Respect for my weenie."

"What do you mean?"

"I don't put any old food in my stomach. I don't wear any old clothes. You know what I'm saying? You've got to respect yourself. You've got to have some standards."

"What about the girl?" Blondie asked.

"What do you mean?"

"Do you want her to be a virgin?"

"Of course."

"Isn't that inconsistent?"

Feller laughed.

"Absolutely."

Blondie woke the next morning, groggy from half-remembered dreams and disoriented by unfamiliar surroundings. He took a long shower. The warm streams coursing down his body gradually focused his awareness on the weight dangling between his legs.

"You're a dangerous weapon, Nessie, but you've never had your trigger pulled."

Chapter Fifteen

Okay. So it *was* the Saturday after Thanksgiving. So people were well fed and their thoughts had turned to Christmas. Did that mean they had to be so damned cheerful?

His mom was the worst. She seemed consumed by the holiday spirit. Already, she was playing Christmas carols on the stereo and singing along with them. Already, she'd baked Christmas cookies—big shortbread jobs cut into stars, candy canes and snowmen, then frosted and sprinkled with colored sugar.

They were hurtling down Route 40 on their way to a monster mall near Baltimore for some Christmas shopping. Blondie could envision the scene: throngs of shoppers pushing and shoving each other to buy ties and toys, sweaters and scarves, toasters and televisions.

He stared out the window at the washed out papier-mâché countryside. He hated winter. Everything was so hard and dead—and cold. Most of all he hated the cold. Every winter, it sank into his body and wouldn't go away until summer.

"You're being awfully quiet today," his mother said. "Is something the matter?"

"My life is half over, I've never been laid, and my dream of love is ended," he mumbled.

"What's that?"

"Nothing," Blondie said.

Blondie glanced over at his mom, somehow afraid she could read his thoughts. She was humming "Amazing Grace." That always seemed to put her into a trance. Blondie watched her from the corner of his eye and noted the look of contentment on her face. Was that something that came with getting older? He could never remember feeling that way. He wondered if his mom had ever felt as desperately attracted to someone as he did to Tammy.

They passed a dilapidated house between a used-car lot and a garden supply store. There were cracked panes in the windows and the rusting carcass of a car on the front lawn. Some boards had come loose, revealing tarpaper beneath. Blondie was sure the house was deserted until a grizzled old man stepped out of the door.

"Billies," he muttered.

His mom heard him. She asked him what he meant. Blondie explained.

"That's terrible," she said when he'd finished. "Those people are just poor."

"Poor doesn't excuse their behavior," Blondie retorted.

"Poor excuses a lot and you'd know it if you'd ever been poor. Ask your father. He grew up in the Depression. What am I saying? I grew up in the Depression. We didn't have any of the things you kids have today."

"Then how come you guys didn't turn out to be billies," he said when she was done.

"Maybe we were lucky," his mom said. "You shouldn't judge others."

What? Was she kidding? That's all anyone did at school, and over the most trivial things—the way someone looked, what they wore, how they styled their hair, what kind of car they drove, and on and on. Anyway, he wasn't buying it. Shakes was poor and he wasn't mean. Of course, he was awfully small.

It took forever to find a parking place. Crazed shoppers knocked into him all afternoon, while Christmas songs assaulted him in an endless and mind-numbing progression. He couldn't find a thing he wanted. As far as he was concerned, the trip was a total bust.

Coming home, they passed a sign announcing the "Sherwood Forest Motel" in Medieval calligraphy. What caught Blondie's eye was the large face of a goateed man in a crested hat—Robin Hood, no doubt. A look at the place convinced Blondie Sherwood Farce would have been more apt. There wasn't a tree for a hundred yards...just a cluster of aging bungalows surrounded by an asphalt parking lot.

His eyes gravitated to a car parked in front of one of the bungalows—a red-and-white Ford Galaxie Skyliner. It looked a lot like the Bear's. What reason would he have to be at a motel in the middle of the day? Even stranger was that the only other vehicle in the lot—a bright blue Nash Rambler—was parked right next to it.

His mom was still in a high state. She began hinting around at what Santa might bring him, as if Blondie were still fascinated by a fat elf in a suit. Blondie knew what he wanted for Christmas and his mom couldn't get it for him.

"Dear Santa, could you please bring me a girl for Christmas. Make her skin clear and fresh, her lips full and red, her hair shiny and dark. Heck, skip the specifications. Her name is Tammy Hollander."

Sincerely,
Blondie Reimer.

* * * * * * * *

"This place can be a real drag," Feller said to Blondie on Monday.

"You're telling me," Blondie agreed, even though they'd only been back at school two hours.

"Let's cut school tomorrow."

"What?"

"Let's cut tomorrow," Feller repeated.

"Why? What's special about tomorrow?"

"Nothing. It's just one more day in the pen."

The thought of playing hooky made Blondie nervous. He hadn't skipped school once in his entire educational career. How could he? His mother was a teacher.

"What would we do?" Blondie asked.

"We could shoot pool at the bowling alley."

"What if we get caught?"

"Tell you what. Come stay at my house tomorrow. Tell your mother I'm taking you to school and bringing you home. You won't be running any risk."

"How about your mom?"

"What will she know? We'll leave and return at the normal time. We just won't go to school."

Feller seemed to have covered all the bases. Blondie still didn't like it, but how could he wimp out in front of his newfound friend?

"Okay," he agreed.

"I'll see if anyone else wants to cut with us."

Dispatch was the only taker. Brick said he didn't like to shoot pool. Feller didn't ask Grouper—"He'd never do anything against the rules," he explained. Blondie found that odd. He considered him a free thinker.

"What about Shakes?" Blondie asked.

"I didn't even ask. He's in a funky mood because Janine dumped him."

It must be awful to be rejected by someone as ugly and insignificant as Janine Raznosky, Blondie thought. Poor Shakes. But the scheme was set and three of them were players. Blondie took a deep breath. He was about to break the rules.

He kept his head low the next morning as they drove through the outskirts of town in Feller's dad's Fairlane. They were fugitives from high school. Blondie was sure Bear would call the police to request an all-points bulletin. He listened for the siren's wail.

Save for the P-mobile, the parking lot was empty when they reached Shady Lanes. As soon as they stopped, Dispatch came out and dashed over to them.

"It doesn't open until 10:30," Dispatch grumbled when Feller rolled down his window.

"It opens at nine on Saturday," Feller said.

"It isn't Saturday."

"It opens at nine every day during the summer."

"It isn't summer, either."

"Well, shit!" Feller said.

Feller suggested they cruise around town in the P-mobile until the alley opened. Blondie balked at that—someone might see them. Dispatch suggested the quarry. Blondie had never been there, but it had acquired mythic proportions in his mind from the stories the guys told about it: the drinking, the lovemaking, the fighting.

Blondie was disappointed. The legendary quarry struck him as no more than a big hole filled with brackish water and dead leaves. Feller insisted it was more romantic in the summer when there were the trees were full and the moonlight bounced off the water. All Blondie could think of was some kid falling in and drowning, his bloated body rising to the surface days later covered with slime.

They shot the shit until 10:15—growing colder by the minute so Dispatch could save gas—then headed back to Shady Lanes. Another car was there when they arrived: a puke-yellow fifty-eight Mercury.

"That's Fred's," Feller affirmed. "He's the day manager."

Blondie pulled up his collar as he went inside, just in case Fred might someday run into his mother. Once he saw Fred, he quit worrying about that. He was a greaser from way back, with a ducktail straight from a mallard and enough pockmarks on his face to rival the Badlands. He was fiddling with the soft drink dispenser. He nodded at Feller and returned to his labor.

"Can we get some balls?" Feller asked.

"Need some balls, huh?" Freddie said, cracking a grin. He went over to a gray metal cabinet and removed a plastic tray of striped and solid-colored spheres. Feller took it and led Blondie and Dispatch to the poolroom, where they began playing "Screw Your Buddy."

Dispatch was the first one eliminated every game. After each loss, he concentrated even harder the next game, staring at each shot as if he were trying to frighten the ball into the pocket. He stroked each shot with a fury, now and then knocking balls off the table.

Feller's approach to the game was more effective. He assumed a relaxed position over the table, lined up each shot with care, and never struck the cue harder than necessary.

Blondie realized his own game was like every other part of his life—prone to excess effort, uncertainty, and fear of failure. Nevertheless, by studying each shot and taking his time, he found he could beat Dispatch most of the time and Feller every now and then.

After an hour or so, a young man stalked into the billiard room. He was big—Blondie guessed 240 pounds—and most of his heft was muscle. He looked like he'd arrived in the world in a piano crate. An apprehensive look flitted across Feller's face. He missed his shot. Dispatch, intent as always on his immediate task, seemed oblivious to the newcomer's arrival.

Under his denim jacket, the man wore a tee shirt with the words "Rodney's Fix-It" hand-lettered across the front. He dropped his tray of balls on the next table and ambled to the wall rack to select a cue. Feller's eyes were glued to his every movement.

"Who's that?" Blondie whispered to him.

"Sh-h-h, he might hear you," Feller replied.

When the man returned to his table, he nodded their way. Feller relaxed.

Blondie and Dispatch and Feller began another game. Dispatch wound up with a long shot. He let fly with a mighty stroke, propelling the cue ball off the rail and high into the air. For an instant, the ivory orb hung against the paneled wall like a miniature moon. Then, as the three of them watched in terror, it began to fall toward the unsuspecting skull of the newcomer. At the last minute, the man moved to his left and the ball smacked down at his feet.

He turned and gave them a peevish look. Feller blanched, but Dispatch stuck out his lower lip and shot the man a defiant look. The little guy had balls.

"A guy could get killed down here," the man said. His face looked like the front of an old Packard—wide, cold, hard. He picked the offending ball from the floor. Blondie expected him to squeeze it into chalky dust. Instead, he walked purposely toward their table. Just when Blondie thought he was going to shove it down Dispatch's throat, he softly set it down.

"I do the same fucking thing..." the man said, "...hit the son of a bitch too hard." A smile flitted across his mouth. He went back to his table.

"Let's get a Coke," Feller said to Blondie. Feller's voice was small and rough, as if it had been pulled through a cheese grater. He pulled Blondie past the lunch counter and into the men's room. He leaned against the door.

"Do you know who that is?" he asked Blondie.

Blondie shook his head.

"That's Mountain Pulaski. He graduated four years ago. Went to North Dakota State on a football scholarship. Played left tackle. Hurt his knee his junior year."

Blondie wondered why Feller was giving him this biography.

"They say he threw Paddy Conroy over a car," Feller said, building up to his punch line. "He's the toughest guy in the county."

Blondie didn't contest Feller's conclusion, though he had no idea who Paddy Conroy was. He didn't need to. One look at Pulaski told Blondie he ate tire irons for breakfast.

"Don't say a word to the guy," Feller warned. "It might be your last."

When they returned to the poolroom, Blondie and Feller were astounded to find Dispatch shooting a game with the brute.

"Oh fuck," Feller whispered to Blondie. "Dispatch won't have the sense to lose to him."

"Dispatch couldn't beat a one-armed epileptic," Blondie reminded him.

While Blondie and Feller looked on, Mountain trounced Dispatch seven games in a row.

"How about one for money?" Pulaski asked. "I'll take three of my balls off the table to start with. Make the four that are left and the eight ball and you win. For a buck?"

"I'm not afraid of you," Dispatch said.

The game was on and Dispatch bore down with his usual intensity. As usual, it failed to compensate for his lack of skill. Soon, Mountain was lining up a shot on the eight ball.

"Corner pocket," he called.

With a smooth stroke, Mountain sent the cue ball straight to its target, where it met the eight ball and propelled it into the corner pocket. For a moment, the cue ball remained motionless, then it began spinning backward. It bounced off a rail and banked into a side pocket.

"You scratched," Dispatch gloated. "You owe me a buck."

Mountain looked at him with eyes of flint. Then he reached into his back pocket and tossed a dollar bill on the table.

"You owe me a rematch, mop-head, but I gotta go." He flicked out his hand and mussed Dispatch's hair. "You're a feisty little pecker," he said, grinning at him. He started for the doorway.

Almost as from someone else's mouth, Blondie found himself addressing Pulaski.

"Excuse me, sir..."

Mountain turned and scrutinized Blondie.

"Have you ever heard of Buford Barnwell," Blondie stammered.

"Yeah," Pulaski answered with a puzzled expression.

"Is he very tough?"

Mountain gave Blondie an astonished look and began to laugh. He was still laughing as he clomped from the room.

"Jesus, that was dumb," Feller said. "Mountain would chew Barnwell up and spit him out without even thinking about it."

"Well, then why are we all so scared of Barnwell?"

"First of all, none of us are Mountain Pulaski. Secondly, I'm not sure we're all as scared of him as you seem to be."

Blondie felt rebuked.

"This is boring," Dispatch announced.

Feller gave him a vexed look.

"Well, then, why don't you suggest something more interesting?"

"Why don't we go down to the Celestial Arts?" Dispatch suggested.

Feller looked at Dispatch more respectfully.

"Not bad," he said.

"What's the Celestial Arts?" Blondie asked.

"It's a nudey show down in Baltimore."

"You mean naked girls?"

"One would hope," Feller answered sarcastically.

"Can we get into something like that?" Blondie asked. He noted a squeak to his voice. "I thought you had to be eighteen."

"They don't care. Brick goes all the time. What do you think?"

Blondie didn't know what to think. He'd never been to a "nudey show."

"Who's there?" Feller asked Dispatch.

"Pam and her Playful Python."

"That could be rich. What do you think, Blondie?"

"Can we get back in time?"

"Sure, we could be back by four and still see a whole show."

Feller and Dispatch were waiting for him to respond. The very idea of what they were contemplating turned his insides to pudding. What if they got caught there? Underage. Looking at naked women. What would his mother think?

"What the hell!" Blondie answered.

It was time to draw the line. He couldn't worry about what his mother thought every time he needed to do something to advance his development as a man. He couldn't—he wouldn't—be a pussy forever.

Chapter Sixteen

Snow polka-dotted the air when they left the lanes. Clumps were sticking to the concrete.

"Maybe we should reconsider," Feller said.

Blondie could live with that.

"Through rain, sleet and snow the P-mobile will go," Dispatch countered.

Feller looked at Blondie, shrugged, and got in. Blondie had no choice but to follow.

"Looks like Christmas out there," Blondie said as Dispatch began plowing down Baltimore Pike, his windshield wipers barely keeping up with the white fluff.

By the time, they entered the endless brick tenements of North Baltimore, the snow had subsided to a few desultory flakes. As they proceeded into the heart of the city, white faces gave way to darker ones. The row houses petered out and the high walls of downtown closed about them in a sooty embrace.

They parked in a side street near the shot tower, from whence union troops had dropped globs of molten iron during the Civil War, watching them cool into cannonballs before they hit the ground. A short walk brought them to The Celestial Arts was just around the corner. Its neon marquee blazed the inscription: "Pam and Her Playful Python. Erotic Dance of Serpentine Proportions."

"Pretensions of art to keep the cops away," Feller scoffed.

Blondie was apprehensive as Dispatch approached the ticket window. What if they had to show identification? What kind of a crime was it to look at naked women if you were only seventeen?

The crone in the booth didn't flinch when Dispatch dropped the bills in front of her. She kept reading a copy of *True Romances* as she handed him the tickets.

Blondie followed Dispatch and Feller through glass doors painted black. He plunged into a vestibule barely lit by a red bulb and bumped into something soft that mumbled…Dispatch. Feller grabbed Blondie's arm and pulled him in the opposite direction. Heavy velveteen curtains brushed against his body and then a stage appeared from the darkness. A shabbily dressed man was standing on the stage holding onto his fly as if trying to control a giant erection. A halfhearted chuckle echoed off the far walls.

Blondie rammed his leg against the metal side of an outstretched seat and then was shoved into it. He hunched down a little in case someone was sitting behind him. When Blondie's eyes adjusted, he realized the theater was almost empty. Only the first row was fully populated.

The comedian on stage continued his lewd slapstick, now and then zinging an insult at someone in the audience. He kept talking about a woman's "snapper." Blondie had never heard the term before, but he knew what the comedian was talking about.

"Is this it?" Blondie asked Feller. He felt disgusted with himself for agreeing to come.

"Be patient. This is one of the comedy acts."

"It's a barrel of laughs."

"See those men on the front row," Feller said.

Blondie nodded.

"They're always here. They all bring hats. When the lights go out, they put their hats in their laps and jack off into them."

Blondie's stomach heaved.

"Why do they do it?"

"They're old and poor. This is their sex life."

After the comedian, there was drum roll and a fat lady appeared on the stage wearing a gold-colored G-string and a matching bra. As a hidden band played strip music, she removed her bra and then the G-string. Blondie was shocked.

"I thought they had to keep something on," he whispered to Feller.

"They do. See. She tied it around her thigh."

Blondie couldn't get over it. He'd seen bare breasts in men's magazines, but she was showing it all. It didn't make him horny, though. She was too much of a heifer.

"Outstanding!" Dispatch exclaimed.

When she was done, the comic came back out and told the audience the woman's name was Samantha and that she'd been voted Snatch of the Year—in 1933! Blondie found himself despising the man.

The band provided a more rousing introduction to the next act. To a few more chuckles, the comic told the near-empty house that this was the moment they'd all been waiting for—the "climax" of the whole performance.

"All the way from Pittsburgh," he said, his voice rising, "the eighth wonder of the sexual world, that peerless piece of pulchritude, Pamela, with her snake Lickety-Split."

Someone clapped.

Blondie was astounded when a beautiful young woman stepped from behind the curtains into the flat circle of light. She couldn't have been more than twenty-five and she had a centerfold's body. In the right clothes, she could've been a campus queen. She wasn't dressed that way. She wore an outfit similar to her predecessor's, only in blue, and carried a wicker basket.

Blondie wondered if she would take everything off like the older woman. He hoped so. She was gorgeous. Tan, unwrinkled skin. Long raven hair. Firm thighs. Bounteous breasts straining at the bra she wore.

"Take it off," a geezer in front yelled. "Show us your snake."

"I'll show you my snake," one of his cohorts answered.

Blondie held his breath. He felt he'd die if he saw her totally nude—but he was willing. She removed her bra. Her breast were sublime.

"For Christ sakes, breathe, Blondie," Feller whispered.

She removed her G-string. Blondie was mesmerized by her dark, feathery crotch. He told himself it was only hair, but it promised succulent delights.

He began to feel lightheaded. Just when he thought he'd maxed out on lust, Pamela raised the ante. She removed the top of her basket and pulled out a six-or seven-foot python. It was iridescent brown and chartreuse, maybe five inches thick in the middle. She held the snake in her right hand, its body coiled around her arm.

The music grew more seductive. Pamela swayed in apparent ecstasy. She moved the snake's head along her body, its tongue flickering over her skin. Still swaying, Pamela shoved the snake's head into the soft fur of her groin.

"Wow!" Dispatch exclaimed.

"Taste good?" one of the front-row denizens inquired.

Pamela wrapped the python around her waist and pulled its tail through her legs so it wiggled out from between them.

"It's gotta be in her crack," Dispatch said.

"What I'd give to be that snake," Blondie muttered.

By the time Pamela disappeared behind the curtains, Blondie was exhausted. He'd never felt such desire. Nessie ached.

Blondie wasn't the only one who'd been so affected. Feller and Dispatch were more than willing to wait the hour and a half it took to see her again, suffering through a procession of burlesque queens well past their primes. When Pamela reappeared, Blondie howled like a coyote.

"Again?" Dispatch asked when she was through.

"Yeah," Blondie whispered.

"No. No." Feller said in a hoarse voice. "It's already four-thirty. We'll be lucky to get home much before dinner now."

Dusk was peeking over the rooftops when they exited. They hurried toward the alley where they'd left the P-mobile. As Dispatch fumbled with the ignition, something clattered onto the street beside them. A broken brick lay beside the front tire.

CRASH! An object struck the car.

"What the hell!" Dispatch exclaimed.

"Motherfucker," someone yelled.

Blondie couldn't see anyone at first. Then he saw movement in the shadows at the end of the street. A couple black kids were standing by a pallet of bricks.

Blondie didn't understand.

"What's the matter?" he yelled. "Why are you throwing those bricks?"

"Get in the car," Feller ordered. He slid into the back seat as Dispatch got behind the wheel.

"There must be some mistake," Blondie shouted at their attackers. "We don't even know you."

"Honky jerk offs, go back where you belong," came the reply.

A brick hit the P-mobile again. A sliver nicked Blondie's neck.

Feller reached out and grabbed Blondie's jacket as the P-mobile roared to life.

"Get your ass in the car before we all get killed."

A brick exploded against the back windshield, spreading a spider web across it. Blondie jumped into the car.

Dispatch rolled down the window.

"Jungle bunnies!" he yelled at the top of his lungs.

"Christ, Dispatch," Feller said. "Would you get moving?"

Bricks rained down around them. Dispatch gunned the throttle and the P-mobile shot down the street. Blondie looked back. Now there were six or seven black youths running after them, bricks in hand.

"Faster," Feller urged.

Dispatch shot through a red light at the end of the street, forcing a yellow Oldsmobile onto the curb. After a mile or so, he slowed down. They were silent for another three or four minutes.

"Why'd they do that?" Blondie asked.

"Because we're white," Feller answered.

That was it? Just because they were white. Blondie felt baffled, offended, betrayed. He always stuck up for blacks. How could they attack *him*?

"You're late tonight," Blondie's mother observed when he got home.

"Yeah, I went up to the bowling alley after school with Feller and shot a few games of pool."

"Are you sure the bowling alley is a proper place for you to be spending time?"

If you only knew, he thought.

That night, Blondie dreamed of a shantytown near a large factory. He was alone and didn't know how he'd gotten there. He entered a door. Inside were a number of tables and chairs. The room was deserted except for a large black dog in the corner. A Wurlitzer jukebox leaned against one wall, its lights glowing like a spaceship. It began playing "Chattanooga Choo Choo." A beautiful dark-haired girl appeared in the middle of the dusty floor, facing away from him. She was naked.

She began gyrating to the sound of the music. Blondie anticipated Pamela, but, when the girl turned, it was Tammy! Blondie was shocked. He was even more shocked when the dog turned into a nude black man with a huge penis. The man laughed and held it out toward Tammy. Blondie expected her to recoil in horror, but instead she ran her tongue along her lips.

Blondie woke in a sweat and had trouble going back to sleep. What was happening to him?

The next time he caught Grouper alone at school, he told him about their trip to the Celestial Arts and about the dream he had.

"Do you think I'm a racist?" he asked Grouper.

"No more than the rest of us white folks—and those black fellows you ran into. You've just had a shock, that's all."

He gave him a look a mother might give a child.

"**Life's a shocking proposition**," he said.

Chapter Seventeen

"Oh God, oh God..." Blondie repeated to himself as the Bear lurched along in front of him, his broad shoulders thankfully shielding Blondie from the prying eyes of his classmates. He didn't have to guess where the Bear was going...or what the subject of the forthcoming discussion would be. He needed a defense. But what could it be? That he'd needed a day off to catch a once-in-a-lifetime strip act?

The bear shoved open the office door, smashing Mrs. Spritz into a file cabinet. She yelped.

"Sorry," Bear muttered.

He knocked on Clapper's door, then eased it open.

"Got another one," he said to Clapper. "Do you want me to handle him, too?"

"Oh yes, certainly," Clapper said, looking mystified.

Bear led Blondie down a short hallway to the teacher's lounge. It contained a Coke machine, a table littered with magazines, several metal-and-plastic chairs, and an aging sofa. Seated on the last item were Feller and Dispatch.

Bear nodded toward the sofa. Blondie sat down beside his comrades. Mr. Bearzinsky put his foot up on one of the chairs. He snarled, exposing his canine teeth, then produced a metal ruler from behind his back. He began brandishing it like a sword.

"Okay," he said, "Who wants to be the first to fess up?"

Feller stared at him and said nothing. Dispatch looked out the window.
"Where's your note, Reimer?"
Note? Had Feller and Dispatch brought a note?
"I don't have one, sir," Blondie said as placating as he could.
"Well, at least I won't have to add forgery to your list of offenses."
List? Was Bear still holding the mouse episode against him?
"Does anyone care to speak before I suspend you all?"
Dispatch opened his mouth, then shut it when Feller pushed his knee into his thigh.
"I admit it looks coincidental," Feller said, "but we apparently all got sick the same day."
"Next," Bearzinsky said. "Something more creative?"
He wanted creative?
"I think I may be diabetic," Blondie looking at the Bear to see if he was on the right track. " Just as I was leaving the house, I went blank. I don't remember yesterday at all."
"Not bad, Reimer," the Bear said.
He rubbed his chin and Blondie relaxed a little.
CRACK! Bearzinsky smashed the ruler down on the table.
"They don't pay me enough for this job," he lamented, lifting his gaze toward the heavens. "Now listen up, you three. Do I need to call your parents at work—and make them twice as angry—or will you accept your suspensions without any more discussion, effective immediately?"
Dispatch and Feller looked at each other. Then, they looked toward Blondie.
"I'd rather you didn't call my folks," Blondie said.
"Deal," Feller said.
Dispatch grunted assent.
"I'm not finished. Before you even think of coming back to school, I want a note from your parents guaranteeing you won't be absent again. Of course, I'll compare any handwriting with your own."
"Of course," Feller nodded as if that were assumed.

"Now, get out!" Bear growled.

Outside, dead leaves tossed like tiny galleons on the frigid wind. The sky was a piece of dry ice.

"That faggot," Dispatch griped. "We should have called his bluff."

"He wasn't bluffing," Feller said.

"I don't care. It's the principle of the thing that bothers me."

"What's that?"

"He's an asshole."

"Who fingered us?" Blondie wanted to know.

"Farber," Feller answered. "He noticed both of us gone. He was joking with me before class today like he knew what we'd been up to and it was okay. So I kinda admitted it."

Blondie moaned in frustration.

"What do we do now?" he asked.

"Let's write each other's notes," Dispatch suggested.

"Didn't you hear what the Bear said?" Feller asked him. "He'll be watching for that."

"Not if we write each other's."

"I don't know," Blondie said. "He's likely to call our parents no matter what. I think we're going to have to tell them."

"Tell them what?" Feller asked. "That we sneaked into a strip joint to see a woman make love to a snake?"

"Well, I'm not telling my old lady," Dispatch said. "I couldn't stand to listen to her lecture."

"So what *do* we do?" Blondie asked.

"We could go up to Shady Lanes and shoot some more pool," Feller suggested.

Blondie couldn't get up for that.

"You guys do what you want. I'd just as soon go home."

Dispatch was happy to drop him off, but Blondie felt strange being home so early on a school day. Everything in the house seemed an accusation of his villainy. He cursed himself for being so parent-whipped.

Why couldn't he just look his mom in the eyes and say, "Write me a note, will you? I had a little run-in with the vice principal and got suspended. No big deal." After all, he was seventeen. He had a right to fuck off once in a while, didn't he?

Nothing told himself alleviated his sense of wrongdoing. Then he remembered something Feller had told him once. He'd called it Muggerood's Theorem: that a male has but one main artery and that it goes directly from his penis to his brain.

"It's a question of which head is in control," he'd explained. "You can't maintain a hard-on and worry at the same time."

Obviously, then, what Blondie needed in this moment of crisis was a gigantic boner. The catch was that he was already worried, so how was he going to get it up? Perhaps the proper environment would do it. He headed for the shower. Soon, he stood behind the glass door, limp member in hand. As the first fingers of warm water began massaging his skin, he searched his mind for a suitable fantasy. His old standby came to mind—an isolated cabin with two horny coeds. However, he'd discovered over the years that the staying power of any fantasy was only three or four showers in a row, and he'd already run out the string.

He ran a number of other possibilities through his mind: a day at a nudist camp, a peephole into the girls' shower at school, a reprise with Linda Lapidus. Nothing was working.

"You're behaving like a worm," Blondie scolded his organ. He quickly apologized. He'd never get hard undermining Nessie's self-esteem. Then he remembered an oldie but goodie. Once long ago—through a crack in a window shade—he'd seen a friend's sister masturbating. Nessie immediately began to show a little spine and, within minutes, Blondie reached a satisfactory climax. The tension flowed from his body.

After donning a fresh pair of jeans and a clean shirt, he stood before the mirror, transformed. This was no wimp staring back at him, no cowering goody two-shoes afraid to confront his own parents. It was the reincarnation of James Dean, a rebel *with* a cause—that cause being to stand up to his parents.

After wolfing down a twin-pack of Twinkies for lunch, Blondie felt ready for anything. The feeling lasted until his parents arrived home. As if out of a bad dream, his mother went directly to the bathroom and noticed that her facial towel was still damp.

"Did you take another shower today?" she asked him.

"Yeah, I was still sweaty after Phys. Ed."

She found the Twinkies' wrapper in the waste can not more than fifteen minutes later.

"Why were you eating junk food just before dinner?" she asked.

"Don't get excited. I ate it a couple hours ago," he replied without thinking.

"You were home early? Why? Were you sick?"

What should he do? Should he tell her he'd been sick? What about his suspension? Blondie felt beads of moisture on his forehead.

His dad turned toward him.

"You haven't answered your mother, Bernard."

"Well, yeah, I came home early."

His voice came out small and squeaky.

"Why, Bernard?"

His dad's tone was much sharper than his mom's.

Think of James Dean. What would he do?

"Nothing's going on at school," he said with a burst of bravado. "It's a drag."

"Are you telling me you didn't go to school because it isn't entertaining enough?"

Blondie cringed at the quantum rise in his dad's tone.

"Did you think I didn't show up at reveille on days I thought there wasn't going to be any war?"

His dad was getting into his military thing: duty, honor, country.

"I didn't feel good," Blondie amended himself.

"Why didn't you say that in the first place?" his mom said. She gave him a look of concern.

Oh God, he was wimping out, playing for sympathy.

"Well, you look all right now," his dad said. "So I expect you'll be at school tomorrow."

"That's going to be a problem," Blondie said.

"Why?" his dad asked, raising his eyebrows.

"I got suspended."

Blondie didn't remember all that happened after that, although it felt like three hours in a sauna with a pack of wolves. The low points of the drama were a teary reproach from his mother and a stern lecture from his father. There were no high points.

Later, his mother gave him a groveling note apologizing to Mr. Bearzinsky for "Blondie's unfortunate and never-to-be-repeated transgression" and begging "his forbearance in allowing her contrite son" to return. Blondie felt like puking. He was going to have to deliver this obsequious piece of crap to the Bear. But at least he hadn't been grounded. His mother had talked his dad out of that.

Still, as he lay in bed that night, staring at the moonlight that fell on the foot of his bed, he judged his encounter with his folks a total defeat.

"James Dean my ass," he muttered to himself. Then he begged Nessie's forgiveness.

* * * * * * * * *

Blondie was snatched from a dream—he remembered only that it was unpleasant—by scraping outside. He leaned across his bed and looked out his front window. Winter had painted everything white. Mr. Potter, fattened by a bulky black parka and floppy galoshes, stabbed at the snow on his driveway with a red shovel.

Blondie slipped on his jeans and slippers and went out on the front porch. The world seemed fresh and pure, open to possibility and free of threat. Potter looked his way with a hostile expression. So much for a threat-free world, Blondie thought.

It was Saturday, the last shopping day before Christmas. Blondie had accepted his mom's invitation to accompany her into town. He had nothing better to do. Besides, he needed to get presents for his parents. That night, he was planning to go out with the gang—except for Feller who'd been grounded by his dad for cutting school. Grouper had insisted upon driving, saying that he hadn't been carrying his share of the "chauffeuring burden." He told Blondie he'd pick him up in his dad's Chrysler. Blondie recalled Feller's warning about Grouper's driving: "He's blind as a cave fish but not nearly so coordinated."

As soon as they reached town, Blondie excused himself from his mom and loped up the street, slipping frequently on the slushy sidewalk. He shoved his way into a gaggle of frenzied shoppers at the Variety Store and grabbed a wallet for his dad. What to get his mom, though?

She liked knickknacks and the Bonanza was full of them: glass balls filled with snow scenes, fake cuckoo clocks, porcelain figurines, silver-plated thimbles. It was too confusing. He bought her a box of chocolates, praying she wasn't on a diet. The odds were fifty-fifty.

On his way out, Blondie saw Bobby Clements in the sporting goods section. He was perusing a set of golf clubs. Working up his nerve, Blondie approached him.

"Do you play?"

Bobby turned his head slowly and gazed at Blondie.

"Oh, it's you," he said. Blondie wondered if Bobby remembered his name. "Not very well," he said, responding to Blondie's question.

Blondie felt his tongue knotting up. He didn't want to say anything dumb to the number-one stud in school.

"How about you, Blondie?"

Clements did remember his name. That was a score.

"Yeah, I play," Blondie said, trying to keep from showing too much enthusiasm. Guys who got too excited over things weren't cool.

"Any good?"

"Low eighties."

Bobby whistled. Blondie felt his chest swell.

"I've been playing since I was ten," Blondie added, hoping Bobby wouldn't think he was bragging.

"You could be on the golf team."

"Fenton has a golf team?"

Percy High hadn't had one.

"Yeah. It plays against the Baltimore schools. I bet you could make it. Talk to Mr. Beasley. He's the golf coach."

Beasley? Blondie's overweight phys-ed instructor?

"He doesn't look like a golfer."

"Beasley's a real klutz," Bobby said. "but he's the coach. He could use you. You could get a letter."

"That so?"

Blondie raised his eyebrows. He'd always thought athletic letters were reserved for macho sports like football, baseball, or wrestling.

"I'll think about it," he said in an offhand manner.

"Do it."

Blondie began to walk away, then stopped and turned back to Clements. He felt inspired—like he always did, just before he did something rash.

"Maybe we could play golf together sometime."

"Maybe. I play baseball in the spring and that takes up a lot of my time, but maybe."

Wow! Bobby Clements would consider playing golf with him! That would put Blondie right up there with Fenton High's elite. He bet Tammy would pay him a lot more attention if she knew he was buddies with Clements.

Back on the street, Blondie noticed the marquee on the Marylander Theater just up the street: *Psycho*. Some Christmas movie. Only in Fenton, he thought.

A car pulled up to the curb across the street.

"Merry Christmas, Blondie!" a woman shouted from the open window.

It was Miss Darlington, her red hair hanging from the car like a Christmas stocking.

"Merry Christmas to you," he called back.

Seeing her boosted his mood even further. She was so cheerful, so positive. He couldn't help looking back her way as he headed down the street. He wished he hadn't.

Something caught in his mind. It took hold and wouldn't let go...a seed of worry and, like a seed, it began to assume color, to take shape. The color and shape was that of her car. There was no denying it. Her late-model metallic-blue Rambler looked a lot like the car he'd seen parked at the sleazy motel on Route 40 the month before—beside the one that had looked like Mr. Bearzinsky's. No, it couldn't be. He remembered how Feller had told him, in a fractured metaphor, that the Bear was married to an old heifer that'd borne him a brood of cubs.

Angry voices jerked him from his speculation.

"Worthless piece of crap!" he heard a man shout. Blondie turned to see figure in the lot beside Ernie's Hardware. Shakes was one. He was standing beside the run-down Studebaker Blondie'd seen at his house and facing a short, stocky man with hedgehog hair and a bullet head. His dad, Blondie assumed. A split paper bag lay on the ground between them. It was surrounded by a swarm of nails.

The man lowered his voice. Blondie could no longer make out what he was saying, but from the way Shakes hung his head, Blondie was sure he was berating him. Without any apparent provocation from Shakes, the man lashed out with his fist and punched Shakes in the shoulder. Blondie was *shocked*. He'd never seen a father hit his son before. For an instant, Shakes coiled like a cobra preparing to strike. Then his shoulders quivered and his arms fell to his sides. He slumped into the car.

Blondie hurried to where his mom had left the car. He let himself in with his set of keys, started the motor, and clicked on the radio. He needed to push the scene he'd just witnessed from his mind. Brenda Lee was singing "Rocking around the Christmas Tree." It didn't help.

During the ride home, he started to tell his mom what he'd seen. He couldn't find the words to begin. It seemed too shameful to discuss.

Blondie's dad was putting up the Christmas tree when they got home. He was playing Christmas carols on the phonograph, the religious kind he liked: "Oh, Little Child of Bethlehem," "Oh Come All Ye Faithful," "Away in a Manger." Blondie preferred bouncier songs like "Sleigh Ride" or "Jingle Bell Rock." But he was in no mood to quibble about his dad's selection of music—or anything he did. He'd seen how bad a dad could be.

That evening, Grouper surprised Blondie by appearing at the front door wearing a stylish wool overcoat, a tartan scarf, and dark gloves. Except for an extra hundred pounds, he could have stepped from the pages of *Esquire* magazine. He held out his hand to Blondie's mom and introduced himself as "Walter Clarence Whipple." He complimented his dad on the way he'd decorated the tree.

"Such a well-mannered boy," his mother whispered to Blondie as he went out the door.

"What'd you come to the door for?" Blondie asked the Grouper. He wasn't sure he wanted his parents to know all his friends.

"Only plebeians just drive up and honk for people."

"Dispatch always honks."

"Precisely my point."

Blondie felt rich, spoiled, in the Whipple's New Yorker. It was brand new, navy blue, and polished to a glimmer. Blondie sank into the soft leather seat. It engulfed him like a mother's embrace. He began to relax.

Not for long. Grouper backed over the curb leaving the driveway, missed the turn out of Heritage Acres, and drove through the first red light they came to.

For a moment, Blondie considered telling Grouper about Shakes and his dad, but he decided against it. They were on their way to pick him up. Blondie was sure Shakes didn't want anyone else to know. What kid would?

"Nice wheels," Blondie said instead.

"Dad has to look good with his peers."

"Because he's a lawyer?"

"A corporation lawyer in Baltimore," Grouper emphasized. "He defends corporations against bogus on-the-job injury claims."

"You mean people fake injuries?"

"Everyone does, according to my dad. He could convince a jury someone mangled his arm in a machine just to dodge work."

Blondie decided not to pursue the subject. He was already bummed out about Shakes' dad. He didn't need to hear about the shortcomings of Grouper's.

"What's that on the radio?" Blondie asked.

"Beethoven's Fifth Symphony."

Was Grouper trying to impress him? Or did he actually like that stuff?

"Do you mind if I change stations?" Blondie asked

Grouper smiled and pushed a button on the dash. The Tokens blared forth: "Weem-o-way, weem-o-way."

Grouper was more talkative than usual, agitated about something he'd heard on the radio that day. An American soldier had been killed in Vietnam. The first one, he said.

"Miss Darlington told us about Vietnam," Blondie said. "She's worried we'll get into a war."

"It sounds like we already are."

Khrushchev's doomsday device came to Blondie's mind again. "The commies are evil. We have to draw the line somewhere."

"Vietnam is a long way from America and the side we're supporting is corrupt," Grouper replied.

Miss Darlington hadn't mentioned that.

Blondie still didn't know where Vietnam was. He supposed it was one of the countries in the Third World. Blondie wasn't sure where the Third

World was either. He always thought of palm trees and half-naked natives when he heard the term.

"What if you had to go?" Grouper asked him.

"Why would I? I'm not going to enlist."

"You have to sign up for the draft when you turn eighteen."

"Yeah, but no one's being drafted. Vietnam isn't Korea."

Grouper pushed out his lower lip and fell into thought. He was the only one in the group who ever talked about politics or current events.

Blondie stared out the window at the red, white and green Christmas lights on Front Street. It almost looked pretty all lit up. A life-sized crèche crowded the corner of Front Street and Home, in front of the armory. A donkey with a missing tail, three wise men in garish garb, and the holy family huddled under a cedar-shingled roof. The Christ-child's nose was broken off.

Grouper shifted his eyes from side to side as he drove. He seemed to be looking for something. Before they reached the cutoff to Shakes' house, Grouper turned.

"Where're we going?" Blondie asked.

He didn't answer. He drove a few more blocks and turned again. A hazy garland of lights glowed in the distance. As they drew nearer, Blondie saw that someone had strung Christmas bulbs in some trees above a frozen pond. Several people were skating on it.

Grouper slowed as they passed. What was he up to? In an instant, Blondie understood. Skimming over the ice in wide circles, like a gull turning in the breeze, was a girl in a long white coat and white gloves. Her dark hair tossed from side to side with each turn.

Blondie hoped she'd look his way, although he didn't know what he'd do if she did. He pressed his face against the cold glass of the car window and watched, mesmerized, until the rink faded from view. A cameo remained in his mind for a long time, a Currier & Ives print. Tammy had never seemed more beautiful.

An approaching car momentarily lit Grouper's face. He was looking straight ahead, but an almost imperceptible smile creased his lips.

Chapter Eighteen

Shakes was waiting on the porch in a rusted lawn chair when they arrived, wearing a thin plaid jacket, his arms wrapped around his chest to fend off the cold. Light spilled from the little rambler, but there was no movement within. The driveway was empty.

Shakes seemed his normal self when he got into the car—whiny and argumentative.

"It's about t-time," he complained.

Blondie watched him furtively for evidence of the altercation he'd witnessed earlier—some mark, some emotion. He detected nothing. Were beatings so common as to be quickly forgotten? Blondie couldn't imagine it.

"W-watch out!" Shakes yelled as Grouper headed for the mailbox backing out. Grouper twisted the wheel sharply.

"Gr-great. Now we're h-headed the wrong w-way."

"Doesn't Barnwell live up here somewhere?" Blondie asked.

"A c-couple blocks up the street and then l-left," Shakes answered.

"Why don't we drive by?"

Blondie felt drawn by morbid curiosity to see the abode of his archenemy. It was as if someone had said, "There's a nest of copperheads in that woodpile over there. Wanna see?" Yet, when Grouper turned up Buford's street, Blondie felt out-of-place, a *voyeur*. Moreover, he pictured Buford's house as something from a horror flick, harsh and forbidding.

His imagination was out to lunch. The Barnwells' house, far from being Dracula's lair, was an ordinary mobile home on cinder blocks—neither freshly painted nor peeling, neither well kept nor slovenly. The thin front lawn was held in check by a knee-high white fence and populated by a plastic flamingo and a lopsided doghouse. The only thing frightening about the place was its banality.

"That's enough," Blondie said. "Let's get out of here."

They swung by and collected Brick and Dispatch, then headed for the Suds Cellar.

"Who's going to buy?" Brick asked when they arrived, fixing his gaze on Dispatch.

Blondie wondered why Brick never volunteered. He seemed gutsy enough and he looked older than Dispatch. Perhaps he felt it was beneath his dignity.

Dispatch reached for his wallet.

"Uh-oh," he said. "I forgot my cards."

Brick turned toward Grouper.

"You could pass," he said.

Grouper hesitated. Blondie could also tell this was a "moment of truth" for him. Would he step over the line? Break the rules?

"Well, I am the most sophisticated," he said.

"Whatever," Brick replied.

The minute Grouper left the car, Brick turned to Shakes and told him to follow Grouper "and see how he does."

Shakes slid out of the car as soon as Grouper lumbered down the short flight of stairs into the tavern. Time dragged by. Other patrons came and went.

"What the fuck? Are they jerking each other off in there?" Brick asked. "I'm thirsty."

Shakes bolted from the stairwell, ran to the car and jumped in. Almost immediately, Grouper sauntered from the Cellar with empty arms.

"He didn't get it?" Bricks shouted. He was outraged.

"Gr-Grouper asked for a s-six Pabst of p-pack."
"Some friggin' sophisticate," Brick groused.
"D-don't t-tell h-him I w-was w-watching."
"They're not the type of people I like to deal with," Grouper explained when he got in the car.
"Yeah, and you're a dufus," Brick said.
"Please gentlemen, I understand your disappointment, but I'm sure there are other ways to get what we want."
"I oughta ream your asshole out with my church key," Brick snarled.
A shadow appeared beside the car.
"It's P-Purdy," Shakes said. "H-he w-wants me to r-roll down the w-window. What should I d-do?"
"Give him the finger," Brick recommended.
"N-no w-way," Shakes said.
Purdy's appearance made Blondie apprehensive. Barnwell was likely to be nearby. Blondie caught sight of Purdy's battered pickup under a light across the lot. He was relieved to see it empty.
"Roll down the window and see what the dickhead wants," Brick ordered.
"You guys aren't having trouble getting beer, are you?" Purdy inquired.
"No, we just come up here to watch all the town drunks," Brick replied.
Purdy ignored him.
"I can get you some beer."
"Why would you do that?" Brick asked.
Purdy shrugged.
"We don't have to be enemies," he said.
"How much?" Brick asked.
"How much beer do you want?"
"A case."
"Five bucks," Purdy said.
"A little high, but I'll chip in," Dispatch chimed in.

"How do we know y-you won't just t-take our f-five and s-split?" Shakes asked.

"If that's the way you feel," Purdy sniffed, "don't give me the money until I give you the beer."

"Sounds foolproof," Dispatch said to Brick.

Brick grunted.

"Okay, it's a deal," he agreed. "We want Pabst."

Purdy walked over to the stairwell and disappeared. Shortly he reappeared holding a grocery bag.

"Look in there and see what it is," Brick told Shakes.

"It's P-Pabst," Shakes confirmed.

They each ponied up a buck and gave it to Purdy.

"Hey, thanks man," Blondie said to Purdy, hoping this marked some turning point in his relationship with Purdy—and Barnwell.

"Ah, it's nothing," Purdy said with a wide smile. He strolled away.

"What'd you go thanking the cocksucker for?" Brick chided Blondie.

"Where next?" Grouper asked.

"How about the quarry?" Dispatch suggested.

As soon as they turned off the main drag, Shakes reached into the bag, pulled out a can and handed it to Brick.

"Nice and cold," he remarked.

He punctured it in the dark with the can opener he wore like dog tags around his neck. He tilted the can up to his lips. Phhwwwwt! Vapor exploded from his mouth and sprayed the front of the car.

"What's the m-matter?" Shakes asked.

"Turn on the light," Brick ordered.

Grouper switched on the overhead light. Brick raised the can to eye level. Mountain Dew.

"I thought you looked," Brick said to Shakes.

"I d-did."

Brick reached in the bag and pulled out a flat piece of cardboard with Pabst printed on it.

"It's just packing material."

"We've been had," Grouper said.

"Go back!" Brick shouted.

Blondie asked Brick what he planned to do.

"I'm going to rearrange Purdy's internal organs," he said.

Blondie had never seen Brick mad before. His whole body bristled. Blondie was impressed—and nervous. Events were spinning out of control.

"Are we sure we're handling this situation rationally?" Blondie asked no one in particular.

"This isn't something we're taking a poll on." Brick bit off each word. "This is personal. You don't prepare someone's taste buds for a Pabst and give him fucking Mountain Dew."

Blondie conceded the point.

Dispatch's counsel: "Kill the son of a bitch."

The pickup hadn't moved.

"I'm surprised he's got the guts to be here," Brick said. "I'm going to clean his clock."

Grouper ground the Chrysler to a halt about ten feet from Purdy's truck. He was as expressionless as usual, but his movements were wooden. Blondie felt tense, too. He hoped Purdy wouldn't show, that he'd gone off with one of his friends.

No such luck. Purdy came strolling around the corner of the diner. Matching him step for step was Barnwell. Blondie sucked in his breath.

"Buford's with him," Dispatch said to Brick.

"I can see."

"What if he joins in?" Blondie asked.

"It doesn't matter."

Blondie had never seen Brick so pissed. He got out of the car.

"Hey Purdy," he yelled at him. "You fat fucking hillbilly jack off. Come over here."

Purdy took a step forward, then stopped. Barnwell didn't move.

"Something the matter?" Purdy asked. Blondie detected a faint tremble in his voice.

"I want our five bucks back."

"No way. You got something to drink."

"Five bucks or it's your ass."

"Get it from Blondie. He owes us a case, anyway."

Brick looked back toward the car.

Oh shit, Blondie thought. He'd forgotten all about that.

"What're you talking about?" Brick asked Purdy.

"Blondie promised us a case on account of Buford not killing him. He never delivered."

Barnwell grinned and stared at Blondie. He was dying inside. Christ, he would've bought the case if they had asked. Why was Purdy telling everyone? He could feel the gang's collective eyes boring into him—into his yellow, lily liver.

"What'd you promise them beer for?" Brick hissed at Blondie through the window. "We would've backed you up."

What a worm he was, Blondie thought, what a craven worm. He'd disgraced the whole club—himself most of all.

"I don't know about that case," Brick growled, turning back to Purdy. "I didn't make any promise about anything. I paid for beer and I want beer, not hillbilly swill."

"What's the matter, Brick?" Buford taunted. "That sodie pop too strong for you?"

"Stay out of this, Barnwell. You're not involved."

"What if I get involved?" Barnwell stepped from under the eaves and took a few steps toward their car.

"Then I'm going to kick your skinny little redneck butt all over this parking lot."

Blondie could feel his stomach jumping. Buford was a tough customer. But then, Brick had about thirty pounds on him and it was all muscle—and Brick was pissed.

Barnwell didn't answer and he didn't move. Instead, he leaned toward Purdy and whispered something to him. Purdy walked over to the door of the Cellar and went inside.

"You're pretty far away to talk so big," Barnwell said to Brick, recommencing the verbal fray. "Why don't you come closer?"

Brick stomped toward Barnwell, tightening his fists with each step, homing in on Barnwell like a slow-moving torpedo. Barnwell took a step backward and cast an anxious glance to his rear.

The door to the Suds Cellar crashed open. Purdy shot from the top of the stairs, followed by a large, muscular-looking young man in a leather jacket. He had a couple days' worth of whiskers on his face.

"Holy Christ," Dispatch said, "it's Merwin Fester."

Blondie'd never heard the name before, but from Dispatch's awed tone, he knew Fester had a reputation.

Brick stopped about six feet from Barnwell. Buford—who'd been crouching—straightened up.

"Hey there, Buford," the new fellow said, "having a problem?"

Blondie could see the guy better under the parking lot lights. He looked to be twenty-two or -three. Sewn onto the left front of his jacket was a patch bearing the "Harley-Davidson" logo. He was wearing jackboots.

"Nothing I can't handle," Buford said, renewed confidence in his voice.

"L-liar," Shakes yelled from the car.

"Eat sh-shit, br-broken m-mouth," Barnwell mimicked.

"Wh-what d-did you s-say?"

Blondie felt Shakes' whole body began to quiver next to him in the car.

"I said eat shit, you stuttering half-wit," Barnwell taunted.

Shakes exploded from the car and ran at Buford. Blondie was astonished. Brick was astonished. Barnwell was most astonished.

When he reached Barnwell, Shakes began flailing his small fists. Buford stepped aside and caught Shakes hard against his left ear. Shakes turned in surprise and Barnwell hit him flush in the face. Blood spurted from Shakes' nose. Shakes wiped his nose with the back of his hand and then gaped at the red smear on his hand.

A sudden rage gripped Blondie. Barnwell was a lot bigger than Shakes. It wasn't fair. He opened his door and stepped outside.

"Well, if it ain't the giraffe," Buford said.

"You son of a bitch," Blondie said, advancing a step or two towards him. "He's half your size."

Buford eyed Blondie warily as Shakes stumbled back toward the Chrysler. Fester and Purdy seemed content to stand by and see what developed.

"Yeah, well, he came at me, didn't he?" Barnwell said.

Blondie detected a hint of apprehension in Barnwell's tone. That thought provided Blondie a momentary rush, but with each step forward, he could feel his anger subside. Oh God, it was going to be just like every other time he wanted to stand up to someone—his body was going to give him away. Blondie willed himself to keep moving forward, but his legs began to feel as if they were filling with water. He was getting dizzy. He stopped.

"Second thoughts, huh, big boy?"

Blondie started to make a smart retort, but his tongue wouldn't move. He felt faint. Blondie inched his way back to the Chrysler and leaned against it for support.

Buford laughed.

"What a bunch of pansies you guys are."

Brick's voice ended Buford's brief gloating.

"I'm not finished with you, asshole," Brick said.

Buford looked over to the man in the motorcycle jacket.

"Ah, they're just soreheads is all," he said to him, as if it was all over.

Brick took another step toward Barnwell.

The newcomer interposed himself between Brick and Buford.

"Maybe you and your friends should just move along somewhere else," he said to Brick.

His voice was soft, non-threatening. He seemed more amused than anything else.

"Maybe you should just kiss my ass," Brick replied.

"Oh God, no," Dispatch murmured.

"What'd you say, peckerface?" Fester asked Brick.

"Have you got shit in your ears or can't you hear?" Brick shot back.

Fester's head snapped back and a wild look came into his eyes. He began striding toward Brick.

"Start the car, Grouper," Blondie ordered, jumping into the front seat.

"Brick, Shakes, get in the car."

When Shakes bailed out, Brick's resolve vanished. He began backing up. The man in the denim jacket balled up his fists.

"Start moving," Blondie instructed Grouper.

As the Chrysler eased forward, Blondie held the door open.

"Run, Brick," he yelled.

Brick turned to see where the car was and then broke for it, with Fester in pursuit. Brick dove into the front seat just as Fester aimed a swift kick at his rear. Fester caught air as Grouper hit the throttle.

Through the open window, Blondie heard Purdy's and Barnwell's laughter. He heard it long after they were out of earshot.

Nobody spoke for a long time.

"What a disaster," Grouper finally said. "An epic loss of face."

"What could I do?" Brick said. "I couldn't fight Fester."

"No one's blaming *you*," Dispatch said.

Blondie could guess who they *were* blaming.

"Who is this Fester, anyway?" Blondie asked. He wished he hadn't said a word. Brick, Dispatch, and Shakes all gave him sour looks.

"One of the roughest guys in the county, that's all," Dispatch finally answered. "He trains horses at Mirandel Farms."

"H-he graduated fr-from F-Fenton f-four years ago," Shakes added.

Grouper drove out to the quarry where they sat around in the dark with no beer to ease their pain. Sentences would begin and then break apart. Everything was all wrong, Blondie thought. They weren't in the P-mobile. They didn't have any beer. They'd been disgraced by the billies. And it was all his fault. He kept silent, willing himself to disappear.

"Ah fuck, let's go home," Brick said after about a half hour.

Just before they got to Brick's house, Shakes said to Brick, "B-buford was sc-scared of y-you."

"That's right," Dispatch agreed.

"I would've cleaned his clock," Brick declared.

"Y-yeah, y-you sure w-would've."

That seemed to revive the group a little.

As Brick got out, he turned to Blondie and said, "I'm sorry if I got on you, man. But you shouldn't have made any deal with Barnwell and Purdy. They're snakes."

Shakes turned to the Grouper, who'd said nothing since they'd left the Cellar.

"Wh-what law w-was at w-work tonight?" he asked him.

Grouper cleared his throat.

"This one is easy. **Never, ever, conduct business with a billy.**"

"Amen," Blondie agreed. He felt like a warmed-over turd.

"We'll get them for this," Dispatch promised when Grouper dropped him off.

"It w-wasn't all that b-bad," Shakes said when they got back to his house.

"You were brave," Blondie assured him.

"Yeah, and l-look what I g-got for it." Shakes held out his sleeve. Even in the dark Blondie could see it was covered with blood. Just what Shakes needed, Blondie thought. His dad smacks him in the afternoon. Buford smacks him in the evening.

Grouper drove Blondie back through Fenton. Near the courthouse, "Silent Night" blared from a loudspeaker. No one was on the streets.

"I fucked up," Blondie said.

He felt he needed to perform some act of penance. But what could it be?

"It doesn't matter," Grouper said. "It's all just stupid kid stuff."

"Then why are we doing it?"

"Kismet, I guess. Fate, destiny. Because we're still in high school."

"How can you always be so calm? Doesn't anything ever bother you?"

"Sure. I just don't know how to talk about some things. Right now, in fact...."

He seemed to be debating telling Blondie something.

"Go on," Blondie encouraged him.

"I set it up to pick you up first and take you home last," Grouper continued. "I wanted to talk to you, but...." He broke off again.

In the distance, Blondie saw something on the road, a dark spot at the far reach of the headlights.

"I don't know how to put this..." Grouper started again. Blondie was trying to give Grouper his attention, but there was definitely something there.

"It's just that..."

Now Blondie could make out what it was—a small deer.

"Grouper, there's a deer on the road," Blondie said.

"This is something I haven't told anyone..."

Grouper was fixated on getting the words out.

"THERE'S A DEER ON THE ROAD!" Blondie yelled at him.

"What? Where?"

The Chrysler hurtled toward the antlered road barrier, now less than a hundred yards ahead.

"I can't see anything," Grouper said.

"Grouper, you've got to slow down now!"

"Oh yeah. Now I see it."

"Then slow down!"

"Don't worry," Grouper reassured Blondie. "I've read about this. Once you shine your headlights in a deer's eyes, it's hypnotized. It won't move an inch."

"What are you saying?"

"I'll just drive around it."

Then they were upon it, almost eye to eye as Blondie remembered later. Blondie could make out the hairs on the deer's hide, its dark perplexed eyes. Grouper swung the Chrysler to the right to go around it. Ignoring Grouper's theory, the deer sprang right into them.

WHUMP! The impact drove them onto the shoulder. Grouper fought the wheel to bring the Chrysler screeching back onto the road surface.

"Why didn't it stay still?" Grouper asked, nonplused.

"I guess it had a different idea."

"Do you think it's dead?"

"What do you want to do? Go back and give it mouth-to-mouth resuscitation?"

Grouper waited until he came to a streetlight, then pulled over. He got out and looked at the Chrysler, then let out a groan.

"The whole left side is smashed."

He slumped against the car, gasping. Drops of moisture peppered his forehead.

"Another disappointment for my dad," he said.

Disappointment? What a strange word for smashing your parents' car.

Grouper pulled a monogrammed handkerchief from his jacket and mopped his brow.

"Don't take it so hard," Blondie said to Grouper. "Your dad probably has insurance."

"I wasn't thinking about the car. My folks can afford to fix it. Blondie, I've got to tell somebody this."

He took a deep breath.

"I've met a girl."

Chapter Nineteen

"I'll bet it's Meryl Dimsell," Feller said when Blondie accidentally spilled Grouper's news. "But I hope not."

Feller was psychic. That was the name Grouper had mentioned. Drat! Feller had guessed Grouper's secret because of his big mouth.

"I've seen him talking with her," Feller added.

So Feller already suspected. That took him off the hook, didn't it?

"Who is she? What's she like?" Blondie asked, giving in to his curiosity.

"She's a senior. Takes business classes. Hangs out with Delores Clitoris and Flossie Wilder sometimes…. a real yokel. And talk about ugly."

"She's not a billy queen, is she?"

"A real slop-highness."

Blondie was perplexed. Grouper disdained billies.

"Then why…?"

"Maybe she's all he can get. Maybe he's fucking her."

"The Grouper?"

"Do you think he's beyond horniness?"

Blondie'd never given Grouper's hormones much thought. Now that he did, it was hard for him to imagine Grouper sexually aroused. He never even made lewd comments about girls. Besides, he seemed too…lethargic? But he *was* a teenaged guy. That implied his basic posture toward life—despite any observable mannerisms—would be fully erect.

"Are you still grounded?" Blondie asked Feller.

"Afraid so."

Blondie told him about the deer.

"It's a good thing no one witnessed it."

"Why?"

"The state patrol charges three bucks a pound for a deer."

That didn't sound fair to Blondie. The deer had ambushed them.

"It must have weighed a couple hundred pounds."

"Like I said, it's a good thing no one saw you hit it. How was your Christmas?"

"Boring. Yours?"

"Boring."

The first two weeks back in school were taken up by semester exams. A little studying pulled Blondie through with an A, 3 B's, and 2 C's—disappointing to his parents, but he was satisfied. He'd be able to get into college with those grades.

Feller slightly bested Blondie's marks and Dispatch, Shakes, and Brick hadn't come close. Grouper wouldn't tell anyone what his grades were.

"Grouper never tells," Feller said, "but I'm sure he does all right. He knows all the answers in class."

Feller asked Blondie again about going to Smith-Reid with him. They'd both taken their college boards a couple weeks earlier.

"Yeah, okay. Why not?"

"Great," Feller enthused, slapping him on the back. "But keep it a secret, huh? I don't want the other guys to feel left out."

Speaking of secrets, Blondie was relieved when Grouper began strolling the halls with Meryl, stunning Brick, Dispatch and Shakes into varying degrees of disbelief. He could quit worrying about Feller revealing his indiscretion.

Blondie hated to admit Feller was right because he liked the Grouper, but Meryl *was* a dog—short and stout and mannish in posture and gait. Her only notable feature was a large mole that clung to her cheek like a leech.

Brick often teased Grouper when he saw him walking with her.

"Hey Grouper, where'd you get that girl?" he'd call out.

Blondie asked Feller why Brick was acting so cruel.

"Beats me. Brick used to go out with Meryl, but I never thought he liked her. I assumed it was because she's supposed to be easy."

Was that why Grouper was dating her? Blondie had trouble believing it. He didn't seem the type to take advantage of anyone.

One thing was for sure—Grouper's coupling changed their group dynamics. It wasn't fun to discuss girls now that Grouper had one. What everyone said about girls—they wore too much makeup, took too long in the john, wouldn't fuck them or fucked the wrong guys (other guys)—now sounded like sour grapes. And then, of course, Grouper spent far less time with them.

Second semester brought few changes. Blondie had the same teachers and in the same order, except now he had Farber for physics instead of chemistry and Miss Darlington for journalism instead of civics.

Blondie promised himself he was going to be more prominent in school. Not just because he was tired of feeling like a cipher, but more from the belief Tammy might notice him if he were a Big Man on Campus. His self-promotion plan had two components. First was getting on the staff of the school newspaper, *The Fentonian*. Second, when the time came, he was going to try out for the golf team.

Blondie's first day in journalism class brought one surprise—Tammy's tall, pig-tailed friend Phyllis was there. It turned out juniors, as well as seniors, could take journalism. Blondie debated whether her presence was bad or good. He decided it would be good if she thought he was pretty swift and bad if she thought he was a nerd. Either way, it was sure to get back to Tammy. Blondie determined to acquit himself well.

From the first day, he displayed a zeal for journalism that soon led Miss Darlington to invite him to join the *Fentonian* staff (she was faculty sponsor). That meant spending an extra hour a day after school on Wednesdays, helping lay out the paper. Blondie was willing to do it, but he didn't have a ride home.

He mentioned his predicament to her.

"Where do you live?" she asked him.

"Heritage Acres."

"Phyllis lives up that way somewhere. Maybe she could give you a ride home."

"She's on the staff?"

Blondie hadn't realized that.

"Why yes, she's the events editor. Next year, when she's a senior, she'll be the managing editor."

"Well, I don't know...."

Even for Tammy, riding around with Phyllis might be pushing things. Blondie weighed the pros and cons. On the con side, Phyllis was unwholesome in appearance, if not personality. On the pro side, she *was* Tammy's friend.

"Do you want me to ask her?" Miss Darlington asked.

Blondie pondered the idea for few more seconds, then acquiesced. School would be out in less than five months one way or the other.

The next day, Miss Darlington told him Phyllis had said it would be okay for him to ride home with her as long as he didn't smoke.

"She said what?" Blondie exclaimed indignantly.

Miss Darlington looked at him in surprise.

"You don't smoke, do you?"

"Well, no."

"Then there's no problem."

Miss Darlington didn't understand. Phyllis was too ugly to be setting conditions.

Blondie felt like a dork the first afternoon he met with the newspaper staff. Everyone had a job but him.

One guy looked familiar. He was almost as tall as Blondie, with dark curly hair and glasses. Blondie remembered seeing him at a couple football games. He'd been carrying a camera with a flash. He seemed a bit nerdy, but friendly.

Blondie introduced himself to the boy.

"I'm Neil Golden," he said, holding out his hand.

A Jew. Blondie hadn't known many Jews.

"What do you do on the paper?" Blondie asked him.

"Sports and photography."

"You cover sports?"

Blondie's respect for him went up.

"Like golf?"

"No. It's the same time as baseball. So I cover baseball."

"Who covers golf?"

"No one right now."

"I'm thinking of going out for the team."

"That's great. If you make it, you can cover golf."

"Me?"

"Why not? Do you have an assignment?"

"No. But wouldn't that be a conflict of interest?"

Golden laughed.

"What do you think this is, the *New York Times*?"

Blondie couldn't believe it. If he made the golf team—which sounded like a snap—he could report on his own matches. Headlines popped into his brain: "Blondie Saves Match With Ace on Last Hole," "Blondie Rally Sinks Baltimore School," "Blondie's Balls Consistently Closest to Hole." Well, maybe that last one wouldn't work. But what a chance to be a self-made hero.

He was in high spirits when the hour ended, high enough to approach Phyllis.

"Hi, I'm Blondie Reimer," he said to her.

She looked at him as if she didn't understand.

"You're supposed to give me a ride home."

"Oh, you're the one. You ride my bus."

Christ, she didn't even know him by name! He'd been answering half the frigging questions in journalism class for a week—and riding the same bus for five months—and she hadn't bothered to find out who he was! How could she help him with Tammy if she was that fucking oblivious?

He walked behind her to her car, noticing every unbecoming thing about her all over again—her tangled hair, her big thighs, her dorky clothes. She stopped at her car, a lime-green 1960 Corvair, and turned to him.

"Hold my books while I get my key out."

Blondie tightened his fists. What was he, her doorman? He forced himself to keep cool. She was his ride home and she *was* Tammy's friend.

Halfway to his house, she asked, "Didn't I see you dancing with Tammy at a CYO dance last fall?"

Blondie's heart jumped, but he kept his cool.

"Tammy, who's that?"

"I could've sworn you were dancing with her. She's real pretty. Dark hair, nice complexion."

"Oh yeah, I remember. She's a cheerleader."

Phyllis went back to watching the road. Tell me more about her, Blondie urged without speaking.

"Do you have an assignment?" she said as she turned into his development.

"Yeah. I think so. Sports."

"With Neil. Good. He's a good writer. He can help you out."

What? Did she think he couldn't write? And what about Tammy? God, he couldn't just bring her up himself.

"Your friend," Blondie blurted, "what's her name again?"

"Who, Tammy?"

Jesus! How dense could she be?

"Yeah, her. Are you good friends with her?"

"Sorta."

"Didn't you get on the bus with her the first day of school?"

"You remember that?"

Oh God, what a gaffe. He'd revealed his hand. Now she'd realize how gaga he was for Tammy. He felt his face go scarlet.

"Once in a while, she spends the night," Phyllis said. "She's nice, but a little dull."

Had he heard right? This pigtailed scag was calling his dream girl dull? It was an outrage. Blondie bit his lip. When Phyllis pulled into his driveway, he bolted from the car to make sure he didn't ruin everything right then and there.

"Goodbye," Phyllis called after him. Her tone was friendly.

Blondie rushed into the house, watched from the window until her car was free of their drive, then let out a shriek of rage.

How could she call Tammy dull? Girls as pretty as Tammy had to be interesting. Phyllis was envious, that was all, Blondie decided, but he wanted to strangle her anyway.

At lunch the next day, Blondie recounted his ride home to the group.

"I can't believe it," he repeated. "Phyllis is such a dog and she has the nerve to criticize Tammy."

Shakes turned toward him and said, "Y-you make m-me s-sick, Blondie."

What was eating him?

"Y-you th-think anyone y-you d-don't like is a d-dog."

"What are you talking about?" Blondie defended himself. "She is a dog. Ask anyone here."

Feller tugged at Blondie's sleeve and whispered to him.

"Maybe Shakes likes her now that Janine dumped him."

Shakes with Phyllis? It was unimaginable. She'd tower over him like a mantis over a fly.

"I h-heard wh-what you s-said, F-feller, and y-you're f-full of sh-shit, t-too."

Feller took umbrage at that.

"Y-you all th-think y-you d-deserve queens. W-well, wh-what m-makes you s-so h-hot?"

Shakes grabbed his dessert bowl—strawberry Jell-O laced with banana bits—dumped it into his mashed potatoes, and stalked away.

"He likes Phyllis?" Blondie asked Feller.

"I don't know. What do you think's bothering him, Grouper?"

A wry smile bent his mouth.

"One man's dog is another man's queen," he said.

Was he talking about Shakes—or himself? Blondie looked down at his plate and Feller shuffled his feet.

"Fuck girls, anyhow," Dispatch chimed in. "They're more trouble than they're worth. Just when you think you're gonna get your hand in their pants, they have to go to the bathroom or they have a fucking conversation with the Virgin Mary."

"Who shot you down this time?" Feller asked him.

"Linda Lapidus. And I even bought her a nice meal."

Shakes didn't show up for their Saturday sortie. On Monday, he wasn't in school when classes began.

"Did you hear about Shakes?" Feller asked Blondie when they met in Farber's chemistry class.

"No, what?"

"He got caught shoplifting at the Bonanza on Saturday."

Now why would he do a dumb thing like that, Blondie wondered.

Chapter Twenty

smegma, n. a thick, foul-smelling, cheese-like, sebaceous secretion that collects beneath the foreskin or around the clitoris.

"Do you think that's what makes girls smell the way they do?" Feller asked Blondie. They were standing before the huge unabridged dictionary in the school library.

"I don't know how girls smell, remember? And how would you? You told me you were a virgin."

"I had my finger in Delores a couple times, though."

That was news to Blondie. It made him feel even more out of it as far as girls were concerned. His only sexual experience to date had been yanking his crank.

"And there was a smell?"

"Yeah. Kinda fishy."

Blondie remembered the riddle Brick sometimes asked: "If girls are made of sugar and spice, how come they smell like tuna fish?" Blondie didn't like to think about that. It wasn't romantic. He didn't like to think about most bodily smells or processes and that included bad breath, body odor, menstruation, urination, defecation, and, of course, farting and belching. The thought of billions of people engaging in such activities on a daily basis was enough to gag a maggot. Moreover, it made him fear for the health of the planet.

"What can we do with a word like this?"

Feller seemed proud of his discovery. Blondie could empathize. It wasn't everyday you discovered a new sex word.

"You can spring it on the unsuspecting." Feller answered his own question.

"Like whom?" Blondie asked.

"Like Mary Cherry."

"H-mm-m."

Making a fool of Mary was appealing. Blondie was sick of her constant sucking-up to Mrs. Buckley and her supercilious airs.

"How would we do it?" he asked Feller.

"Doesn't Bucky hand out a sheet of vocabulary words every week?"

"Yeah."

"And doesn't she ask us to write a short story using each word at least once? Then, doesn't she ask for volunteers to read their stories? And doesn't Mary Cherry always volunteer?"

"All true."

"Then it's simple. We just add a word to the list."

"Mary'd never use a word like that," Blondie argued.

"What if she believed the definition was something she liked?"

"Yeah?" Blondie found himself beginning to smile. "Any ideas?"

"What about 'the essence of masculinity?'"

Blondie nodded, but he still didn't see how Feller was going to pull it off. It was already Tuesday, the day Bucky gave out the vocabulary list. Feller seemed unconcerned. He said he'd take care of it over lunch.

When Blondie entered Bucky's class, Feller shot him a satisfied smile. He pulled a sheet of paper from his desk. Somehow, he'd obtained a copy of Bucky's latest vocabulary list.

Shakes' seat was empty for the second day. Blondie wondered where he was. Shoplifting wasn't a school offense. Anyway, Feller told him

Shakes had only swiped a Mad magazine—not exactly a felony. Blondie couldn't rid himself of the feeling he was somehow responsible for Shakes' slipup.

Bucky's class proceeded as usual. She bombarded the class with a hail of fatuous observations about English literature while Mary Cherry cheered her on. Toward the end of the period, Bucky asked for a volunteer to help distribute the week's vocabulary list. Mary's hand shot up, but before Bucky could select her, Feller zipped to the front of the room. He ripped the bundle of lists from Bucky's hands. No one but Blondie noticed the sheet of paper Feller slipped on top the stack.

"It's nice to see you so involved, Paul," Bucky said to him.

"I just love words," he replied.

Feller put the top sheet on Mary's desk.

"I expect something creative on Friday," Buckley told them.

In the hall after class, Blondie asked Feller what would happen if Mary looked the word up for herself.

"She won't. She'd trust that old goat Buckley with her twat."

Shakes returned the next day. He sat down by Blondie in first-period trig without saying a word. A strawberry crescent blemished his cheek—the sign of another beating, Blondie guessed. He felt sorry for him.

"What happened?" he asked.

Shakes didn't reply. He just stared straight ahead with a pissed-off expression on his face.

By the time class was over, Blondie was angry, too. He grabbed Shakes by the arm. Shakes winced and Blondie realized there were more bruises beneath his shirt.

"What's eating you, anyway?" Blondie demanded.

"Y-you probably th-think I d-did it to impress y-you."

"To impress me?"

"All of y-you. Y-you think I j-just d-do th-things to get in t-tight with the gr-group."

Shakes was defiant, his face mottled with maroon, a cowlick shooting from his hay-like hair. A riled bantam rooster, Blondie thought.

"What are you talking about? Why would I think that?"

Shakes didn't answer. He set his mouth in a firm line.

"Well, why *did* you do it?" Blondie challenged him.

Shakes' mouth began to twitch and a look of anguish gripped his face.

"I d-don't kn-know."

"You don't know. You mean it was an accident."

"No. I w-wanted to t-take the m-magazine."

"Didn't you have the money?"

"That w-wasn't the issue."

"I don't understand."

They were at the end of the hall. Shakes grabbed his arm and pulled him toward the outside door.

"We're not supposed to go outside now," Blondie said.

"N-not s-supposed to," Shakes mocked.

Outside, Blondie waited for Shakes' explanation.

"I n-never d-do anything," he said after a few seconds.

Blondie was bewildered.

"I w-wanted to d-do s-something d-different."

"Shoplifting? That's different all right," Blondie said sarcastically.

"S-something I'd n-never d-done. S-something n-no one w-would expect."

"To prove what?"

"That I w-was s-somebody."

Blondie couldn't make the connection.

"A r-real p-person," Shakes went on.

"Who ever said you weren't a real person?" Blondie asked.

"It's j-just the w-way you all treat m-me. L-like I'm n-not equal."

What the hell was Shakes talking about? They treated him like everyone else, didn't they? Okay, so maybe not quite the same. But what did he expect? He was kinda strange looking and he stuttered. With those deficiencies, he couldn't expect the same respect as a Feller or a Brick. That was unrealistic—and unreasonable.

"Your shoplifting didn't make anything better," Blondie pointed out to him.

"N-no. It m-made th-things a l-lot w-worse. My d-dad h-hates m-me. My m-mom d-doesn't trust m-me. And I c-can't sh-shop at B-bonanza anymore."

Shakes was acting as distressed and disoriented as a hurricane survivor. He was giving Blondie the creeps. Nonetheless, Blondie reached out his arm and put it around Shakes' shoulder.

"What the fuck," Blondie said. "Life goes on, right."

Somehow that boosted his spirits.

"Y-yeah. Wh-what the f-fuck."

The whole group was at lunch, including Grouper, who usually ate with Meryl.

"It's nice of you to join us," Feller said with mock graciousness.

Grouper nodded.

"Y-you're n-not b-becoming p-pussywhipped, are y-you?" Shakes asked Grouper.

Blondie considered it a positive sign for Shakes to pull someone's chain. He was coming around.

"Actually, pussywhipped is a misnomer," Grouper began, but before he warmed to his subject, Brick interrupted.

"Didn't I see you hanging around the hall with a ninth grader?" he asked Dispatch.

"She adores me. She'll do anything I ask."

"You mean like fuck you?"

"Well, no."

"Then what's the point?"

"It's not out of the question," Dispatch countered.

And so it went. Another verbal jousting match filled with insults and imprecations. He'd affiliated himself with clowns. They'd never attain the first rank of school cliques. On the other hand, they were the most entertaining bunch he'd ever been with. He couldn't help feeling a little proud to be one of them.

Phyllis didn't see it the same way.

"You don't seem like those bozos you hang around with," she commented on the way home from the *Fentonian* layout session that afternoon.

He knew she meant it as a compliment, so Blondie restrained himself from hanging her by her pigtail. Instead, he asked Phyllis about herself—her family, her likes and dislikes. He wasn't interested in the slightest, of course, but currying Phyllis' favor was an essential part of his grand plan to make contact with his darling.

Anyway, he had the emotional reserves to indulge Phyllis today. That afternoon, he'd received his first story assignment from Miss Darlington. She'd asked him to cover the girls' field hockey game the following Monday. It wasn't the Baltimore Colts, but you had to start somewhere.

"That's great," Phyllis said when he told her. "That shows Miss Darlington has confidence in you."

Girls were so strange. A week ago, Phyllis had acted as if she couldn't care less about him.

"Thanks for the ride," he said when she let him off.

"I'm happy to do it," she said, smiling broadly.

The next day, Feller gave him a ride in. Blondie asked him if he'd noticed the bruise below Shakes' eye.

"Yeah."

"What can we do?" Blondie asked.

"What can anyone do? It's *his* dad."

"That doesn't give him a right to beat him, does it?"

They rode in silence for a while, passing snow-cloaked houses and denuded trees. Winter seemed to last forever.

"You're right, though. We should do something," Feller said as they entered the school parking lot. "Let me think about it."

The next afternoon, Blondie attended a "try-out" for those interested in being on Fenton High's 1962 golf team. Only three kids were in the gym when he arrived. That boded well. A golf team required six players.

Mr. Beasley huffed in, red-faced, his belly hanging out from his too-tight shorts. He stared at them while he caught his breath.

"Are you guys here for golf?" he asked, as if expecting a different group.

There was some coughing and looking away. One guy nodded.

"Hum-m-ph," Beasley muttered, scrutinizing them.

"You're tall," he said to Blondie.

"Sorry, sir."

"What do you shoot?"

"Mid-eighties." Blondie figured there was nothing to gain by over promising.

Beasley squinted at him.

The door banged open and two guys entered. They wore identical khaki slacks and Madras shirts. Joe Colleges, Blondie thought.

"Testerman and Carrington, where've you been?"

Beasley's voice showed its first strain of excitement.

"Are we late?" Carrington asked in a deep, manly voice. He was one of those guys whose face was shadowed with whiskers by the end of the day.

Beasley turned back to the group and announced, "Everyone's on the team. Be here in two weeks."

Beasley hadn't watched them swing or anything. He was just what Bobby had said—a fat and lazy slob. Blondie didn't cotton to the idea of Beasley as his coach, but he was ecstatic about making the team.

"Letter sweater, you're almost in hand," he said to himself. That couldn't fail to make an impression on Tammy.

At supper, Blondie told his family about his score.

"That's wonderful, Bernard," his mom said.

"Be sure not to miss any practices," his dad advised. "Discipline is the key to winning."

And that was it for his big news. His mom began to clear the table and his dad jumped up to get ready for the monthly meeting of his military group. He always wore his dress blue uniform and spit-shined shoes.

On his way out of the house, he looked Blondie in the eye and said, "Never admit defeat on the links. Never."

His expression was grave.

"What are you talking about, Dad?"

"Defending our way of life begins on the playing fields."

That night, Blondie couldn't get Shakes' accusation out of his mind. The next day, he waited until everyone but Grouper had left the lunch table.

"Do you think I treat other people like they're not real?" he asked him.

Grouper paused in his consumption of chocolate pudding.

"Like whom?"

"Like anyone," Blondie answered.

"Like me?" Grouper asked, licking the last remnants of brown from his spoon.

"Not you." Grouper could be exasperating with all his questions. "Shakes, for example."

"Is that what he said?"

"Could you just answer the question?"

Grouper looked up, bug-eyed, like a turtle emerging from its shell.

"Most of us are closet solipsists," Grouper said. He took a napkin and cleaned his spoon.

Solipsists? What was he talking about?

"A solipsist is someone who believes only he exists," Grouper continued, as if Blondie had spoken aloud. "Everyone else and everything else is only an illusion, a product of his mind."

"If that was true, I'd make Barnwell disappear and Tammy fall in love with me," Blondie commented.

"I admit the theory has limited practical application."

"So what about Shakes?" Blondie asked again.

"He apparently doesn't think you take him seriously."

"I take him seriously," Blondie protested. "I just think he's a little weird."

Grouper smiled, his eyes turning from those of a turtle to those of an owl.

"Everyone's weird," he said. "If we could each see into each other's minds...."

The thought made Blondie shiver. What if Tammy knew all the bizarre stuff he thought?

By the time Bucky's class rolled around the next day, Blondie was consumed with anticipation. With any luck, Mary Cherry would fall into Feller's trap. As it happened, Feller's plan worked like a charm. When Bucky asked for volunteers, Mary's hand shot up on cue.

"Very well, Mary," Bucky beamed. "I know you'll have something thoughtful for us."

Mary stood and turned to the class, a vainglorious look upon her face.

"This is a love story," she announced.

Feller turned around and gave Blondie a sly look.

"Anne had been at college for almost a month," Mary began, "and was filled with *exuberance*..."

That was one of Bucky's words.

"She loved to read books and she became *imbued* with knowledge. But she yearned to meet the man of her dreams. One *fulgent* day, she saw him standing across the quad. He held himself so erect. His *smegma* seemed to permeate the air between them..."

Grouper brayed. Mary paused.

Blondie looked over at Feller. He had his face buried in his hands. His shoulders were heaving.

"Never had Anne felt anything like this before," Mary continued. "It was a *revelation*, like *extrasensory perception*. She could almost taste his *smegma*..."

Grouper howled and Feller made a choking noise. Blondie was biting on his lips to keep from laughing out loud.

Mary looked toward the back of the room, perplexed.

"What's that word you're using?" Bucky asked.

"What word?" Mary asked.

"That word you're using in connection with the young man."

"Smegma?"

"Yes, that one. I don't know that word."

Mary stared at her uncomprehendingly.

"But it's on your list," she said. "It means the 'essence of masculinity.'"

Feller ducked under his desk, drawing stares from nearby students.

"Epilepsy," Blondie explained.

"That word is definitely not on my list," Bucky said. "Show me what you're talking about."

Mary pulled a sheet of paper from her notebook and took it up to Bucky. Bucky laid it on the desk beside her list.

"See," she told Mary. "It's not there. I think someone is pulling your leg."

Mary whipped around and stared Feller's way. She appeared stupefied to find his desk empty.

"Let's see if there is such a word," Bucky said pleasantly. She got up and waddled over to the wooden stand that held her huge Webster's dictionary. She fumbled around for a few minutes, searching for the right page. Then, she stabbed her finger down on the page.

"Ah, here it is!" she exclaimed.

Bucky kept her head down for quite some time. When she turned around, her face was white.

"Well?" Mary asked.

"Someone *is* pulling your leg. Someone not very nice."

Panic gripped Mary's face. She sprang to the dictionary. When she found the word, she shrieked.

Feller was prone on the floor, his chest heaving, his face suffused with color. Blondie felt his face turning purple from the strain of not laughing. He leaned into the aisle to hide his face.

The rest of the class had grown curious.

"What's it mean?" Sarah Quirk asked.
"It's not a fit word," Bucky said.
Freddy Finster jumped up and ran to the dictionary.
"Freddy, you sit right back down," Bucky ordered.
It was too late. Freddy turned back to the class with his hand over his mouth.
One of his friends yelled to him: "What's it mean?"
"It's some stuff that gets on a guy's dick."
"Penis, Freddy, penis," Bucky shouted.
The class erupted in gales of laughter.
"Dismissed!" Bucky yelled.
Feller rolled out the door. Even Grouper was struggling to maintain his composure. Blondie's ribs ached. He went over to Feller and held out his hand. They began to roar.

Chapter Twenty-One

The spine-clenching sound of metal grinding metal shrieked across the night. Sparks showered from the open doorway, where Joe Caldane was working late on a 59 Edsel with a crumpled rear fender, smoothing a jagged edge with a metal sander. He was wearing a black knit cap and heavy goggles to protect his eyes. A container of Bondo and a rubber hammer lay on the ground next to where he knelt.

Blondie, Feller, Brick and the Grouper huddled behind a shrub at one corner of the post office, thirty feet from the rear bay of Frank's Auto Repair. Their breaths crystallized in the frigid air and floated before them like tiny clouds. Blondie shivered and rubbed his hands together. He was cold, but mostly nervous. He'd never confronted a grown man before.

Feller asked if everyone was ready and then he, Blondie and Brick began marching across the lot, their feet scraping against the frosty pavement. Blondie thought of the showdown in the *Gunfight at the OK Corral*.

Caldane never moved from his work until Feller tapped him on the shoulder. Then he switched off the sander, stood slowly, and pulled his goggles down around his neck. He was a little taller than Blondie had remembered and more muscular, though quite a bit shorter than he was and not as heavy as Brick. He squinted at them with the eyes of an eel.

"Mr. Caldane, we're friends of your son's," Feller stated boldly, though Blondie thought he detected a trembling in his voice.

"So?" His tone was belligerent, as was his posture.

"Well, uh, we've noticed a few times, uh...." Feller was having trouble, although he'd already gone over his spiel once with the Club. A thin line of moisture formed above his lips.

"You've noticed what?"

Caldane was hostile and moving toward ballistic. Blondie watched his shoulders and arms tighten and his hands curl into bludgeons.

"We think you're beating him," Blondie blurted out.

Caldane turned toward him. His jaw was as hard and square as a steam shovel bucket. His eyes burned like portholes into the Inferno. Blondie retreated a step.

"Who said that?"

"It really doesn't matter who said it...." Feller began in his most diplomatic tone. Caldane switched his gaze to him. ".... what matters is that it stops."

Caldane put his whiskered jowl close to Feller's cheek. Their noses almost touched.

"Or what?" he said.

Fear flickered across Feller's eyes. His jaw moved, but no sound came forth.

"Or we're gonna kick your redneck ass," Brick replied.

Blondie ignored Brick's oxymoron. He was relieved to hear something forceful from their side.

Caldane turned toward Brick. He thumped him in the chest with his thumb.

"I'm not afraid of you...." he said, "....or you or you," he added to Feller and Blondie.

Now what, Blondie thought. Were the three of them going to duke it out with him?

"There's more of us," Feller said. "Hey, Killer," he shouted toward the post office.

An enormous shadow emerged from the shrub. Blondie often forgot how big Grouper was because he knew he was a pacifist—i.e., pussy—but across the lot, he loomed large.

Caldane's manner shifted. He unclenched his fists and stepped away from them.

"What do you want?" he asked less belligerently.

"We want you to quit beating on Jerry," Feller demanded.

"I never said I did."

"Well, if we hear that you did or see evidence that you did, we'll be back," Feller threatened, "and next time we'll unleash Killer. Got it?"

Caldane eyed them for a few seconds, weighing his options.

"There's no problem here, okay. I got no quarrel with you boys," Caldane said with a forced smile.

Later, in Feller's dad's Fairlane, they shared a hoot over their big bluff.

"Can you imagine?" Feller said, "We backed the prick down by threatening him with the Grouper."

"Watch yourself, Feller," Grouper boomed at him, "or I'll rearrange your face."

That made them laugh all the harder. Blondie was still chuckling when he went to bed. But he knew he was laughing from relief. Mr. Caldane was a scary guy.

"We gotta get laid, Blondie," Feller said to Blondie on the way to school one day the next week. "I feel embarrassed being a virgin."

"No one knows but me."

"I'd be embarrassed if you didn't know. Christ, I'm seventeen."

Why was Feller getting agitated now? They'd existed in the same sorry state of deprivation their whole lives. Maybe it was some biological clock. Maybe if you hadn't been screwed by a certain age, you began to go nuts.

"Do you have someone in mind?" Blondie asked.

"Delores."

"Delores Clitoris?"

"It's really Delores Humphries."

"I thought you had too much respect for your weenie," Blondie reminded him.

"I must have been out of my mind. Anyway, I'll be eighteen in a few weeks. Wouldn't it be a kick to lose our virginity together. Sorta like blood brothers. What do you say?"

Blondie thought it was a bizarre notion.

"Who would I get?" he asked hesitantly.

"Delores has a friend. Flossie Wilder. Chances are she'll be as easy as Delores. That's how girls divide up."

"According to who does it?"

"Yeah. What do you say?"

Screw a stranger? The idea was even more intimidating to Blondie than screwing someone he knew. But he knew Feller was right. A guy had to get laid sooner or later, even if it wasn't romantic or even fun.

"Okay," he agreed.

"Great. I'll set it up."

So he wasn't going to lose his cherry to someone he was nuts about. He'd been hoping it would be Tammy. Realistically, though, what were the odds? It was too much of a long shot to count on. Anyway, girls liked guys to be experienced. Tammy would need someone knowledgeable to initiate her into the mysteries of love.

When Blondie saw him at lunch, Feller gave him a funny smile.

"What are you grinning about? Did you set something up with Delores?"

"Not yet."

"Then what is it?"

"I heard something."

"Yeah?"

"Guess who likes you?"

Blondie's heart speeded up. Someone liked him. Could it be Tammy?

"Who?"

"Phyllis."

"Phyllis?"

Feller's grin grew wider.

No, Blondie told himself. It couldn't be.

"Who says so?"

"Pam Ferris. She hangs out with them. Phyllis told her to keep it a secret, but she told Delores."

It wasn't fair. He didn't even like Phyllis. He'd only been nice to her to get to Tammy. What a pickle. If Tammy found out Phyllis liked him, she'd never go out with him. That's the way girls were. On the other hand, if he discouraged Phyllis, she'd be hurt and tell Tammy. Tammy wouldn't go out with someone who'd hurt one of her girlfriends. That's the way girls were.

"Oh, fuck."

Feller kept grinning.

"It's not funny."

"Oh yes it is," Feller said.

Blondie was depressed for three days. His pick-me-up came with the throaty roar of the P-mobile that Saturday night. Blondie hadn't been in it since before their run-in with Purdy and Barnwell—and Fester. He'd forgotten how attached he'd grown to the chrome-and-steel beast. He found the P-mobile's luminescent dash lights strangely comforting. They made him feel like he and the others were Captain Nemo and the crew of the Nautilus, denizens of the depths, comrades of the dark.

The whole club was on hand, including Feller, who'd finally come off his grounding, and Grouper, who'd missed a number of sorties "squiring Miss Dimsell around," as he put it.

"Did your little lady take the ring from your nose tonight?" Brick asked him.

Feller said he wanted to shoot some pool at Shady Lanes before they got to the main event of the evening, which, as usual, was to be drinking beer and bullshitting in the P-mobile out at the quarry. When they arrived, Purdy's pickup was hunkered in a corner of the lot.

"What's that billy doing here?" Brick asked.

"Let's just ignore him," Feller suggested. "We'll take care of him some other time."

Easier said than done. When they entered, Purdy turned from the counter and said: "Hey Shakes, how's your face?"

"Eat sh-shit," Shakes responded, causing a few adults to look his way. Purdy just laughed.

"Easy, guys," Feller said. "We came up here to shoot pool."

Mountain Pulaski was knocking balls around by himself in the poolroom. When he saw Dispatch, he smiled.

"Hey mop-top, how about a game?"

"Sure."

The rest of them paired off. Blondie against Feller. Brick against Shakes. Grouper sat in a tall chair in the corner and watched.

After a while, Blondie went to the bathroom to relieve himself. While he was there, Mountain stomped in and entered one of the stalls. Blondie heard his belt buckle clank against the floor and then a few grunts.

Blondie combed his hair and was just leaving when Purdy came in.

"Well, if it ain't the giraffe," he said.

"Watch yourself," Blondie said with as much menace as he could muster.

"Why should I? I saw what happened between you and Buford. He looked at you sideways and you came unglued."

Blondie hated hearing it, mainly because it was true. He *had* backed away from Buford. And now Purdy was messing with him.

Blondie had a brainstorm.

"Say Purdy, who was that guy with you and Barnwell that night?"

"Are you kidding? You don't know? That was Merwin Fester?"

"Who's he?"

"What a dumb fuck you are. He's the toughest guy in the county."
"Is that right? Gosh, Feller told me it was someone named Mountain."
"Pulaski? No way. Fester would kick his butt."
"Is that a fact? I'd heard this Mountain guy was pretty tough."
"Shit. He's no fighter. He's just big."
A prodigious fart boomed from Mountain's stall. Purdy looked his way.
"But Pulaski could probably kick Buford's ass...." Blondie began.
"Listen, I'm not sure Mountain could take me," Purdy said, growing cockier.
"Oh come on…"
"You think I'm some pushover?" he challenged.
"Pulaski would whip you so fast it would make your head spin."
"Yeah? I'd like to see him try."
The stall door crashed open and Mountain emerged, boiling with anger. The color drained from Purdy's face.
"You set me up," he accused Blondie.
Blondie smiled at him.
"Boy, you got a big mouth," Mountain said to Purdy.
"Hey, look, Mountain, that asshole set me up."
"All that shit seemed to come out of your mouth on its own," Mountain said to him.
"I was just kidding. You know, just shooting my mouth off. That's not very smart, is it?" His voice had shriveled to a nun's whisper.
"You got that right."
"But it's no reason for you to get pissed off, is it?"
Beads of sweat formed around Purdy's forehead, a garland of fear.
"I'm not pissed off any more," Mountain said.
"Good."
Mountain's fist flew out from his side and popped Purdy squarely on the nose. Purdy fell to the floor like a trap door had opened beneath him. Blood began to spurt from his nose and, to Blondie's amazement, he began to cry like a baby.

"I thought you weren't pissed," Purdy sniveled.

"I'm not. I just figure life's about living and learning. My guess is that if I hadn't popped you one, you wouldn't have learned a goddamn thing."

"I'm gonna get you for this," Purdy threatened Blondie between spasms of tears.

"You didn't learn anything, did you?" Mountain said. "I oughta pop you again."

Purdy cringed and hunkered in the corner.

"I don't know this guy well..." Pulaski said to Purdy, tilting his head toward Blondie.

"Blondie," he volunteered.

"...but you and this Buford pussy better leave him alone. If you don't, I'm going to take you on like a meat grinder. Understand?"

"Yeah," Purdy moaned.

"Okay my friend," Mountain said to Blondie, "let's leave this turd where he belongs. In the latrine."

Blondie felt exhilarated walking back to the poolroom stride by stride with Mountain. He'd redeemed himself. So what if he hadn't been the one to strike Purdy. He'd set it up. That was good enough. The guys would approve.

Blondie was right. It was the liveliest night ever out at the quarry. The constant snap of church keys biting into cold and willing beer cans punctuated their animated conversation.

"T-tell us h-how P-Purdy cried," Shakes said.

"Just like a baby," Blondie said. Then he imitated him. They loved it.

"Was Mountain pissed?" Brick asked.

"Like a bull whose nuts have been dipped in Ben-Gay."

Grouper acclaimed it as their first real victory against the "insidious forces of billiedom."

Their conversation moved on to the subject at hand: beer. When Brick said he preferred draft beer to bottled, Dispatch said: "Speaking of draft, I had to go register for the draft last week."

"What, you're eighteen now?" Feller asked him.

"Let's not talk about the draft," Brick said. "It's depressing."

"What difference does it make?" Dispatch said. "There's no war going on."

"Yes, there is," Grouper voice rumbled through the car.

"Where?" Several of them challenged him.

"In Vietnam."

"Where the hell is that?" Brick said.

"Next to Cambodia and Laos."

"I've never heard of those places," Brick said.

"Why do I bother trying to educate you Philistines?" Grouper asked. "Don't any of you ever read the paper."

Blondie stayed out of the fray. He knew Miss Darlington worried about Vietnam, just like the Grouper, but he didn't agree. He had too much faith in President Kennedy. He would never send American boys over to some no-name place halfway around the world.

"It can't be much of a war if I've never heard of it," Brick argued.

"Well, I'm sure as hell not going into the army," Dispatch said.

"I hope I never get drafted," Grouper said.

"Who'd draft you?" Brick said. "You're so far out of shape you couldn't pass the physical."

"Y-yeah, and y-you've g-got flat f-feet," Shakes added.

"I'm not in that bad shape," Grouper answered.

"If the shoe fits, sit on it," Brick said. "The only thing you're in shape to do is drink beer."

"Better than anyone else," Grouper boasted.

"Bullshit!" Brick retorted. "I could drink you under the table."

"I'd like to see that."

The gauntlet had been thrown.

For the next two hours, Blondie, Feller, Dispatch, and Shakes watched while Brick and Grouper matched each other beer for beer.

Empty after empty was placed on the P-mobile's dash. At one point, Blondie counted eighteen.

Dispatch had to return to the Suds Cellar twice for replenishments.

Brick's speech began to slur as the gang gabbed about everything from Mrs. Buckley's rump to who was screwing whom. Grouper, on the other hand, continued to speak clearly in his *basso profundo,* although Blondie noted he remained silent during their sexual speculations. Yet he was the only one with a girl. Blondie wondered if he and Meryl were *doing it.* He didn't figure Grouper was the kind who would tell—and he was glad for that.

Suddenly Brick's head slumped against the window.

"Are you okay, Brick?" Feller asked.

"H-he's p-passed out," Shakes said.

"Looks like you won," Blondie said to Grouper.

Grouper didn't answer.

"I said it looks like you won."

Grouper still didn't answer.

"Turn on the lights," Blondie said to Dispatch.

The Grouper was staring straight ahead with a glazed look. His face had turned green.

"Grouper? Grouper!" Feller screamed at him.

Blondie shook Grouper. His huge head lolled to one side and his eyelids fell shut.

"Jesus, he doesn't look good," Dispatch said.

Blondie grabbed Grouper's wrist and felt for a pulse.

"I can't feel any pulse," he said with alarm.

"How can you tell with all that blubber?" Dispatch asked.

"See if he's breathing," Feller said.

"I can't tell," he said, alarmed.

"What's up?" Brick asked, emerging from his stupor.

"Something's wrong with the Grouper. He's not breathing."

"He's dead. I drank that sucker under the table."

At the word "dead," Blondie's heart stood still. What if Grouper were dead?

Blondie raised one of Grouper's eyelids. His pupil was barely visible. When Blondie let go of the lid, Grouper's eye stayed open. Only white showed.

"He's fucking dead!" Brick repeated gleefully.

"It isn't funny, Brick," Feller said to him.

Blondie heard the worried tone in Feller's voice.

"We better get him to a hospital," Feller said. "And quick."

The P-mobile shot out of the quarry, spewing rocks and bring angry shouts from interrupted lovers.

Halfway to the main road, the Grouper sat up and said, "Who won?"

They stared at Grouper in disbelief and then all heads turned to Brick who'd passed out again in the front seat.

"You, I guess," Feller said.

"Not much of a contest, was it?" the Grouper said.

That night became known thereafter as *The Night the Grouper Died and Came Back to Life.*

Chapter Twenty-Two

Girls got wet! Why hadn't anyone ever told him? When they'd been subjected to two days of sex education in ninth grade health class, the teacher had shown them all kinds of diagrams and anatomical drawings with all the detail and sex appeal of blueprints. Never once did she mention the incredible fact that girls got wet. Now, for the first time ever, Blondie'd put his hands in a girl's underpants, then given away his lack of experience by asking if she'd had "an accident." What a gaffe.

"It's all right," Flossie told him. "I think it's sweet when guys haven't played around too much."

Sweet? Wimpy—that's what it was.

What a gaffe. But how was he supposed to know? For the first time ever, he'd put his hands in a girl's underpants and he'd asked her if she'd had an "accident"!

He and Flossie were in the back seat of the P-mobile, parked by the rock quarry. Feller'd rented the P-mobile from Dispatch for five bucks, explaining that they needed something "roomy." Feller was in the front seat with Delores, but he and she had disappeared below the seat back several minutes before.

Blondie's right hand remained secure in Flossie's panties. He found it immeasurably exciting, though he wasn't sure if it was the act so much as the thought of it—forbidden fruit of the first magnitude. Just as exciting was the incredible and unexpected development that Flossie was fondling Nessie. Blondie didn't know girls did things like that.

Happy as Blondie was with the present state of affairs, he kept thinking he should move along. After all, the object of the evening was to get laid. With his free hand, Blondie felt along his pants leg until he felt the outline of the foil package Feller had given him. Feller'd advised him to put the contents on his member "at the appropriate moment." But now that the moment had arrived, Blondie decided he didn't want to fool with the damned thing. It would detract from his mood.

"Do you think we should go a little further," Blondie whispered.

"What do you have in mind?"

"Well, you know what guys like."

"You want me to go down on you?"

What had she said? The very thought of Flossie putting her mouth around Nessie made Blondie feel weak. But for some reason he'd never understood, getting a blow job didn't count as much with other guys as getting laid—and, of course, it still left one a virgin.

"Thanks for the offer, but that wasn't quite I meant," Blondie said.

"You want to make love?"

"That's it."

"Okay. How do you want to do it?"

Holy shit! Why was she bringing up all these options? How many ways were there? She didn't seem to understand. He wasn't after the exotic or gymnastic. He just wanted to get the job done.

"The usual way," he answered.

"For a car, you mean? Okay, you sit there and I'll sit on top of you."

That wasn't what he'd meant, either. But he decided he'd be better off letting her take the lead. She seemed to know what she was doing. When she put Nessie up inside her, Blondie moaned. It felt so good he thought he was going to go off right then.

Flossie began to sway her hips.

"Don't do that," Blondie told her.

"Don't you like it?"

"Yeah. But I don't want to come right away."

"Okay."

He looked at her face, trying to see her expression. Was she as excited as he was? It was too dark to tell.

From the front, Blondie heard a sudden inhalation and Feller's voice murmuring "Oh God, Oh God...." Jesus, Feller had gone off. Blondie felt pressured to finish before Feller and Delores sat back up. He'd feel dumb if they were watching. He told Flossie to go ahead and "move."

She rotated her hips a couple times and raised and lowered her bottom on his lap and that was it. For a mind-stopping instant, his brain shut down and all he could feel was a pleasurable warm stream pass through his body: Muggerood's Theorem.

"Finally, finally, finally," Blondie said to himself when his brain switched back on.

As soon as she got off him, Flossie stuffed some Kleenex into her panties and pulled them up. She was efficient. Blondie liked that. He was even more surprised to find he kinda liked *her*. Because she was a friend of Delores's, he'd expected Flossie to be marginal-looking and wear too much makeup, but she wasn't and didn't. In fact, she had pretty long blond hair and a fairly cute face. As a bonus, her legs were outstanding. Best of all, she thought he was smart and witty. How could he not like someone that perceptive?

On the way home, when they were nearing Flossie's house, she nestled up to him and whispered, "I liked it with you."

Her words, and the shy way she spoke them, affected him.

"I'm glad," Blondie said.

After they dropped her off, Delores spent most of the time on the way to her house fussing about her permanent. Blondie wondered how anyone could talk about a hairdo after getting laid. Girls were something else. For him, getting laid had been *monumental*. It was the first time in his life when, for even the smallest time, he'd forgotten who or where he was.

Once Delores was out of the car, Feller asked, "Well? What'd you think?"

"Worth the price of emission," Blondie said.

Feller laughed.

"Virgins no more!" he shouted

Blondie couldn't wait to tell the Grouper about his big score, though he told himself to be cool about it. After all, Grouper'd had a girl for a couple months and he didn't want to let on that he'd been a virgin before. So what he told Grouper when he had a chance to be alone with him was "Feller and I had a pretty hot night last Saturday."

Grouper raised his eyebrows, but didn't say anything.

"Don't you want to know who it was?"

"Okay, who was it?" Grouper asked, as if drawing his voice from some hidden cavern in his body.

"Flossie Wilder. Do you know her?"

"I've heard Meryl talk about her. Isn't she a tenth-grader?"

Now why did he bring that up? He was missing the point. Blondie couldn't just grab him by the shirt and say, "Don't you understand? This is major. I got laid!" Anyway, Grouper seemed out of sorts.

"Is something bugging you?" Blondie asked him.

"Meryl and I have split the sheets," he mumbled. "We're just not a good match."

"I never thought she was worthy of you," Blondie offered in consolation.

Grouper gave him a sharp look.

"What do you know about worthy?"

What had he said? It wasn't like Grouper to get peevish.

"Meryl's okay," Grouper said. "She's just not what I want—or need."

Blondie was impressed by the pains Grouper was taking to avoid saying anything negative about Meryl. It was more-or-less expected for guys to badmouth girls when the romance was over—and absolutely required if ending it had been the girl's idea.

Although he and Feller hadn't made any plans to follow up what Feller called, borrowing on baseball jargon, the Night of the Twin Killing, it wasn't long before Feller asked him if he wanted to "double-date" again. Blondie was game. Sex was terrific.

"Do you think they'll want to do it again?" Blondie asked him.

"I know they do."

When Blondie told his mom he had another date, she asked him if he had a girlfriend.

"Not a girlfriend."

He didn't think of Flossie that way.

"Don't you like her?"

"I just met her. I hardly know her."

Upon reflection, Blondie thought it a strange thing to say about the only girl he'd ever been "intimate" with.

"Are we going to be seeing each other regularly?" Flossie asked when they got together with Feller and Delores the following Friday night.

"Probably."

"Don't you think you better use a...well, you know."

"I should," Blondie conceded.

But, when the time came, he passed again. Whipping on a condom was easy to contemplate in advance, but when Nessie began tugging at his corduroys, Blondie couldn't interrupt the natural progression of events—Muggerood's Theorem again.

Afterwards, Flossie put her lips to his ear and whispered, "You could get me pregnant, you know?"

"If I did, I'd marry you," Blondie said.

"What?"

She seemed startled.

"If I got you pregnant, I'd marry you," he repeated.

"You'd marry me?"

"If I got you pregnant."

"No one's ever said anything that nice to me before."

"Well, I mean it. A guy has to be responsible for his actions."

Later, Blondie told Feller what he'd said.

"What? Are you cuckoo? It would wreck your life to marry a girl like Flossie. She isn't going anywhere."

"She's nice."

"As nice as Tammy?"

"Well, no. But how do I know I can get her?"

"You won't if you're a defeatist." Feller paused. "I think it would be best if we kept our little foursome quiet for a while," he added.

"Why?"

"It's not going to do your reputation any good to be going around with Flossie. And it sure isn't going to help mine going around with Delores Clitoris."

"I don't have a reputation," Blondie said.

"Maybe not. But you don't want to get a negative one."

The routine had been established. Every Friday or Saturday, he and Feller took the girls out on a date, but never anywhere too visible like the Marylander Theater or a teen dance. Blondie felt a little guilty hiding his relationship with Flossie that way. He was sure she knew what he and Feller were doing. She never said anything, though.

Winter slowly gave birth to spring. Mornings turned brighter, afternoons warmer. Buds appeared on trees, early cherries blossomed. The Orioles were off at spring training—and his dad was again talking about how this could be the year they won it all.

On the way to school one morning in April, Feller suggested they take in another CYO dance.

"You mean take Flossie and Delores?"

Was Feller changing the rules?

"No. I mean just us. Look, we can't spend all our time with them. The school year's coming to a close. Don't you want to try for a real girlfriend?"

Blondie reckoned he did, but he felt like it would be cheating on Flossie.

"What if they show up?" he asked.

"They won't. I found out Delores is having a slumber party at her house that night and Flossie is going."

That seemed safe enough, so Blondie agreed. He hoped Tammy would be at the dance and that her dad, Phyllis, Purdy and Barnwell wouldn't. He almost broke even. Phyllis and Tammy's dad weren't there, but the others were.

Blondie noticed Tammy immediately. She was wearing a burgundy sweater with a chain of fake pearls around her neck. She was as desirable and unapproachable as ever.

Purdy and Barnwell watched him all evening, but they kept their distance. Blondie figured he was under Mountain's protection. He hoped it would last.

Blondie was surprised when Dispatch showed up with Meryl. He asked Feller what was going on.

"I guess Dispatch figures if Meryl would put out for Grouper, she'd put out for anybody," he said.

"Doesn't Dispatch care what Grouper thinks?"

"Dispatch? Are you nuts?"

Feller began scoping out the "talent."

"See you later, buddy," he said, as he eased across the dance floor and made a beeline for a pretty junior in Blondie's journalism class.

Most of the kids were shaking and gyrating as The Sensations belted out "Let me in, wee-oo." Yet, no one had asked Tammy to dance. Blondie didn't get it. He'd have thought she'd have danced every dance. Maybe all the guys were afraid of her. She was so poised, so graceful…a queen.

Blondie wondered if he could work up the nerve to dance with her again after making a fool of himself in front of both her and her dad. Worse, now her best friend liked him.

Then, Elvis's voice wafted across the smoky air, slow and resonant, to the fateful refrain of "Can't Help Falling in Love," and Blondie knew he had to ask her at all costs. The music pulled his feet across the floor to where she stood. She gave him the same surprised look as before when she accepted his invitation and, as before, she buried her face in his chest as if she were his alone.

Blondie felt as if he held a treasure in his arms and was duty-bound to protect and cherish it all his life. He understood exactly what Elvis was singing about. He couldn't help falling in love with Tammy.

Just before the music ended, she looked up at him.

"Aren't you dating that Wilder girl?" she asked.

Chapter Twenty-Three

How did girls find things out? He and Feller had been so careful to keep their love lives a secret—at least outside their group. Of course, Blondie realized, nothing prevented Delores and Flossie from spreading the news. Why hadn't they thought of that?

"I just never thought girls like Delores and Flossie communicated with girls like Tammy," Feller said.

Sometimes Feller could be so dense. No matter now. The news had reached Tammy, scotching any scheme—unformed as it might be—for getting together with her. He hadn't even been able to reply to her question at the dance. He'd just stood blankly before her as she'd smiled and walked away.

It didn't appear there was any point in keeping his involvement with Flossie a secret any longer. When Flossie asked him for the third or fourth time to accompany her to Mass, he felt he had no reason to refuse.

"Are you serious? You're taking Flossie to Mass?" Feller said. "That's like a 'coming out' to Catholics. It makes a statement."

"I already told her I would."

Feller threw up his hands.

Blondie realized it wasn't just for Flossie. He'd never been to a Catholic Mass before. He wanted to know why Catholic girls were different—especially since Phyllis had informed his that Tammy was one too.

His parents were shocked.

"That's Popery," his dad, a lifelong Baptist said. "Catholics baptize babies before they even know what it means to accept Christ."

Hell, Blondie thought, I don't know what it means to accept Christ either.

"Don't eat any fish," his mom warned.

Sunday brought the smell of new life. Daffodils and crocuses were erupting from the small strip of earth his mom had tilled and planted in front of their house. Baby leaves unfurled from the ash on the front lawn. Blondie was glad it had survived the winter.

Flossie's folks lived on the other side of town in an older development called Sycamore Hills, although there weren't any sycamores. There weren't any hills, either. Their house was a well-tended brick bungalow, 40s style, with a picture window and a concrete porch. Flossie said it wasn't half as nice as his, but Blondie thought it was okay.

Mr. Wilder, who managed the carpet department at a Sears Roebuck in Baltimore, was slight with light-brown hair and close-set eyes, younger than Blondie would have expected. He was nice enough to Blondie—almost deferential, in fact—but he didn't have much to say. Flossie's mom, blonder and better fed, was much the same way.

He took an immediate liking to Flossie's five-year-old brother Ted, a skinny and hyperactive towhead. Blondie teased him about Roy Rogers, his hero. He told him Gene Autrey was quicker on the draw.

"Is not," he squealed.

"Is too," Blondie said, making a gun with his thumb and index finger and pointing it at Ted.

"I think he likes you," Flossie said.

Maybe he could be a role model, Blondie thought. He promised himself never to disappoint the little tike.

Flossie looked sharp to him this morning in a light-blue seersucker dress and heels, her light hair gleaming in the morning sun.

She basked in his approval for a minute or two, then slipped her hand into his and said, "Let's go. Mom and dad and Ted will come along a little later."

She directed him to a fieldstone church halfway to Percy and set back from the road in a grove of oak trees, embraced by their stout limbs. A cemetery lay to one side, its headstones rows of Mah Jongg tiles.

Blondie found Catholicism a lot more impressive than what he'd grown up with. The priest wore a long scarf trimmed in gold. The altar boasted silver goblets and candlesticks. The balustrade in front was white marble. And there was a lot more ritual...a lot of kneeling and praying and signs of the cross by the priest...boys in robes scampering back and forth performing mysterious tasks. He could only guess at the meaning of any of it because almost the whole service was in Latin.

Nonetheless, he knelt respectfully on the padded wooden rail while the priest chanted "Doh-mee-nus voh-bis-cum" and the massed worshippers answered, "Et-cum-speery-tutu-oh."

"What's it mean?" Blondie whispered to Flossie. "Why is it in Latin?"

"Sh-h-h."

"Don't you care what they're saying?"

"No."

"Then why do it?"

"Because I'm Catholic."

Blondie was glad Flossie didn't mind his questions. All she seemed to care about was that he was there with her. Blondie wondered why Feller had been so concerned about his coming.

He found out on Wednesday.

"Why are boys so rotten?" Phyllis asked Blondie on the way home from the *Fentonian* staff meeting.

"What do you mean?"

"All they care about is sex."

"That's not all," Blondie argued without conviction. Since he'd met Flossie, thoughts of sex occupied a large percentage of his waking moments—and nearly all his sleeping ones.

"You're one to talk," she snapped.

"What did I do?"

"You've been hanging around with that Wilder girl."

Phyllis' fingers were turning white around the steering wheel.

"Who told you that?"

Had Tammy told her?

"I saw you in church Sunday."

Of course. She was a Catholic too. Blondie wondered why he hadn't seen her there.

"It's not what you think."

Why was he feeling so defensive? It was none of Phyllis' business.

"I bet you're taking her to the prom."

Huh? What was Phyllis talking about? He hadn't even thought about going. Anyway, the prom was over a month away.

"Look, Flossie and I aren't going together."

"You're just having sex with her, is that it?"

Blondie felt his face ignite.

"What I do is my own business," he said.

"And who I drive around in my car is my own business, too."

"What do you mean by that?"

"I mean I don't think I should let a boy in my car who doesn't believe in the sanctity of women."

"Jesus Christ!"

"Blaspheming won't help, either."

She was a nut—and she was acting like a wounded lover. Feller'd been right. She did have a crush on him.

When Phyllis dropped him off, she told Blondie he could find another ride back from the *Fentonian*.

"No one else comes this way," he protested.

Her smile was spiteful as she backed from the drive.

When the phone rang that evening and his mom said it was for him, Blondie was sure it would be Flossie. But it was a male voice, one he didn't recognize.

"What about tomorrow? After school?"

Blondie was confused, but the voice sounded familiar.

"Tomorrow for what?"

"Golf. It's supposed to be warm again. We could get in nine holes before dark if we left right after class."

It was Bobby Clements! What had inspired him? Golf the next day? It was out of the question. He had things to do. It was a school night. But then...a chance to play golf with Clements. It might be the start of a real social life. Blondie had to make it happen.

"Do you have wheels?" Blondie asked Bobby.

"No. I thought you would." Bobby sounded disappointed.

"Just a second."

Blondie set the phone down and went downstairs to the family room. His parents were watching a Milton Berle special.

"Could I borrow the Pontiac tomorrow?"

No way the Dart was cool enough for Bobby Clements.

"What for?" his dad asked. His tone wasn't promising.

"I want to play golf after school with a friend."

"Play on Saturday. I want the Pontiac for a meeting tomorrow night."

"Not that old Order of whatever it is," his mom said.

"Military Order of Merit," his dad stated.

"What's so important about playing tomorrow, dear?" she asked.

"It's just with the coolest guy in school."

His mom gave his dad a knowing look.

"Well, Francis, don't you think you could miss one meeting?"

"There's a war going on, Betty," he pleaded.

"What war?"

"In Vietnam."

There it was again.

"Well, it doesn't involve us," his mom answered. "Anyway, I'm sure Kennedy can take care of it."

His dad wilted.

"Well, okay," he said. "But be careful. That car's just a year old."

"What could happen? I'm only going up to Meadowbrook."

"Keep your eyes on the road."

Parents! They acted like you couldn't piss in a pot without their help.

"It's a deal," Blondie told Bobby over the phone.

Blondie felt like a big shot driving the Pontiac to school the next day. True, it wasn't a hot rod or anything, but it was almost new and it *was* a Pontiac. Blondie drove as slowly as he could into the lot hoping someone he knew would see him arrive. But only Phyllis was there and, thankfully, she didn't recognize him in his parents' car. Blondie didn't want another scene.

Blondie was surprised at Bobby's clubs when he dumped them in the trunk after school. They were decades old and rusty—his dad's no doubt. The irons didn't even have flanges on the bottom.

It was warm. Blondie buzzed the electric windows down. He wondered what he should talk about with Bobby. Girls? No, he'd heard that truly cool guys seldom talked about girls. College? Maybe. Sports? Yeah, that should be safe.

"How's baseball practice going?" he asked him.

"The season's underway. We've already played a game."

Blondie felt stupid. He should've known that. Sports was his beat. He pulled into a service station and about a couple Cokes. He handed one to Bobby.

"Where are you going to college?" Blondie asked as they headed out again.

"Nowhere if I don't get a scholarship."

"You'll get a scholarship. You're the best athlete in school."

"That may not be good enough."

Why was Bobby being so negative? Guys like him were supposed to have reservoirs of self-confidence. Maybe he *should* talk about girls. He knew Bobby was scoring there.

"Your girlfriend's a knockout."

"Yeah," Bobby responded with little enthusiasm.

"Are you going to marry her?" Blondie asked.

"Who told you that?"

Bobby stared at him.

"No one told me," he answered. "It's the talk around school."

"What do they know?"

What the hell was eating him? Blondie told himself not to let Bobby's grouchiness drag him down. It was a beautiful day. They were on their way to play golf. What could be better?

Blondie turned on the radio:

"*Duke, Duke, Duke, Duke of Earl, Duke, Duke....*"

Life was sweet. Moments later the bouncy beat of "Hey, Baby" by Bruce Channel jumped from the speakers.

"Do you always sing along with the radio?" Clements asked Blondie.

"Was I singing?" Blondie asked. What a dork he was.

"No, it's okay."

Blondie peeked over at Bobby. He had his eyes shut. His arm was half out the window and his head rested on it. The breeze billowed his hair.

As they neared the golf course, the road twisted along the creek. Blondie finished his Coke and tossed it out the window. He turned and looked back to make sure it hadn't shattered on the road. The next thing he knew, they were flying through the air. Blondie'd missed the curve! He turned just in time to see the looming trunk of a huge tree. The Pontiac came to a crashing stop against it. A spider web of cracks spread across the windshield.

"Are you okay?" Blondie said to Clements.

"I'm fine...but you just wrecked your parents' car."

It sounded so formidable to hear someone else say it.

"Well, so much for golf," Bobby added.

Those words were even more frightening to Blondie. He couldn't give up his chance to play with Bobby. Who knew when he'd get another?

"We can still get in nine holes," Blondie said on an impulse.

"How? We can't even get there."

"I'll call a tow truck. They can drop us off on the way."

"How'll we get home?"

"I'll call Dispatch. He owns a car."

"Yeah, I've heard of it. What's he call it? The Pussymobile?"

Clements chuckled.

Blondie trudged up the road to the clubhouse and called a tow truck. The driver, an overweight older man with graying sideburns, was surprised when Blondie asked him to let them off at the course.

"Your parents know about this?"

"Sure."

"Should I call them?"

"No. What for?"

"That's what I thought. Well, I got the car, so I guess I don't need to worry."

Maybe his parents would be glad he was still alive and not get too mad, Blondie thought. He didn't believe it.

Watching Bobby play was a humbling experience for Blondie. He could tell Bobby had spoken the truth when he said he didn't play often. Every once in a while, he spun a shot off into the woods. But when he hit one right, it was awesome, even with his old beat-up clubs. He had a natural rhythm a pro could never teach. Blondie felt depressed thinking about it. The one sport he was pretty good at and Bobby could be better if he wanted to.

Dispatch proved a complete asshole about picking him and Bobby up after golf. He bitched about "being inconvenienced" the whole way back into town. He didn't seem to care that he was getting a chance to drive a school hero around. Bobby sat in the back seat and smiled, amused by Dispatch's fulminating. His worries seemed to have disappeared.

Blondie was surprised by Bobby's house. It was small and run down. A heavy-looking woman peered out the window. She had a beer can in her hand.

When Bobby got out of the car, he said "Maybe we'll do it again sometime. I'll drive next time."

He laughed and walked away.

"Where's the car?" his dad asked as soon as Blondie entered the house. Blondie conceded it was a reasonable question. He'd been trying to think of a good answer all the way home.

"You'll be glad to know I wasn't injured...." Blondie began.

"Are you telling me you wrecked my new car?" Tiny arteries on his dad's nose flared.

"*Our* new car, Francis," his mother corrected from upstairs.

"The important thing is that I wasn't hurt," Blondie repeated.

"Not yet," his dad answered venomously.

"There was no way to avoid it."

"Someone hit you?"

For a moment, Blondie detected concern in his eyes.

"To be honest, it was a tree."

"You couldn't avoid a tree? What are you saying? Did it jump out in the road in front of you?"

"There's no need to be sarcastic, Dad."

His dad's fury subsided and he said, "Well, I suppose it is a bit treacherous on that road after dark."

"It wasn't dark," Blondie let slip before he thought of what he was saying.

"It happened on the way up."

"Tell me I didn't hear what you just said. Are you telling me you played golf AFTER YOU WRECKED OUR CAR?"

His dad became incoherent after that. All things considered, Blondie thought as he lay in bed later, it had been his dad's worst scene.

Grouper found Blondie's tale of woe amusing, as did the rest of the guys. Blondie had expected more sympathy from Grouper, since he'd wrecked his father's car.

"There must be a law to fit this happenstance," Feller said to Grouper.

"Yes. A rather obvious one. Blondie's little incident can be seen as a metaphor for life...."

Blondie resented Grouper terming his crash a "little incident."

"**Never assume the road ahead is straight**," Grouper finished.

"Oh, fuck your laws," Blondie said.

Blondie's dad calmed down some after his insurance agent told him most of the damage was covered. But Blondie knew he wouldn't be driving the Pontiac again soon. Of more immediate concern was how to get back and forth to the *Fentonian* staff meetings. There was a possible way out. He could ask Phyllis to the prom. It was an awful prospect, but Blondie figured he could always back out later. By then, the school year would be near its end.

There were only three drawbacks to the plan. First, Phyllis might turn him down. Second, the thought of asking Phyllis to the prom made his stomach turn. Finally, if Flossie found out, she'd be hurt.

In the end—on Tuesday night and still without a ride home from the layout session—Blondie called her.

"What do you want?" Phyllis asked. Blondie could almost feel frost forming on the receiver.

"I was thinking about what you said the other day and I realized that you probably like me...."

"Are you crazy? What a conceited statement."

It wasn't going right.

"I was calling about the prom...." Blondie's voice trailed off.

"What about the prom?" Her voice was much softer.

"Well, I thought that if no one had asked you yet...."

"Yes?"

"....that maybe you'd go with me."

The other end of the line was silent for several seconds.

"What about Flossie Wilder?"

Why was she making this so difficult?

"We're just friends."

"I can imagine what kind of friends you are."

"Anyway, I don't think I'll be seeing her much more."

Why had he said that?

"Really?"

Blondie sucked in his breath. Once a liar....

"Really."

"Well, okay."

"You'll go with me, then?" Blondie asked.

"I guess."

Blondie waited for Phyllis to offer him a ride home the next day. She didn't.

"Was there something else?" Phyllis asked.

Blondie cleared his throat.

"I just wondered if maybe you could…uh…give me a ride home tomorrow after the staff meeting."

"I think I get the picture." Her voice was tight. Then she sighed. "Oh, why not?"

"Hey thanks."

After he hung up, Blondie wiped his forehead. He was surprised at how moist it was. He felt like a Judas. He'd sold Flossie out for a ride home from the school paper.

Chapter Twenty-Four

The sun blazed like a new rivet. In the distance, the tents of ten thousand Turks dotted the endless sand. At the top of a rise, Thomas Edward Lawrence sat poised on his white stallion, long rows of mounted cavalry to his right and left. He raised his arm and a restless murmuring issued from the assemblage. When he let it fall, a mighty shout ripped the silence and an army of Bedouins descended upon the barren plain, caftans billowing. A swarm of dark and deadly moths.

In the darkness of the theater, Blondie's soul fused with that of the celebrated Lawrence of Arabia.

He was at the head of that pack, his courage a mountain, his resolve granite. He'd been born to lead, to dare the heroic, to change the world. He knew it.

The movie ended and the lights came on.

"That was neat," Flossie gushed.

Her comment annoyed him. What Lawrence had accomplished wasn't *neat*. It was *colossal*. She hadn't understood. For her, the movie was entertainment. For him, it was destiny. Blondie was sure a girl like Tammy would understand the fever in his brain, his great need to elevate himself above the crowd. He was just as sure Flossie never would.

He'd driven most of the way to Baltimore not just because *Lawrence of Arabia* was too new to be showing at the Marylander, but because he didn't want to be seen with her. Whenever anyone asked him about

Flossie, he told them he "dated her sometimes" and let on he was "playing the field." His desire to keep his love life hidden had become even more imperative since he'd asked Phyllis to the prom, a piece of news he'd yet to share with Flossie.

He couldn't deny it—he was using her. He told himself the kind thing to do would be to let Flossie go. Their lives were headed in different directions. They had different dreams. But he couldn't cut the cord. He'd become a *sex junkie*.

Ever since his first night with Flossie at the quarry, he'd been infected with a virulent case of lust. He couldn't get enough sex. The best explanation he could reach was that his body was trying to recover from years and years of virginity.

When Flossie invited him over to "watch television" the next weekend—letting slip that her parents would be gone—his fledgling inclination to do the right thing got trampled by his runaway libido.

"What's this girl's name again?" his mother asked when he told her his plans for the weekend. Blondie knew she knew. She was just irked that he'd never brought Flossie over to the house to meet her.

"Are you sure she's a nice girl?"

"What's the test?"

"Don't be a smart aleck, Bernard. You know what I mean? Does she have nice parents?"

"I suppose."

No way was he going to tell his mom he was spending the evening at a girl's house with her five-year-old brother as chaperone.

Blondie's next assignment for the school newspaper was Fenton's first home baseball game. The Flyers were taking on Percy, his old school. Blondie had mixed emotions, but finally decided he'd pull for Fenton.

Blondie visited Mr. Kegley, the baseball coach, to gather some "background" on the game. He found him slumped in a chair in his office, a stout man with plastered-down hair and dandruff. He bit his fingernails while Blondie interviewed him.

"Do you think Fenton will have any problem with the Panthers, coach?" Blondie asked.

"We better not. They're a bunch of turkeys."

It wasn't the quote he'd been looking for.

"Would you care to elaborate on that?"

"Not really." Kegley picked at his nose, found something of interest and wiped it on his pants leg.

"Well, then, do you have any particular game strategy?"

"Yeah, beat the shit out of them," Kegley answered expelling a fingernail from between his lips.

Blondie thanked the coach and went out to watch the players prepare for the game. A chill breeze blew across the diamond. Blondie stood by the edge of the field and shivered as boy-men in Fenton's colors tossed balls at each other. Dust clouds nipped at their dancing feet.

Blondie saw Neil Golden wandering along the first base line, snapping shots of the team practicing. After a while, he loped over to Blondie.

"Covering the game?" he asked Blondie.

"Yeah."

Blondie didn't want to act like it was any big deal. After all, Neil was just a junior and he was too earnest, too talkative, and too approachable. He didn't hold anything back like cool guys did.

Still, Blondie kinda liked him, especially since he'd learned Neil detested Mary Cherry. He'd told Blondie he considered her "a vacuous parrot with the intellectual depth of furniture wax."

Blondie had been surprised at the strength of his emotion.

"Is that all?" he'd joshed.

Neil had explained that Mary had told his history class that her father told her the Holocaust "hadn't been as bad as it's been portrayed."

Blondie had been shocked. This was the girl universally acclaimed the school genius?

"You gonna write about Bobby?" Neil asked him today.

"If he does anything."

"He will. I'll try and get a good shot for your story."

Blondie headed for the stands. They were half empty. He chose a seat far from anyone. After he sat down, a man in a trench coat and a fedora clambered up the steps and seated himself next to him.

A fat man in a mask and chest protector came out and swept home plate. The Fenton cheerleaders raced onto the field. Blondie was amazed—he hadn't known they performed at baseball games. He wasn't complaining, though. As soon he caught sight of Tammy, he warmed to his task. Maybe she'd notice him in the stands and realize the important function he was performing. Blondie began scribbling in his notepad: "Tammy Hollander dazzled the crowd with her enthusiasm and gymnastics, setting the stage for the arrival of the Flyer nine." That would make a great lead.

The game wasn't close, a real bore. By the end of the second inning, Fenton held a six-run lead. It grew inning by inning thereafter. But Blondie was fascinated by Bobby Clements. The athleticism he'd revealed sparingly as a golfer was fully manifest when playing a sport he knew. His movements were graceful and controlled—he never put more energy into a swing or throw than it required. And yet, he threw the ball straighter and hit it harder than anyone. He was a man among boys.

In the fifth inning, Bobby smashed a fastball, a line drive that had home run written all over it. Just as the ball began to sail over the fence, the Panther center fielder leaped high and speared it. Blondie resented him for that.

The man next to him wrote something on a piece of paper. The next inning, when Bobby made a good play in the outfield, the man made another notation.

"I'm a reporter for the *Fentonian*," Blondie said to the man. "Are you a reporter, too?"

He laughed.

"I can't write for beans. Nah, I'm an assistant baseball coach at Maryland. Just doing a little scouting."

"Are you interested in Clements?"

"He's got some talent," the man said with no particular emotion.

Some? What was he talking about? Blondie figured the man was just keeping his cards to himself.

In the eighth inning, with the game well put away, Clements looped a ball between the right fielder and the center fielder. Blondie could tell by the way Bobby sped down the first base line that he was going for a double.

While Blondie watched the right fielder cut off the ball, something happened. He heard a gasp from the crowd, like air rushing from a flat. When he looked back toward first, Clements lay on the ground, grasping his knee, his face taut with pain.

"What happened?" Blondie asked the man in the hat.

"Caught a spike on the bag."

Coach Kegley ran onto the field and felt Clements' leg. Then he and one of the second-stringers lifted Clements to his feet and hobbled him off the field. The cheerleaders never stopped cheering.

After the game, Blondie headed for the locker room. Clements was dressed and preparing to leave.

"How's your leg?" Blondie asked him.

Clements shook his head.

"I don't know. It's my knee."

Clements sounded worried.

"Serious?"

"It's happened before. If my ankle gets twisted, my knee pops out."

"Have you seen a doctor?"

"I've been avoiding it. Coach told me I have to now."

"I'm sure it's nothing serious," Blondie encouraged him.

"I wish I was."

The next day, Feller grabbed him in the hallway.

"I got a letter from Smith-Reid yesterday," he told Blondie. "I'm in." His excitement was palpable. "Have you heard yet?"

Blondie shook his head. Feller's news made Blondie nervous. He thought he'd have heard first if he was going to be accepted. After all, he'd scored higher on his college boards than Feller, and his grades were about as good. What if Feller were accepted to Smith-Reid and he weren't?

Blondie's worrying was for naught. When he got home, a buff-colored envelope bearing the Smith-Reid logo was in the mailbox. Blondie ripped it open. The letter read: "*Dear Mr. Reimer: As dean of students, I'm pleased to advise you that you've been accepted for admission to Smith-Reid College beginning the fall semester....*"

Hot dog! Smith-Reid had been his first choice all along. He'd checked it out and it had passed muster: well-regarded academically, a strong English department, several courses in creative writing, small, but not too small. Out of town, but not too far away for him to come home once in a while. And, most important, his buddy would be there with him.

"That's great news!" his mom enthused when he told her. His dad agreed.

That evening in bed, he imagined how college would be: inspiring lectures by learned professors in ivy-walled classrooms, stimulating philosophical conversations in smoke-filled coffeehouses, and rousing sports victories in Romanesque gymnasiums and stadiums. He also envisioned rivers of beer, endless parties, and ravishing and willing co-eds.

He broke the news to Feller in Farber's class the next day.

"Blood brothers forever!" Feller said.

Blondie's spirits were high. They soared even higher when he passed Tammy on the way to English class and she smiled at him! His first thought was that she'd felt the vibes he was giving off, the confidence of a soon to be collegian. More likely, he thought a minute later, it was because he'd asked Phyllis to the prom. If so, maybe it was worth it.

For once, his optimism lasted the whole day. However, as he was passing the teachers lounge on his way out of school, he happened to glance into Miss Darlington's homeroom and saw the Bear talking to her. Her eyes were red and wet. That night, Blondie wondered what it meant. Were they having an affair? Had they been their cars he'd seen at that motel last fall?

The thought disgusted him. Miss Darlington was young, fresh and sweet. The Bear was an old fart, probably in his forties. Besides, he was married. What could Miss Darlington see in him? He also remembered, with some agitation, what Feller had told him once—that the Bear "had trouble keeping it in his pants." Jesus, what if it were true?

Blondie was relieved when Miss Darlington seemed her normal self in journalism class the next day. She was focused on the day's lesson: the difference between news stories and features. She asked each of them to choose a news story from that day's paper and write it as a feature story.

Blondie picked an article about the Cuban exiles who'd been caught in the Bay of Pigs invasion the year before. They'd all been sentenced to 30-year prison terms. He began: "Roberto Morales sits alone on a rusty steel cot in a rotting prison in the jungle, repulsing hordes of giant cockroaches with his bare feet. He contemplates the irony that left him in this vermin-infested sty, while those who encouraged his brave act sip strawberry daiquiris on Miami beaches...."

He made most of it up—including Roberto Morales—and thought it was pretty dreadful, but Miss Darlington selected his piece to read to the class anyway. Blondie felt flattered. But when he was leaving class, he detected on her face a wistfulness that bordered on despair. For an instant he felt an impulse to put his arm around her. He wondered if the Bear was causing her grief. He told himself it was none of his business.

Blondie knew he was bent on self-destruction when he found himself headed toward Miss Darlington's home room after his last class was over—and after waiting an additional ten minutes for the halls to empty.

At first, he thought her classroom was deserted. All he saw when he peered through the slightly open door were vacant desks and the bank of windows opening to the field outside. As he was about to turn away, he heard a sound from within.

Blondie eased open the door. Miss Darlington was sitting on a wooden shield above the radiators in the rear of the room. Her back was turned toward him and she was curled into a ball. He heard her sigh and her shoulders rise and fall. Then, she began to shake and moan.

He crept toward her, with no idea what he was going to do, his heart thumping. When he reached her, he willed his hand toward her, but it stayed at his side. For long moments, he stood rooted in place, listening to her agony. Finally, he coughed to make himself known.

She started, twisting violently toward him, her eyes wide.

"Bernard, why on earth are you spying on me?"

Her skin was blotched and her eyes raw. She looked wild, desolate.

"I'm sorry..." he began and could go no further.

For a moment, they just stared at each other.

"I saw you crying yesterday, Miss Darlington...."

"It's no concern of yours," she snapped. Then she sighed. "I'm sorry. You didn't deserve that. And please call me Sandy."

Blondie couldn't bring himself to do it.

"It's the Bear, isn't it?" he asked, surprised at the anger in his voice.

"What do you know?" she asked, grabbing his arm.

"I saw your cars at a motel."

He no longer doubted it.

"Oh, God." She shut her eyes and sighed. "Who else knows?"

"Nobody as far as I know. I never said anything."

She relaxed a trifle.

"It's not what you think," she said.

He gave her an encouraging smile. She returned a wry one.

"What am I saying? It's probably just what you think."

Blondie felt his shoulders slump.

"You can't understand why I'd be attracted to him, can you?"

Blondie shook his head.

"He's so sure of himself, so authoritative, so...."

"Married," Blondie offered.

"Yes." She sighed again.

Funny, he'd always thought of her as so much older than himself. He knew it was no more than five or six years, but she was an adult and he was a kid. At this moment, he saw her as a girl.

"He called it off yesterday, didn't he?" Blondie asked.

"No. I did."

She began sniffling.

Blondie sat down beside her and put his arm around her. She let him hold her for a long while until she stopped crying.

"Thanks," she said, gathering herself and standing. She picked up her satchel and walked from the room without looking back. Blondie remained on the wooden counter, staring absently at the patterns the pale light threw onto the far wall.

Later, Blondie shared the episode with Grouper after eliciting a pledge of secrecy.

"What do you make of it?" Blondie asked him. "Why would someone like Miss Darlington fall for someone like the Bear?"

"**Everyone is desperate for love**," he said.

"Desperate enough to turn a dickhead into a Don Juan?"

"Every time."

Grouper gave him a knowing smile and Blondie realized Grouper was no longer talking about Miss Darlington.

"Or a cheerleader into a Cleopatra?"

"Even that."

Chapter Twenty-Five

Flossie heated spaghetti for Ted and parked him in front of the upstairs television. She told him to go straight to bed after watching The *Flintstones*.

"Abba dabba doo," he replied.

Then she led Blondie down to their rec room. A large Zenith TV monopolized one corner of the orange shag carpet and a fake painting of an Alpine scene hung on one wall.

Flossie wanted to snuggle with him on the couch and watch *Rawhide*. She seemed to prefer snuggling to sex. That made him feel a trifle inferior. She could take sex or leave it. He had to have it.

Again tonight, after but a few kisses and touches, Blondie felt the hot hand of lust take hold of him.

"You want to do it now...here?" Flossie responded to his suggestion. She looked at him as if were a lunatic, but he knew she wouldn't deny him. She never did.

But the couch was all wrong. It was too short. It was too soft. A guy could break his back. How would he ever explain that to his mom?

A long oak table stood upright near the bottom of the stairs. Blondie rushed over and stood it on the floor.

"This will do," he announced.

"That's our old dining table. It'll be hard and cold."

"I'll put my sweater under you."

Blondie thought it a gallant touch, a bit of Sir Walter Raleigh.

Flossie was still hesitant, but she took off her skirt and stood before him in her panties. Blondie found her legs gorgeous in the faint light from the TV screen—slender and silver.

He helped her up on the table and slid off her panties. The sight of her most female part hoisted his member to high noon. Blondie frantically unbuckled his pants and pulled them and his underwear down to his ankles. He didn't have the patience to untie his sneakers.

Just as he was ready to spring onto the table, Flossie sat up and stared beyond him. Her eyes were eggs.

Blondie turned his head. At the foot of the stairs, in rabbit pajamas, Ted was watching them in wonder. Large gray ears flopped over on each side of his head,

"I want some milk," he said.

Driving home, Blondie told himself he'd crossed the line. He was mentally diseased. His blunder at Flossie's house proved it. There had to be a name for what he had, *lustus profundi*s or something like that. The cure would be long and painful—something like making out with Phyllis.

It was obvious he'd never gain control of his illness if he kept seeing Flossie. He phoned her when he got home and told her he needed to cool it with her for a while.

"Boys don't quit dating girls because they get too horny around them," she said. "It must be something else."

"It's not good-bye or anything. I just feel rotten about what I'm doing to you."

"You're not doing anything to me." Desperation laced her tone. "I like you."

"I like you, too. That's the problem. I like you too much to bring you down. Don't you understand?"

"No." Her voice quavered.

"You've got to try," Blondie said as he hung up.

He felt crummy, but he was determined. What else could he do? She wasn't the one. Was it right to keep making love to her knowing that?

Blondie vowed to devote more time to his journalism, his golf, his studies—any activity that fit the connotation of *wholesome*. If his lust got too great...well, he could always pull his pork like a really caring guy would do.

Feller made it clear he wasn't about to follow Blondie's course of action.

"I don't get it," he said. "You're on your own on this. I still want to get laid."

Blondie told Grouper of his decision.

"Appropriate under the circumstances," Grouper agreed.

They were at Grouper's Overlook, imbibing Pabsts. Grouper had bought it at the Suds Cellar. He'd forced himself to go back and get it right, saying it was a "matter of face."

Blondie told Grouper about the plans for college he'd made with Feller. He was hoping Grouper might invite himself along. He realized he felt a strong affinity for the big fellow.

"Smith-Reid, huh? Sounds good," he mused. "I wish I could go somewhere like that."

"What's stopping you?"

He made a sound like the moan of a distant foghorn.

"My dad has decreed that I should go to an Ivy League school," Grouper said.

"You think you could get in?"

"I don't know. I'm an extracurricular washout. That's pretty important to those schools. If I can't get, my dad wants me to go to one of the Philadelphia schools."

"Don't you have a vote?" Blondie asked.

"One would think." Grouper belched. "But you don't know my dad."

Grouper took the church key and popped another beer.

"You don't seem to like your dad much," Blondie said.

"He's a pompous, arrogant prick," Grouper said.

Blondie couldn't remember ever hearing anyone speak so harshly of their father.

"Then why do you care so much what he thinks?"

"I've asked myself the same question a thousand times. I can't find an answer. Somehow pleasing him seems to be important, even though I seldom do."

"You get good grades. You stay out of trouble."

"He likes that all right."

"Then what....?"

"He doesn't think I'm ambitious enough, athletic enough or...."

Grouper stopped and Blondie realized he was choking up.

"Or?"

"Manly enough."

Grouper forced the words out.

Not manly enough? Grouper wasn't the Mountain Pulaski type, but he was just as manly as he was.

"That's bullshit," Blondie said.

"I appreciate your feeling that way."

In bed that night, Blondie wondered what kind of father could cause someone like Grouper to be so negative.

* * * * * * * *

Thursday afternoon, Blondie stood on the ninth tee at Meadowbrook, waiting for the ferret-faced boy to tee up the ball. His name was George and Blondie didn't like him. The main thing he didn't like about George was that, although he had a girl's swing, he'd somehow managed to keep pace with Blondie for eight holes. They were tied at four holes apiece with one left.

Because Blondie was new to the team, Beasley had him playing sixth man—the last spot, the one reserved for the poorest player. Blondie resented that. He knew he was better than most of the others on the team.

Beasley had crept up to him as Blondie was walking between the eighth green and the ninth tee. He was wearing a pair of loud checked shorts, his spindly legs knobby as a crab's.

"How're you doing?" he'd whispered.

"We're tied, coach," Blondie had told him.

Disappointment had broken out all over his face.

"That's okay," he said in a sudden change of heart. "Here's the situation. Everyone else is finished and so far, we've had two wins, a tie, and two losses. So, whether we win the match or not is up to you."

He looked Blondie straight in the eyes to make sure he grasped the significance of the situation.

"Now, I want you to go after this little peckerhead…"

Beasley stopped and rubbed the whiskers on his chin. He scowled.

"Is there anything else, coach?"

"I hate their coach. I've never beaten the son of a bitch. This is the best chance I've ever had. Don't fuck it up."

Beasley walked off a few paces, then looked back and yelled, "Don't be nervous."

Now, George carefully placed his tee in the ground, centered his ball on it, and aligned his driver behind the ball. Then, he arranged his feet in the same precise way he'd done for eight holes and took two or three practice swings.

What a dork, Blondie thought.

Finally, he was ready, sighting down the fairway, aiming between two large maples on either side of the fairway fifty yards away. He waggled the driver back and forth behind his ball.

Hit the fucking thing, Blondie urged under his breath.

George drew the club back and, with the same jerky rhythm as his practice swings, somehow brought the clubface into contact with the ball. There was a loud crack, followed almost immediately by another sharp report as George's ball hit the maple guarding the left side of the fairway. Dead smack center. It bounced all the way back onto the tee.

Blondie was astounded. The little shit hadn't hit a bad drive all day. What a break!

George pulled out his three wood. Again, he went through his ritual, this time aiming the ball farther to the right.

THWACK! The ball leapt off the clubface and BAP! He nailed the tree on the right. Again, the ball bounced back onto the tee.

Blondie had trouble hiding his glee. He looked up the fairway and saw Beasley hiding behind a bush. When George turned to collect his thoughts, he jumped out and pumped both fists in the air.

On his next attempt, George hit the ball straight down the fairway. But he was laying three. All Blondie had to do was avoid making the same mistake and victory would be certain.

As soon as Blondie saw his ball split the fairway, he let out a sigh of relief. How could he possibly lose now? He hadn't shot worse than a five all day and George would have to play well from here on in to get six.

George's drive was a good twenty yards behind Blondie's, so he hit next. He seemed flustered and knocked his bag over while taking out his seven iron. But George put his shot onto the middle of the green, about thirty feet from the pin.

Blondie had a routine nine iron to the pin. He felt confident now. He was Arnold Palmer at the Masters. He felt his brows knit together into Arnie's determined squint. Keeping his eyes locked on the ball, Blondie took his club back smoothly and hit his best shot of the day.

He watched the ball soar high in a straight line with the pin and then begin to fall. It was right on top of the pin. It could go in! To Blondie's amazement and horror, his ball landed on top of the pin, bending it. For an instant, the ball seemed to balance there, and then the pin straightened, catapulting Blondie's ball about thirty feet to the right and into a sand trap.

He couldn't believe it. Blondie turned his face to the heavens and mouthed the word "Why?" Then, he looked over at George, as if expecting him to say, "You were robbed. Go ahead and pick your ball out of the sand and place it near the pin."

George was looking away. Nonetheless, Blondie could see that the corner of his mouth had curled into a slight smile.

Blondie looked toward the bush where Beasley had been hiding. He was sitting behind it in the grass, his fists pressed against his head. In a moment, he recovered and came rushing up to Blondie like a buffalo in heat.

"Forget about it," Beasley encouraged. "You were robbed. But you're still a shot up on him. Just get the ball out of the trap and two-putt. He'll never make his putt from where he is."

Blondie appreciated Beasley's support and took up his task with fresh resolve. He strode confidently into the trap. No point in letting George have any inkling of how much he hated sand shots.

Blondie focused his eyes on a point an inch behind the back of the ball. That was where he wanted his club to hit. He took his sand wedge back in a graceful arc and let it drop into the yielding sand. There was a splash of gold against the sky and the momentary rising of the ball. It landed on the edge of the green, but instead of skittering forward, it began spinning backward. Blondie watched it hang for an instant on the edge of the trap, then roll back in.

Full-scale panic set in. Blondie's one-stroke lead was gone. George looked at him with a smirk. From the corner of his eye, Blondie saw Beasley tearing leaves off a nearby tree.

His confidence wavering, Blondie swung again. He half-expected to catch the ball thin and rocket it over the green and into the firmament. But somehow, shaky arms and all, he scooped the ball from the trap and dropped it two feet from the pin.

Blondie allowed himself the pleasure of turning toward George and grinning. George looked ill. Blondie marked his ball and waited for George to putt. If he missed his thirty-footer and Blondie made his tap-in, the match was his.

George bent over his putter in his peculiar hunchbacked way. When he stroked his putt, Blondie saw it was way too hard and off line to the left. But somehow, the grain of the grass slowed the putt down and, as Blondie watched in horror, it began to break to the right. It was headed straight for the hole!

The ball began to slow. When it reached the edge of the cup, it ran out of gas and stopped. Blondie turned toward Beasley and smiled. From behind, he heard a clunk. When Blondie turned, the ball was out of sight and George was grinning.

"It fell in," he said in a snotty tone.

Blondie's stomach tightened like a fist. He could no longer win. He had to sink his two-footer to tie.

As Blondie surveyed his putt, it began to grow. Three feet. Four feet. Ten miles. Blondie forced himself to calm down. It was straight in, he told himself. A beginner could make it. An octogenarian could make it.

His pep talk wasn't working. His arms felt like two-by-fours, knotted and stiff with tension. He aimed the ball right for the center of the hole, but somehow, he flinched. Not much. Just enough that the ball caught the rim, circled the cup, and perched on the back edge.

He'd lost!

Blondie turned to Beasley for sympathy, but he wasn't there. Testerman and Carrington, the number one and two men, were looking at him as if he'd molested their sisters.

It wasn't fair. He'd hit the shot. He'd been robbed.

Blondie heard Beasley talking to someone as he approached the clubhouse.

"And then he hits the fucking pin..." Beasley was saying as if Blondie'd plotted with the pin to lose the match.

"Tough shit, Beasley," a voice answered. "You lost again. That's fifty big ones."

Blondie could guess whose voice that was.

Over dinner, Blondie's mom asked him how he'd performed at "his golf thing."

"I blew the match for us," he told her.

"That's wonderful," she said, "and I have some good news for you, too."

"Didn't you hear what I said?"

"I knew you'd do well. Now, let me tell you my news. We're going to New York state for the summer."

"What are you talking about?"

"Dad's been accepted into a master's program at the state university at Potsdam."

"What does he need a master's degree for?"

Why were parents so weird? Just when you thought you were finally settled, they went and changed things.

"Your dad," his mom said proudly, "is considering teaching military history at the college level."

That would be dangerous to the security of the nation, Blondie thought.

"Anyway, we thought you'd be pleased. You can come up with us and explore the area around Potsdam. There are mountains to hike, lakes to swim in, and plenty of golf courses."

"No."

"You don't want to go?"

His mom cocked her head, as if she couldn't believe what she was hearing.

"No."

"It'll be fun," his mom persisted.

Now his dad was looking over and his look wasn't friendly.

"We're not leaving you here alone," he said firmly.

"Why not? I'll be eighteen by then. A grown man."

His father wasn't convinced. Blondie argued with him for a while, then let his mother—who'd unexpectedly taken a sympathetic turn—take over.

"Francis, we shouldn't make him. Perhaps it's unreasonable to expect an 18-year-old boy to spend the summer with his parents."

Unreasonable didn't begin to describe it, Blondie thought.

"I don't care, Betty," his father said, "I don't think we can trust Blondie. He's been suspended from school. He stays out until all hours doing who knows what with that gang of his. He wrecked our car!"

Christ, why was he dragging all that stuff up again? Anyway, how could he seriously expect him to hang out with him and his mom all summer? The boredom would be deadly. On the other hand, having the house to himself all summer...now that had possibilities.

Blondie waited for an opportune moment and stomped off to his room as if upset. He figured his mom could handle his part of the argument. Indeed, after a fractious row, she came up to his room and told him his father had agreed he could remain in Fenton. His mom always won.

Blondie couldn't sleep that night. Over and over, he heard the sound of the ball hitting the top of the pin and saw his last putt spin out of the cup. It was unbearable. He had twice the ability of that geek-necked runt he'd been playing. But talent didn't seem to count if one couldn't produce under pressure, he conceded. And he couldn't deny it. He was a *choker*.

Chapter Twenty-Six

Friday was a bad day. Feller came up to him first thing in the morning to offer his condolences on the golf match.

"Sorry you fucked up," he said.

Then Miss Darlington expressed some reservations about his article on the match—"Ugly Hole Ruins Day." She suggested he change the title and run it without the two paragraphs detailing the "awful stroke of misfortune" that caused "ace ball-stroker Reimer" to double-bogey the last hole.

He knew she was trying to do the right thing by journalism, but she didn't understand. He couldn't "let the facts stand for themselves." The facts said he'd blown the match. Tammy would read all about it.

But that was just the warm-up. That evening, he received a phone call.

"Hi, it's me," Flossie said. She sounded far away. "Why haven't you called?"

"It's only been a week. I think we need more time apart."

"I have something I need to tell you."

Don't tell me you love me, Blondie thought. I couldn't handle the pressure.

"What is it, dear?"

That was a good touch. Show some caring. Blondie smiled in appreciation of his magnanimity.

"I'm pregnant," Flossie said.

The room began to spin. Thoughts rushed his mind in such a multitude his brain locked up. He couldn't speak.

"Now I guess we'll get married, huh?" Flossie said.

Her voice sounded different—soft as always, but more forceful. And her She suddenly seemed fearsome to him.

"It better be pretty soon," Flossie continued. "We wouldn't want people to think we had to."

Emotions coursed through his body, tripping muscles willy-nilly. His jaw popped. An eyelid twitched. A foot spasmed. He was coming undone.

"You're not saying anything, Blondie."

"I'm thinking," he finally uttered hoarsely.

"You mean about how we'll tell our parents and all that?"

Why was she pressing him so? He was fighting to gain control and she kept launching new horrors his way, each a more frightening extension of the initial one—Flossie was pregnant. And he was responsible.

Visions of fatherhood nuked Blondie's mind. He'd never get a college degree or a decent job. He could see the future now—trapped in poverty in a tacky little bungalow with a loving, but unimaginative, wife and a kid who'd slobber, snot, and shit all over him.

He couldn't do it. He wouldn't do it. That was all there was to it.

"I can't," he mumbled into the phone.

"Can't what?"

"I can't marry you." He cringed at the sniveling despair in his voice.

"You mean you lied to me?"

Her voice, a whisper now, shouted betrayal at him.

"No. I meant it then."

"But now that it's happened, you're backing out. It's my problem, is that it? Even though you were the one who always wanted to do it...even though you wouldn't take any precautions."

She was right. He was a wretch. Feller'd been right, too. He should've worn a rubber. If only he could put one on now. He'd put it on his head. That was where the worst leak had occurred.

"Look, maybe you're mistaken," Blondie said, trying to gin up a little hope.

"I don't think so."

Her voice was hard now, in a tone he'd never heard before. She was in control.

"How about an abortion?"

"It's illegal, remember. Besides, I'm a Catholic."

"Adoption?"

"Are you serious? You think I'd give our baby away?"

Our baby!

"Well, what else is there?"

"There's nothing else, Blondie. You've told me all I need to know. I'll be seeing you."

"But what are you going to…"

She hung up.

Oh heel of a thousand heels. He'd fucked up Flossie's life when she'd trusted him. Where were his noble intentions now? He was running from the consequences of his behavior like a puppy that'd fouled a carpet. But he had to save himself, didn't he? He assured himself most guys would do the same thing in this situation. True, a nit-picking voice agreed, but most guys were moral worms.

"Do you want some chicken, Blondie?" his mom called to him from the kitchen.

Was she kidding? The idea of eating anything made him want to retch.

"No thanks."

"That's not like you," she replied.

You don't know the half, he thought, as he headed for his room and, hopefully, the oblivion of sleep. First the golf match, now this. If he had any honor, he'd commit *seppuku* right this minute. He wondered how much it would hurt.

He had to talk to someone. He called Grouper and asked if they could get together the next evening. Just the two of them. He instructed Grouper to bring some beers—a lot of them.

Sure enough, when he showed up, a case of Pabst was in the back seat of his dad's Chrysler. It looked brand new.

"My dad fixed it right away," Grouper said. "He may get pissed at me, but he always fixes my mistakes. He reminds me of that on a regular basis."

Grouper drove up to his overlook. Once he'd parked, he pulled a can from the container and punched it open with a church key. He handed it to Blondie. Then he opened one for himself. He pushed his doughy torso into the soft leather seat and breathed deeply.

"Well, what should we talk about tonight?" he asked.

Strangely, now that he was with Grouper, Blondie couldn't bring himself to talk about Flossie. He wanted to talk about anything but her.

"What's the deal between you and Miss Spalding?" he asked Grouper instead. "The truth."

Grouper chuckled.

"I'll tell you, Blondie, if you promise to keep it to yourself."

"Cross my heart," Blondie said, guzzling the beer. He was determined to push his problems from his mind.

"Last year, about this time, I stayed late at school one night to finish a science project. I heard some noises from a classroom down the hall. It sounded like a woman moaning. I thought maybe someone had been hurt. I opened the door and turned on the lights and there was the Bear humping Miss Spalding." Bearzinsky! That prick! He'd drilled Miss Spalding too. What a philandering fuck. He had to pay. Blondie's anger momentarily pushed all thoughts of Flossie away. But after it subsided, they came right back. After a few more beers, he could hold it in no longer. He told Grouper about Flossie's "condition."

Grouper turned toward him and put his big paw gently on his shoulder. "What is life?" he asked.

What did that have to do with anything?

"Life is consequences," Grouper said. "Consequences that spin a web around you. The older you get, the more consequences you've created. The web gets tighter and tighter until you're trapped by the results of everything you've done."

Trapped! Blondie could identify with that.

Blondie waited for Grouper to continue, but he didn't. Instead, he quickly downed two more beers. Blondie, with a recklessness born of lost hope, matched him. Soon, he felt his brain slowing down and strange perceptions bubbling to the surface of his consciousness. Like how Grouper's head looked like a balloon blown slightly forward by the wind. Or how there was a strange light off in the trees to their right.

He watched the light jump across the dark and disappear.

"A light in the forest...." he said poetically.

"Life is like that," Grouper said.

"Sbeginning to sound like life is like everything," Blondie said, his tongue struggling to form words.

"A very astute observation, my boy. Life *is* like everything.... everything is life."

Grouper's voice drifted off. Blondie feared he'd fallen asleep.

"I'm not planning to marry her," Blondie said.

"I guess you don't have to," Grouper answered lethargically.

"I said I would, though. I have no honor ash all."

The self-pity in his voice disgusted him. He also was getting seriously drunk. His dad would think that was disgusting. But he didn't care. He needed to.

"Well, I suppose each person must follow his own code."

"But I told her I'd marry her if I got her pregnish."

"Here, have another beer."

"Thanksh."

Grouper breathed in and out loudly a few times.

"Don't be too hard on yourself, Blondie. **It's easy to be noble in advance.**"

"Ish that a law?"

"I suppose it is."

"Good, I needed one."

Blondie looked out the window and saw the light again. Now, it seemed to be hopping.

"Look at that," he said to Grouper.

"H-mm, that's weird," he said.

"Maybe it's a fartgeist."

"A what?" Grouper said.

"Brick saysh farts sometimes spontaneously ignite and glow in the dark like shpirits."

"You don't believe that."

"No."

Blondie counted the empties on the dash twice. He was sure there were either thirteen or fourteen. Unless there were twelve.

"Gotta pee," Grouper announced. He opened the door and crashed into some nearby bushes.

The light in the woods drew closer.

Stuporously, Blondie watched it dart from here to there.

Blondie pointed his finger at the light and cocked his thumb.

"POW," he said.

The glow stopped moving, then headed straight toward him like a guided missile. His door flew open and a beam of light smacked him right between the eyes.

"All right, buster, where's your partner?" a voice barked.

"Who're you?" Blondie said.

The beam—Blondie now could see it came from a flashlight—began whipping around the interior. It reflected off the row of beer cans and then passed slowly along them.

"I knew you were drinking. I could tell by the way you drove up here."

"Didn't drive. Grouper drove. He always drivesh that way."

"You're in trouble, buster. You don't look like you're twenty-one. Show me your license."

"Can't."

"You don't have one?" The voice rose.

"No. I can't get up."

A hand grabbed his jacket at the shoulder and ripped Blondie from the car.

"Stand right there."

As soon as the hand released him, Blondie began to sway back and forth.

"Now slowly remove your wallet and show me your license."

Blondie reached for his wallet. He got it out of his pants pocket before he lost his balance and fell into his invisible inquisitor.

"Sorrysh," he said as the light fell to the ground.

"Shit," the voice came from near Blondie's feet. "I just had this fucking uniform cleaned."

Blondie staggered to his feet.

"Let me helpsh you."

Blondie held out his hand to his fallen antagonist, only a dark shape in the night. The shadow struggled upright without his help.

"I'm going to take you in, boy. Now, show me that license."

"Dropped it."

The flashlight painted a white circle on the ground, illuminating Blondie's wallet. A hand materialized from the night, snatched it up and flipped it open.

"Aha," the voice said. "You're not twenty-one."

"I never said I wush."

"Okay, forget your pal. We're leaving. You follow me."

"No keysh."

"What?"

"Ish not my car. And, something elsh."

"What?"

"I'sh too drunk to drive."

"Well, get in my car."

"Okay. One morsh thing."

"What now?"

"I think I'sh going to throw up."

"Oh God, why did I get this call? I could have been busting whores."

"I won't tell," Blondie promised.

"What are you mumbling?"

"If yoush go, I won't say you wersh here. No one will know yoush fucked up."

"I DIDN'T FUCK UP," the voice roared.

Suddenly, the mournful baying of a coyote floated across the night. A very old coyote.

"What's that?" the cop said.

"Animal?" Blondie offered.

The baying turned into the whoop-whoop-whoop-yip-yip of a chimpanzee, a chimp with a deep voice.

"All right, smart ass. You're coming in, too."

"You'll have to catch me," Grouper boomed from the woods. "Watch the mud holes."

"Well, I'll just take your partner in, then," the cop called back.

"I've got your ke-eys," Grouper yodeled.

"WHAT?"

"You left them in your ca-ar."

The dark figure groped around his belt.

"Goddamn," he muttered.

"Make you a de-al," Grouper sung out.

"No way," the cop said.

"No keys then."

"What's the deal?"

"We'll leave if you do. Okay?"

"How about my keys?"

"I'll put them back on your seat. Deal?"

"Deal."

There was a long sigh. An owl hooted in the distance.

A little later, Grouper called out, "You can go now."

"What if I don't?" the cop asked, suddenly assertive.

"I'll go take your keys again."

"Ah shit," the cop finally said. He stomped away. Blondie heard his steps Shortly, a car door opened, a motor roared to life, and the cruiser sped away.

A moment later, Grouper exited the woods.

"What if he'sh waiting for us to come out?" Blondie asked.

"He wouldn't want anyone to know about this little episode, now would he?"

Grouper laughed.

"You mean we beat the law?"

Blondie couldn't comprehend it.

"You could say that."

"Well, fuck-an-A."

And, for a while, their triumph pushed Blondie's troubles from his mind. The next morning, thought, he felt pretty punk. It didn't help that his dad kept eyeing him suspiciously. He was still slightly hung over on Monday.

"I hope you feel better for the junior-senior picnic," Feller said.

That rang a faint bell.

"When is it?"

"Next week, dummy. Tammy will be there."

And Flossie wouldn't, Blondie realized. She was only a sophomore.

A if he'd read his mind, Feller said: "I heard about that number Flossie did on you." A smirk flew across his face.

"What do you mean?"

"Oh Blondie, I'm pregnant," Feller mimicked in a falsetto voice.

Blondie grabbed his arm.

"What are you saying?"

"Easy, Blondie," Feller answered, removing Blondie's hand. "I didn't think you'd fall for it."

"Flossie's not pregnant?"

"Not hardly."

"Then why.... ?"

"Meryl put her up to it. Flossie told her you said you'd marry her if you got her pregnant. After you dumped Flossie...."

"I didn't exactly dump her."

"....Meryl dared her to put you to the test. She was with Flossie when she called."

"Goddamn dames!"

"Yeah," Feller agreed. "It's terrible what men have to go through to get laid."

Chapter Twenty-Seven

The scene reminded Blondie of a painting he'd once come across in his mom's book of French impressionists: bathers in colorful garb beside a slow river, strollers in fancy clothes and parasols, people relaxing in the sun. Only here, the bathers were in much skimpier outfits, the strollers were in tattered jeans and tee shirts, the river was a chilly mountain lake, and a bunch of guys were playing softball on a makeshift diamond nearby. No one had been playing softball in the painting. It was Fenton High's annual junior-senior picnic.

Here and there, radios on scattered blankets were blaring forth the latest hits—"Soldier Boy," "Slow Twistin'," "Mashed Potato Time"—and a few pale bodies were jerking to the bouncier tunes. It was a bright May day and everyone were giddy.

Not Blondie. All he could think about was how his life had unraveled. His dad was still pissed at him over the car—even though it was fixed, his dad claimed it "pulled to the left"—and because he wasn't going to New York with them. He'd agreed to take that awful Phyllis Scarff to the prom, just a couple weeks away. He'd messed up a pretty good thing with Flossie. Coach Beasley regarded him as a loser, even though he'd beaten his man at golf every time since the first match. And, though Barnwell and Purdy had quit taunting him in the halls, Blondie was still apprehensive. He knew they still wanted a piece of him. All things considered, his chances of surviving high school—at least without substantial psychological, emotional or physical damage—remained slim.

All the way up to the lake, he'd listened to the rest of the guys talking about what a thrill it was going to be to see the girls in their swimming suits.

"O-oh-oh, h-how about L-linda L-lapidus?" Shakes said, biting his clenched fist.

"Or Ethel Philbin?" Feller cooed.

Blondie hadn't been able to get into any of that. Now he and the rest of the Club were lying around on some old army blankets his dad had lent them. Shakes was complaining that his made him itch.

"Bring your own blanket next time," Blondie snapped.

"Wh-what's wrong w-with you?"

Grouper paid them no attention. He lay on his back—taking up a whole blanket—with the president's book *Profiles in Courage* propped up on his great gut. With his light-colored swim trunks and pale body, he looked like a beached white whale—"Moby Dickless," Brick called him The rest of the group—except for Dispatch, who went off looking for Meryl—slopped suntan lotion on themselves and stared aimlessly around. Feller called for a "strategy session" to decide what to do.

"We c-could p-peek in the girls' l-locker r-room," Shakes suggested.

"That's cool," Feller answered sarcastically.

"We could get drunk," Brick offered.

Everyone looked at him.

"How?" Feller asked.

"I brought a pint in my duffel bag."

Feller groaned.

"We could get kicked out of school for that."

"Well, this sitting around doing nothing stinks," Brick said. "I don't know about you bozos, but I'm going to see if I can get into the softball game."

"Not a bad idea," Feller agreed.

Brick stood up and trudged off, followed by Feller and Shakes.

"Aren't you coming, Blondie?" Feller called back.

"Nah. I just want to relax."

"Suit yourself."

He didn't bother to ask Grouper, who'd fallen asleep in the sun.

Blondie sat with his arms around his knees and surveyed the situation. The pols, chops, brains, and jocks had already formed into clusters and staked out their turf—except today many of the athletes and cheerleaders were mingling openly. Blondie noticed Bobby Clements talking to Ethel Philbin. Their conversation seemed intense.

A few kids swam in the lake, although none stayed in long and all came out shivering and clasping their arms around their chests. Blondie guessed the water would be warmer where it was shallower, near a sandy beach at one end. Maybe he'd wander over later and get wet.

His interest in doing so soared when he saw a group of girls heading that way and Tammy was one of them! She was wearing a bright red one-piece swimsuit. Blondie had never seen her so meagerly clad. The outline of her pert breasts beneath her suit and her bare legs jolted every neuron in his brain. Blondie scarcely noticed the other girls, who swirled around Tammy like dust around a comet. But he could tell from her sexless gait that one of them was Phyllis. Drat, drat, drat!

Blondie decided to approach the situation cautiously. He loped halfway to the beach, then ducked beneath the shadow of a large oak. He wondered what to do next. Meanwhile, he couldn't help watching Tammy. She was like Venus, just emerged from the sea, her motions as graceful as the waves upon the lake.

A couple of the girls stuck their feet in the water, then shrieked.

"Blondie!" Phyllis called.

Damn! He'd been caught watching.

She waved to him and invited him over.

Blondie tried to act casual as he strolled from the shadow. He felt like a dork in his jeans and tee shirt when they were all in bathing suits. He thought he detected a flicker of amusement in Tammy's eyes as he approached.

Phyllis seemed beside herself to see him.

"Isn't this fun?" she gushed.

"Sort of."

He was in a dicey situation. If he acted too nice to Phyllis, Tammy would think he was smitten by her. But if he behaved poorly to her, Tammy would resent him for mistreating her friend.

"Are you having a good time?" Phyllis asked.

"Sure." Blondie screwed his face into a smile.

"I think you know Tammy."

Tammy was still looking at him. Blondie couldn't read her expression.

"Well, we've never been introduced," Blondie said.

"Tammy, this is Bernard. He's taking me to the prom."

Oh, pain. She'd gouged him twice. Bernard? How could she call him that? And why did she have to mention the prom?

Phyllis put her hand on his arm. Blondie fought his impulse to slap it away.

"Phyllis has told me all about you," Tammy said, smiling devilishly.

What did that mean? Had Phyllis been filling Tammy's head with crap about her and him?

"Why don't you join us?" Phyllis said.

Blondie noted the multi-colored spread of beach towels a few yards away.

"Yes, why don't you?" Tammy chimed in. "For some reason, guys seem to be avoiding us."

There was no way Blondie was going to pass up her invitation. He hurried back to where the Grouper lay and grabbed his gym bag.

"Where're you going?" Grouper asked groggily.

"Some girls invited me to join them."

"Is Tammy one of them?"

"How did you know?"

"Don't get anyone pregnant."

"Very funny."

The men's locker was a concrete bunker filled with wooden benches and wire baskets stacked in racks. Blondie put his clothes in one of the baskets and slipped on the new trunks he bought just for the picnic. To his dismay, they were tight and revealing. He prayed he wouldn't get an erection. This was no time for Nessie to make a spectacle of himself.

Unclothed, Blondie was acutely aware of how thin he was. His arms were bicycle handles, his ribs bird cages, his rear end almost a no-show. None of the girls seemed to notice. Most had their eyes closed, soaking up the sun. Jesus, girls were sensual when they just lolled about. Blondie instructed Nessie to disregard the observation.

Phyllis had placed a towel beside her for him. Blondie was glad to see that Tammy lay on the other side of it. She was lounging on her back, her face hidden behind a huge pair of sunglasses. The contours of her body imprinted themselves upon his brain and, Blondie was sure, into his genetic code so that all future generations of male Reimers would be attracted to girls with figures like hers.

The next few hours flowed like molasses, slowed further by Phyllis' constant chattering about school happenings or details of her life—where she'd lived as a child, her family, her hobbies. Blondie did his best to act interested, but his mind was preoccupied with the awesome awareness that his angel lay to the other side of him.

Every so often, the other girls started a conversation among themselves. Blondie listened attentively. He'd always wondered what girls talked about. He was relieved to find they didn't talk about boys the way boys talked about them—at least not around him. They discussed movies and records, new clothes, who was going with whom, dumb things their mothers made them do, what they'd be doing in the summer. Stuff like that.

Tammy didn't talk as much as most of the girls, but Blondie did pick up a few things about her. She liked silk dresses. She detested her little brother. She thought Tab Hunter was divine. She liked that goopy song "Johnny Angel" by Shelley Fabares. She thought about being an actress.

Only once did Tammy speak directly to him, asking what it was like to be new at school.

"A little scary," he told her, surprised at his candor. "But, when you move around, you meet new people, learn different things."

"I've always lived in Fenton," she said with a trace of regret.

Eventually, the bellowing of the Bear told them it was time to go home. Blondie tarried long after the girls had left for the women's locker room. He was caught in the cloying grip of a contentment he'd never felt before.

When Blondie finally reached the men's locker room, it was nearly empty. Brick, fully dressed, was lacing up his sneakers. Blondie found his basket, but his jeans weren't in it.

"Where are my jeans?" he muttered to himself.

"How should I know?" Brick snapped as he left the building.

What was going on? Had someone put on his jeans by mistake and left the rest of his clothes? It made no sense. He had no choice but to pull on his tee shirt and sneakers and run for the bus, still wearing his swim trunks.

As he drew near the buses, he saw two guys standing near one of them waving at him. Purdy and Barnwell. What did they want? Purdy pulled a pair of jeans from behind his back and began flapping them in the breeze. They'd stolen his jeans! Son of a bitch. He started running toward them, shoving his way through groups of stragglers. Purdy and Barnwell disappeared into the swarm of buses.

As he pushed through a group of girls, they began giggling. He stopped and turned around. Mary Cherry stood in their midst, her hand clamped over her mouth and her eyes wide in shock. What the hell was going on?

He shot them an angry, confused look.

"Your shirt," one girl said.

"What about my shirt?"

What were they talking about? It was an ordinary white tee shirt.

"The back," she added.

Blondie ripped off his shirt and turned it around. On the back was a grease-pencil drawing of a face, with a penis for a nose and testicles for eyes. Beneath was the caption: "Mr. Bearzinsky is a dick."

Blondie didn't have to guess who the perpetrators were. He wadded the tee shirt into a ball and raced for the buses.

Feller stood by one of the buses holding his gym bag.

"Where the hell have you been?" he said. "I thought you were going to miss the bus. Hey, where are your pants? You can't get on the bus like that."

"Purdy and Barnwell took my jeans."

Feller reached into his bag and took out a gray windbreaker.

"At least put this on."

"Got to find them," Blondie said.

"The motors are going," Feller said. "You've got to get on the bus."

Dozens of staring eyes roamed over his body as he picked his way down the aisle to the back of the bus where the rest of the Club was sitting. Grouper, monopolizing one corner, was the color of a rutting salmon, purple-pink from too much sun. His fried lips were even puffier than usual. Shakes was squashed into the other corner, a blissful look on his face.

"What's with him?" Blondie asked.

"He drank the whole pint of Brick's whiskey," Feller said.

No wonder Brick was pissed.

"At least it's keeping him quiet," Feller added. "He created a ruckus in the park by mooning a couple football players. I thought they were going to kill him."

Gears began grinding as the buses lurched forward. ,Blondie was glad Tammy wasn't on his bus. She'd think he was a real dink, running around with no pants on.

They reached the main road before Blondie looked behind. As soon as he did, he began pounding on the back window. Seated in the front seat of the bus behind were Purdy and Barnwell. They were holding up his jeans and shooting him the finger. What had changed? Why were they challenging him now?

"Those assholes," Feller said when he saw what was happening.

"Wh-what's g-going on?" Shakes asked, stirring from his stupor.

Feller pointed out the back window.

"They stole Blondie's pants," he explained.

"Are y-you n-naked?" Shakes asked Blondie, causing several heads to turn.

"Christ, shut up!" Blondie barked.

"I w-was j-just asking."

Shakes looked out the back window. Purdy bobbed Blondie's jeans up and down, as if they were a prize fish. Shakes began unbuckling his jeans.

"What are you doing?" Blondie cried.

Shakes pulled his pants and his underwear down around his knees and pressed his tiny alabaster butt against the back window.

"No, no..." Blondie begged.

Behind them, Purdy and Barnwell were furiously shaking their fists at Shakes. Blondie was more worried about the look on the bus driver's face beside them. He was enraged. He began honking his horn.

"What's going on?" a voice boomed from the front of the bus. A large figure rose from the front seat. It was the Bear! When had he gotten on?

The frantic honking accompanied them up the road as Shakes remained stuck to the rear window.

"Get down in your seat, Caldane!" Bear yelled. "You could get killed riding like that."

Everyone looked back.

"He's got his pants down," a girl shrieked.

Animal hostility seized Bear's face. He began hurrying down the aisle. He was after fresh meat and Blondie knew where he was going to find it—pressed up against the back window.

The bus lurched around a curve and Bear sprawled into the aisle. Brick dragged Shakes down onto the seat.

"Put your pants on," he hissed at him. Shakes tugged at his pants, which were wrapped around his ankles, and fell face first onto the floor. Brick grabbed him by the back of his shirt, as if he were a kitten, and lifted him upright while Feller pulled up his pants. By the time Bear, now covered with dust, reached the back of the bus, Shakes was fully clothed.

"What were you doing, Caldane?" he shouted at him.

Shakes looked up at Bear with swimming eyes, then flopped against Brick.

Bear bent over and smelled Shakes' breath.

"He's been drinking!" Bear shouted, as if proclaiming the discovery of penicillin. "Where's his bag?"

Brick held it out to him. Bear ripped it open and withdrew an empty pint bottle of *Ancient Turkey*.

"Ah ha!" he cried. "I was right. Caldane, you're out."

Bear's outburst revived him.

"Wh-what do y-you m-mean?" he stammered.

"You're suspended."

Blondie felt sorry for Shakes, but he was glad Bear hadn't suspended him again as well. His mother would weep and his dad would go ballistic.

Bear started back up the aisle, then turned.

"Where are your pants, Reimer?" he asked, as if Blondie's bare legs had just registered.

"Lost 'em," Blondie mumbled.

"You're on thin ice, too, Reimer. One more thing...."

He stomped off without finishing.

It was all Purdy and Barnwell's doing, Blondie thought. Anger welled inside him.

"Will you come with me when we off the bus?" Blondie asked Brick.

"What for?"

"I'm getting my jeans back."

Brick's eyes drew into slits.

"Yeah, I'll be glad to."

When their buses rolled to a stop in front of the school, Blondie saw Barnwell and Purdy leap from the door of a nearby bus. He and Brick bolted from their seats, but got caught in the herd of departing students. By the time they forced their way out, Barnwell and Purdy were halfway across the parking lot, heading for Purdy's pickup.

"Hey, you assholes!" Brick yelled at them as he and Blondie charged forward.

"What do you want, Brick?" Barnwell yelled back, stopping beside the tailgate.

Purdy stood beside him, grinning and displaying Blondie's jeans.

"Blondie wants his pants back."

"Well, let him ask for them. Politely."

"Give me my clothes," Blondie demanded, now almost upon them.

"Say please."

Blondie lunged for Barnwell and grabbed his shirt.

"Listen, you skinny hillbilly fuckface…."

Barnwell pushed him away.

"Oh, it's a fight you want, is it?"

"I'm not afraid of you."

And, for once, Blondie noted, he wasn't. His righteous anger flowed like a torrent in a millrace, empowering his arms and his voice. He liked that feeling. Maybe this time he would follow through.

"Well, good," Barnwell answered, his small teeth and tight lips a zipper across his face. "I wondered when you were going to quit hiding behind Brick's skirts."

"Who wears skirts?" Brick growled.

"Easy, Brick, I got no quarrel with you," Barnwell said. "It's the giraffe here who wants a fight. You want a piece of me, Mr. Giraffe?"

It was taking too long. There was too much talk. Blondie could feel his anger begin to subside. Don't let me down, he begged his body. But he felt fear begin to seep in.

"If you had another brain, you'd be a half-wit," Blondie forced himself to say. He wasn't going to retreat, no matter what.

Now Barnwell lunged at Blondie. Brick stepped between them.

"This isn't the time or place," he advised.

"When and where then?" Barnwell demanded.

"The quarry. Next Saturday night at eight."

Why was Brick playing the promoter, Blondie wondered, as the last drop of his anger evaporated.

"Come on, Purdy, give him his jeans back," Brick said.

Purdy looked to Barnwell, who nodded.

Purdy threw Blondie's pants at his feet.

"Saturday night," Barnwell reminded Blondie as he got in his car. "I'll let everyone know so you can't back down."

Jesus, what had gotten into Brick's head? Blondie was going to have to fight Barnwell in front of a frigging mob. He could see the poster in his mind: "Razorbones Barnwell vs. The Giraffe Kid. Scheduled for fifteen rounds—but come early. It may not last that long." He was as good as dead.

Chapter Twenty-Eight

Blondie was hardly amazed when Mr. Farber told him he was wanted in the principal's office. He'd always figured Farber and the Bear were in a conspiracy against him. He was just surprised he hadn't been called first thing in the morning.

When he got to the office, Mrs. Spritz directed him back to the teacher's lounge. The Bear was standing by the pop machine, looking out the window. His broad back seemed to fill the far wall. Blondie had been looking forward to a showdown with the Bear ever since Miss Darlington had told him her story, but now that he was alone with him, Blondie felt apprehensive.

"I suppose you think that was funny," Bearzinsky said without turning around.

"What's that?" Blondie asked, his heart beginning to thump.

"That obscene thing you wore all day yesterday at the picnic."

All day?

"There were children there, you know," Bear continued.

Children? Did he mean the juniors?

"I should have given you the thumb yesterday along with Caldane. You're their leader, aren't you?"

Blondie was both surprised and pleased at Bear's remark. The leader of the B & F Club? He'd never thought of himself as the leader of anything.

But "B" could stand for Blondie as well as Brick, he realized. He hoped the Bear wouldn't notice his smile.

"Did you think I wouldn't find out?" Bear asked, finally turning to face him. He didn't seem angry, just disappointed. Blondie realized he was trying to shame him.

"What are you talking about?" Blondie asked.

The Bear's face contorted in a sudden rage. He rose up on the balls of his feet. Blondie wondered if a student had ever been mauled in the teacher's lounge. Perhaps he was about to partake in a precedent-setting event.

"Do you think my face looks like a penis?" Bear shouted at him.

"Not exactly," Blondie replied.

"Not exactly?" His fury doubled. "You're going to learn some respect, Reimer. How would you feel about not graduating with your class?"

Not graduate? Could Bear do that? Blondie'd just about finished all his classes and he was passing them with ease. The thought of spending even one extra day at Fenton High was terrifying.

"I didn't even do it," Blondie blurted, feeling the familiar and unwanted craven tone enter his voice.

"Bullshit!" Bear roared. "Mary told...."

He stopped, aware of his error.

Mary Cherry! Of course, she would have been the one to rat on him.

"Anyway," the Bear said, regaining control, "I wouldn't plan on graduating if I were you."

Blondie felt routed. He'd been planning to get the best of the Bear ever since he'd found out what a heartless philanderer he was, but once again the Bear had gained the upper hand. Blondie felt sweat trickle down his back. Not graduate?

Bear put his foot up on the arm of one of the chairs. "Unless you bring both your parents in here to discuss a more appropriate punishment," he added with a smug smile.

Bring his parents in to hear about how he'd worn a dick on his back at the school picnic? That was worse than not graduating. His parents would never forgive him. Goddamn Buford!

"Now go on back to class and think about it," Bear commanded.

Blondie felt like a scarecrow, spineless, half a man. He began to slink away, his neck bowed, his back curved.

"You know, I had you pegged for a troublemaker the first day of school," Bear added, "when you started that ruckus with Buford."

What? Bear was blaming him for that?

"That's crap and you know it!" Blondie shouted. "Buford's nothing but a fucking hick and a bully."

"What was that word you used?" Bear asked wide-eyed.

"Hick," Blondie emphasized.

"No, the one before that."

"What? Fucking?"

"You can't say 'fucking' in my presence," the Bear shouted. "Don't you have any respect for your elders?"

Blondie couldn't stand it any longer. He felt himself going over the top.

"You don't like 'fucking'? You're the biggest fucker in this school. You fucked Miss Darlington. No, that's not quite right. You fucked her over."

The Bear's face seemed to collapse inward.

"What do you know? Who else knows?" He voice wavered.

"I know you cheated on your wife. I know you hurt the best teacher in this school."

Blondie could feel the power of his righteous wrath. It felt good.

"Now, wait a minute," the Bear said, "it wasn't like you think. Sandra came after me."

Blondie enjoyed hearing the pleading in his voice.

"Oh no, she didn't," Blondie retorted. "Anyway, she wasn't the first. Miss Spalding, too. And who knows who else."

"Who's telling you these things?"

The Bear's eyes darted.

"Never mind."

"Who else knows?"

"No one," Blondie said. "I didn't tell out of respect for Miss Darlington."

Bearzinsky sighed and sat down. Blondie took a chair opposite him.

"You have to understand, Bernard. It's my job to keep order in the school," he said. "Heaven knows, Clapper won't do it...can't do it. There's a lot of pressure. Sometimes you make mistakes."

Was he apologizing?

"Maybe I was wrong about you," Bear went on. "But if I've been a little tough, it's was because I thought that's what you needed."

Spare me, Blondie thought.

"Believe me, inside I really like you...."

Give me a barf bag. Blondie didn't say it.

"I wasn't really going to keep you from graduating. I just wanted to meet with your parents and make sure we launched you from high school on the best footing."

Blondie didn't change expression, although elation was building in his chest. He was backing the cocksucker down! Blondie had gained power over an adult. Not just any adult, either. The fiercest of them all.

"I might let it go," Blondie said. "If I graduate on time...."

"Of course, of course, my boy."

Bear shot him a smile.

"....and if you immediately end Jerry Caldane's suspension...."

A flash of anger crossed his face and disappeared.

"Of course."

"...and if you apologize to Miss Darlington in writing for what you did."

The Bear choked.

"What? I can't do that. I can't put it down in writing."

"Oh yes you can," Blondie rejoined. "You don't have to worry. Miss Darlington wouldn't want anyone to know either. But she'd have that letter in case you ever pulled something like this again."

"No, absolutely not." Bear's face was resolute.

"Suit yourself. But if I had a marriage and a job dependent upon writing one little note, I think I'd do it."

Blondie stood and took a step toward the door.

"Wait, wait...."

Moisture haloed the Bear's forehead.

"Can I trust you to deliver it? And she has to get it outside of school. I don't want it lost in the hall for anyone to pick up."

"Sure, I'll deliver it. And I want to read it too. I want to make sure you don't weasel out of this."

Blondie noted the firmness in his voice. He sounded like a hanging judge.

"Okay, okay," the Bear said. "But just between us, okay?"

"Don't you think you can trust me?" Blondie said with a final turn of the screw.

The Bear was waiting for Blondie after his last class. He called him over as inconspicuously as he could, then watched until the last student had gone around the corner before handed Blondie an envelope.

Blondie opened it and took out the note.

Sandra,
I'm sorry to be so late with this apology. I've been despondent since our breakup, but it was the best thing given our situations. I was wrong to ever get involved with you. I'll always have the highest regard for you. Please forgive me.
                                                            John

The Bear waited for his reaction.

"Okay, I guess," Blondie said.

"Just between us, right?" Bear asked again.

"Of course."

The Bear looked full into his eyes, seeking reassurance. Blondie turned and trotted off. He waited for her near a tree beside the teacher's parking lot. Overhead the sky was cloudless and cornflower blue. For one instant, all was right in the world. Blondie licked the flap of the envelope and sealed it.

Several teachers got into their cars and departed before Miss Darlington emerged from the building carrying a worn satchel. The sun glinted off her auburn hair. He watched her walk toward him in her half-graceful, half-coltish way. He realized he felt an affection for her. Not like the one he felt for Tammy, though. Something different.

She gave him a wondering look when he approached her, but she seemed pleased. After she put her satchel in the car, he handed her the note.

"What's this?"

"I don't know," Blondie lied. "Mr. Bearzinsky told me to give it to you."

"John?" She grew even more curious. Blondie could tell she was dying to open the envelope. He could also tell she didn't want to do it in front of him.

"It's none of my business," he said, walking away.

When he looked back, she was sitting in her little blue Rambler, reading the note. After she was through, she crushed it into a ball and threw it in the back seat. When she passed him on the way out of the lot, she waved. She looked a lot more hopeful than he'd seen it for some time.

Grouper was shaking his head slowly from side to side when Blondie joined him at school the next morning.

"Unbelievable, unbelievable...."

"What are you babbling about?" Blondie inquired.

"Dispatch and Meryl. They're getting married."

"You've got to be joking," Blondie exclaimed. "She's a pig."

Grouper's head jerked back.

"Sorry, I forgot," Blondie said.

"Don't let it worry you," Grouper said. "There's nothing left between us."

"But why? Dispatch couldn't possibly love her."

"Agreed. But he has a reason—the one that unites most high school couples in matrimony."

"You're kidding. He knocked her up?"

"You nailed it."

Blondie looked at the Grouper to see if he was pulling his leg. His face was as expressionless as a frog's.

"How does he know she isn't faking? Remember what Meryl put Flossie up to?"

Grouper shrugged.

"Dispatch is determined to go through with it. He says it's the right thing to do. He's set the date for soon after graduation."

Blondie felt diminished. He'd fled from his obligation to Flossie, yet here was Dispatch, the last person Blondie would have expected to act honorably, sacrificing his whole life for a known pregnancy-faker. Christ, he couldn't count on anyone to be consistent, even when all it took was behaving poorly.

That evening, the phone rang when he was getting a peanut-butter-and-jelly sandwich in the kitchen. It was Flossie.

"What do you want?" Blondie asked sharply

"Are you mad at me?"

Blondie put his hand over the receiver and took a deep breath. He wanted to be mad at her, but he realized he liked hearing her voice.

"No, I guess not."

"What I did was pretty crappy, huh?"

"Yeah."

"Meryl made me do it. She said you didn't like me enough to marry me."

What could he say to that?

"But that's all right," she added. "I mean we're both too young to think about things like that. Anyway, that's not why I did it."

"No?"

"It was because Meryl told me you were taking that Scarff girl to the prom. I felt upset. I wanted to get back at you."

Hearing Flossie tell it, he couldn't blame her.

"The prom doesn't mean anything to me," Blondie assured her. "I don't even want to go. I'm only going with her because I need a ride home from the *Fentonian*."

"Really?"

"Hope to die. How could I like Phyllis? She's a dog."

Flossie didn't say anything for a minute.

"Does that mean you'll see me again?"

"Look, if it makes you feel any better, I'll leave the prom early and meet you somewhere."

"I'd like that."

After he hung up, Blondie wondered why he'd put himself in such a bind. What could he tell Phyllis to get out of the traditional post-dance dinner? Oh well, he'd worry about that tomorrow. Tomorrow was another day. Wasn't that what Scarlett O'Hara always said? Of course, Blondie realized, Scarlett had been a championship-caliber airhead.

Chapter Twenty-Nine

"I don't see why you're so afraid of Barnwell," Feller said to Blondie. "You've got four inches on him and he's just as thin as you are."

They were at Feller's house, lying on the twin beds in the attic room, with the overhead light on. Blondie'd asked to spend Friday night with Feller. He didn't feel like being alone with his folks the night before his execution.

"I don't like to fight," Blondie said.

"No one does. But sometimes you have to."

Why was everyone so brave was someone else was doing the fighting?

Feller's question was a good one, though. Why did Barnwell inspire such fear in him? Was it because he seemed so ready to fight? Or was it just Blondie's cowardice?

"Barnwell was afraid that night when Brick went after him," Feller said What we need to do is to make him a little more afraid of you."

"How?"

"I don't know. Let me think about it."

Blondie watched while Feller thought. After a while he asked him how he was doing.

"Nothing yet."

"Grouper thinks it's all pretty dumb," Blondie said.

"What is?"

"Squabbling with Barnwell, chasing after girls, getting drunk...."

"Grouper's been known to get drunk."

Blondie flopped over on his back and put his hands behind his head. "Is this the way people get to be adults?" Blondie asked.

Feller laughed.

"In Fenton, it is."

"Has anyone from Fenton ever amounted to anything?"

"Are you kidding?"

That's what Blondie figured. Fenton didn't provide the proper culture for greatness. It was the wrong petri dish.

Quicker than Blondie thought possible, Saturday evening rolled around. There was a notable lack of chatter in the P-mobile as Dispatch pointed it down Oakspring Lane toward the quarry. Grouper had refused to come—he said he couldn't stand the sight of blood, especially that of his friends. Each of the rest of the gang had assured Blondie he had a chance, but Blondie could tell none of them would put money on it.

Only Feller seemed in good spirits. He'd told Blondie he'd come up with an idea that might help him. But Feller said he wouldn't divulge it until they were near the quarry.

Dusk was approaching. Blondie looked out the window at the high scudding clouds streaking across the moon. New leaves tossed against the silver sky like dark schools of fish. Ahead, Blondie saw the dark tunnel of trees that ended at the quarry. The P-mobile plunged onward into that heart of darkness.

Blondie could wait no longer.

"Are you going to tell about this secret strategy or yours before or after Barnwell beats me up?" he asked Feller.

"No need to be sarcastic. Okay, here it is. Yesterday, I told Harold Bull you were a karate expert."

"That's it? That's your big plan?" Blondie's voice rose.

"Calm down. Bull's a friend of Barnwell's, see. I bet anything he passed my information along."

"But I'm not a karate expert. I don't know anything about karate."

"Just act like you do. Put your fist out like this," Feller said, unaware his hand was lost in shadow, "and put one leg in front of the other with your knees bent. Then, yell out some Chinese phrases."

"I don't know any Chinese phrases."

"Try 'Moo Goo Gai Pan' or 'Foo Yung.'"

"Those are Chinese meals," Blondie retorted.

"You think Barnwell knows Chinese? Barnwell doesn't even know American. He couldn't tell chicken-fried steak from chicken shit."

"What's this charade supposed to accomplish?"

"If it works, Barnwell may back away from the fight."

"And if he doesn't?"

"Then you may have a problem."

There was no sign of Barnwell or Purdy when they arrived at the quarry. There were few cars at all. It was too early for the neckers. Even in Fenton, etiquette required taking one's date out for a shake and fries before trying to rip her clothes off.

Dispatch circled the quarry, an ominous black hole in the twilight. He pulled into an open area, about forty or fifty feet from a cream-colored Edsel. No one spoke. No one opened a beer from the case they'd brought along.

"For God's sakes, you guys, loosen up," Blondie squawked. "Go ahead and get drunk. Whatever's going to happen isn't going to take long, so don't plan your whole evening around it."

Brick slapped him on the back.

"That's the spirit, Blondie. It only hurts for a while, right?"

"That isn't what I meant."

"Maybe B-buford w-won't show," Shakes offered.

Shakes had become a real booster of Blondie's since finding out Blondie had persuaded the Bear to let him back into school.

"Yeah, maybe Buford's not so gutsy as he talks," Feller said.

A quarter hour later, a set of low beams crawled around the bend, followed by another. The first set stopped thirty feet away, shining themselves at the P-mobile. The dark void behind the lights was the shape of Purdy's truck. A door opened. A moment later, a shadow formed in front the lights.

"Okay, Reimer, let's see your stuff," the shadow figure called.

It was Barnwell all right.

All heads turned toward Blondie.

"Do what I told you, Blondie, and good luck," said Feller, holding out his hand.

"Y-yeah, g-good luck," Shakes added, offering his hand as well. Dispatch and Brick followed suit.

"Come on, you guys, quit being so fucking grim. I have a chance."

"Sure," Brick agreed half-heartedly. "You have a chance."

The car door seemed to weighed a ton. Like the door of a vault, he thought, a *funeral* vault. Blondie stumbled on the gravel as he stepped from the P-mobile. Barnwell remained a silhouette against the glaring headlights.

"You wanted me, Reimer," Barnwell taunted. "Well, here I am. Come and get me."

Blondie didn't move. He didn't want to move. He couldn't move. He told himself the worst that would happen was that he'd get beat up. That didn't help.

"Not so brave when there's no one beside you, are you, Mr. Giraffe? What would it take to get you mad? Calling you yellow? Well, I think you're yellow."

Blondie felt long roots growing out of his sneakers, planting him in place.

"I saw you lying by that scaggy Phyllis Scarff at the picnic," Barnwell continued. "Are you sweet on her? Do you ever get in her snatch? I wonder if it's as ugly as her face."

Was Barnwell crazy? Did he think insulting Phyllis would make him mad?

"Or is it that cute little Tammy Hollander you're sweet on? She's just so sweet...." Buford's voice was mocking, probing.

Blondie knew what Barnwell was doing. But he still didn't like the jerk talking about Tammy.

"You know what? I heard Tammy sucks dicks."

"LIAR!" Blondie screamed out.

"Oh, did we hit a little nerve there. It's true, though. I know a guy can prove it."

"You don't know shit, Barnwell," Blondie snarled, surprised and relieved to feel genuine anger awakening his leaden legs.

"What's that you said?"

"You heard me."

"No I didn't. Come a little closer and tell me."

Blondie took six or seven steps toward Barnwell, until he was an arm's length away. Recalling Feller's counsel, Blondie leapt into the air, shot one fist out and yelled "Moo Goo Gai Pan." He landed with one foot raised in menace. He gave a low growl, then added "Foo Yung!"

Barnwell seemed confused, somewhat wary. Feller's ploy was working.

"Take back what you said about Tammy," he barked at Barnwell.

"It's true."

"She wouldn't even go out with you, let alone do something like you said."

"I didn't say it was me."

"Well, whoever told you that is a fucking liar."

"What did you say?" Barnwell asked him, not in a challenging way, but as if he hadn't heard.

Christ, Blondie wondered, was he deaf?

"I said whoever said Tammy does what you said is a fucking liar."

"Is that right?" Buford asked in a merry tone.

"You bet your ass that's right," Blondie retorted.

Why was Barnwell acting so happy?

"As a matter of fact, it was Merwin Fester."

Merwin Fester? What was he saying? Tammy would never go out with a scumbag like him. Her father wouldn't let her, anyway.

"Tammy'd never go out with a shit-shoveler like him and you know it."

"What'd you call him?"

"A shit-shoveler. Isn't that what he does? Clean horse's stables?"

When Blondie heard a door open from behind Purdy's truck, his instincts told him he'd made a big mistake. Slow steps crunched on the gravel behind Barnwell and then a large shadow coalesced in front of the car.

"Shit-shoveler, huh?"

It was Fester. Oh god. He was going to die. They were all going to die. From what he'd heard about Fester, he could take all of them.

"You know, I've heard just about all I want to hear from you and your pussy friends," Fester said. "You live up in them fancy houses in them new developments and you think you're hot shit. People like me and Buford grew up around here. We never asked for none of your kind to come here. But seeing as how you have, I guess we should give you the kind of welcome you deserve."

Blondie's heart was a runaway colt. It was tripping so fast he expected a geyser of blood to spurt from the top of his head. Maybe he'd have a heart attack, he thought. That would spare him having all his bones broken and becoming a quadriplegic cauliflower with tubes of plant food in his abdomen.

Blondie staggered back a few feet. Fester took two slow steps toward him.

"There's more of us here," Feller called from behind him.

Blondie was surprised—and impressed. His buddies were risking their necks calling out to Fester like that.

"Am I supposed to be afraid?" Fester scoffed. "You're just a bunch of little high school weenies. Anyway, we're not so alone, either."

Blondie heard a couple more doors open behind Barnwell, although no one came forward. Maybe it would be a Mexican standoff, Blondie hoped.

"I want this one," Fester called to the phantoms behind him. Blondie knew he meant him. The sand had run out of the hourglass. All the dodging and darting he'd done for seventeen years had merely postponed the inevitable, perhaps made it worse. Instead of facing and conquering any number of lesser tormentors, perhaps building some confidence and fighting skill, he'd avoided them all only to face the biggest gorilla of them all with nary a split decision behind him.

Fester sauntered toward him. Blondie couldn't see his face, but he could see the wide expanse of his shoulders, the square cut of his jaw, the massive size of his fists. There was nowhere left to hide, no place to retreat. The choice that remained was whether to die an ignominious coward or a courageous fool. It was an easy decision.

Blondie jumped at Fester, kicking out his leg and yelling "Long Duk Dong" as loud as he could.

Fester snickered.

"Where the fuck do you get off? You don't know karate from your ass."

"How do you know?"

"Because I've been studying it."

Was Blondie hearing right? This guy, who looked like he ate automobile grills for breakfast, knew karate? Blondie's prospects were worse than he'd thought. It was no longer a case of getting beat up. It was a matter of keeping his corpse in one piece. Time to run.

Blondie turned and smacked into Dispatch.

"What're you doing out here?"

Dispatch ignored him.

"You know what I heard, Fester?" Dispatch said to him. "I heard your mother swims after troop ships."

Blondie gasped. What was Dispatch doing? He was waving a red flag in the beast's face.

"I also heard your older sister gangbanged the whole football team a few years ago."

Fester roared.

"I'm going to kill you first, you little weasel."

"Don't be mad at me," Dispatch said in a calm voice. "I just said I heard it. I didn't say I said it."

What was he doing? Imitating Barnwell?

"Yeah? Well, I'd sure like to meet the guy who did."

A deep voice boomed from behind Blondie.

"It was me. I said it."

"Pulaski," Fester said, startled.

"Yeah, it's me, you bona fide turd-for-a-brain."

The P-mobile's lights came on, turning the space between the two cars into a blazing arena. Dispatch grabbed Blondie's arm and pulled him to one side.

"Where'd he come from?" Blondie asked Dispatch.

"Feller said Barnwell would pull a double cross. He asked me to get Mountain to come."

So Feller had had a plan...a real plan.

"Why's he helping us?"

"Because he hates Fester's guts. Fester knocked up his sister."

The two gladiators jockeyed for position in the circle of light. Blondie was spellbound. He'd never been around a big fight, not one between two guys with reputations. The air crackled with tension.

"Well, I guess it had to happen sooner or later," Fester said to Pulaski.

"It's been too long coming for me, Fester."

Blondie heard other people arriving. Lovers from all over the quarry had interrupted their probing and parrying to watch Merwin Fester and Mountain Pulaski square off.

"You don't know fuck about karate," Pulaski said to Fester. "You couldn't even spell it."

"Your sister wasn't any brain trust neither," Fester replied. "If she had any smarts, she wouldn't have got herself knocked up."

"Shut up about my sister," Pulaski yelled. He rushed Fester.

There was a resounding crack as Fester hit Pulaski flush on the cheek. Blondie's stomach clenched. Fester hit Pulaski again, in the stomach. The blow sounded like a butcher's axe striking raw meat.

Pulaski doubled over for an instant, then stood back up. Fester hit him a glancing blow to the face as Mountain dodged. Then Mountain reached out and grabbed Fester in a crushing bear hug. He squeezed Fester tighter and tighter. Fester gasped for air. Just when Blondie thought Fester would pass out, Pulaski dropped him to the ground and jumped on his chest with both feet. Fester groaned. Pulaski squatted over Fester and began pummeling his face. Blondie watched a trickle of blood flow from Fester's nose and turn into a river.

A motor started. The headlights on the far side of the arena began to recede. Purdy and Barnwell were deserting their pal.

Blondie ran to Mountain and grabbed his arm.

"You better stop," he said, "or you're going to have a homicide on your hands."

Mountain shook his head as if waking from a dream. He rolled off Fester and pulled himself upright.

"Stay away from these guys," he said, sweeping his arm to include the whole group. "They're my friends."

"Suits me," Fester wheezed. "I don't want anything to do with them."

Fester looked around.

"Where're Barnwell and Purdy?" he mumbled, his mouth full of marbles.

"They ran out on you, buddy," Pulaski said.

"How'll I get home?"

"I'm sure you can walk five miles. You seem to be in good shape."

"I'll kill that Barnwell," Fester muttered.

On the way home, Blondie asked Feller why he hadn't told him Pulaski was in the Edsel .

"You might not have stood up to Barnwell by yourself."

"Hey, I did, didn't I?"

Blondie felt brighter than he had for a long time.

* * * * * * * * *

Blondie knew something was wrong the minute he entered school. There was an eerie silence in the halls. Boys congregated in open doorways, frightened looks in their eyes. Girls wandered aimlessly with tears on their cheeks. It was Hiroshima. A bomb had dropped.

Feller rushed up to him.

"Have you heard?"

"Heard what?"

"Bobby Clements ran head-on into a bridge abutment Saturday night."

Blondie was stunned. A buzzing sound filled his ears.

"He's dead?"

"He was going about 70 miles an hour."

The buzzing grew louder, filling up Blondie's head so that Feller's words had no place to go. They made no sense, anyway. What he'd said was as incomprehensible as someone saying, "President Kennedy's been shot." People like Bobby didn't die. They were immortals. If someone like him could die, then they were all in peril.

He wandered down the hall with Feller toward first-period trig in a trance. He scarcely noticed his fellow students, who appeared as zombie-like as he felt. Except for Tammy. She was in a circle of girls sobbing her heart out. Well, why not? She'd cheered for Bobby all year long at almost every sports event.

Blondie wanted desperately to talk to Grouper. He'd be able to add some perspective to this tragedy. Blondie caught up with him in Mrs. Buckley's English class and asked if he'd heard about Bobby's accident.

"Maybe it wasn't an accident," he whispered.

Bobby killed himself? It was unimaginable. Blondie was sure, for once, Grouper was mistaken. The Bobby Clementses of the world didn't kill themselves. They had no reason. People like Bobby owned the world.

But throughout the day—a day marked by hushed classes and fumbling explanations by teachers—bits of information settled like fallout. And each one chipped at Bobby's smooth hard image.

Bobby's scholarship had fallen through because of his knee. Ethel was going to New York to be a fashion model. She'd told Bobby she'd be dating other guys. Someone even said Bobby'd been smoking marijuana with a some college guys earlier in the evening.

"It m-must've b-been the drugs," Shakes opined at lunch.

"If Ethel Philbin cut my water off, I'd want to end it, too," Dispatch said.

"Maybe it was being a high school hero with no vision of glory ahead," Feller chipped in.

Blondie didn't know what to think. He asked Grouper for his take on the matter.

"I don't know why he did it, but I'm sure he felt he had good reason," Grouper said.

"That's it?" Blondie was irked. "You don't even sound like you care."

"I liked Bobby. I'm sorry he won't be around. But I also feel I have to honor his decision. A person must have some shred of free will."

What the hell was Grouper talking about? For once, Blondie found the big fellow's explanation unsatisfactory.

"Since you're so smart," he said acidly, "you should be able to apply some law to Bobby's death."

Grouper nodded, then hunched over in his seat for a long time.

"**People die.**" he finally said.

"That's it? That's not very profound."

"Perhaps not, but it's the most absolute law in life."

Blondie was just as disappointed by Grouper's assessment of the big fight. He said he doubted it marked the end of any of their troubles with billies. As far as Blondie was concerned, Grouper'd missed the whole point, which was that Blondie had avoided getting killed and it looked like Barnwell and Purdy were off his back for good. Indeed, the next time he ran into them in the hallway, they just gave him dirty looks and kept on walking. Furthermore, because there'd been so many witnesses to the showdown, the B and F Club had achieved a touch of notoriety. Blondie had even heard himself spoken of as "ready to do battle with Merwin Fester," a rumor he did nothing to dispel. He enjoyed seeing kids move aside when he walked down the hall.

"You're a genius, Feller," Blondie told him at lunch the next day. Feller didn't demur. But Blondie had scant time to dwell on the fight. The school year was coming to a close. Graduation was less than two weeks away. Before that came finals—and the prom was next weekend.

Feller told Blondie he'd invited Delores.

"Don't you care what people are going to think?" Blondie asked him.

"You know, I really don't."

Blondie admired Feller for that. Anyway, he had no grounds for questioning Feller's choice for a date when he was taking Phyllis.

His mom didn't care whom he took. She was ecstatic that he was going at all.

"This shows that you're one of them at last," she said.

One of whom? She didn't get it. He didn't want to be part of Fenton High, just the B & F Club.

His dad showed his support by offering to let him drive the Pontiac.

The school rocked with anticipation. "What should I wear?" "Who's taking whom?" "Where're you going afterward?" Almost everyone was involved in some project in support of the "Spring Fling," as Mrs. Buckley had named it, displaying, Blondie believed, the limits of her creativity. Boys' Shop was building sets for the dance. Art Class was making decorations. The Electronics Club was wiring the gym for sound. Others were assigned to set up chairs or serve punch the night of the prom.

Midway through the week, Mrs. Buckley announced the King and Queen of Spring, the lucky couple who would preside over the Prom. To no one's surprise, Ethel Philbin was named Queen. The surprise was whom was named King. It was Bobby Clements. Most everyone thought that was a classy move. He would've earned the title if he'd stuck around. Of course, it meant Ethel had to sit on a dais beside an empty throne. Blondie wondered how she'd feel about that.

"The pr-prom. Big f-fucking deal," Shakes said at lunch midway through the week.

"You're not going then?" Feller said to him..

"I'd r-rather w-watch two fleas f-fuck."

Blondie could understand his feelings. He hadn't had a date since Janine Raznosky threw him over months before.

"How about you, Brick?" Feller asked.

"Count me out. There's a triple boxing card in Baltimore Saturday night."

"How about you, Grouper?"

"I'll be there," was all he'd say.

Of course, Dispatch was taking Meryl, who had outraged almost everyone in the Club by proclaiming her "engagement" to Dispatch all over school, even though Dispatch couldn't afford an engagement ring. That didn't bother Blondie, thought. They *were* getting married in a little over two weeks. That was good enough for him.

Blondie was glad no one had asked whom he was taking. Of course, everyone knew it was Phyllis. He just couldn't stand to say it aloud.

But the night wasn't going to be a total loss. He and Feller had come up with a plan. About eleven, Delores was going to "get sick" and Blondie was going to have to drive her and Feller home. He'd offer to take Phyllis home, too, if she wanted. But he was prepared to be gallant and let her stay at the dance alone if she wanted. Heck, he'd even offer her taxi fare.

Once they were rid of Phyllis, they'd pick Flossie up at her house and go skinny-dipping in some pond Delores knew about. Blondie'd never done that before. He found the idea both exciting and scary. He was excited at the thought of watching two naked girls traipse around in the moonlight. At the same time, it made him nervous to think about two people seeing him naked who'd never seen him that way before. He didn't expect any disparaging remarks, though. They were all at risk.

Blondie was a little concerned that Purdy and Barnwell might show up, but Grouper told him not to worry.

"Billies don't go to proms," he assured him. "They don't like to dress up."

"I don't see why you're so afraid of Barnwell," Feller said to Blondie. "You've got four inches on him and he's just as thin as you are."

They were at Feller's house, lying on the twin beds in the attic room, with the overhead light on. Blondie'd asked to spend Friday night with Feller. He didn't feel like being alone with his folks the night before his execution.

"I don't like to fight," Blondie said.

"No one does. But sometimes you have to."

Why was everyone so brave was someone else was doing the fighting?

Feller's question was a good one, though. Why did Barnwell inspire such fear in him? Was it because he seemed so ready to fight? Or was it just Blondie's cowardice?

"Barnwell was afraid that night when Brick went after him," Feller said What we need to do is to make him a little more afraid of you."

"How?"

"I don't know. Let me think about it."

Blondie watched while Feller thought. After a while he asked him how he was doing.

"Nothing yet."

"Grouper thinks it's all pretty dumb," Blondie said.

"What is?"

"Squabbling with Barnwell, chasing after girls, getting drunk...."

"Grouper's been known to get drunk."

Blondie flopped over on his back and put his hands behind his head.

"Is this the way people get to be adults?" Blondie asked.

Feller laughed.

"In Fenton, it is."

"Has anyone from Fenton ever amounted to anything?"

"Are you kidding?"

That's what Blondie figured. Fenton didn't provide the proper culture for greatness. It was the wrong petri dish.

Quicker than Blondie thought possible, Saturday evening rolled around. There was a notable lack of chatter in the P-mobile as Dispatch pointed it down Oakspring Lane toward the quarry. Grouper had refused to come—he said he couldn't stand the sight of blood, especially that of his friends. Each of the rest of the gang had assured Blondie he had a chance, but Blondie could tell none of them would put money on it.

Only Feller seemed in good spirits. He'd told Blondie he'd come up with an idea that might help him. But Feller said he wouldn't divulge it until they were near the quarry.

Dusk was approaching. Blondie looked out the window at the high scudding clouds streaking across the moon. New leaves tossed against the silver sky like dark schools of fish. Ahead, Blondie saw the dark tunnel of trees that ended at the quarry. The P-mobile plunged onward into that heart of darkness.

Blondie could wait no longer.

"Are you going to tell about this secret strategy or yours before or after Barnwell beats me up?" he asked Feller.

"No need to be sarcastic. Okay, here it is. Yesterday, I told Harold Bull you were a karate expert."

"That's it? That's your big plan?" Blondie's voice rose.

"Calm down. Bull's a friend of Barnwell's, see. I bet anything he passed my information along."

"But I'm not a karate expert. I don't know anything about karate."

"Just act like you do. Put your fist out like this," Feller said, unaware his hand was lost in shadow, "and put one leg in front of the other with your knees bent. Then, yell out some Chinese phrases."

"I don't know any Chinese phrases."

"Try 'Moo Goo Gai Pan' or 'Foo Yung.'"

"Those are Chinese meals," Blondie retorted.

"You think Barnwell knows Chinese? Barnwell doesn't even know American. He couldn't tell chicken-fried steak from chicken shit."

"What's this charade supposed to accomplish?"

"If it works, Barnwell may back away from the fight."

"And if he doesn't?"

"Then you may have a problem."

There was no sign of Barnwell or Purdy when they arrived at the quarry. There were few cars at all. It was too early for the neckers. Even in Fenton, etiquette required taking one's date out for a shake and fries before trying to rip her clothes off.

Dispatch circled the quarry, an ominous black hole in the twilight. He pulled into an open area, about forty or fifty feet from a cream-colored Edsel. No one spoke. No one opened a beer from the case they'd brought along.

"For God's sakes, you guys, loosen up," Blondie squawked. "Go ahead and get drunk. Whatever's going to happen isn't going to take long, so don't plan your whole evening around it."

Brick slapped him on the back.

"That's the spirit, Blondie. It only hurts for a while, right?"

"That isn't what I meant."

"Maybe B-buford w-won't show," Shakes offered.

Shakes had become a real booster of Blondie's since finding out Blondie had persuaded the Bear to let him back into school.

"Yeah, maybe Buford's not so gutsy as he talks," Feller said.

A quarter hour later, a set of low beams crawled around the bend, followed by another. The first set stopped thirty feet away, shining themselves at the P-mobile. The dark void behind the lights was the shape of Purdy's truck. A door opened. A moment later, a shadow formed in front the lights.

"Okay, Reimer, let's see your stuff," the shadow figure called.

It was Barnwell all right.

All heads turned toward Blondie.

"Do what I told you, Blondie, and good luck," said Feller, holding out his hand.

"Y-yeah, g-good luck," Shakes added, offering his hand as well. Dispatch and Brick followed suit.

"Come on, you guys, quit being so fucking grim. I have a chance."

"Sure," Brick agreed half-heartedly. "You have a chance."

The car door seemed to weighed a ton. Like the door of a vault, he thought, a *funeral* vault. Blondie stumbled on the gravel as he stepped from the P-mobile. Barnwell remained a silhouette against the glaring headlights.

"You wanted me, Reimer," Barnwell taunted. "Well, here I am. Come and get me."

Blondie didn't move. He didn't want to move. He couldn't move. He told himself the worst that would happen was that he'd get beat up. That didn't help.

"Not so brave when there's no one beside you, are you, Mr. Giraffe? What would it take to get you mad? Calling you yellow? Well, I think you're yellow."

Blondie felt long roots growing out of his sneakers, planting him in place.

"I saw you lying by that scaggy Phyllis Scarff at the picnic," Barnwell continued. "Are you sweet on her? Do you ever get in her snatch? I wonder if it's as ugly as her face."

Was Barnwell crazy? Did he think insulting Phyllis would make him mad?

"Or is it that cute little Tammy Hollander you're sweet on? She's just so sweet…." Buford's voice was mocking, probing.

Blondie knew what Barnwell was doing. But he still didn't like the jerk talking about Tammy.

"You know what? I heard Tammy sucks dicks."

"LIAR!" Blondie screamed out.

"Oh, did we hit a little nerve there. It's true, though. I know a guy can prove it."

"You don't know shit, Barnwell," Blondie snarled, surprised and relieved to feel genuine anger awakening his leaden legs.

"What's that you said?"

"You heard me."

"No I didn't. Come a little closer and tell me."

Blondie took six or seven steps toward Barnwell, until he was an arm's length away. Recalling Feller's counsel, Blondie leapt into the air, shot one fist out and yelled "Moo Goo Gai Pan." He landed with one foot raised in menace. He gave a low growl, then added "Foo Yung!"

Barnwell seemed confused, somewhat wary. Feller's ploy was working.

"Take back what you said about Tammy," he barked at Barnwell.

"It's true."

"She wouldn't even go out with you, let alone do something like you said."

"I didn't say it was me."

"Well, whoever told you that is a fucking liar."

"What did you say?" Barnwell asked him, not in a challenging way, but as if he hadn't heard.

Christ, Blondie wondered, was he deaf?

"I said whoever said Tammy does what you said is a fucking liar."

"Is that right?" Buford asked in a merry tone.

"You bet your ass that's right," Blondie retorted.

Why was Barnwell acting so happy?

"As a matter of fact, it was Merwin Fester."

Merwin Fester? What was he saying? Tammy would never go out with a scumbag like him. Her father wouldn't let her, anyway.

"Tammy'd never go out with a shit-shoveler like him and you know it."

"What'd you call him?"

"A shit-shoveler. Isn't that what he does? Clean horse's stables?"

When Blondie heard a door open from behind Purdy's truck, his instincts told him he'd made a big mistake. Slow steps crunched on the gravel behind Barnwell and then a large shadow coalesced in front of the car.

"Shit-shoveler, huh?"

It was Fester. Oh god. He was going to die. They were all going to die. From what he'd heard about Fester, he could take all of them.

"You know, I've heard just about all I want to hear from you and your pussy friends," Fester said. "You live up in them fancy houses in them new developments and you think you're hot shit. People like me and Buford grew up around here. We never asked for none of your kind to come here. But seeing as how you have, I guess we should give you the kind of welcome you deserve."

Blondie's heart was a runaway colt. It was tripping so fast he expected a geyser of blood to spurt from the top of his head. Maybe he'd have a heart attack, he thought. That would spare him having all his bones broken and becoming a quadriplegic cauliflower with tubes of plant food in his abdomen.

Blondie staggered back a few feet. Fester took two slow steps toward him.

"There's more of us here," Feller called from behind him.

Blondie was surprised—and impressed. His buddies were risking their necks calling out to Fester like that.

"Am I supposed to be afraid?" Fester scoffed. "You're just a bunch of little high school weenies. Anyway, we're not so alone, either."

Blondie heard a couple more doors open behind Barnwell, although no one came forward. Maybe it would be a Mexican standoff, Blondie hoped.

"I want this one," Fester called to the phantoms behind him. Blondie knew he meant him. The sand had run out of the hourglass. All the dodging and darting he'd done for seventeen years had merely postponed the inevitable, perhaps made it worse. Instead of facing and conquering any number of lesser tormentors, perhaps building some confidence and fighting skill, he'd avoided them all only to face the biggest gorilla of them all with nary a split decision behind him.

Fester sauntered toward him. Blondie couldn't see his face, but he could see the wide expanse of his shoulders, the square cut of his jaw, the massive size of his fists. There was nowhere left to hide, no place to retreat. The choice that remained was whether to die an ignominious coward or a courageous fool. It was an easy decision.

Blondie jumped at Fester, kicking out his leg and yelling "Long Duk Dong" as loud as he could.

Fester snickered.

"Where the fuck do you get off? You don't know karate from your ass."

"How do you know?"

"Because I've been studying it."

Was Blondie hearing right? This guy, who looked like he ate automobile grills for breakfast, knew karate? Blondie's prospects were worse than he'd thought. It was no longer a case of getting beat up. It was a matter of keeping his corpse in one piece. Time to run.

Blondie turned and smacked into Dispatch.

"What're you doing out here?"

Dispatch ignored him.

"You know what I heard, Fester?" Dispatch said to him. "I heard your mother swims after troop ships."

Blondie gasped. What was Dispatch doing? He was waving a red flag in the beast's face.

"I also heard your older sister gangbanged the whole football team a few years ago."

Fester roared.

"I'm going to kill you first, you little weasel."

"Don't be mad at me," Dispatch said in a calm voice. "I just said I heard it. I didn't say I said it."

What was he doing? Imitating Barnwell?

"Yeah? Well, I'd sure like to meet the guy who did."

A deep voice boomed from behind Blondie.

"It was me. I said it."

"Pulaski," Fester said, startled.

"Yeah, it's me, you bona fide turd-for-a-brain."

The P-mobile's lights came on, turning the space between the two cars into a blazing arena. Dispatch grabbed Blondie's arm and pulled him to one side.

"Where'd he come from?" Blondie asked Dispatch.

"Feller said Barnwell would pull a double cross. He asked me to get Mountain to come."

So Feller had had a plan...a real plan.

"Why's he helping us?"

"Because he hates Fester's guts. Fester knocked up his sister."

The two gladiators jockeyed for position in the circle of light. Blondie was spellbound. He'd never been around a big fight, not one between two guys with reputations. The air crackled with tension.

"Well, I guess it had to happen sooner or later," Fester said to Pulaski.

"It's been too long coming for me, Fester."

Blondie heard other people arriving. Lovers from all over the quarry had interrupted their probing and parrying to watch Merwin Fester and Mountain Pulaski square off.

"You don't know fuck about karate," Pulaski said to Fester. "You couldn't even spell it."

"Your sister wasn't any brain trust neither," Fester replied. "If she had any smarts, she wouldn't have got herself knocked up."

"Shut up about my sister," Pulaski yelled. He rushed Fester.

There was a resounding crack as Fester hit Pulaski flush on the cheek. Blondie's stomach clenched. Fester hit Pulaski again, in the stomach. The blow sounded like a butcher's axe striking raw meat.

Pulaski doubled over for an instant, then stood back up. Fester hit him a glancing blow to the face as Mountain dodged. Then Mountain reached out and grabbed Fester in a crushing bear hug. He squeezed Fester tighter and tighter. Fester gasped for air. Just when Blondie thought Fester would pass out, Pulaski dropped him to the ground and jumped on his chest with both feet. Fester groaned. Pulaski squatted over Fester and began pummeling his face. Blondie watched a trickle of blood flow from Fester's nose and turn into a river.

A motor started. The headlights on the far side of the arena began to recede. Purdy and Barnwell were deserting their pal.

Blondie ran to Mountain and grabbed his arm.

"You better stop," he said, "or you're going to have a homicide on your hands."

Mountain shook his head as if waking from a dream. He rolled off Fester and pulled himself upright.

"Stay away from these guys," he said, sweeping his arm to include the whole group. "They're my friends."

"Suits me," Fester wheezed. "I don't want anything to do with them."

Fester looked around.

"Where're Barnwell and Purdy?" he mumbled, his mouth full of marbles.

"They ran out on you, buddy," Pulaski said.

"How'll I get home?"

"I'm sure you can walk five miles. You seem to be in good shape."

"I'll kill that Barnwell," Fester muttered.

On the way home, Blondie asked Feller why he hadn't told him Pulaski was in the Edsel.

"You might not have stood up to Barnwell by yourself."

"Hey, I did, didn't I?"

Blondie felt brighter than he had for a long time.

* * * * * * * * *

Blondie knew something was wrong the minute he entered school. There was an eerie silence in the halls. Boys congregated in open doorways, frightened looks in their eyes. Girls wandered aimlessly with tears on their cheeks. It was Hiroshima. A bomb had dropped.

Feller rushed up to him.

"Have you heard?"

"Heard what?"

"Bobby Clements ran head-on into a bridge abutment Saturday night."

Blondie was stunned. A buzzing sound filled his ears.

"He's dead?"

"He was going about 70 miles an hour."

The buzzing grew louder, filling up Blondie's head so that Feller's words had no place to go. They made no sense, anyway. What he'd said was as incomprehensible as someone saying, "President Kennedy's been shot." People like Bobby didn't die. They were immortals. If someone like him could die, then they were all in peril.

He wandered down the hall with Feller toward first-period trig in a trance. He scarcely noticed his fellow students, who appeared as zombie-like as he felt. Except for Tammy. She was in a circle of girls sobbing her heart out. Well, why not? She'd cheered for Bobby all year long at almost every sports event.

Blondie wanted desperately to talk to Grouper. He'd be able to add some perspective to this tragedy. Blondie caught up with him in Mrs. Buckley's English class and asked if he'd heard about Bobby's accident.

"Maybe it wasn't an accident," he whispered.

Bobby killed himself? It was unimaginable. Blondie was sure, for once, Grouper was mistaken. The Bobby Clementses of the world didn't kill themselves. They had no reason. People like Bobby owned the world.

But throughout the day—a day marked by hushed classes and fumbling explanations by teachers—bits of information settled like fallout. And each one chipped at Bobby's smooth hard image.

Bobby's scholarship had fallen through because of his knee. Ethel was going to New York to be a fashion model. She'd told Bobby she'd be dating other guys. Someone even said Bobby'd been smoking marijuana with a some college guys earlier in the evening.

"It m-must've b-been the drugs," Shakes opined at lunch.

"If Ethel Philbin cut my water off, I'd want to end it, too," Dispatch said.

"Maybe it was being a high school hero with no vision of glory ahead," Feller chipped in.

Blondie didn't know what to think. He asked Grouper for his take on the matter.

"I don't know why he did it, but I'm sure he felt he had good reason," Grouper said.

"That's it?" Blondie was irked. "You don't even sound like you care."

"I liked Bobby. I'm sorry he won't be around. But I also feel I have to honor his decision. A person must have some shred of free will."

What the hell was Grouper talking about? For once, Blondie found the big fellow's explanation unsatisfactory.

"Since you're so smart," he said acidly, "you should be able to apply some law to Bobby's death."

Grouper nodded, then hunched over in his seat for a long time.

"**People die.**" he finally said.

"That's it? That's not very profound."

"Perhaps not, but it's the most absolute law in life."

Blondie was just as disappointed by Grouper's assessment of the big fight. He said he doubted it marked the end of any of their troubles with billies. As far as Blondie was concerned, Grouper'd missed the whole point, which was that Blondie had avoided getting killed and it looked like Barnwell and Purdy were off his back for good. Indeed, the next time he ran into them in the hallway, they just gave him dirty looks and kept on walking. Furthermore, because there'd been so many witnesses to the showdown, the B and F Club had achieved a touch of notoriety. Blondie had even heard himself spoken of as "ready to do battle with Merwin Fester," a rumor he did nothing to dispel. He enjoyed seeing kids move aside when he walked down the hall.

"You're a genius, Feller," Blondie told him at lunch the next day. Feller didn't demur. But Blondie had scant time to dwell on the fight. The school year was coming to a close. Graduation was less than two weeks away. Before that came finals—and the prom was next weekend.

Feller told Blondie he'd invited Delores.

"Don't you care what people are going to think?" Blondie asked him.

"You know, I really don't."

Blondie admired Feller for that. Anyway, he had no grounds for questioning Feller's choice for a date when he was taking Phyllis.

His mom didn't care whom he took. She was ecstatic that he was going at all.

"This shows that you're one of them at last," she said.

One of whom? She didn't get it. He didn't want to be part of Fenton High, just the B & F Club.

His dad showed his support by offering to let him drive the Pontiac.

The school rocked with anticipation. "What should I wear?" "Who's taking whom?" "Where're you going afterward?" Almost everyone was involved in some project in support of the "Spring Fling," as Mrs. Buckley had named it, displaying, Blondie believed, the limits of her creativity. Boys' Shop was building sets for the dance. Art Class was making decorations. The Electronics Club was wiring the gym for sound. Others were assigned to set up chairs or serve punch the night of the prom.

Midway through the week, Mrs. Buckley announced the King and Queen of Spring, the lucky couple who would preside over the Prom. To no one's surprise, Ethel Philbin was named Queen. The surprise was whom was named King. It was Bobby Clements. Most everyone thought that was a classy move. He would've earned the title if he'd stuck around. Of course, it meant Ethel had to sit on a dais beside an empty throne. Blondie wondered how she'd feel about that.

"The pr-prom. Big f-fucking deal," Shakes said at lunch midway through the week.

"You're not going then?" Feller said to him..

"I'd r-rather w-watch two fleas f-fuck."

Blondie could understand his feelings. He hadn't had a date since Janine Raznosky threw him over months before.

"How about you, Brick?" Feller asked.

"Count me out. There's a triple boxing card in Baltimore Saturday night."

"How about you, Grouper?"

"I'll be there," was all he'd say.

Of course, Dispatch was taking Meryl, who had outraged almost everyone in the Club by proclaiming her "engagement" to Dispatch all over school, even though Dispatch couldn't afford an engagement ring. That didn't bother Blondie, thought. They *were* getting married in a little over two weeks. That was good enough for him.

Blondie was glad no one had asked whom he was taking. Of course, everyone knew it was Phyllis. He just couldn't stand to say it aloud.

But the night wasn't going to be a total loss. He and Feller had come up with a plan. About eleven, Delores was going to "get sick" and Blondie was going to have to drive her and Feller home. He'd offer to take Phyllis home, too, if she wanted. But he was prepared to be gallant and let her stay at the dance alone if she wanted. Heck, he'd even offer her taxi fare.

Once they were rid of Phyllis, they'd pick Flossie up at her house and go skinny-dipping in some pond Delores knew about. Blondie'd never done that before. He found the idea both exciting and scary. He was excited at the thought of watching two naked girls traipse around in the moonlight. At the same time, it made him nervous to think about two people seeing him naked who'd never seen him that way before. He didn't expect any disparaging remarks, though. They were all at risk.

Blondie was a little concerned that Purdy and Barnwell might show up, but Grouper told him not to worry.

"Billies don't go to proms," he assured him. "They don't like to dress up."

Chapter Thirty

"What do you think?" Phyllis asked, posing for him in the entrance to her living room. She was wearing an old-fashioned satin gown with puff shoulders and a slight—and as far as Blondie could tell, unnecessary—décolletage. It was orange-pink with lace around the sleeves and hem. Her face was radiant.

What could he say? He thought it was the most ridiculous outfit he'd ever seen. But he couldn't tell her that, not on her prom night.

Phyllis' father, a short, plump, balding fellow with a camera, smiled at Blondie and waited for his answer.

"You look super," Blondie said. He remembered what Grouper'd told him once: "**With ugly girls, you always have to lie.**"

Phyllis beamed at him. For an instant, Blondie was happy for her—and he knew he should feel flattered she was so proud to be with him. But he didn't want to carry his magnanimity too far. She *was* unattractive and she *was* his date.

He reminded himself to be patient. Under the scheme he and Feller had concocted, three hours was the most he'd have to endure with Phyllis. Then, freedom and fun!

Blondie suffered three flashbulbs in the face before old man Scarff put his camera away. Then Phyllis' mother, a tall woman with a hatchet nose, gave Phyllis her good-bye.

"My little girl.... a grown woman," she gushed.

When Blondie opened the car door for Phyllis, he caught Feller with his hand up Delores' skirt. Blondie prayed Phyllis hadn't seen that. She might want the same thing from him. Feller had been acting goofy ever since he'd picked him up at Delores' house. He suspected Feller had dipped into old man Humphries' liquor cabinet.

Miss Darlington was collecting tickets at the gym door. A man about her age in a crew cut and glasses stood beside her. Miss Darlington introduced him as her date. He looked like someone who might treat her right. Blondie hoped so.

"Oh my god, it's beautiful," Phyllis said when she stepped inside the gym.

The walls were covered with huge sheets of butcher paper jam-packed with crayon trees and flowers. Here and there a rabbit or fawn peeked from the foliage. Real tulips in pots surrounded a portable platform. In the center was a large wooden rose. Two of its petals had been sculpted into seats.

"Jesus Christ!" Feller exclaimed. "Look at that fucking flower!"

"Paul, watch your language!" Phyllis scolded.

"You know what it reminds me of, all pink and opened up...." Blondie heard Feller whisper to Delores.

A half-pickled Feller. Just what he didn't need. Blondie was depending on Feller to maintain some decorum. It would be impossible for him to handle the evening if Feller didn't. On the other hand, Blondie wondered if he could make it through the evening sober himself. He remembered Dispatch's vow to smuggle a pint into the dance "come hell or high water."

"Grain alcohol, too," he'd bragged. "My brother brought some home from college."

Blondie didn't see Dispatch anywhere. Anyway, he wasn't sure how much he wanted to risk getting caught drinking. Another screw-up and he'd have to spend the summer with his folks.

As Phyllis chattered away, Blondie canvassed the scene. He had to admit with all the decorations and all the kids dressed to the nines, the occasion seemed adult, almost elegant. Maybe they were growing up.

Blondie spied Grouper dipping from a punch bowl. In a tux, he looked more like a killer whale than a grouper. He offered the drink to a tall girl beside him. She had bony shoulders and buck teeth. Blondie guessed she was his date. He saw Rudy Tilly, too. He appeared to be staring at him.

Then Tammy walked in the door and everyone else disappeared. She was wearing a white silk gown that tapered to her waist, then fell straight to the floor. Her dark hair was pulled high atop her head in tight curls. A thin gold necklace ringed her neck. She was more than a queen tonight. She was an *empress*.

When he finally was able to take his eyes from her otherworldly aura, he wanted to ram his head into the gym's concrete wall. Holding her arm, squiring her around with the smug smile of someone who'd just leaped two social classes in one bound, was Harold Slusher! Blondie couldn't believe it. Harold Slusher. Sure, he was junior class president, but what a geek! He had a flat top, acne, and thick glasses. That added up to zero.

As soon as Tammy saw Phyllis, she dragged Harold over to where she and Blondie were standing with Feller and Delores.

"You look luscious," Tammy said to Phyllis. Tammy gave Blondie a warm smile. Was because she was pleased to see him or because he'd performed the saintly sacrifice of inviting Phyllis to the prom?

"Say hi to them, Harold," Tammy said.

"Hi," Harold said disinterestedly.

The lights dimmed and the band began to play. Blondie felt the tune pass through him like a knife. It was "The Way You Look Tonight"—his and Tammy's song, even if she didn't know it.

Blondie watched as Harold led Tammy out onto the floor. Agony of agonies. His true love not only was dancing with someone else to their song, she was dancing with a geek.

"Why'd Tammy come with him?" Blondie asked Phyllis.

"What's wrong with Harold?"

"He's a nerd."

"Well, I think he's nice…" That figured. "…besides, he was the only one who asked her."

"The only one who…. ?" More anguish. Blondie contemplated the wall again. With a good running start, he could knock himself unconscious. Then he could quit thinking the obvious: if Tammy'd accepted an invitation from Harold, she would surely have accepted one from him.

"Aren't you going to ask me to dance?" Phyllis asked Blondie as the song drew to a close.

Blondie'd never thought about that prospect. When he'd contemplated the prom at all, which he'd tried to avoid doing, he'd seen it as little more than a blur from eight o'clock to eleven when Delores was scheduled to get sick.

Phyllis tugged Blondie onto the floor and placed his arms around her. Blondie gazed forlornly over her shoulder at Tammy and Harold as they danced. It was an outrage against nature. He and Tammy belonged together.

"Isn't it something?" Phyllis said. "Everyone thinks Tammy's so popular and just one boy asked her to the prom."

"Well, how many asked you?" Blondie snapped.

"Two—plus you, of course."

Two others? That was preposterous. Who else could be so demented?

"Jerry Caldane was one," Phyllis said.

Shakes did like Phyllis. Grouper's words came back to him: "One man's dog is another man's queen." And, tonight, Shakes was at home alone and Blondie was taking his dream girl to the prom—and hating every minute.

"Who else?" Blondie demanded.

"That's my secret." She gave him a coy look.

He wanted to get away from her worse than ever. His first break came when Feller announced he had to take a leak. Blondie immediately discovered the same urge.

"Are you having fun?" Feller asked impishly as they walked away from their dates.

"I'd rather spend the evening with a proctologist."

Dispatch called to them from the refreshment table where he stood with Meryl. She watched the two of them approach with unveiled distaste. In her tight-fitting lavender gown, she looked like a linebacker in drag. If she was pregnant, it didn't show.

"Pour yourselves some ginger ale," Dispatch said when they reached him.

"We already have to pee," Feller whispered to him.

"Do as I say." Dispatch winked.

Blondie and Feller poured some Canada Dry into plastic cups and headed for the bathroom. Dispatch followed behind, with a mischievous look on his face.

The restroom was crowded with formally attired and serious-looking young men preening and combing their hair, or holding their members daintily over the urinals.

Dispatch shoved Blondie and Feller into a stall and shut the door. The three of them crowded around the toilet while Dispatch removed a small silver flask from his inside pocket.

"One hundred and ninety proof," he said to Blondie. "It'll make Phyllis look like a princess."

"That's impossible."

"If you drink enough, it'll make you blind."

"That might do it," Blondie said. "Fill it up."

Dispatch poured a small amount into each of their glasses.

Blondie couldn't taste the alcohol. He didn't see how it could help if he couldn't even detect it. He experienced a sudden rush of mellow haziness and reassessed.

"Good stuff," Blondie complimented Dispatch. "I feel better already."

"I feel better already," Feller mimicked in a high-pitched voice.

They began to giggle.

Heavy shoes thudded outside the stall door.

"What's this, six legs in a stall?" a familiar voice exclaimed.

Was it Farber? If so, they'd been had. He'd have to go to New York with his family. Worse, he'd probably have to repeat his whole senior year with the upcoming teen mutants—and the Bear, Mrs. Buckley, Purdy, Phyllis. His mind seized up.

"Looks pretty strange to me," the voice continued. "You guys aren't up to something unnatural, are you?"

A teacher wouldn't say that. Blondie looked at Feller who looked at Dispatch who cracked open the stall door.

Grouper stood before them, grinning.

"Asshole," Dispatch said.

Feller invited Grouper into the stall. It was a mistake. They could barely move. Nonetheless, they managed to kill the remainder of the flask.

Blondie asked Grouper about his date.

"I've already forgotten her name. She's the daughter of a friend of my dad's. He was adamant that I come tonight. He said it was important I learn the social graces."

"I got some news," Dispatch announced.

"What's that?" Feller asked.

"Mountain joined the army."

What? When? He couldn't do that, Blondie thought. He was their protection.

"A couple weeks ago," Dispatch went on. "He said he was tired of the whole bullshit Fenton scene. He's going to Fort Bragg for basic training. He's going to be a paratrooper."

"Not good," Feller said, sharing Blondie's concern.

Grouper belched and said, "My friends, let us never forget this sacred moment. I anoint you all into the Sacred Order of the Commode."

"Hear, hear," Blondie added with more volume than he intended. The grain alcohol was short-circuiting his brain.

"You're primed," Feller said to Blondie.

"Where were you?" Phyllis said when Blondie returned. "I hope you weren't smoking."

"Not smoking. Better than that," Blondie replied merrily.

"You've been drinking!" Her eyes opened wide in horror. She put her nose up to his mouth. "I don't smell anything."

"Get your face away from me," Blondie thundered.

"That wasn't nice," Phyllis snapped.

Things weren't going too badly, Blondie thought. Phyllis was already pissed at him. That should make his getaway easier.

The lights came back on full bore, searing his eyeballs. When Blondie regained his sight, Miss Spalding was on the stage with a piece of paper in her hands. She walked over to a microphone.

"My dear students and fellow faculty members," she simpered. "Tonight is the last dance for our graduating seniors...."

There was a chorus of whoops and cheers. Blondie couldn't tell who was cheering harder—the seniors or the juniors.

"Soon, they'll be headed off to college or to jobs, to take their place in responsible adult society and make us all proud...."

"Who wrote that drivel?" Feller bellowed, creating a small stir.

"But they'll always remember the girl or guy of their dreams," Spalding continued.

Blondie again remembered Shakes' story of Miss Spalding's motorcycle accident. Always before, he'd imagined she'd landed on her face. Tonight, he was sure it had been her cranium.

"We, the remaining students and faculty, dedicate this song to all of you as we crown our King and Queen of Spring."

The lights dimmed again and a spotlight flooded the stage. The band began to massacre "Stardust" and a number of girls started to sob. Ethel Philbin materialized inside the circle of light, wearing a stunning blue gown and carrying a bouquet of roses, tears flowing down her cheeks. She composed herself and marched regally toward the dais.

"Isn't she beautiful...." washed back and forth across the gym, along with

"such courage" and "how can she stand to do it?"

After Ethel seated herself beside the empty chair, Miss Spalding said, "Our King can't be here with us tonight...." Her voice began to crack. "He's sitting on a much more impressive throne next to the grandest king of all...."

Ethel went to pieces and started bawling. Several of her princesses helped her to the ladies' room.

"What a travesty," Feller said.

He was right. Only Fenton High could have pulled it off.

"Don't you two have any sensitivity?" Phyllis snapped at Blondie.

"I didn't say it."

"He's your friend."

"Yeah. You should stick up for me," Feller said.

"You're drunker than I am," Blondie said.

"You're drunk?" Phyllis asked Blondie.

"Just kidding. What reason would I have to get drunk?"

Blondie looked at her through foggy eyes and smiled. Behind her, he noticed Rudy and Mary Cherry. Again, Rudy seemed to be watching him.

The band began playing "Stranger on the Shore." Blondie looked up at the colored balls of light spinning overhead—and nearly fell over.

"I thought you were a nice boy," Phyllis said to him.

"I am."

"You're smashed," she said in disgust.

"But I am nice."

She glared at him, hands on hips.

"Come on, let's dance," he said, taking her in his arms.

She hesitated for a second, then said, "Well, all right...." and gave him a hopeful smile.

Blondie began gliding back and forth with her to the music. For a moment, with the alcohol coursing through his brain, he almost forgot it was Phyllis. He tried to imagine she was Tammy, but she was too bony for that. Still trying to work himself into a friendlier mood, Blondie lowered his hand on her back. It brushed against a ball of fabric.

"What's that?" he asked.

"That's my bustle."

"Your what?"

"My bustle. Didn't you notice it at my house?"

Phyllis seemed disappointed when he admitted he hadn't.

"It's just for decoration," she explained. "Women used to wear them in ante-bellum days—before the Civil War."

"You're wearing a dress from before the Civil War?"

"Honestly, Blondie, you're acting so stupid."

"How's it stay on?"

"It just snaps on."

"Yeah?"

Curious, Blondie flicked the bustle with the back of his hand. It fell off on the floor.

"What'd you do?" Phyllis cried.

"I think I knocked your bustle off."

Phyllis looked stricken.

"Watch out!" Blondie heard someone yell, then he heard a thud.

A girl in a yellow organdy gown lay sprawled on the floor. A couple guys snickered. The fallen girl began to cry.

"What the hell is this?" her date asked, picking up the wayward bundle of cloth.

"It's her bustle," Blondie pointed at Phyllis.

"Well, put it back on your butt where it belongs," the young man growled at Phyllis, shoving it at her. She looked at it in shock, unmoving. Blondie took the offending garment.

"This is the worst night of my life," she hissed, turning her back on him.

"Don't you want your bustle?" Blondie held it toward her.

"Go away."

"You need a ride home."

"I'll get one," she said, biting off each word.

This wasn't the way Blondie had planned it. He felt badly that he'd embarrassed her. But, on the positive side, it was just ten-thirty.

Blondie drifted through the crowd until he found Feller dancing with Delores in erotic embrace. He tapped him on the shoulder.

"We're in luck. We can leave now."

"I'm beginning to enjoy myself," Feller said.

"Look, if you want to rut, let's go somewhere else."

"Am I being obvious?" Feller asked.

"Does Davey Crockett wear a coonskin cap?"

"What's that in your hand?"

"A bustle."

"A what?"

"Never mind. Let's go."

On the way out, Blondie spied Mrs. Buckley. She was wearing a brown dress with a ring of feathers around her collar. With her fat rump, she looked like a wild turkey. Blondie walked over to her and handed her the bustle.

"Mrs. Buckley, I'd like you to have this. Someday, when you're old and gray, remember me by it."

"What is it?"

"It's a bustle," he said authoritatively.

"That's the last thing I need."

As soon as he was outside, Blondie began to shout "It's over!" again and again.

After they were all in the car, Blondie explained what had happened.

"Phyllis will never speak to you again," Feller said.

"That's the best part."

Flossie was waiting for them at her house, watching out the picture window. She seemed unsure of herself, but happy to see Blondie.

"Where to, my love?" Feller said to Delores.

She guided Blondie through town and north toward the Pennsylvania state line. After they passed through the light at Milton, she told Blondie to take the next turn, a road so narrow and overgrown with trees it seemed like a lava tunnel. A wooden gate materialized at the end of the tree-lined lane. Blondie slowed the car.

"I thought you said the pond was in the middle of nowhere," Feller said to Delores.

"There wasn't any gate last year."

"What do you think?" Blondie asked Feller.

"We're here now," Feller said.

Blondie got out of the car and opened the gate. It swung shut behind them after he drove through. A short distance further, the road forked.

"Right, I think," Delores said.

Blondie missed the turn and drove into tall grass.

"Blondie's four sheets to the wind," Feller said to Flossie.

"Are you sure we should be doing this?" she asked Blondie.

"No. But I'm sure we're going to."

He cut loose with a rebel yell.

"All right!" Feller said.

"Why do you guys get so much out of getting drunk?" Delores asked.

"For the same reason you get so much out of getting laid," Feller responded.

"That's mostly to please you."

"Well, it sure does."

Except for the moon's reflection upon it, Blondie would've missed the pond. It was smaller than he'd expected, less than a hundred feet across. He pulled off the road and parked.

"Are you sure it isn't too deep?" Flossie asked.

"Positive," Delores said. "When I was here with Bobby.... oops."

"Bobby who, Delores?" Feller asked.

"Never mind."

"Bobby Clements, perhaps?"

"So what?"

"When were you skinny-dipping with him?" Feller asked. "He's been going steady with Ethel for three years."

"Maybe it was before that."

"You would've been in seventh grade."

"What do you care? You know I've been with other guys."

"I'm not jealous, believe me."

"I was afraid you'd say that."

"Well, is anyone going to get in?" Flossie asked. "If not, I'd just as soon go somewhere and get a Coke and some fries. It's chilly out here."

"Hell yes, we're going to do it," Feller said, ripping off his bow tie and cummerbund.

Blondie followed suit and soon there was a mound of pants, jackets, shirts, and underwear on the seat between him and Flossie.

"How come Feller and I are the only ones without any clothes on?" Blondie asked.

"Yeah, what's the deal?" Feller said to Delores.

"I'm not going to undress in front of everyone."

"Me neither," Flossie said.

"Am I missing something here?" Feller asked. "Aren't we all going to be naked in the pond?"

"That's different," Delores said. "Now, get out of the car while we get ready. Both of you."

"Girls!" Feller exclaimed.

Blondie was glad the water was still warm from the day's sun, but that was all he was thankful for. As soon as he stepped into the water, his feet sank into slimy mud.

"It wasn't like this last year," Delores said.

"Is it the same pond?" Feller asked irritably.

"I don't know. Why are you getting angry?"

"Well, let's make the best of it."

"What should we do?" Blondie asked.

"Swim, I guess," Feller replied.

"I'm not swimming out there in the dark," Flossie said.

"Why not? You think there are sharks?" Feller demanded. He softened his voice said, "Okay, okay, let's just wade where it's shallow."

"We came out here to wade?" Blondie was incredulous.

"How do I know what to do?" Feller said to him. "I've never been skinny-dipping before. I just know it's supposed to be sexy."

Once Blondie got used to the squishing between his feet, it wasn't so bad. He enjoyed watching Flossie and Delores prance around in the nude in the moonlight. It appealed to his romantic sensibilities.

He went over to Flossie and put his arm around her.

"Are you having fun?"

"Yeah, but can we quit soon?"

"Isn't it great to let the breeze caress your body?"

"There isn't any breeze."

"It's the idea, though. Don't you see?"

"You're drunk."

"That's not relevant."

Blondie heard a motor.

"Holy shit!" Blondie yelled, "Someone's coming."

Headlights appeared at the gate.

They began scrambling from the water. At the edge of the pond, Blondie stepped on something sharp. He screamed.

"What is it?" Flossie cried, wading over to him.

"I cut my foot."

"Let me help you."

Leaning against her, Blondie limped back to the car. He turned on the overhead light. His toe was bleeding.

"Here," Flossie said, throwing him her panties.

Blondie looked at her.

"It's all right. They've been bled on before."

Blondie wrapped the panties around his toe, then started to pull on his pants.

"Forget your clothes," Feller said. "Let's get out of here."

"We can't drive down the road naked."

"We can dress after we're through the gate."

"I don't think I can drive with my foot like this," Blondie said.

"Give me the keys, then," Feller ordered.

With much knocking about and cursing, they exchanged placed. Feller started the Pontiac and swung it around toward the gate. He stepped on the accelerator. The wheels spun briefly, spraying gravel into the dark, then caught.

Ahead, the other car—Blondie could see it was a white Mercury—began to turn away from them at the fork. Maybe it wasn't coming their way after all. Then it stopped. When their headlights hit it, Blondie could make out two people inside, a boy and a girl. The boy had a flat top and was wearing a tux. The girl's shoulder were bare. He couldn't make out their faces.

Feller turned on the overhead light.

"What're you doing. They'll see us," Blondie shouted at him.

"That's okay."

"What do you mean?"

"Can't you see who it is?" Feller asked. "It's Rudy Tilly and Mary Cherry. This could be rich."

"Are you nuts? I don't want them to see us like this."

Blondie began covering himself with loose articles of clothing.

Feller coasted the Pontiac up to the Mercury as Rudy and Mary watched apprehensively. For an instant, the headlights lit the gate behind Rudy's car. Blondie was dismayed to see a small sign on one post: *George and Helen Cherry*. Of all the places Delores could have picked for their nude nocturne, she'd chosen Mary's homestead.

When Mary recognized Blondie and Feller, she started to wave. Her hand stopped in mid-air, then flew to her mouth. Rudy looked straight at Blondie. His mouth drew tight.

"I guess they've never seen four naked people in one car before," Feller said.

He rolled down the window.

"Pardon our lack of attire," Feller apologized to them. "We weren't expecting company."

Chapter Thirty-One

Graduation—a Friday afternoon—arrived sunny and hot, hot enough to turn graduation gowns into mini-saunas. Inside the gym, Blondie fidgeted with the tassel on his cap, trying to remember whether it was supposed to hang to the left or right. In his black robe, he towered above his classmates like a dark angel.

Feller was checking out his "look" in a pocket mirror his mother had lent him, practicing various smiles for effect—confident, happy, smug, gratified. He screwed his face into a madman's grimace.

"Just right," he said, grinning at Blondie.

Dispatch was attempted to balance his cap on his thick shag of hair. Shakes was trying to cope with his oversized gown, which overflowed his small frame and formed an inky puddle around his feet. Brick was nowhere to be seen.

Blondie figured Grouper had already taken his place on the raised platform from whence school dignitaries would consecrate them into the ranks of the satisfactorily schooled. In a brief message over the public address system the previous Monday, Mr. Bearzinsky had surprised the whole Club—the whole school—by announcing Grouper as class valedictorian. He hadn't sounded happy about it.

"Grouper? I thought sure it would be Mary Cherry," Blondie had commented to Feller.

"Everyone did, including Mary. Would you believe it? Grouper had all A's. Mary had one B. She took it well, though. She told Grouper he must have cheated."

"Does this mean Grouper is going to make a speech?"

The thought made Blondie nervous.

"That's what the valedictorian does."

Later in the week, Grouper told him the Bear had begged him to step aside in favor of Mary.

"Of course," Grouper rumbled, "I told him that wouldn't be right. It would be a violation of school procedure."

Now it was 3:45 p.m., 15 minutes until launch time, when an armada of bobbing mortarboards would be loosed upon the waiting crowd outside. Blondie could envision his mom and dad sitting stiffly on their metal seats, craning their necks for the first sign of the soon-to-be graduates.

He noticed Barnwell putting on his gown in the corner, alone. Purdy couldn't be with him today. For a moment, Blondie felt a tremor of sympathy for him. He had no future and he had to know it. Then Barnwell looked his way and glared at him, and his sympathy vanished. His kind didn't deserve a future.

The boys and girls were paired—boys in black, girls in red—for their march to glory and Shakes had drawn Mary Cherry by the luck of the alphabet. He and Feller had plans for her.

"Keep your head down when you go down the aisle," Feller advised Shakes.

Blondie had been coupled with Ethel Philbin, a circumstance that, a couple weeks before, he would have considered a score of major proportions. But not anymore.

At 3:50, Bucky began forming them up. She spoke to them as ladies and gentlemen, as if their imminent graduation at last had rendered them worthy of respect. Blondie took his place beside Ethel, resplendent in her scarlet robe, a queen to the last. Her face was gorgeous as always, but there was no joy upon it. He felt out of place, an interloper. Bobby was the one who should have been marching beside her. Knowing that wouldn't have happened anyway—paired as they were according to last names—did little to lessen his discomfort.

The aluminum doors of the gym crashed open and the repetitive strains of "Pomp and Circumstance" washed in. With a few loud belches and simulated farts—Blondie suspected one or two were real—the Class of 1962 snaked forward, squeezing itself from the gym and into the bright afternoon. A multitude of keyed-up parents turned their faces toward them in collective beatitude.

Splitting the crowd was a colonnade of rose arches—thorny rose branches wrapped around flexible metal rods—supported by members of the junior class. Miss Spalding had begun the tradition several years before. She termed it her "greatest inspiration."

Sweat gathered between Blondie's shoulder blades. The velvety robe stuck to his arms and back like masking tape. Nonetheless, he strode on proudly, chin up. Ahead, he saw Feller whip out a pair of sunglasses and put them on. Mr. Farber appeared from nowhere and yanked them off.

Beyond and above the flowery passageway, Blondie saw Grouper seated beside Mr. Clapper and the Bear on the plywood platform. He was wearing a black suit and gray tie. He seemed serious, but calm, as did Mr. Clapper, whose serenity bordered, as usual, on comatose. In contrast, the Bear's expression was as sour as if he'd just licked a day's run of postage stamps. Mrs. Buckley labored up the short flight of stairs and plopped onto the empty chair next to him. His look grew more grim.

Blondie suspected Bearzinsky had one goal for the afternoon's proceedings—to escape with his dignity and that of the school untarnished. He knew it would be in vain. The fix was on and in a matter of seconds Mary Cherry would receive a long-overdue comeuppance.

Blondie watched as the first few couples disappeared into the shady tunnel—first the A's, then the B's (including Barnwell), then the C's...Caldane and Cherry. He smiled in anticipation.

As Shakes and Mary arrived at the arch held by Neil Golden and his partner, Neil dipped the bough, snagging Mary's cap on its thorns. When Mary reached back for it, Nancy Cochrane bowled her over and then tripped on her fallen body. A brief domino effect snared two more girls and sent them sprawling before Mary managed to pick herself up and run off after Caldane, who'd marched on, stride unbroken, in the dirge-like rhythm Mrs. Buckley had taught them.

Phyllis was one of the first juniors Blondie came to after he entered the rose tunnel. Her eyes were darts. As he passed beneath her bough, razors raked the back of his head. A warm trickle began running through his hair. He put his hand to his head. It came back streaked with blood.

"Bitch," he muttered to Phyllis. A nearby woman gasped at his language. Ethel, looking stricken, hurried on ahead.

"It wasn't my fault," he mumbled to her when he caught up. He felt stupid.

His mood improved when he passed beneath the arch Tammy held and received a friendly smile. Apparently, she wasn't holding his buffoonish performance at the prom against him. But what difference did it make? He'd never connect with her now. There were no teen dances during the summer and he'd never summon the courage to give her a call.

With a flurry of banging knees and shifting chairs, the class seated itself, facing directly into the sun. A squeaky voice issued from the glare.

"I want to welcome each and every one of you to the 22nd annual graduation ceremony at Fenton High School," Clapper began. "Twenty-one groups of earnest and aspiring young men and women have passed before you and gone out into the world to make their mark...."

"Like Merwin Fester," Feller whispered from several rows ahead.

"...doctors, lawyers..."

"...butchers, bakers, and candlestick makers...." Feller interjected, drowning out Clapper.

"Sh-h-h," Mary Cherry hissed at him.

"Every class is different..." Clapper went on, then he seemed to lose his place and everyone heard Bear's voice echo through the speakers, "No, over here, Mr. Clapper. This is the next line. Is the mike on?"

"Oh yes. This class is unique, not just because no other class was born in the same year..."

Feller groaned.

"...but because you're graduating in a year that is very significant in American history. This year marks the one hundred and eighty-sixth anniversary of the American Revolution. Never again will we be able to say that."

A few parents coughed.

"This class is unique..."

Clapper broke off again and there was more whispering followed by Clapper's voice inquiring, "Did I already say that?"

Some of the seniors began to laugh. Clapper sputtered to a stop and turned the ceremony over to the Bear. He kept his comments to a minimum, making a few cutting remarks about the class's "high jinks" during the year.

"Now he calls them high jinks," Feller said loudly, causing more tittering.

"Most of all," the Bear concluded, "high school prepares our students intellectually. We're proud that several students attained the highest academic marks. Only one, however, earned straight A's in all subjects for all four years. As you might expect, we're quite proud of that student...." Bear seemed to be having trouble getting the words out. "....who will speak on behalf of all the graduating seniors of 1962. It gives me great pleasure to present to you this year's valedictorian, Mr. Walter Clarence Whipple, Jr."

Blondie heard loud clapping behind him. A large, bald man in a business suit was banging his palms together as hard as he could. Beside him, an Amazon in a green dress and a blond wig followed suit. Blondie was surprised. Grouper acted like his parents paid him no mind.

Grouper stood and lumbered toward the microphone where he loomed above the crowd, a shadowy pillar against the sky. Blondie heard the rustling of the small sheaf of papers Grouper placed on the lectern. He bent toward the mike and cleared his throat. When he began speaking in his deep bass voice, it sounded like the voice of God.

"Thank you, Mr. Bearzinsky, your example has always proven instructive," he said, almost without irony. "Good afternoon parents, faculty and fellow students. I've spent some time researching valedictory speeches. What I've discovered is that they almost always consist of paeans to the faculty for their efforts on our behalf and exhortations to the students to make the world a better place. As a consequence, they're uniformly predictable and fatuous. I beg your indulgence as I depart from this formula."

There were a few murmurs from the crowd. The Bear's face widened in apprehension.

"As Mr. Clapper so redundantly pointed out," Grouper continued, "we're a unique group of students. But does anybody know who we are? Let me ask each graduating student to consider whether his or her classmates or teachers truly know who he or she is?

"Let me speak for myself. I've spent four years here at Fenton High and very few know me. Sure, I hang around with a group of guys, but we all play our accepted roles and seldom do we delve beneath our facades. We mainly spend time protecting our fragile egos and polishing our personas through rote performance of traditional adolescent behavior."

Blondie felt strange hearing Grouper say that. Blondie'd never felt so tight with any group and now Grouper was saying they didn't know each other. Was he saying they were a bunch of phonies? Was it true?

"None of my teachers ever made an attempt to get to know me—except for Miss Spalding. However, I'm not sure anyone else can ever know who we are in any meaningful way. The more important question is whether we know ourselves. Fenton High graduates, I ask you: *Do you know who you are*?"

Grouper's voice boomed over the mike. Several seniors near Blondie shifted in their seats. Blondie sneaked a glance at his parents. Their faces were attentive, but devoid of comprehension. Mr. Whipple stared at the stage. He didn't seem pleased.

Blondie was sure Grouper wasn't talking to him. He knew who he was—or at least who he would be one day. He'd be another Jack Kennedy or Lawrence of Arabia or Ernest Hemingway. So what if he wasn't that person yet. In time, he was sure he'd grow into the image of himself he carried inside.

Grouper's voice rumbled on like an approaching storm.

"When we first arrive in the world, we're formless, but we have the potential to become anything we want: poets, politicians, scientists, saints, inventors, industrialists. By the time we leave grade school, however, we've been molded by the expectations others have placed on us. In high school, it gets worse. Our parents' and teachers' expectations increase. Peer pressure becomes enormous.

"I know most of you parents out there have largely forgotten what high school is like. You don't need to remember, because I suspect it's not much different from the rest of your lives. At its best, high school is exciting, a breathtaking adventure composed of learning new things, meeting new people, sharing ideas and feelings. At its worst, it's involuntary immersion into an insensitive and intolerant—often bullying—conformity. Hardly a breeding ground for change, let alone progress.

"After all, high school is the forge for the archetypes of adult society: those who seek success with their looks; those who seek success with their bodies; those who seek success with their brains; those who seek success with their fists."

The Bear's face twisted in consternation.

"The world is in peril," Grouper warned, his voice rising to baritone. "For the first time in history, we must contemplate the end of civilization. Much as we don't like to think about it, at any instant we and all our kind could be incinerated in a hail of radioactive firestorms.

Around the globe, billions of humans live in abject poverty, nonetheless breeding millions of new mouths to feed. In the United States, disparities in income are alarming and unjustifiable, with people of different colored skin relegated to poverty and social inequality. Look around you—it is now more than 10 years since the Supreme Court ruled that segregation is illegal. Yet, Fenton High still has no black students."

Again, the crowd stirred. On stage, the Bear's eyes had drawn into one long squint.

"There's a secret war going on in a place called Vietnam, a place few students even know of. Yet, if it continues, it will suck many of us into its bloodthirsty jaws...."

The Bear sat forward on the edge of his seat. Blondie could tell he wanted to quiet Grouper. He wondered if he'd dare.

"In the face of these threats, these injustices, most of you choose to change the channel, to tune out, to continue lives of graceless materialism and smug conventionality."

Blondie sensed an undercurrent of anger. The crowd felt challenged, perhaps attacked, and he knew that wasn't why they'd come. They'd come to see their children graduate and go home feeling proud and fulfilled.

"But today, you come here hopeful, hopeful that we, the next generation, can solve these problems and preserve the planet from extinction. But how can we? We are your *clones*. What can we do but recreate the same world we inherit? The best within us has been driven underground by meaningless classroom lectures and by a high-school culture that celebrates hard drinking, hard fighting, hardheadedness and hardheartedness...."

Grouper paused.

"....This is my advice to the parents gathered here today: *Don't count on us!* **Most of us will never recover from high school.** At least one of us won't even survive it."

The audience gasped. Beside him, Ethel Philbin began to weep. Blondie could see, though he couldn't hear, the Bear gnashing his teeth. He looked as if he were about to spring upon him and rip out his larynx. Grouper caught his look.

"My time appears to be drawing to a close. Before I sit down, I feel I owe my classmates a few words of advice. Here they are. Flee Fenton! Flee Fenton as fast as you can and go as far away as you can. Thank you."

Grouper turned and smiled at Mr. Bearzinsky, then ambled back to his seat.

Blondie waited for someone to clap, but silence reigned. Blondie felt embarrassed for Grouper, so he clapped his hands once, hoping someone would join in. No one did.

The Bear strode to the mike and grabbed it in a stranglehold. With a tight jaw, he snarled a brief thanks to Grouper for his "unusual perspectives." Then, forcing a smile, he announced the awarding of diplomas. The first row of students stood and began shuffling toward the platform. Mrs. Buckley rose and took a clipboard to the Bear. He began reading names from it as students rolled past, picking up their certificates from Mrs. Buckley. When Blondie received his, Mrs. Buckley said, "I'm very pleased that you and your friends are graduating on schedule." She smiled like a jackal.

When all the diplomas had been given out, the FHS Glee Club sang "Climb Every Mountain" from the Broadway musical *The Sound of Music*. It was full of brave and sappy thoughts about overcoming all obstacles until one found his or her dream.

Parents' eyes filled with tears. Graduates' chests swelled. In spite of what Grouper had said, everyone seemed sure the Class of '62 was going to conquer the world.

Clapper returned to the mike and mumbled a few more words like a benediction. He opened his arms wide like Christ embracing the world's sinners and "presented" the FHS graduating class to the world. Mortarboards rocketed skyward as parents rushed to their little darlings, swelled with pride that they'd been ratcheted up one more notch in life.

Students sought each other out for hugs and handshakes and affirmations of enduring friendship. It was an orgy of self-congratulation.

Soon his mom and dad surrounded him. His dad shook his hand. His mom hugged him with tears in her eyes.

"Please don't be weepy, mom," Blondie whispered to her. He burned with embarrassment until he realized all his classmates were being similarly victimized.

That night, the guys drove out to the quarry to celebrate—all except Grouper. His parents had insisted on taking him to an expensive restaurant in Baltimore for a graduation dinner. The celebration never came off. The group was moody, out of sorts. It didn't stop the flow of beer, but it did stop the words.

Blondie wondered what they were all thinking about? Was it about what Grouper had said? Had he put a spell on them? Or was it just uneasiness at facing the end of one part of their life with no clear idea what to do next?

Feller ended their reverie by saying, "Well, it's been a pisser." Blondie didn't know whether Feller meant graduation, the past year, or their entire high school careers. Regardless, he was sure Feller was right. Shortly afterward, Shakes got wiped and threw up in the car.

In bed that night, Blondie found himself walking under the rose arches again. This time, only girls held the ends of the rods.... and they were all naked. Flossie was one.... and Delores...and Tammy. They were watching him with admiration in their eyes. He liked that.

When Blondie came to Mary Cherry, he was confused. She was a senior. Why was she holding a rose arch? He turned to his partner. It was Ethel Philbin in her blood-red graduation gown. But he was wearing something else: a white letter sweater with a big red "F" on it. An assortment of small gold footballs, basketballs, and baseball bats was attached to it. He felt an overpowering apprehension as he looked ahead, down the dark tunnel of roses.

As he walked on, a point of light appeared ahead. It grew larger as he drew nearer. He reached the end of the archway and found himself in a concrete room. It was empty except for a long dark object standing upright in one corner—a shotgun. Blondie felt a terrible dread.

He woke to a still house. Goosebumps forested his arms and legs.

He'd been Bobby in the dream. But why? And what had he been so afraid of? He thought about it for a long time until an answer began to form in his mind. Perhaps it was what had driven Bobby to his desperate act, the thought Blondie feared more than any other: *that nothing extraordinary was ever going to happen in his life.*

Chapter Thirty-Two

Summer at last. Warm, languid, golden. It came filled with images of a more secure and agreeable time. Blondie could remember his mother crooning to him when he was a child, her voice husky and sad, as she sand the bittersweet standard "Summertime" about the soft life of someone whose father was rich and whose mother was good-looking. He remembered her voice and the words like a comforting embrace.

Had she really sung to him that way? He was no longer sure. He was sure, however, that his daddy wasn't rich and his momma was no longer good-looking. But no matter. They were getting along better now and soon they'd be leaving for New York.

His life wasn't without worry, however. Since graduation, Blondie had been wrestling with what Grouper had said in his speech. Why had he said the group hardly knew each other? Blondie had never felt so close to anyone as he did to Feller and Grouper. He finally felt bothered enough to call Grouper and ask if they could get together and talk. Grouper told him he'd been grounded.

"My father was 'displeased' by my graduation remarks. He said they were an attack on his generation. He took the whole thing personally."

"Perhaps it was because of all the other parents there," Blondie said.

Grouper harrumphed.

"My father could care less about anyone in Fenton. He refers to Fenton culture as a high society of rubes. No, he's angry because I don't value what he does, don't respect what he's accomplished."

"Have you heard from Yale yet?" Blondie asked to change subjects.

"They turned me down. They said I didn't display the leadership qualities they were looking for: I hadn't been in student government, I hadn't participated in extracurricular activities."

"So?"

"So I guess I'm going to the University of Pennsylvania. It's the best school that took me."

"That'll be all right, won't it? It's got girls. It's not far away."

"I'd rather have gone to college with you guys. But Father thinks you're a bad influence."

A bad influence? That was a crock. Maybe they weren't Ivy League material, but they weren't dope smokers or juvenile delinquents, either. Anyway, Grouper had always been a willing participant in their activities.

Blondie finally got around to why he'd called.

"I'm sorry if my comments upset you. They weren't meant for you." Over the phone line, Grouper's low voice seemed to percolate from a deep well. "They were meant for all those who never attempt to find out who they are—or why they're here for that matter."

"My dad says everything is part of God's plan." Blondie didn't know why he said it. Perhaps, he thought later, he just wanted Grouper's reaction.

Grouper snorted.

"You don't believe in God at all, do you?"

"No."

Blondie had suspected as much. Still, he was amazed at the casual, almost dismissive, way Grouper had answered, as if the matter were of little consequence. In spite of his own uncertainty about the almighty, Blondie'd never dared consider himself an atheist. What if he denied God's existence and he were wrong? God would bust his balls...*forever.*

"If you're going to live life true, you have to be a free agent," Grouper continued. "That means doing without any crutches for your soul—myths, drugs, self-delusions, religion or whatever."

Free agent. Blondie liked the sound of it. It had a rebellious ring. He flashed on James Dean in *Rebel Without A Cause*. But what did any of that have to do with the Grouper? He was no James Dean.

The second Saturday after graduation, Dispatch got married in a ceremony as bare-boned as a fossil. The only people invited were Blondie and Wanda Wanamaker (a friend of Meryl's). Blondie was surprised Dispatch had chosen him—he didn't feel that close to him. By default, he was best man.

Dispatch wore a worn-looking herringbone suit that fit him like a body bag. Meryl wore a garish yellow dress with a blue bow, while Wanda, Meryl's maid of honor, was decked out in a beige suit that flattered her as much as the runs in her stockings. Blondie wore the only suit he owned, a green worsted his parents had bought him for his 17th birthday. It pinched him in the armpits and crotch.

Mr. Butler, the justice of the peace, was tall and officious. He made the four of them sign a battery of forms whose purposes Blondie couldn't fathom. He asked Dispatch and Meryl a multitude of questions to make sure they knew what they were doing. Blondie knew they didn't, of course, but what Justice Butler didn't know was that Meryl was pregnant—or supposed to be.

Though the ceremony was as brief and compelling as an oil change, Butler didn't make it through before succumbing to an allergy attack. His eyes watered and he sneezed during several critical pronouncements. Dispatch endured the service stoically, but Blondie could tell he was distressed. Who wouldn't be, marrying a bimbo like Meryl?

Blondie experienced his own discomfort when the justice asked if there was anyone present who knew of any reason why Dispatch and Meryl "should not be joined together." Blondie could think of several, the main one being that marrying Meryl meant the end of Dispatch's life. But it wasn't his show, so he kept quiet.

"Where are you going on your honeymoon?" Blondie asked Dispatch after the ceremony.

"We're going to Philadelphia for the weekend," Meryl answered for him, as excited as if they were off to Rio.

"We're going to see the Liberty Bell," Dispatch added, with a hint of irony.

The following day, Mrs. Potter fell down the stairs. Blondie didn't see it—it happened inside their house. He only saw the ambulance pull up and two guys in white bring her out on a gurney. She looked like a loaf of bread beneath the sheet as they wheeled her to the back of the van. Mack was beside himself, gesturing at the medics and pacing around the ambulance after they deposited her in it. The next day, his mom reported that Mrs. Potter had broken her hip and would be in the hospital for a spell.

"She's pretty old, you know," his mom said.

Blondie just grunted.

"Mr. Tilly says Mack is pretty broken up."

Blondie couldn't believe the bastard had any feelings. Anyway, how did Mr. Tilly know how Potter felt. Was he friends with the old goat?

Blondie saw Rudy mowing their back yard the following day and thought about going over and asking him. But he realized whatever slim bond had linked them during the school year had been broken—if not before prom night, certainly at the Cherrys' pond.

Blondie's eighteenth birthday fell the day before his parents were to leave for New York. His mom had baked a cake with white frosting and a silver golf club on the top. It was spiked with eighteen yellow candles shaped like tees. She lit them all, then challenged him to blow them out in one puff. He did. His dad took pictures. So this was the way someone became a man, Blondie thought.

After they finished eating, his mother glanced over at his dad. Her expression was serious.

"Now?" she asked.

His dad shrugged and looked at Blondie with a pained expression.

"There's something we need to tell you," his mom said, although his dad didn't appear to be involved. "Come with me."

Blondie followed her up the stairs to his parents' bedroom. She shut the door and asked him to take a seat on their bed.

"Remember how I promised to tell you something when you turned eighteen?" she reminded him.

Blondie hadn't forgotten. He was sure what it would be: he'd been adopted. That would explain a lot of things, like his hair color and why he felt so little connection with his dad. He'd already prepared himself for the news.

His mom's face screwed into in a look of anguish. Blondie was afraid she was going to cry.

"Francis isn't your real father," she said.

He'd guessed correctly.

"And you're not my real mother, right?" he volunteered.

She looked at him in shock.

"Look, I can handle it," Blondie said. "I know you love me."

"But Bernard, that's not what I'm trying to tell you. Of course, I'm your mother."

This was getting more complicated.

"Then I don't understand."

"Your real father was a captain in the army," she continued. "I met him in Missouri when I was visiting your grandmother in the fall of 1943. Howard was tall and handsome. His hair was the color of butter...."

So that's where he'd gotten his coloring. He could feel his breaths cycling slowly and shallowly, his lungs caught in the grip of uncertainty. The axis of his life was turning with each word from his mother's lips.

"We were so in love. We were going to get married, but he was on a two-week furlough and, by the time we were sure, he had to report back to duty.

He was killed on some small island in the Pacific not long afterward. I received two letters from him...."

Her voice broke. Blondie felt her pain. She *had* known love. Why had he doubted it?

"I'd known Francis all along. He was a soldier too, although he was never called to war. He was stationed at the Pentagon where I was working as a secretary. He liked me. We'd gone out a few times to movies or restaurants. But I'd never thought about marriage."

"Then why....?"

"Soon after I found out your dad had been killed, my body told me I wasn't alone. Unmarried women didn't have babies in those days. I didn't know what to do, who to tell. I told Francis. He immediately offered to marry me. So, just before Christmas, we got married."

Blondie slumped on the bed and tried to make sense of it. It wasn't the kind of story he ever would have expected. It sounded like the plot for one of those stupid daytime shows housewives watched—*Edge of Night, Secret Storm, Brighter Day*.

"Tell me about him," Blondie said.

A happy look creased her eyes and lips.

"Howard was brave, decisive, kind, the type of man any woman would want. He had an inner strength, a sureness about himself—and passion. That's something I've never had from Francis."

For a moment, the sad look returned.

"Please don't be angry with me for keeping this from you so long," she continued. "I didn't want you to ever question that you had two parents who loved you. But I can understand if it's a crushing thing to hear. I hope you're not too disappointed."

Crushed? Disappointed? That wasn't what Blondie was feeling at all. He felt *elated*. His father had been a lover, a hero! And Blondie was his lineage. Even more, Blondie now had a secret in his past, a damned good one. He was *special*.

"I always wondered what you saw in dad," Blondie said. "No wonder you find him so boring."

His mother's eyes flashed in anger, but when she spoke, her voice was soft.

"Francis is a hero too. He accepted you as his own son and brought you up with all the love and care a father could give."

Blondie chose not to quibble with that. For a while, they just looked at each other. Blondie realized neither of them understood the etiquette for such a situation.

"Would you like to see a picture of your dad?" she asked after a while.

Blondie wasn't sure. What if he didn't look like a warrior? What if Blondie didn't look like him? He nodded anyway.

His mother reached out and grabbed a lacquered Chinese box she kept on her bureau. She opened it and removed a small square object wrapped in tissue paper. She pulled the paper aside to reveal a silver frame with a sepia photograph inside. She held it out to Blondie. He took it gingerly in his hands.

The man in the picture was handsome and proud, his hair the color of butter. He stared out at Blondie with a confident look tinged with a trace of humor. Ribbons were pinned to his uniform. Blondie asked his mom if he'd killed anyone.

"I don't know. Not when I knew him. He hadn't even gone to war. The ribbons were for leadership and marksmanship."

"Can I look again?" Blondie asked as he gave the picture back to her.

"Of course, any time."

She looked into his face for a few moments longer, then kissed him lightly on the cheek and walked from the room.

Blondie's initial rapture gave way to a slight queasiness. He wasn't who he thought he was. Still he liked being the son of Howard, even if he didn't know his last name.

A few days later, his parents were gone and, for the first time in his life, he faced a lengthy time alone. It was a delicious prospect.

Chapter Thirty-Three

As Blondie remembered it, the Beer Bank was Dispatch's idea. He, Feller and Dispatch had been riding around in the P-mobile, engaged in a hypothetical discussion about how many beers the Club drank in an average week when Dispatch suggested they research the issue—"do a study."

"That's not feasible," Feller argued. "We're too drunk by the end of the evening to remember how many beers we've had."

"We could keep all the empties and count them up," Dispatch answered.

"Right," Feller scoffed.

"Wait a minute, Feller," Blondie said. "Dispatch may be on to something. We might find out we play a major role in the local economy."

"What? On the index of leading alcoholics? Anyway, where are we going to put them? I guarantee my parents won't be impressed by a mountain of Pabst cans in the corner."

"There's always my house," Blondie volunteered. "But I don't want a pile of empties on the floor. We need something to put them in."

Dispatch jammed on the brakes and wheeled the P-mobile through a gas station.

"Where're you going?" Feller asked.

"To Safeway."

Dispatch drove straight to the loading dock behind the store. It was empty except for one large corrugated box. Fortunately, it was a large one. According to the legend on the side, the box had once safeguarded 144 rolls of toilet paper from the hazards of cross-country trucking.

"Appropriate," Feller commented.

It was too big to fit in the car, so Blondie held it outside the window as Dispatch inched his way back to the Reimers' house to keep the wind from ripping it from his grip. They installed it in a corner of the family room.

Feller asked Blondie if he had a couple pieces of wood.

"What for?"

"Just trust me."

"I've got a ruler. My mom has one, too."

"Bring them to me…and some adhesive tape and a crayon."

Feller made a cross from the two rulers and taped it to the box. He wrote "R.I.P." beneath it.

"That's kind of sacrilegious." Dispatch said.

"Exactly," Feller answered.

"But it gives the wrong message," he argued. "Drinking is about having fun."

"All right, Dispatch, what's your idea?" Feller demanded.

"I don't know. Why can't we just think of it like a bank? Where we put our deposits."

"I suppose they *are* deposits," Feller conceded. "Good for five cents each if we take them back."

"Why not call it the Beer Bank," Blondie suggested.

"Yeah," Dispatch agreed.

Feller crossed out his first effort and wrote "Beer Bank" in big letters across the box.

"Should I take the cross down?" Feller asked. "A bank with a cross—that's a mixed metaphor."

"Who gives a shit?" Dispatch said.

"How many empties do you think it'll hold?" Blondie asked.

"Hundreds," Feller guessed.

"Do you think we can fill it?"

"We have all summer."

While Dispatch was backing the P-mobile out of his driveway, Blondie happened to glance over toward Potter's house. Potter was standing on the front porch, arms crossed, watching them. He gave Blondie the creeps.

There was good news on the horizon, though. A few days later, Dispatch told him Barnwell and Purdy had taken jobs out of town.

"Jobs? Barnwell? Purdy? What could they do?" Blondie asked.

"Someone said they were flipping burgers at the beach."

Beach? What beach? Dispatch didn't know and Blondie realized he didn't care. All that mattered was that they were out of his hair for the summer.

Weeks merged with each other in a repetitious sameness. Days of sleeping late, shooting pool or just hanging out around the house. Nights cruising in the P-mobile with the gang or having them all over for suds and conversation. And occasional nights of passion with Flossie on his parents' queen-sized bed.

Day by day, the Beer Bank grew. By mid-July, the box was half full. Sweet, sweet, no-school-in-sight summertime. What could go wrong?

Then came *the call*. It was late and he'd just crashed after a number of beers at Grouper's Overlook with the gang. The phone's ring blew away the beginning of a dream. 1:30 a.m.. Who would call him at that hour?

His mom.

"Where've you been?" She sounded pissed.

"Bowling with the guys," he lied, his head muzzy with barley and hops.

"Are you sure?"

Her voice was harsh. What was eating her?

"Sure. What's the matter?"

She began crying.

"How could you....?"

How could he *what*? What did she know anyway? She was three hundred miles away.

"Orgies...."

Orgies? Blondie'd never heard his mother use the word before.

"What are you talking about?"

"And drinking."

Sweat broke out on Blondie's brow. She was getting closer to home. Somehow, his parents had found out he'd been having a good time.

"I don't know what you're talking about, Mom."

"It's all in a letter I received today."

"What letter?"

"A letter from Fenton. It tells all about what you and your despicable friends have been up to."

She began sobbing.

"Who sent it?"

"I don't know," she sniffled. "It isn't signed." Her voice hardened. "Your dad and I have decided. I'm coming straight home."

Blondie's breath disappeared. She couldn't come home. Summer was barely half over.

"Don't be rash," Blondie pleaded. "It sounds like some crank to me."

There was silence at the other end.

"Well, what does the letter say?" Blondie asked.

"How can you be so cool? What's happened to my little boy?"

"Nothing, mom. I just don't know what you're talking about. What's it say?"

"It says you've been having orgies every night in our house. With naked girls and loud music and lots of alcohol."

"Yeah?" That sounded pretty neat. Then, indignation welled within him. He'd been wrongfully accused...to a degree.

"It's all lies," Blondie said. "It's must be that crazy Potter next door. Mom, he's a psycho. He watches me all the time."

"Well, Mr. Potter is a little strange," Blondie's mother conceded. "He told Francis our crab grass was invading his lawn. *Our* crab grass."

She stopped crying.

"Tell me the truth, Bernard. Have you had any girls over?" she asked.

"Well, Flossie's come over a few times...." Blondie figured he had to confess to something. "...but we just watched television. I always had her home by midnight. You can ask her parents."

His mom was silent. Blondie could almost hear the gears shifting in her mind.

"How about the part about drinking?" She returned to her inquisition. "You haven't been drinking, have you?"

"Mom, I don't even like the taste of beer."

That wasn't a big lie. He still wasn't sold on the taste of beer. He just liked the results.

"Well, I would like to stay up here with Francis."

Blondie felt the hook wriggling from his skin.

"The letter *is* written in terrible English," his mom said with distaste. Blondie realized his mom had turned the corner. To an elementary school teacher, no accusation could stand under the weight of poor grammar.

After a few more minutes of verbal dodging and weaving, his mom's agitation dissipated and she hung up. He'd talked her out of coming back early! Blondie flopped his head down against the pillow and exhaled. He hadn't dodged a bullet—it had been a mortar shell.

His relief soon gave way to resentment. So many accusations and so few of them true!

Blondie had just tucked his brewing hangover back into bed when the phone rang again. Blondie was surprised when he looked at his clock. Nine hours had passed. It was Dispatch.

"I need to talk," he said.

"Shoot."

"Not on the phone. Can I come over?"

"Sure."

Within the hour, the P-mobile belched up to their house in a blue fog. Dispatch plopped down on his mom's flower-print sofa, his face a scowl.

"What's the problem?" Blondie asked.
"Marriage."
"You're not getting along with Meryl?"
"What's not to get along with? She adores me."
Dispatch stared at his mom's painting as if it were a firing squad.
"Then what is it?"
Dispatch pursed his lips. He placed his fingertips together.
"There isn't any baby."
"No baby?"
"I kept waiting for Meryl's belly to swell, but it didn't. Yesterday, I found a box of Tampax in her closet. I could tell it had just been opened. When I confronted her, she told me she'd had a spontaneous miscarriage."
"You've been had," Blondie said.
"I know. And I've got to get out of it."
Dispatch's jaw tightened. He looked like he could eat luggage.
"Why don't you get a divorce?"
"You have to have a reason unless your partner wants a divorce too. But Meryl loves being married. It's what she's always wanted to be—the little lady of the house."
Little?
"So what can you do?" Blondie asked.
Dispatch turned his face toward Blondie. Blondie sensed his eyes burning behind his bangs.
"What can *we* do, you mean."
"Me? Where do I come in?"
"I've got a plan."

Chapter Thirty-Four

A breeze blew up. On a summer evening, that meant rain. Blondie, in tee shirt and shorts, began to shiver. He looked up at the sky. It was growing dark, but it was still clear. He and Dispatch were sequestered in a copse of dogwoods about fifty feet from where Fishers Lane began a steep decline before it dead-ended at the bottom of the hill.

"I don't see how this can work," Blondie said.

"It'll work," Dispatch replied, his jaw set. "You just wait and see."

He was wearing a hunter's camouflage jacket over a pair of canvas pants. Instead of a gun, he held an old Brownie camera with a flash attachment.

"I can't believe you talked Shakes into fucking your wife," Blondie said.

"It wasn't easy. Even Shakes has standards. I promised to lend him the P-mobile once in a while. Anyway, he's never been laid before. I told him Meryl was all right."

Blondie had picked Dispatch up in the Dart—his folks had taken the Pontiac to New York. It now was hidden by bushes on a spur off the dirt surface of Fishers Lane. The plan had been set. Shakes had talked Meryl into picking him up near his house for a "quick tryst" as soon as Dispatch left. For his part, Dispatch had told Meryl he wouldn't be home "until way after midnight."

"How do you know *she'll* go through with it? After all, she's your wife."

Dispatch gave Blondie a disbelieving look.

"I've got faith in Meryl. She'd fuck anybody who asked her."

It bothered Blondie that Dispatch said it so casually. If Blondie ever got married, he wouldn't want his wife to be unfaithful. But then, Dispatch's marriage couldn't be confused with the real thing...like the kind of marriage he'd have, say, with a girl like Tammy.

The wind picked up. It sounded like a migration of rattlesnakes as it whipped its way through the leaves. The sky had turned charcoal.

"It's going to rain," Blondie said.

"It can't rain," Dispatch responded, as if that settled the matter.

"Why're we here so early?"

"Just in case. I told Shakes to get here as soon as he could. But who knows? Meryl may have more class than I think. She may not want to fuck him until the sun's down."

Time passed. Shadows merged and filled the spaces between the trees. Dispatch began melding into the darkness.

"Are you sure Shakes knows where to come?" Blondie asked.

"I told him to stop before the road heads down the hill. Anyway, I brought him out here for a trial run day before yesterday."

"What if someone else comes along?"

"No one else will come here. They're all afraid of the hook man."

"Who?"

Blondie looked around.

"Some homicidal maniac who preys on young lovers. They say he's about six-six, wears an old felt hat, and has a hook for one hand. The way I heard it, he put his hook through some guy's gut and then raped his girlfriend."

"Who says?"

"I don't know," Dispatch grouched. "It's just common knowledge."

"Has anyone ever seen him?"

"Supposedly—about five or six years ago."

"And he was back here on this road?"

Blondie heard the quiver in his voice.

"For Christ's sake, Blondie. If such a thing ever happened, don't you think it would have made the papers?"

"How do you know it didn't?"

"Because I looked," he answered sheepishly.

The wind picked up and the temperature went down. Goosebumps materialized on Blondie's legs. Why hadn't he worn long pants? Because it'd been a scorcher that day, he reminded himself. He asked himself how he'd allowed himself to be dragooned into participating in such a ridiculous scheme—trying to prove Meryl was an adulteress by taking a picture of Shakes screwing her. Dispatch had told Blondie he needed him along for "moral support," but there was nothing moral about what they were doing.

"No one will believe you just happened to be walking in the woods with a camera when one of your best friends drove up and began copulating with your wife in *your* car," he'd told Dispatch.

"I'll tell the judge I was suspicious and followed them here."

"But one of your best friends?"

"Happens all the time."

"Dispatch," Blondie'd said as tactfully as he could, "your wife isn't very good-looking."

"Look at the other side, though. Shakes isn't either."

The rest of the "plan" called for Shakes to undress Meryl and then pull her down on top of him in the P-mobile. When Shakes stomped his heel against the window, Dispatch would run over and photograph the two of them in full rut.

Blondie heard thunder in the distance.

"It's going to rain," Blondie repeated.

"It can't rain. It'll ruin my pictures."

Soon, it was so dark Blondie could no longer see Dispatch at all. Dispatch pulled a flashlight from the pocket of his hunting jacket and switched it on. The beam shot straight up and turned his face into a Jack-o-Lantern.

"You look like hook man now," Blondie said. "Why don't you put that on the ground?"

Dispatch leaned the flashlight against a tree.

"I'm freezing," Blondie said.

"You're cold? Why didn't you say so. I've got a turtleneck in my inside pocket."

Dispatch pulled a brown turtleneck from his jacket. It fit Blondie like a corset, but it helped.

Soon Blondie heard the sound of a thousand tiny drums beating. *Rain*. The first drop landed on the end of Blondie's nose, the second on the top of his left ear. After that, he couldn't tell. It was a real gusher.

Dispatch put his hood up. He looked like a sorcerer.

"You'll scare Meryl to death if you creep up on her like that," Blondie told him.

Soon, the turtleneck Dispatch had given him was soaked. Blondie's hair was plastered down on his forehead. Rivulets of rainwater ran from his scalp into his eye sockets, then under his nose and into his mouth. Blondie stamped his feet up and down to warm up, knocking the flashlight over. It went out.

Dispatch felt around in the dark until he found it. Blondie heard him click the switch. Nothing.

"That's the end of that," Dispatch said.

"What if they don't come? How are we going to find my car in the dark?"

"We can always follow the road."

"Yeah, but will we see the turnoff?"

"Don't worry. Shakes will show up. He knows we're out here."

Blondie thought he heard a noise in the woods. His heart banged against his collarbone.

"Did you hear that?" he asked Dispatch.

"Hear what?"

"It sounded like steps."

"Maybe it was the hook man," Dispatch said.

"Come off it, Dispatch, that's not funny."

There was a crash and the sound of trees splintering. The whole forest lit up. Blondie gasped when he saw a face loom from the dark.

"Keep cool, Blondie, I'm not the hook man," Dispatch said.

Huge rolls of thunder rumbled through the woods. Now and then jagged bolts of electricity ripped the night.

"What if a tree falls on us?" Blondie asked.

"What if we get hit by a runaway subway?"

Blondie granted that Dispatch had a point. He *was* acting wimpy. He resolved to keep his mouth shut and die quietly and nobly of whatever dangers stalked them. After interminable wet moments, a shaft of light appeared.

"Here comes a car," Dispatch said. "Let's hope it's Shakes."

Dispatch crept closer to the road. The grill of the P-mobile emerged from the downpour like the toothy grin of great white about to snack on a swimmer. Blondie had never been so happy to see it.

The road had turned into a quagmire and when Shakes tried to stop, the P-mobile slid another twenty feet. It stopped on the edge of the steep decline.

"Okay, now we listen for the signal," Dispatch instructed.

"Are you crazy? We can't hear anything but rain and thunder."

"You're right. We'll have to guess when they're getting it on."

"How are we going to figure that out?"

"Well, let's think. How long does it take a guy to pull down a girl's pants and get his dork out?"

"You gotta leave time for foreplay," Blondie pointed out.

"With Meryl? Foreplay for her is undoing her garter belt."

The P-mobile's inside light came on. Now, Blondie and Dispatch could see Shakes and Meryl, though the cascading rain blurred their images.

"Shakes is smarter than I thought," Dispatch said.

Shakes held up a quart bottle of beer and gave it to Meryl.

"What's he doing?" Dispatch grumped. "He doesn't have to get her drunk. Doesn't he realize it's raining?"

Shakes and Meryl passed the bottle back and forth for about ten minutes. Then, both their heads disappeared.

"The trap is sprung," Dispatch said with satisfaction.

The car starting rocking.

"Okay, watch the window," Dispatch commanded. "Watch for a foot."

"With socks or without?"

"Be serious, will you? My life is on the line."

There was a movement against the window.

"Was that his foot?" Dispatch asked.

"I don't know. It happened too fast."

"What do you think? Should we charge them?"

"Why not? You first."

Dispatch jumped from the bushes and rushed the P-mobile. As he reached it, he slipped and slid on his back halfway under the car.

Meryl's head popped up, then Shakes'. They were both buck-naked as far as Blondie could tell. He retreated into the bushes.

Shakes rolled down the window. The raucous sounds of *Palisades Park* blared out into the night, then the radio switched off.

Meryl's trembling voice sailed on the wind. "Who's there?"

"I'm t-telling y-you, there's n-no one out there," Shakes reassured her.

"This is where the hook man hangs out. I asked you not to bring me here," Meryl complained.

"I had to."

"What do you mean you had to?"

"I m-mean it's wh-where I always t-take a new l-lover," Shakes adlibbed.

"Oh, Shakes, you're so sweet. I wish I could get Dispatch to be as romantic."

"Let's g-go b-back to what we w-were d-doing," Shakes said.

Blondie could tell from Shakes' tone of voice that he was not without enthusiasm for his task.

"Look out the window first and make sure it's all right. Don't you have a flashlight?"

"There's one in the g-glove c-compartment."

Soon, a beam of light shot from the window. Blondie ducked lower into the bushes.

Just before Shakes pulled the flashlight back into the car, he looked down. His eyes rose from their sockets when he saw Dispatch's face staring up at him from the mud.

"AIEEE!"

"What? What is it?" Meryl cried in alarm.

"N-nothing," Shakes said, recovering. "I j-just h-hit my wrist against the d-door."

"You didn't see anything, did you?"

"Of c-course n-not. Even the hook m-man w-wouldn't come out on a night l-like this."

"I thought you said there wasn't any hook man."

"J-just k-kidding."

"If you're sure there's no hook man, let's turn the light off. It's more romantic in the dark."

The window rolled back up and the light went off. The P-mobile faded into the gloom.

Blondie heard Dispatch fumbling around in the mud.

"The flash bulb fell out," he whispered to Blondie. Then, a minute later, "I got it."

There was enough light in the roadway for Blondie to see Dispatch rise by the front of the car. The interior exploded in light as Dispatch released the shutter on the Brownie. Meryl screamed.

Branded on the back of Blondie's mind was the image of Shakes' face. He'd been looking out the window as the flash had popped. He was still looking out at the night, blinded when Dispatch took another shot. Shakes began yelling, his voice muffled until he remembered to roll the window down.

"You d-dumb s-son of a b-bitch!" he shouted at Dispatch.

Meryl had never quit screaming.

"It's the hook man!" she repeated over and over.

"Wh-where are y-you, you d-dork? You blinded m-me."

"Calm down, Shakes," Dispatch said. "I'm right in front of you."

"Darrel!" Meryl yelled.

A booming maniacal laugh drowned out the sound of the storm.

"Heh, heh, heh. I got you now, you cheating Jezebel. Got you right in the act with my best friend. And to think I trusted you."

Meryl switched on the overhead light and shrieked again.

Dispatch's face and body were covered with mud, his hair clumped together in frightful formations...a slime monster.

"God d-damn, D-dispatch," Shakes said, "you l-look like the C-creature from the Bl-black L-lagoon.

"You scared me," Meryl accused him.

"Heh, heh, heh. You haven't seen the worst of it yet. I got you right here on film. Committing adultery with my friend. It's Splitsville now."

"What're you talking about?" Meryl asked.

"I'm talking divorce. I'm talking freedom."

Dispatch opened the back door and jumped in the P-mobile.

"Shit, l-look what you're d-doing to the s-seat!" Shakes exclaimed.

"It's my fucking car, isn't it?"

Blondie listened to them quarrel through the open window, debating whether to join them. Even the rain might be better than sitting in a car with two nudey loonies and a mud man.

"You never said you wanted a divorce," Meryl whined.

"Well, I didn't until I found out what you've been doing behind my back," Dispatch said with as much umbrage as he could muster.

Meryl stared at him for a moment longer and then began to giggle. She laughed so hard she rolled over on Dispatch, pinning him to the seat.

"Oh, Darrel, no one will believe you just happened to be out here with a camera. Anyway, you only got our faces."

"I did? Well, let me get another shot."

Dispatch reached into his pocket for a flash bulb. By the time he put it in the camera, Meryl had donned her skirt and was holding her blouse in front of her chest.

"Go ahead, take your picture. People will wonder why your buddy was sitting around naked with your wife."

Dispatch squeezed off another shot.

As if a corresponding light had gone off in her head, Meryl turned toward Shakes.

"You were in on this all along, weren't you?"

Shakes looked away.

"I'm g-getting d-dressed," he announced, reaching for his jeans.

"You didn't really want to make love with me, did you?"

For a minute, Blondie thought Meryl was going to cry.

Ah shit, he told himself, and wandered out of the bushes. It was just too fucking miserable to hold back any longer.

"Blondie!" Meryl gasped.

She looked at Dispatch.

"Did you ask all your friends?"

"I needed a witness."

"You're so dumb for being so smart, Darrel. None of this is going to get you anywhere."

"We'll see," Dispatch said, sticking to his guns.

"Can I get in?" Blondie asked. "I'm freezing."

"Sorry, Blondie," Dispatch said. He slid over on the back seat. Blondie sat down on a film of mud.

For a moment, they all looked at each other, as if they were four strangers in a lifeboat. Then, Blondie felt a slight shift beneath them.

"Oh shit!" Dispatch yelled.

"Wh-what is it?" Shakes cried.

"We're moving."

"That's n-not p-possible," Shakes argued. "I've got it in park."

"You parked too close to the edge of the hill!" Dispatch shouted at him.

"I p-parked j-just where you t-told me to, d-damn it," Shakes yelled back.

Blondie rubbed his eyes. It couldn't be true. He wasn't sitting in a car with three total idiots sliding down a steep grade at the end of Fishers Lane. But he knew better. He also knew nothing could stop them from sliding all the way to the bottom—and, worse, that Dispatch would never be able to drive the P-mobile back up the slippery slope.

Chapter Thirty-Five

America's blonde goddess was dead, overdosed on sleeping pills at the age of 36. The country was in shock. Blondie didn't know what to make of it. It was as if her death had called into question the American dream.

More upsetting to Blondie was a short announcement on the back page of *The Mayhew Courier*. It was an obituary notice for an Arnold Pulaski, age 23, who'd been shot by a sniper near the village of Tan An 20 miles southwest of Saigon. Mountain had been "in-country," as Blondie had heard the expression on television, for just six days.

Mountain was dead. But the marriage of Dispatch lived on. According to the Grouper, who'd accompanied Dispatch to court, the judge had termed Dispatch's petition for divorce "farcical and impertinent" before delivering his unfavorable verdict.

"Well, there could be worse things than being married to Meryl," Dispatch said to Grouper and Blondie a couple days later.

Blondie and Grouper just stared at him.

"Couldn't there be?" Dispatch pleaded.

Frank Sinatra had sung that "love and marriage went together like a horse and carriage," but Blondie was beginning to wonder. Maybe they weren't as closely related as he'd thought. He didn't like to reflect on that. If love and marriage weren't slices of the same pie, maybe his love for her was no guarantee they'd make it in marriage—as if getting together with her was any more than the wildest pipedream in the first place.

It was ridiculous for him to even think about her. He hadn't seen her since graduation day. Anyway, he was still involved with Flossie, although he'd begun experiencing an edginess when he was around her. He realized he'd felt a similar feeling before, always when something was about to come to an end. He could recall several times, even before his father told them he'd been reassigned, when he'd already begun letting go of his friends. Perhaps it was the sixth sense of an army brat who'd moved every year or two.

The following evening, with Flossie, he felt that old sensation. They were on the sofa in their family room watching television. Flossie acted skittish whenever he tried to get close.

"What's the matter?" he asked.

"Will we still be going together when you're at college?"

Blondie hadn't thought they were "going together" now. He preferred to think of their relationship as steady dating rather than going steady, although he wasn't sure anyone else would grasp the distinction.

"It would be selfish of me to keep you from dating other guys," Blondie answered magnanimously. He'd been expecting the question.

She returned a skeptical look.

"Are you going to date other girls?"

"That's part of going to college…meeting new people."

"Sleeping with them?"

Blondie shrugged. What did she expect him to say? He was beginning to feel lousy.

She eased his hand from her thigh.

"That's no reason to change what we have," Blondie said.

"With everyone else I've ever known, I've accepted them dating other girls. No matter how I felt about it, I always made it okay. I can't do that with you."

She seemed small, shy, frightened, loving. The look in her eyes tore at his heart. She truly cared about him. He'd known all along.

He let his eyes meet hers. What could he do? Flossie was nice-looking, but not beautiful like Tammy. And she wasn't college material. She might even love him, but what future did they have?

"Well, I guess that's it then," he said.

Why did he feel so guilty? So low? She was the one calling it off, wasn't she? When tears came to her eyes, he had to look away.

After he'd taken her home, he felt a hole in his heart—and his ego. For months, Flossie had been there to reassure him he was someone desirable, someone special. How could he let go of that? But how could he go on, stringing her along, knowing the inevitability of their parting. He told himself he'd done the noble thing.

Loneliness assailed him the next morning. Blondie knew he could sink into the worst kind of self-pity if he couldn't get rid of it. He needed to share his misery and he knew Grouper wouldn't be sympathetic. Instead, he called Feller and arranged a bull session at the quarry.

He knew he'd made a wise choice when, as the beers were going down, Feller agreed with his decision.

"I'm in the same boat with Delores," Feller said. "I just don't want to cut my water off before I can get in with some sweet co-ed."

Blondie didn't like hearing it that way. It sounded too cold. But wasn't that what he'd been thinking?

"We're still together on Smith-Reid, right?" Blondie asked him.

"Blood brothers to the end," Feller answered.

Blondie felt a little loopy driving Feller back to his house. He thought maybe that was why he was being so paranoid. He could swear he and Feller were being followed. He'd first noticed the car near the shopping mall after they'd turned onto the main road. It had been too dark to get the make, but it wasn't hard to spot—one of its headlights was out.

The car followed the Dart all the way through town, duplicating the one turn he made. Blondie told himself it was a coincidence. Just to make sure, though, he made a sharp turn onto Maidenspring Lane a couple miles from Feller's house. Not many people went down it at night.

"Where are you going?" Feller asked.

"I think we're being followed," Blondie said.

Feller turned just as the one-eyed auto turned onto the road behind them.

"It's missing a headlight."

"Yeah."

Feller strained to discern the car's make, but he finally told Blondie it was too dark. It didn't matter. Blondie knew what the car would be: a 1959 black Buick, with upswept tail fins like a bird on the wing...a dark raven sweeping along behind them, bringing doom.

"It's Potter," Blondie said dismally.

Moreover, his ploy to see if they were being followed now struck him as extremely ill advised. Each revolution of the Dart's wheels was taking them further and further from the relative safety of Fenton—and in only a few miles Maidenspring Lane dead-ended at a deserted farm.

"We could stop and confront him," Feller said. "There are two of us. We should be able to handle him...."

His statement, begun in confidence, faded to a wish. He too had seen Potter working in his yard, shirtless, a miniature bison.

Blondie didn't get it. Why did Potter hate him so? Was it because he'd spent his youth in the pen and most of his time since with his humpbacked crone of a mother and hated anyone who appeared to be enjoying life? It wasn't right. For having a little fun, he and Feller were going to die, strangled by Potter's stubby fingers or beat to death by his ham-hock fists.

Blondie ransacked his mind for a way out. Perhaps, they could apologize. But what for? They could hide in the woods that were flying past at dizzying speed on either side of the car. No time for that, though. Or they could stay in the car with the doors locked. But windows were vulnerable to swift-moving tire irons.

"Isn't there a dirt road off this one?" Blondie asked.

"Yeah, you're right," Feller said. "But I don't know where it goes."

"Doesn't it connect with Wheelhouse Road?"

"I don't know."

Why didn't Feller know? He was the one who'd grown up here.

"Someone told me it did," Blondie stated emphatically, hoping assertion would help prove fact.

"That's good enough for me," Feller said. "How far is it?"

"It's coming up soon. Can we turn onto it without Potter seeing us?"

"I don't know. He's right behind."

Blondie flinched as a bat flew in front of the windshield. The demons were out tonight.

"Stop!" Feller yelled, as if an elephant had wandered onto the road ahead.

Blondie jammed on the brakes, skidding on the gravel and catapulting loose stones into the dark. For a moment, Blondie feared he'd stopped too short. The headlights of their pursuer ballooned in size. He was going to crash into them!

"Now hit it! Let's lose him." Feller said.

Just before the seemingly inevitable collision, Blondie took his foot off the brake and stomped down on the accelerator. A barrage of loose stones clattered against the car behind them as the Dart shot forward. The headlights in the rearview mirror shrank.

Blondie rounded a corner and Feller screamed, "There it is!"

Barely visible in the tangle of dead brush along the shoulder was a small gap. Blondie skidded around the turn and onto the dirt road, then killed the lights. For an instant, they careened on the edge of disaster, then the tires caught hold. Blondie stomped on the brakes and looked back. There was a brief explosion of light in the space between the trees, then darkness.

Blondie turned the lights back on and sped away.

At first, Blondie felt relieved. He was going to live through the night. Fantastic. Then, anger welled. Why should they have been frightened half out of their wits? Who was Potter to push them around?

"We've got to do something about that asshole," he said to Feller.

"Why don't we run up to him and ram our faces into his fists?" Feller suggested.

"I'm serious. He's a menace to society. He's a psychological cripple, an evil man."

"And un-American," Feller joshed.

"We've got to do something," Blondie maintained.

"What are we going to do? Tell the cops?"

"Why not? Isn't there a law against following decent people around in the middle of the night?"

"What decent people?"

"We were just minding our business," Blondie argued, his voice rising.

"We're two underage guys who were just out in the middle of a pasture drinking," Feller reminded him.

"But who knows that?"

"Anyone who looks in the back seat."

Blondie turned to see a six-pack.

"We can toss it," Blondie said.

"WHAT?"

"Okay, we can put it in the trunk."

"You're serious about this, aren't you?" Feller asked.

"You're damned right. I'm tired of being pushed around just because I'm a kid. Anyway, I'm not a kid anymore. I'm eighteen now."

"That'll get the police's attention," Feller said dryly.

Within minutes, they were in the parking lot at the highway patrol barracks on Baltimore Pike, the six-pack hidden in the trunk.

"I'll do the talking," Blondie said.

"It's your show. Just don't aim your breath at anyone."

Blondie strode into the gray flagstone building, noting the yellow and black Maryland flag over the entrance. He lived in a free state in a free country. He had rights. Feller trudged behind.

A portly, balding man in uniform eyed them from behind a chest-high wooden counter.

"What's the problem, boys?" he asked.

"Sir, we're being harassed by a homicidal maniac," Blondie blurted out. "not to mention a real asshole."

Feller lowered his head and rubbed the bridge of his nose.

"Is that so?" the officer said. "And where and when did this alleged harassment occur?"

"On Maidenspring Lane. Just a few minutes ago."

The officer held up a buff-colored form. It had been filled in with a pencil.

"That's mighty interesting. I just received a report from a gentleman who says two boys in a green Dodge Dart nearly ran him off the road on Maidenspring Lane. I wonder what kind of car you might be driving."

"Now, wait a minute," Blondie protested. "Can't you see what he's up to?"

"Who?" the officer asked.

"The selfsame asshole I was telling you about. Potter, right?"

The officer's eyes tightened.

"Listen boys, I don't have to tell you anything. A citizen has the right to make a complaint without fear of reprisals."

He was protecting Potter from them?

"But just to rest your mind, I will tell you this. The name wasn't Potter."

"What? Let me see that form."

Blondie reached for the paper in the patrolman's hand. The officer caught his wrist in a steel grip.

"Son, you're skating on the edge. I don't know what happened out there, but I'll be willing to drop the matter if the two of you leave right now."

"That's not right," Blondie argued. "We're law-abiding citizens just out for a drive."

"At eleven at night on a dead-end road? Seems a little unusual to me. You know, harassing a citizen with your car could buy you a nice room for the rest of the night—if you don't mind bars across the windows."

"I think we can be big about this," Feller interjected. "We can forgive and forget."

Blondie glared at the officer, his wrist still in his grip. The officer tightened his fingers and Blondie winced.

"What do you say, blond boy? Can I get back to my paperwork or should I come out and scout around your car?"

Blondie's resistance collapsed.

"Just trying to do our duty, sir," Blondie whispered through clenched teeth.

"I'm sure," the officer replied, releasing Blondie's arm. "Well, good evening, gentlemen."

"Fuck!" Blondie exclaimed as soon as they were outside.

"Who do you think it was?" Feller asked.

"It was Potter. He just used another name."

After dropping Feller off, Blondie's mind fastened on a fact that had been lost in the heat of battle. Potter lived next door to him! And he'd had plenty of time to make it home.

Sure enough, when Blondie turned into their cul-de-sac, Potter's Buick was parked in his drive. Blondie was surprised that no lights showed through the windows. Had he already gone to bed or was he lurking beneath their front porch? Blondie took a careful look around before he got out of the car. He saw nothing amiss.

Once inside, Blondie locked the front door and went upstairs to his parents' bedroom. He'd been sleeping there during the hot nights of August because it offered better circulation. He pushed his parents' ancient Capehart stereo against the bedroom door. One couldn't be too cautious with a lunatic next door. Blondie stripped to his briefs and hopped into bed. There was a faint light on the far wall. Someone was still up at the Tillys.

Blondie tried to still his mind by thinking of something besides Potter. But his menacing bulk shadowed every thought. Then Blondie remembered what Potter had written his parents...all-night orgies. The idea of that gave him something else to ponder. He could feel his right hand begin to close into a circle. No, he told himself, it wouldn't be appropriate to flog his dog after such a harrowing encounter.

Nonetheless, a line of naked girls soon paraded before his closed eyes. He was a sultan and it was time to make his annual selection of harem girls. Each girl showed her wares as she passed. Blondie began to moan. Down the line he could see Tammy coming. Her body was perfect, like a statue come to life. Nessie began pushing against his jockey shorts. Yes, this was the way to get a grip on life, he thought.

The line of girls stopped. Blondie opened his eyes. His harem girls vanished. He'd heard a creaking noise...like a door opening. Something moved and Blondie's heart stopped. It was his reflection in the vanity mirror.

Blondie heard another creak. It sounded like a footstep on the stairs. He cocked his right ear toward the noise. There was no doubt...someone was climbing the stairs!

Potter was coming for him and he wasn't going to be denied. Blondie's imagination sketched every detail of the steel shank he'd be carrying. Potter would disembowel him, then eat his entrails. Blondie felt as if his quivering intestines were trying to crawl out of his body and hide under the bed.

"Who's there?" he called out.

The words seemed deafening inside his head, but were swallowed up in the stillness of the house. He cried out again. The steps stopped outside the door. The doorknob began to turn. The bolt slid open and the door smacked into the Capehart.

"Y-a-a-gh!" Blondie yelled as he sprang from the bed. He tugged at the handles on the nearest window until it flew open. Tiny wires punctured

Blondie's skin as he dove headfirst through the window onto the shed roof. He'd forgotten to remove the screen.

"Help! Help!" Blondie screamed, jumping up and down on the shed roof. "Murder!"

Light burst from the windows in neighboring houses. The first person to appear was Mr. Tilly. He was wearing a bathrobe and house slippers, and carrying a fireplace poker and flashlight. He swung the beam back and forth across Blondie's back yard.

"Up here," Blondie yelled at him.

Mr. Tilly shone his flashlight on Blondie. He suddenly realized he was wearing nothing but his briefs.

"What's the matter?" Tilly asked as other rumpled bodies appeared behind other points of light. Soon, there was a small crowd. Blondie saw Rudy join the group. He was fully dressed.

"It's Potter," Blondie yelled at the growing throng. "He's gone berserk. He's got a knife and he's trying to break into my room."

Behind him, Blondie heard the door banging against the Capehart. He leapt to the ground and ran over to Mr. Tilly and the others.

"Potter?" someone repeated.

"Yeah. He's flipped. He's gone mad from living all alone with his mother…incest, I bet."

The small band crept toward the front of Blondie's house in nightgowns, pajamas, and other nighttime apparel, bunched together, as if expecting at any moment the frenzied attack of a crazed ex-con.

When they turned the corner onto the front lawn, a light came on next door. To Blondie's astonishment and chagrin, Mr. Potter—in dingy coveralls—strode onto their porch. He crossed his arms and gave the group a malevolent stare.

Mr. Tilly scowled at Blondie.

"I thought it was him," Blondie said sheepishly.

They heard a shout and the group fell back. The front door opened. Feller backed from its yawning maw.

"Christ, am I glad to see you, Blondie," he said when he caught sight of him. "Something awful's going on inside your house. I heard screaming from your bedroom."

"You were in my house?"

"Yeah, I came back to see if you wanted me to stay over, what with that nut Potter next door."

Feller noticed Potter standing on his porch and blanched.

"How'd you get in?" Blondie asked.

"You gave me a key, remember? Right at the start of the summer. So I could donate to the Beer Bank if you weren't home."

"Be quiet about that," Blondie whispered to Feller. For the first time, he noticed the Fellers' Fairlane parked along the curb below.

There was an embarrassed rustling as neighbors became aware of their dishabille. Robes drew tighter and eyes turned away. People began heading for their homes.

"I wouldn't want to be in your shoes now," Mr. Tilly said, throwing his gaze Potter's way. A couple of the other neighbors directed vicious looks his way. He guessed next time they'd let Potter have him.

So Potter hadn't been the one in his house. Blondie was sure it had been he following them down Maidenspring Lane, though. He'd seen his Buick…well, he was pretty sure he had. Anyway, it had to have been Potter who'd written his parents in New York. Who else would have done it?

The next time the Club went out drinking, Feller told everyone about their evening, elaborating on every detail. Blondie thought he was way too descriptive of his plunge through the upstairs window. For the first time Blondie could remember, Grouper laughed aloud.

"**Hell hath no furies like a wimp's fears,**" he said.

Chapter Thirty-Six

His folks arrived home two days early. His mom gave him a hug, then a probing look, as if to ask whether he'd been involved in any more mischief. (Blondie was glad he'd scrapped the Beer Bank the week before when they'd topped it off.) His dad's look was hesitant, as if he were unsure of his standing.

Blondie had given the matter some thought during their absence. How could he feel the same about Francis knowing he wasn't his real dad? He decided he couldn't. The funny thing was he liked him *better* knowing that. His measuring rod wasn't as severe for a step dad as for a father.

Another good thing. He immediately noticed that his mom and dad were getting along better. The tension that had calcified their every interaction for months was no longer evident. Blondie figured they must have reached some resolution, if only to carry on. Maybe that's what people meant by commitment. It didn't seem romantic in the slightest, but Blondie was beginning to wonder if the reality of relationships was ever a matter of romance. Perhaps romance was something within oneself—an aspiration, a figment of the imagination—that one applied to the world rather than discovered there.

Whatever had changed, Blondie was glad they were back. Since he and Flossie had broken things off, he'd found the house an increasingly lonely place—and the guys weren't enough. Actually, he realized he was beginning to tire of all the nights he spent drinking and bullshitting with them. Most evenings, he came home with his brain in a fog, slept late, and woke up with a hangover. What was the thrill? Where was the gain?

The only evenings that had seemed fulfilling were those infrequent occasions when he and Grouper had gone up to the Overlook to "ruminate," as Grouper put it. There, they spoke not just of what was going on, but of the *meaning* of things. Blondie felt he could tell Grouper anything—his dreams, his most hidden feelings. Thus, he hadn't hesitated to share his growing disinterest in the B & F Club's capers.

"**You can't be a kid forever,**" was all Grouper had said.

After his parents settled in, Blondie decided to ask Francis the question that had been fluttering inside his mind ever since the night Potter had followed him and Feller home.

"Dad," Blondie said. He wanted to use that word.

His father looked up from the paper.

"The Birds lost yesterday," he said.

"Dad, I need to know something."

"What's that, Bernard?"

"Did you know about Potter when you bought our house?"

"Know what?"

Geez, was he playing dumb or what?

"About him killing a man."

"Killing a man? Mr. Potter never killed anyone," his dad said. "Who told you that?"

"Rudy."

"Well, he doesn't know what he's talking about."

His dad seemed annoyed.

"He wasn't in prison?"

His dad put his paper down. His eyes softened.

"Mr. Potter was in jail for a few months as a kid. He stole a car and got caught. I don't think we should judge him too harshly for that. He's had a hard life, caring for his mother and all. She's not quite right in the head you know."

She's not quite right in the head? Blondie debated telling his dad about how Potter had been tormenting him. So he hadn't killed anyone. He was still a bad actor. On the other hand, Blondie figured he didn't deserve to be called a murderer if he wasn't. He resolved to straighten Rudy out.

Blondie excused himself and headed for the Tillys, although he felt a little nervous about seeing Rudy again. He might still be pissed about their encounter at the Cherrys' pond.

As he started up the steps to their front porch, Blondie happened to glance at the white Mercury in the drive. It was the same car Rudy'd been driving the night of the prom. One of the front headlights was broken, the glass held together with electrical tape. Blondie felt like a medicine ball had been dropped on his stomach.

"Why, Bernard, what a pleasant surprise," Mrs. Tilly said when she opened the door. Mr. Tilly, who was lounging in a Barcalounger in his Sunday pants and a sleeveless tee shirt reading the paper, was less friendly. He curtly nodded his head and went back to the funnies. Blondie guessed he hadn't forgiven him for his late-night alarm the week before.

Rudy was at his desk building a plastic model of a battleship. His room was filled with miniature planes, ships and cars. What a juvenile hobby for someone who'd been senior class president!

"You're a prick," he said to Rudy when he turned.

Rudy sat back in shock.

"You know what I'm talking about," Blondie said, the heat of his anger driving him on. "You're the one who followed me the other night, aren't you?"

Rudy blushed and then shrugged.

"I was just coming home," he said.

"Maidenspring Lane's not on your way home."

Rudy said nothing. Defiance was in his eyes.

"You sent that letter to New York too, didn't you?"

"So what?" Rudy's said indignantly. "You and your ilk think you're such hot shits."

Ilk? Hot shits? Was Blondie hearing this right? Rudy, super politico of their class, upset because he thought the B & F Club acted superior?

"What are you talking about?"

"The way you treat people...."

"Who?"

"Mary Cherry for one. And Phyllis."

Phyllis? He cared about Phyllis? First Shakes and now Rudy. Was Blondie nuts or blind or both? How could anyone care about Phyllis?

"You asked her to the prom, didn't you?" Blondie probed.

Rudy's look affirmed it.

"We've been dating all summer," he said. "She told me how you treated her that night."

For a moment, Blondie was speechless. The peckerhead was playing the gallant knight.

"I ought to punch you out," he finally said.

"Asshole," Rudy replied.

Blondie could see this was getting nowhere. And he *was* in Rudy's house.

"The two of you deserve each other," Blondie said as he stomped off.

What a turn of events! All this time he'd been fearing Potter, blaming him for being a tormentor, and his only sin was being a cranky old coot who guarded his yard like a bull terrier.

When Blondie rounded the corner of his house, he was surprised to see Potter standing on their porch. Blondie jumped back and peeked around the corner. He was talking to his mom, who was standing in the doorway. She was looking at him in a consoling way. Blondie ducked behind the chimney as Potter made his way down the stairs and across their lawn to his house.

"What was Potter doing here?" Blondie asked his mom when he got inside.

"His mother died this morning," she answered. "Poor man. He doesn't know what to do with himself. She was all he had."

Blondie felt a pang of sympathy he wouldn't have thought possible even moments before. Maybe everyone, no matter how shitty they seemed, had feelings. It was an awesome possibility. But it wasn't the first thing on his mind. The first thing on his mind was death.

Bobby, Mountain, Marilyn, Mrs. Potter. The body count was rising. What had Grouper said? *People die.* Blondie'd known that intellectually, but never before had it had any emotional force. Suddenly, intimations of mortality whispered to him from every quarter. Thinking that life was so…*terminal*…was almost unbearable.

* * * * * * * *

The trip to Ocean City was Shakes' idea. They were in the P-mobile drinking beer at the quarry several nights after Blondie's folks returned—everyone but Grouper. Shakes was griping about summer coming to an end.

"I d-don't w-want to just g-go back to school," he said.

Shakes and Dispatch had been accepted to the University of Maryland and decided to go.

"What are you going to do, Shakes, stop the clock?" Brick asked.

Brick didn't like talking about college. He hadn't applied. With his grades, it would have been futile. He was planning to join his dad in his grocery wholesale business.

"I mean w-we ought to d-do something."

"Steal a car, beat our meats, what?"

"C-come on, Brick, that's n-not what I meant."

"What did you mean, Shakes?" Feller asked.

"R-raise h-hell."

"That's it? That's your idea? Raise hell?"

Shakes was briefly cowed by Brick's sarcasm.

"We c-could g-go to Ocean City," Shakes offered, watching for the group's reaction.

Nobody said anything.

"Over L-labor D-day weekend," he added.

"Hm-m-m," Feller murmured.

Blondie'd been to Ocean City once with his parents. He remembered it as a seedy version of Atlantic City: large, white-shingled houses transformed into run-down hotels, an old and splintery boardwalk, tiny shops with tawdry merchandise. And the smells…fried fish, cotton candy, salt air and saltwater taffy. But what Blondie remembered most were the kids. Ocean City belonged to teenagers.

The notion of one last madcap escapade suddenly seemed enticing. A little craziness might lessen the weight of recent events: Bobby's suicide, his breakup with Flossie, Rudy's betrayal. It might be good for his mental health to blow his mind in one ultimate, three-day-long, beer-guzzling, girl-chasing sortie.

"It *could* be fun," Blondie allowed.

"What would we do?" Brick asked, still skeptical.

"We c-could g-get drunk," Shakes said.

"We could get laid," Dispatch said.

"We could get arrested," Brick added.

"You're being too negative, Brick," Feller said. "Shakes and Dispatch are both right. We could get drunk *and* laid."

"The place has to be cheap," Brick said.

"And sleazy," Dispatch added. "So we don't arouse any attention."

"Cheap and sleazy, huh?" Feller said. "I don't think that'll be any problem."

It had been decided.

"What about Gr-grouper?" Shakes asked.

Blondie had almost forgotten him.

"Do you know what's going on with him, Blondie?" Feller asked.

"Same old, same old…problems with his folks," Blondie lied. He didn't feel comfortable telling them Grouper had lost interest in their company.

"Y-yeah, old m-man Whipple is pretty w-weird."

"Blondie, why don't you get in touch with Grouper and tell him our plan," Feller suggested.

Blondie realized he wanted him to come, even if he chose not to join in some of their activities. His presence would provide a steadying influence.

He realized the hopelessness of his cause the minute he heard Grouper's voice over the phone. It was lifeless. He invited him along anyway, making the jaunt sound as appealing as he could.

"I'm not in the mood for getting drunk and talking nonsense," Grouper responded.

"You seem to need a little merriment," Blondie said.

Grouper snorted.

"What can I say to change your mind?" Blondie asked.

"There's nothing you can say. I just don't feel like going. My life isn't right. I can't seem to find solid ground."

Blondie could identify with that.

"Look, you're not alone. I've been feeling a little off-center myself. Can we talk about it?"

"When?"

"Tonight?"

The line was silent for a while before Grouper agreed.

The night was so clear and bright there were shadows. Moonlight cast a frost-like sheen over the pasture and flooded the woods with a silvery fog. Blondie envied the moon. It was remote, detached, dignified. He wished he could be like that.

Grouper had been distant and grumpy the whole way up. He'd slumped against the door with his arms across his chest. However, after a few beers, and as Blondie shared his concerns, he gradually came to life.

Blondie told Grouper he'd felt a foreboding ever since Bobby's suicide. Marilyn's, Mountain's and Mrs. Potter's deaths had substantially compounded it.

"Have you been thinking of your own death?" Grouper asked.

"A little, I suppose. But that doesn't feel like what it's about."

"What then?"

"More like death is going to impact my life even more in the future."

Grouper laughed.

"I can guarantee you that."

Through the open windows, crickets fiddled and an owl romanced the moon.

"It bothers me to think that death is the end of everything," Blondie said after a time, "that's there nothing more."

"Maybe that's all people want eventually...an end to things. Relief."

Grouper's prosaic tone bothered him. He told Grouper so.

"What is it you want?" Grouper asked with a trace of exasperation. "Do you want me to tell you death is tragic...that it isn't fair...that it makes a mockery of life?"

Blondie realized that was precisely what he wanted to hear.

"Death is just part of the rules of the game. As Bobby showed, it can also be an option."

"That's pretty existential," Blondie complained.

Grouper sat up and clapped his hands.

"Existential! By God, I have taught you something."

"Get hosed."

After a few more beers, Blondie told Grouper about Rudy's betrayal.

"You shouldn't have been surprised," Grouper said. "You challenged his values."

"Me? I never said anything to him about anything like that. I just helped him with his homework."

"Don't you see, just by being the way you are, you rejected Rudy and everything he believed in...."

Grouper clamped his huge hand on Blondie's shoulder.

"....Rudy is a small-town guy, a play-by-the-rules guy. He's invested his whole life doing things the way Fenton told him they were supposed to be done. He's going to resent anyone who calls any of those rules into question—especially from someone who has to help him through school."

Blondie looked away, out through the windshield. Empty beer cans on the dash formed a row of steel tombstones that obscured the view of Fenton below. Blondie could feel it coming to an end—the nights drinking with the Club, the nights talking with Grouper. Inevitably, the bonds would be broken. Was that the sense of doom he was feeling?

"I'm not going to the University of Pennsylvania," Grouper said after he'd killed another beer.

"How come?"

"My dad wants me to stay on there and get a law degree. I don't want to be a lawyer."

"Have you told your folks?"

"No."

"Won't your dad be disappointed?"

"Yes. But I can't repeat his life."

"Where will you go to school?"

Blondie wondered if it was too late for Grouper to get into Smith-Reid. Wouldn't that be great? He and Feller and Grouper all at the same place?

"Where I go to college is not an important issue for me at this time."

The way he said it gave Blondie the creeps. Again, he wondered what was going on with him. It had to be more than not wanting to go to college where his dad wanted him to go. He felt uncomfortable probing, though.

"It's your life," was what he finally said.

"Exactly. That would seem to give me a great deal of say about it."

Blondie could think of no reply. He was beginning to have trouble thinking of anything. His thoughts were slowing down, spacing out. The alcohol.

"Maybe we should go back," he said.

"No, not yet."

Blondie felt Grouper's hand apply a trifle more pressure on his shoulder. He looked his way, but he was looking straight ahead.

"I envy you, Blondie," he said seconds later.

Blondie was astonished. How could Grouper envy him when his whole life was off-kilter?

"You have ability and you have a dream, one that might come true," Grouper continued.

"What? My writing? All you've ever read of mine is a silly poem and some abysmal articles in the school paper."

"True. But they show me you have a talent, one that will point your direction."

Blondie didn't feel any sense of direction.

"You're smarter than I am," Blondie said. "I wish I had your mind."

"No, I don't think so. It's more a burden than a blessing. Anyway, being smart isn't the same as being talented. It doesn't tell you where to go."

Grouper slumped back in his seat.

"You underestimate yourself, Blondie."

He said it in almost a loving way.

"Before we're all blown away to the four winds, there's something I need to tell you...." Grouper halted.

He sighed and it was as if all the noises of the night were sucked into his breath.

"This is harder than I thought."

Grouper dropped his hand from Blondie's shoulder.

"Go ahead," Blondie encouraged him. "You can talk to me."

Blondie couldn't understand why Grouper was being so hesitant. What could he possibly have to say that would shock him? That he'd cheated on a test, swiped a record, peeked up a girl's skirt?

"I never had a girlfriend before Meryl...."

Blondie hoped Grouper wasn't going to start bemoaning her loss. There was no way he could sympathize with him over that.

"...not because I could never get one, though that might have proven true. I never even tried."

"Well, I guess that's okay," Blondie said, relieved. So Grouper was afraid of girls. So what? They all were to one degree or another.

Grouper fell silent. Blondie wondered if he'd said something wrong.

"I've never told anyone this..." Grouper began again. This time Blondie didn't interrupt. "...I've never found girls that appealing."

"What *are* you trying to say?" The sense of dread he'd felt before returned.

"I think you know."

Blondie felt a tremor along his neck. Grouper was telling him he was a guy who liked guys! That made him a.... Blondie refused to let the word into his brain. But images popped up. Images of guys doing things to each other—*disgusting* things. It couldn't be true. Not his *best friend*.

"What about Meryl? You were banging her," Blondie argued.

Grouper waved his hand dismissively.

"I never said that. If I intimated it, it was a lie. I never touched her. At first, she thought I was just being shy or playing the gentleman. But she figured it out. She called me a...pervert."

Grouper's words broke in anguish.

"How can you be so positive?"

Surely, there was room for doubt. Perhaps he was just unusually shy around girls.

"That's the sixty-four-dollar question. It's not something you want to acknowledge. My first inkling came when I was fourteen and visited my cousin in D.C. He was fifteen. One night, after our parents had gone off to some function, he asked me if I wanted to play 'blind man' with him."

"Blind man?"

"It was just a name he'd made up...." Grouper said in a monotone. "He asked me to strip to my shorts and get into bed with him in the dark. Once we were under the covers, he took off his underpants and asked me to do the same. Then, we stroked each other until we were both spent."

Blondie shuddered. He couldn't help it. What Grouper was talking about was *gross*.

"It was just a lark to my cousin," Grouper continued, his words as slow and steady as a lava flow. "But to me it was a revelation. It explained why I'd never been attracted to girls."

An even more disturbing thought wormed into Blondie's mind.

"You never think of *us* that way....?"

"I wouldn't say 'never,'" Grouper answered in a whisper.

Blondie asked no more. He wanted to bolt from the car. He felt himself in the grip of an ever-growing horror.

"That time with my cousin was the only time I've ever done anything with a guy." Grouper said after a while. "But I've had desires...."

"Maybe they'll go away," Blondie offered, his voice trembling.

Grouper snorted.

"Not likely. When I think of someone at night, someone I'd like to be with, it's not a girl. And, yes, my parents know. They won't admit it, but they know. I see it every time my father looks at me. His look hurts more than I could ever describe."

Grouper's voice cracked again. Blondie looked out the window into the darkness, forcing his thoughts to slow down. He noticed that the owl had stopped hooting and the crickets had quit chirping. Was the whole world holding its breath? Listening in?

"Is that why you hate billies so?" Blondie asked to keep the stillness from overwhelming him.

"Let's just say there's a natural antipathy between those who celebrate brutish maleness and those who supposedly fall on the more feminine side of life."

There was a cynical edge to Grouper's words.

"Why are you telling me this?" Blondie asked.

"Did you ever feel there was something so big inside that you'd explode if you didn't get it out?" Grouper asked, looking toward him. Blondie was glad he couldn't see his face.

"That's how this thing feels to me," he went on. "Keeping it in for so long has made me feel so alone, like no one else in the world has any idea who I am—as if I'm not authentic, not *real*."

For a moment, Blondie could empathize with Grouper's distress: to carry such a big secret inside, to try and contain its pressure. He could identify with that. Wasn't that how he felt about Tammy? He could imagine how much more burdensome Grouper's secret had to be.

Blondie tried to process what Grouper had told him, to find a way to let his words in and still think of him as before. Wasn't that what a friend was supposed to do—accept someone as they were? Then why was he having so much trouble doing it? He realized it was because of an even more frightening thought lingering in his mind. He had to pursue it.

"But me?" Blondie pressed. "Why are you telling *me*?"

Grouper's shoulders trembled. Blondie feared he was going to cry. He didn't know how he would handle that. He reached across the car and put his hand on Grouper's shoulder. Even if he didn't understand all that Grouper was trying to tell him—even if he found parts of it monstrous—he owed him some comfort in his distress. Grouper's trembling stopped.

When he spoke again, his voice was tremulous and faint.

"Because I love you...."

Before Blondie could stop himself, before he was aware of any thought whatsoever, he lifted his hand slightly from Grouper's shoulder. He prayed Grouper hadn't noticed, but he knew Grouper noticed everything.

"....and maybe because I dared believe you might accept me for what I am."

There was a momentary catch in Grouper's deep voice and a shuddering throughout his whole body. For an instant, Blondie considered tightening his fingers around Grouper's shoulder in a firm grasp of support. But he couldn't do it. What if Grouper misunderstood? What if he touched him back?

"Sure, Grouper, sure," Blondie said instead. "You know we're buddies."

For a few seconds, Blondie felt proud of himself for extending himself that far. Then he felt ashamed. His words had fallen well short of what Grouper needed—and already it was much too late to add to them.

On the way back to Grouper's house, Blondie attempted to make small talk with him, as if nothing momentous had happened. But, as he lay in bed later, questioning his every word and gesture, he knew he'd botched some critical and irretrievable moment in time and that, all good intentions aside, things would never be the same between him and Grouper again.

Chapter Thirty-Seven

Everyone was *psyched*. The zaniness had started as soon as they'd made the big buy—five cases of Pabst in Baltimore County. They'd put most of their treasure in a large cooler Feller'd copped from his folks. One case remained up front for on the way.

The radio, on full blast, bombarded them with "The Loco-motion" by Little Eva, the "Wah-wahtusi" by the Orlons, and "Palisades Park" by Freddy Cannon. When "The Stripper" came on, Shakes began to take his shirt off.

"Leave it on," Brick ordered. "I don't want to get sick."

Long before they reached the endless steel-and-concrete hump of the Chesapeake Bay Bridge, Shakes was blasted. Every time they passed a car full of young people headed their way—and there were plenty—Shakes stuck his head out the window and shouted "R-raise H-hell!" as loud as he could.

Two guys in a red MG took umbrage at Shakes' enthusiasm and shot him the finger as they approached the high point of the bridge. Shakes' response was to drop his shorts and stick his skinny butt out the window. While tilting white sails sliced across the deep blue of the Bay, Shakes mooned both halves of Maryland.

Dispatch stopped for gas. After placing the pump in the tank, he headed for a pay phone. Anger masked his face when he returned.

"I thought I had Meryl ready to give me a divorce," he told them. "I offered her my new car. I know there's someone she likes at the store where she works."

"So what happened?" Blondie asked.

"She said she'd be happy to take my car, but no divorce."

"That's a bunch of shit," Brick said.

"L-long d-distance shit," Shakes added.

"I'm sure there's a moral in this," Feller said. "Too bad Grouper's not here. Blondie, you're not too bad with words. Why don't you take a shot?"

Blondie wasn't sure it was appropriate for him to be postulating laws in Grouper's absence—even thinking about Grouper left him feeling unsettled—but he couldn't resist the flattery. After giving the matter some thought, he said, "**Never spend good money for bad news.**"

"Not bad," Feller nodded. "Not bad."

Dispatch's call served to remind Blondie of an important fact. No matter how many sorties the group went on, or how far they traveled, they couldn't escape the pesky, insistent reality of the rest of their lives.

The P-mobile hurtled onward, over the flat brown and green arm of Maryland's eastern shore, past marshes of beige reeds and brackish water, past small farms and towns and occasional groves of trees. Road signs chronicled their progress. Ocean City—56. Ocean City—33. Ocean City—12.

They reached the outskirts at 7:30, as the sun was going down, its last rays painting the whitewashed buildings a tawny gold and turning their windows into fire.

The mournful voice of Ray Charles crooning "You Don't Know Me" drifted from the radio. It was the lament of a lover whose adored one has no idea of his devotion.

The song made Blondie sad. He thought of Tammy.

"We better get laid," Dispatch said when they reached the city limits. "It took us a lot of gas to get here."

"What're you worrying about?" Feller asked. "We all chipped in. Anyway, we're *all* going to get laid. We've got to believe that."

"I heard some girls from Fenton were coming over this weekend," Dispatch said.

"Who?" everyone asked at once.

"I think Delores…"

Feller groaned. A couple weeks before, he'd given her the pink slip. He'd been avoiding her ever since.

"And Mary Braithwaite and the Thompson twins."

"Dogs," Brick said.

"And someone told me Tammy Hollander was coming with her parents."

Blondie felt a rush in his chest. But what were the odds he'd run into her? This was the big weekend of the year for Maryland's teenagers. Thousands upon thousands of them would be scrabbling around the city like sand crabs.

No one had thought to make reservations, so they prowled the narrow streets for a half hour, checking out one hotel after the other. All were full.

"Good job, Dispatch," Brick said.

"Me? I never said I'd get a room."

Several blocks from the boardwalk and farther from the center of town than they wanted, they discovered a droopy inn grandly named the *Georgian*. A vacancy sign peeked out a window. Blondie volunteered to go in.

The screen door failed to close behind him. The lobby reeked of beer and vomit. Sand on the linoleum grated with each step he took. Blondie was encouraged. The *Georgian* seemed to be everything they were looking for.

A frowzy woman on the far side of middle age greeted Blondie like a long-lost friend. She wore a flowered cotton dress and a faded rose in her hair. She was drunk.

"I'm Kitty." She held out her hand.

Blondie didn't know if she wanted him to kiss it or what. He decided on "or what" and gave it a polite shake.

"Your sign says you have rooms."

"I always have rooms," she complained.

"Do you have two together?"

"Not good ones."

Understood, Blondie thought.

"I'd like to see them anyway," he said.

Navigating her way on unsteady legs, Kitty led him up two flights of creaking stairs and toward the back of the building.

The first room was a wreck. Split wallpaper curled toward the ceiling. Splinters forested the floor. All three cots sagged in the middle like over-raced thoroughbreds. A rusted sink huddled in one corner, its faucet dripping.

The adjoining room was better. It didn't have wallpaper or a sink and the bedsprings were close to horizontal. There was even a slight view of the ocean.

"How much?" Blondie asked.

While she puzzled it out, Blondie studied the thick sacks under her eyes, footlockers for years of disappointment.

"Can you handle twenty-five a night?" she finally asked.

Blondie looked at her.

"That's for both rooms," she added.

Five bucks per person per night? That was a bargain.

"Sure."

By the time Dispatch parked the P-mobile—no mean feat in a town of small streets lined with "no parking" signs—and they'd carried their gear to their rooms, it was eight-thirty.

Shakes opened the cooler and downed two more beers. The rest of them piled onto the sagging cots. Feathers exploded from holes in the mattresses.

"I think you've had enough," Feller said to Shakes. "Some of the rest of us are planning on drinking this weekend."

Blondie just wanted to crash, but the lure of the boardwalk was too great for the others. A beer or two each replenished their energy and spirits. They almost dragged Blondie out the door with them.

In four blocks, they reached the north end of the boardwalk. Heading south, they passed bevies of young females in swimsuits or Bermuda shorts and tee shirts. They giggled and chirped in what Blondie guessed was some sort of oceanside ecstasy. The most identifiable—and common sound—was the word "he."

As he walked along, listening to the crash of the sea and feeling the salt air scrub the day's sweat away, Blondie began to feel rejuvenated. He'd had doubts anything would come of their trip to the ocean, but he was growing more optimistic. There were so many girls. They had to have come for the same reason as the guys.

As they drew nearer the center of town, shops began to crowd the aging wooden walkway offering suntan lotions, tacky souvenirs, tee shirts, and food of all kinds.

Shakes was still smashed. He suggested they crawl under the boardwalk and look up through the cracks to "see what they could see."

"Great idea," Feller scoffed. "All the girls are wearing bathing suits or shorts."

"We could walk all night, but, eventually, we've got to make our move," Dispatch said, while casting a voracious look at some passing girls.

The group appointed Dispatch and Feller, who were considered the cockiest, to try and negotiate a deal with the next worthy group of girls—meaning girls who were not too young or too ugly to take back to their rooms.

"You guys get out of sight," Feller ordered the rest of them.

"N-now w-we can get under the b-boardwalk," Shakes enthused.

Blondie felt like an untouchable hiding under the rotting timbers. He saw no reason he shouldn't have stayed with Feller and Dispatch. He was presentable. Brick grumped beside a piling, while Shakes put his eye against an overhead knothole, hoping for a "beaver shot."

A clatter of sandals and clogs announced approaching quarry. Four of them. Blondie could see through the aging boards that, in spite of the late hour, they all still wore swimsuits.

"Good evening, ladies," Blondie heard Feller say.

There was some giggling.

"No need to hurry," Dispatch added.

The girls stopped. Blondie allowed himself a dose of optimism.

There were several minutes of "Whatcha doing?" and "Where you from?" and that sort of thing. Then, Feller went for the sale.

"We have a whole cooler full of beer in our room," he said.

"H-hey, that's j-just for us," Shakes squealed from below.

"What was that?" one of the girls asked.

"Oh, I'm sorry," Feller said. "I forgot to introduce my friends."

"What friends?"

"Guys, you can come up now," Feller called.

Blondie felt stupid crawling from beneath the boardwalk. Shakes lost his balance and fell back into the sand, emitting a loud belch.

"Who's that?" one of the girls said with disgust.

"Don't mind him," Feller said. "He's just a little drunk."

Blondie decided a couple of the girls weren't too bad. Of course, there was no guarantee he'd get one of them. Even if not, the idea of four scantily clad females in their rooms was most appealing.

It was going well. Feller and Dispatch had begun walking back toward the *Georgian*, with the girls chatting and laughing beside them.

"Which one d-do I g-get?" Shakes shouted from behind.

The girls turned and looked at him. He was wearing baggy checkered Bermudas and a T-shirt with a picture of a horse on it. Beneath its hooves was printed the word "Stud." Sand coated his arms and legs.

"He's not part of the deal," one of the girls said.

"I g-gotta have a g-girl," Shakes said.

"Maybe you could skip tonight," Feller suggested to him.

"N-no w-ay. I p-paid the s-same as everyone else and I sh-should g-get l-laid like everyone else."

The girls stopped walking.

"I thought this was just for some beer and conversation," a cute brunette said to Feller. "Isn't that what you said?"

"Ignore him," Feller said. "He's out of it."

"N-not out of it," Shakes retorted. "S-sick."

He struggled to the railing and let his lunch go in a yellow-brown torrent.

The girls disappeared like spring snow.

"Jesus Christ," Brick said.

"Let's call it a night," Blondie suggested.

Everyone agreed.

Chapter Thirty-Eight

Morning light roosted on Blondie's face, dueling on the insides of his eyelids with the remaining narcosis of several cans of beer. Blondie looked over at Feller's sheet-shrouded body. His face was as smooth and serene as a child's. They were in the back room, the "premier suite." as Feller had dubbed it. He'd convinced the others it was his due for founding the Club.

A continuous clattering resounded from the other side of the wall. It sounded like a Nazi column goose-stepping up the stairs. What were all these people doing up so early? Blondie grabbed his watch from the floor. It was already ten o'clock.

Blondie pulled on his shorts and a tee shirt and wandered out to the main room. Brick lay face down on his bed like a hit-and-run victim. Dispatch was already in the morgue, covered complete by a sheet. Shakes sprawled on his back, arms and legs at all angles, like a broken doll. He was snoring loudly.

Blondie eased open the door and slipped into the hall. He ambled down the decaying floorboards to a large balcony above the front entrance and plopped down in one of the metal rockers. He propped his feet on the balustrade and let the sun knead its warmth into his arms and legs.

He watched the morning traffic, mainly girls and guys streaming toward the beach with radios, coolers, blankets and other paraphernalia. He felt remote and godlike form his perch above the street.

Blondie heard someone join him on the balcony. It was a young man in flowered surfer shorts, nothing else. He was sipping something from a paper cup.

"Hi, I'm Donald Duck and I don't give a fuck," he said. He held up his cup. "Bacardi and Coke," he explained, though Blondie hadn't asked.

Blondie resented the intrusion. After a while, Blondie stole a closer look at the interloper. He was about six feet tall and lean, his tan belly taut as rawhide. He seemed preoccupied with drinking his rum and staring at the sky.

When he caught Blondie looking at him, he started talking again. He told Blondie he was a native of Dundalk, a sophomore at the University of Maryland, and a member of the school's lacrosse team. He straddled the railing and leaned back against the wall, letting the sun wash over his freckled face and reddish hair.

"Nirvana," he said.

A few minutes later, another young man, wearing a U. of Md. tee shirt over jockey shorts, wandered out to the porch. He was drinking a beer and scratching his testicles.

"This is George," the Duck told Blondie. "Around campus, he's known as Gross George."

He was shorter and fatter than his friend, with a rodent's face and rat hair. He had a vacant look in his eyes and Blondie doubted it was because of the beer.

Without pretext, Donald told Blondie a few stories about George: how he'd shown up uninvited at a snotty sorority party in jack boots and a motorcycle outfit...how he'd mooned the University librarian...how he'd thrown up on a visiting soccer team's bus and dared anyone to do anything about it.

"We're both members of Chi Chi Chi fraternity," Donald concluded with a burst of pride. "Tri-Chi."

George wandered around the porch, tugging at his privates as if he couldn't get them where he wanted.

"Hey George, do something gross," Donald said to him.

George went over to the railing and yelled down at some passing girls, "Is it too early in the morning for a little SOMF action?"

The girls glanced up at George in horror and hurried off. George went back inside.

"What was that word he used?" Blondie asked.

"What? SOMF? You don't know that one. It's big on campus. They put it on every issue of the school newspaper. S-O-M-F...sit on my face."

"You learn something every day," Blondie commented.

"Yeah," Donald agreed. "Say, what's your name?"

"Blondie."

"That figures. Want a drink?"

Blondie started to say no, then thought, "what the hell" and followed Donald to a room a couple doors down the hall. George was lying on the bed stark naked.

"Christ, George," Donald said to him with mild disapproval.

He turned to Blondie.

"Rum or beer?"

"Beer's fine."

Donald handed him a lukewarm Hamm's. Blondie hated Hamm's, but he didn't want to appear ungrateful.

Donald asked him what college he went to.

"I just graduated from high school in June," Blondie said.

"Hey, man, you're in for some good times then. College is a blast."

Blondie scrutinized the two of them. Were they what people meant by "college men"? They didn't act any differently from the B & F Club. He'd thought college guys would be more mature, more intellectual, their conversation laced with references to famous writers and philosophers. He hoped they weren't typical.

"Where are you going to go to college?" Donald asked.

"Smith-Reid, I think."

"You oughta come to Maryland. We party all the time, don't we, George?"

George had fallen asleep.

"I need to get back," Blondie said.

"Well, if there's anything else we can do...."

As soon as he opened the door to their room, Blondie's eyes were drawn to a girl sitting cross-legged on one of the unmade beds. She was wearing a tank top and a pair of panties, and sipping one of their beers.

"This is Marianne," Feller informed him. He was combing his hair in front of the mirror. Brick and Dispatch were sitting on Dispatch's bed, leaning against the wall and gawking at Marianne as if she were an apparition. Shakes was still passed out on the bed, limbs akimbo.

"Hello," Blondie said.

"Hello yourself," she responded.

Blondie couldn't believe it. A girl in their room—and she was cute. He shot Feller a questioning look.

"Go on and sit by her," Feller said.

Blondie walked over and sat down beside the girl. She had long dark hair and a trim body. Her breasts were small, but her nipples punctuated her cotton shirt in a provocative manner.

"Marianne's staying across the hall with some other girls," Feller said slowly, as if he thought Blondie might miss the significance of his words.

"With my sister Patty," she said.

"They go to Central Tech in Baltimore."

"We're Techies."

"Marianne likes her back rubbed," Feller continued.

Where the hell was Feller getting all this? Blondie hadn't been gone a half-hour.

"Rub her back, Blondie."

"Would you like your back rubbed?" Blondie asked Marianne.

"Oh, yes."

He began rubbing her back, beneath her shirt. Her skin was smooth and soft. Blondie felt himself becoming aroused.

"Ask her if she'd like her front rubbed," Feller said.

Blondie eagerly complied.

"Oh, no," she said. "I don't know you."

Blondie was pleased she wasn't offended.

There was a knock at the door. Dispatch got up and opened it. A piggy-looking girl with strawberry blonde hair marched in.

"What are you doing to my sister?" she demanded of Blondie.

"Rubbing her back," he answered blithely.

"Well, rub yourself."

Blondie felt too mellow to respond.

"Is that your sister?" Feller asked her. "I should have known. There's a real resemblance."

The newcomer took Feller's remark as a compliment and softened. Feller introduced everyone in the room except Shakes.

"My name's Patty," she said.

"Have a beer, Patty," Feller offered.

Patty liked the idea a lot and soon sat beside Marianne nursing a Pabst. Dispatch, pursuing a plan of his own, took a seat on the floor near Patty. Not even eleven o'clock and two girls in the room. Things were looking up, Blondie thought.

"Are there any more of you lovely ladies over there?" Feller asked.

"Two more of my friends," Patty responded.

Perfect, Blondie thought. Right across the hall.

A few more beers and Marianne and Patty became downright chummy. Marianne was letting Blondie kiss the back of her neck. Patty, mollified by alcohol, watched dreamily as Dispatch stroked her legs. Feller stood in one corner watching, a smile on his face.

A sudden creaking pulled all eyes to Shakes. He'd begun to twitch, a weird expression tugging his still-closed eyes. His lips moved, forming unspoken words. While the group watched, he turned onto his stomach and pulled his knees under him, pushing his backside into the air. With a self-satisfied moan, he cut loose a ferocious fart.

"My God!" Patty screamed. She jumped from the bed and dashed through the door. Marianne remained seated for a second or two as if in shock, then she too ran from the room.

Blondie smelled it next. His nostril hairs stood on end. His eyes began to water. He rushed to the window and pushed his head as far out into the sea air as he could without falling. Almost immediately, Blondie was pinned against the side of the window by Feller and Dispatch, also gasping for air. Blondie heard Brick begin to curse, then a thud. He assumed Brick had kicked Shakes in the ass.

Blondie felt outraged. Couldn't they ever pull anything off with any class? No wonder Grouper had pulled away. For a moment, Blondie wondered what he was doing. He had an uneasy feeling he'd let him down.

Later, as they were walking down the boardwalk, Dispatch claimed he'd seen Shakes' flatulence.

"You can't see a fart," Brick said.

"It was like a shimmering green fog. Really. If you looked closely, you could see it."

"It better be gone when we return," Brick said to Shakes.

Shakes, come alive, argued that it hadn't really been so bad.

"The paint's coming off the fucking walls," Brick replied.

"Be fair, Brick," Feller said, "the paint was already coming off the walls.

They were on their way to the beach to sunbathe. Feller had decided they were too pale to "get lucky."

"Girls like guys to look healthy," he'd argued.

Already, the day was a scorcher. The sun poached in the sky above, while, in the distance, ghost puddles danced across asphalt streets. No one was brave enough to go barefooted.

When they reached the beach, they spread their towels near a group of girls. Blondie felt the sun attack his skin as soon as he removed his shirt. Applying suntan lotion only made him feel like a French fry in hot lard.

Blondie glanced over at the girls. They were just average, but, realistically, Blondie figured average was about the best they'd do. Feller was the only one in the Club he considered good-looking and one attractive guy wasn't enough to bring home a bunch of beauties.

For the moment, thought, he wasn't worried about it. He was at the beach. The sun was out. There was nothing he had to do. Blondie shut his eyes and let his mind fall away.

Brick's voice in his ear brought him back.

"Look at Shakes," he said.

Brick had buried him in the sand. Only his face was showing.

"Does he know?" Blondie asked.

"No, he passed out again."

Blondie saw Feller gesturing at him from behind Brick.

"Let's take a walk," he mouthed without making a sound.

Feller headed away from the group and Blondie followed. Brick and Dispatch started to come as well, but Feller waved them back.

"Someone's got to watch out for Shakes," he told them.

When they were away from the others, Feller said, "We'll never score with the others around."

Blondie didn't tell Feller he wasn't concerned about it. He wouldn't have understood.

"Why don't we scout up what we can this afternoon and make our own arrangements for tonight?" he suggested.

When Blondie shrugged, Feller told him to walk ahead and whistle if he saw anything good coming.

"That will give me time to get my head in gear for the official presentation of our line."

"What's that?"

"We're two college freshmen—girls go for college guys—from Yale who just sailed down from New Haven on our dad's yacht."

"Do you think they'll believe we're college guys?" Blondie asked.

"How can they tell?"

Recalling Donald and George, Blondie realized Feller had a point.

It didn't matter anyway. He and Feller struck out. They talked to four different groups of girls and, while the girls seemed to enjoy their attention, they weren't interested in getting together later.

"For years, people have been telling me that high school guys and girls come to Ocean City over Labor Day to get laid," Feller griped. "Someone forgot to tell the girls."

"Maybe they have boyfriends back home," Blondie said.

"Maybe they're a bunch of lesbians."

Blondie flinched at the term—and Feller's use of it, almost as an obscenity. He'd been wondering whether to say anything to Feller about Grouper's "confession"—he felt he needed to share it with someone. Feller had just answered the question.

When Blondie and Feller got back to where they'd left the group, a circle of people was standing around their towels. Shakes lay in the middle, still buried in sand.

"C-can't move. P-paralyzed. B-bad b-beer. S-somebody h-help m-me."

"Oh, Jesus," Feller said. "Brick and Dispatch must've gone for a snack," Seven or eight adults, plus a couple small children, stared at Shakes curiously, as if he were a sea monster washed onto the shore. Blondie hurried over to him. His face looked like it had been scalded. Blondie began digging him out.

"C-cant m-move," Shakes repeated, near tears.

"Get hold of yourself, Shakes" he growled, embarrassed by the spectacle. "You're just buried in sand."

"Who d-did it?" Shakes asked angrily.
"Brick, I guess."
"Oh."
After they freed him, Blondie and Feller walked Shakes back to their hotel room. They found Brick and Dispatch with long faces.
"Nice going, guys," Feller scolded. "You went away and left Shakes buried on the beach."
"We've been robbed," Dispatch said.
"What do you mean?"
"Most of our beer is gone."
"What?"
"Yeah, there's just one case left. You know how long that will last."
"Who did it?" Feller demanded.
Dispatch shrugged.
Marianne bounced in, still in her underpants, sucking on a Pabst. Her eyes were manic.
"Where'd you get that beer?" Brick demanded.
Marianne walked over and sat down on the bed beside Blondie.
"Rub my back," she demanded.
Blondie couldn't resist.
"What are you doing, Blondie?" Brick reproached him, "These bitches stole our beer."
"Marianne," Blondie purred, "where'd you get that beer?"
"From Patty. She has a whole cooler full."
Brick stomped from the room and started pounding on the door across the hall.
"There's no one there now," Marianne said. "They locked me out, too."
"Where did you come from then?" Feller asked.
"The porch."
"Well, you tell that ugly sister of yours we want our beer back," Feller said.
"Not ugly," Marianne said with slurred words. "My big sister."

"Big sister?" Blondie asked. "How old are you?"

"Fourteen."

Feller slapped his forehead. Blondie quickly removed his hand from her back.

"You better go," he told Marianne.

"You're no fun," she accused before sulking from the room.

Blondie looked at Feller, who looked at Brick, who looked at Dispatch, who looked at Shakes.

"What do we do now?" Blondie asked. "One case of beer and we don't leave until day after tomorrow."

"L-let's drink what we've g-got," Shakes volunteered.

"Brilliant," Brick muttered.

Nonetheless, that's what they did, reminiscing about the past year and all their triumphs and misfires until one by one, they each nodded off. If the girls across the hall returned, no one heard them.

Chapter Thirty-Nine

They'd fucked up. Dispatch was the first to realize it. While they were still stumbling around in the afterglow of the previous night's indulgence, Dispatch reminded them it was Sunday.

"So what?" Brick said.

"Blue laws?" Feller asked.

"Blue laws," Dispatch answered.

Now Blondie remembered. It was illegal to sell alcoholic beverages in most Maryland counties on the Sabbath.

"How about Delaware?" Feller said.

"I don't know anything about Delaware cops—or courts," Dispatch replied.

"And I don't plan on finding out."

Dispatch was adamant.

"They s-sell b-beer in B-baltimore C-county on Sunday," Shakes offered.

"Christ, that's a three-hour drive each way," Dispatch said.

"Then you better get started," Brick ordered.

"Me? Why me? I didn't take the beer."

"You got the car. You got the card."

"I won't get back until after four," Dispatch argued.

"We can live without your company that long," Brick replied.

Thus began what ever after was known as "The Long Run."

Blondie begged off from breakfast when the others went. He felt like being alone. His head was full of thoughts he didn't want to share with anyone else, the main one being that he was finding their company taxing. He lay on his rumpled sheets facing the window. A faint breeze swayed the gauzy curtains back and forth. Tiny flecks of dust hung in the air and caught the light, blazing like miniature suns. A fly buzzed.

He didn't hear the soft footsteps until they were beside him. It was Marianne. She'd put on striped cotton shorts and wore a stiff white blouse. With her hair freshly washed and pulled back into a knot, she looked innocent, almost prim.

"Are you mad at me?" she asked Blondie.

"I'm not mad."

"My sister can be a real bitch."

Marianne paused, as if waiting for him to say something.

"Are you having a good time?" Blondie asked.

"Oh, yes," she said. "At least I think so."

"It's all right if you're not."

She sat down on the bed beside him.

"It's so hard to tell," she said.

Blondie considered it a profound statement.

"Do you want to rub my back?" she asked, brightening.

"Not this morning. Nothing personal. I have a headache."

It was true he had a headache. It was a lie that he didn't want to rub her back. But she was only fourteen. He had to draw the line somewhere.

"I'm sorry about the beer," Marianne said.

"It doesn't matter."

"Why don't you steal it back?"

"You haven't drunk it all?"

Blondie was amazed.

"No. Patty and our friends have been drinking rum."

"From Donald Duck."

"Yeah, he's nice."

Everyone to their taste, Blondie thought.

"Where is the beer?"

"In our closet. It's pretty warm."

Why not steal it back? Blondie didn't want any, but if the rest of the group did....

Retrieving it was easy. Marianne told Kitty her sister had locked her out of their room. Kitty, already or still in a boozy haze, delivered up a duplicate key. In no time, two cases of Pabst were hidden under Blondie's bed. Blondie couldn't suppress a wry smile at the thought of Dispatch driving all the way to Baltimore County for no reason.

"You won't tell your sister?"

"No, I like you."

Blondie wished she weren't fourteen.

"Thanks," Blondie said as she left. She was all right.

The guys were impressed when they returned from breakfast to find their purloined cases returned. After congratulating Blondie, they lit into the beer. It was flat from hours without refrigeration, but no one complained.

Around one, Feller suggested they'd better start "scouting" or they'd have another "nooky-less" night.

"You coming?" Feller asked Blondie.

Blondie shook his head.

"You got something up your sleeve?"

Blondie shook his head again.

Feller waited until the others had gone, then sidled over to him.

"It's about yesterday, isn't it?" he whispered. "You think you'll do better alone."

Blondie nodded to be agreeable. What could he say that Feller would understand? He just didn't have the heart for going through it again: pleading their case to some girls, being rejected, getting drunk, then acting as if something significant had occurred.

After Feller left, Blondie splashed some cold water on his face and put on his cutoffs and a tank top. Might as well look as skuzzy as the rest of the teens. He grabbed a sheet and some suntan lotion and headed for the far end of the beach. When he found an open space, Blondie smeared large quantities of the lotion all over his face, arms, torso and legs, then plopped down on the sand. He gave his mind over to the rise and fall of his chest, the warmth of the sun, the sound of the waves. One by one, the last snippets of thoughts fell away.

When Blondie woke, the shadow from a nearby pier covered him. He guessed it was about five o'clock. Time to reconnect with the guys.

They weren't at the *Georgian*. He briefly wondered where they'd gone. What if they'd met some girls and were having a grand time? Blondie realized he didn't care.

A growling in his stomach reminded him he hadn't had a thing to eat all day. He headed back toward the boardwalk. If he couldn't find the guys, at least he could get fed.

He was walking past a beachwear shop when a movement inside caught his eye. He stopped and peered inside. A girl was trying on a straw hat. She was wearing a white blouse and blue Bermudas. Her arms and legs were the color of honey and just as smooth. She stepped up to a mirror. It was Tammy. She was alone.

Blondie debated going in and speaking to her. He could say he'd just happened into the shop. He couldn't think of what he'd say next, so he continued on his way. But, when he reached the intersection, his legs rebelled. He couldn't just walk away. It was now or never. No matter what happened, he had to speak to her.

Blondie padded back up the cracked sidewalk. Just as he reached the shop, Tammy came out.

"Oh, hi, you're here," she said after a moment's hesitation.

"What a coincidence," Blondie responded.

He waited for her to walk away. She didn't. So he said something else. A second later, he'd forgotten what it was. He was sure it had been inane.

"I'm here with my folks," she said.

"Where are they?"

"They went out to eat with some friends and play bridge. They won't return before midnight."

Was he making that up or had Tammy just said she was alone for the evening? Blondie shook his head to make sure he wasn't hallucinating. Tammy gave him a curious look.

"Just clearing my head," he said.

"Do you have a cold?"

"No. I just have something in my head."

Good Christ, what was he saying?

"Did the rest of your group come?"

She knew about his group. That had to mean something.

"Isn't Paul Feller one of your friends?" she asked.

Did she have the hots for Feller?

"Why do you ask?"

"No reason."

He stood motionless for years. He could feel himself aging before her eyes, but he couldn't think of anything else to say.

"I was on my way to have some dinner," she said, turning to leave.

"Yeah, there's a nice little Mexican place not far from here."

A miracle. His tongue had come unstuck. Was it too late?

"I don't know it."

"I could take you."

"Okay."

That he was walking with Tammy, talking with her, going to dinner with her...it was beyond comprehension. Night after night, Blondie had fantasized being with her and now it was happening. He found it even more incredible, moments later, to be eating refried beans and enchiladas with her. It was as if they were a regular couple.

He wondered if she had any idea how she affected him? Her dark hair, her sloe eyes and crimson lips...no woman could ever have been this lovely. Not Helen of Troy. Not Elizabeth Taylor. Not even Sandra Dee. He was coming unglued.

Overhead, a wooden fan turned slowly, stirring the sultry air. Don't pass out, he told himself. Remember where you are. Remember *who* you are, he added. A college guy. Well, almost.

To hide his nervousness, Blondie asked Tammy about herself. He was surprised to observe that she, like he, was choosing her words with care. For a while, they spoke of high school and mutual acquaintances. She teased him about Phyllis, but backed away when she noticed his sour expression.

"She's not very pretty, is she?" Tammy said. "Not much personality either.

She's pretty dull."

Wasn't that what Phyllis had said about Tammy?

"I thought she was your friend."

Tammy shrugged.

Blondie mentioned he'd signed up for the draft.

"Do boys have to sign up?"

"There's a war going on," Blondie explained.

She'd never heard of Vietnam.

She told Blondie she was miffed at her parents for not buying her a car.

"I don't have a car of my own either and I'm a senior," Blondie said.

Tammy laughed.

"No. I'm a senior. You're a graduate."

"You're right, of course," Blondie agreed, laughing too.

She was appropriately impressed when he told her he was going to college, although she admitted she'd never heard of Smith-Reid.

"Are you planning to go?" he asked.

"I guess."
"You're not sure?"
"My folks want me to," she said.
"What do you want to do?"
"I don't know. Get a car."
A car? That was her goal?
"You know what I'd like?" Tammy said.
"What's that?"
"A beer. I haven't had one since I got here."
"I've got some beer," Blondie said, "but it's kinda flat."
"That's okay. I don't have much taste for it anyway. I just want to get a buzz on. You wouldn't believe how boring my folks are."

Outside, the sun had dropped below the rooftops. A firefly flitted past Blondie's eyes and disappeared among the new stars of the night. He took Tammy's arm and led her to the *Georgian*.

"I shouldn't go in," she told him. "It wouldn't look right. Me there with a room full of guys."

The room was still empty, although there were two more cases of beer stashed under the bed. Dispatch must have returned from the other side of the bay and left again. Blondie changed into jeans and a long-sleeved cotton shirt. He grabbed a can opener and a six-pack.

"Let's have one now," Tammy urged when he got back outside.
"Where?"
"Down the alley. Behind the hotel."

This wasn't the way he'd expected her to be, sneaking behind a building for a beer. But what the hell? Blondie pulled the church key from his pocket and opened the beer for her. It sprayed his shirt and she laughed. She took the beer and emptied it in three swigs.

"What now?" Blondie asked when she'd finished.

"Let's go back to my room and drink the rest of them," Tammy suggested.

Blondie was beginning to think he was making up the whole scene. She was inviting him to go with her alone to her room? To drink beer? His mind was doing cartwheels.

The sky was roseate by the time they reached her motel. At the door, Blondie leaned over and kissed her.

"I always figured you for shy," Tammy said.

"I am."

"You don't act it."

Tammy pulled a key from her shorts and let them in. The room was chilly from the air conditioner. She turned it off and jumped onto the double bed. Blondie popped open a beer for each of them and sat down beside her.

Tammy began talking about growing up in Fenton and the people she'd known. Blondie was interested at first. Her life was so different from his. She'd known the same people all her life. But, as she kept talking, Blondie began to wonder if the people in Fenton were *all* she knew or cared about.

"Don't you have a dream?" he asked after a while.

"Sure. I'd like to have a cherry red Corvette."

"I mean, don't you sometimes lie awake at night and picture yourself doing something extraordinary?"

"You mean like running around at the school picnic wearing a tee shirt with an obscene picture on it?"

Blondie blushed, then laughed. He'd asked for that. He *was* being awfully serious.

After another beer, Tammy rested her hand on his leg. Blondie felt like a warm drug had entered his blood stream. He began to feel amorous. He pulled Tammy to him and kissed her. She didn't resist. He did it again, longer.

"Do you like kissing me?" he asked her.

"Yeah. It feels good."

Blondie rubbed her back, pressing her against him. He could feel she was a little flat chested, but she was soft. Growing bold from the alcohol, Blondie ran his hands over her breasts. Tammy shivered, but didn't stop him. Her kisses grew more passionate.

When *was* she going to stop him? Nice girls were supposed to make a guy work for it. He didn't want her to hold out too long, of course, but she was supposed to show some resistance.

She never did.

Soon, they were making love with each other—passionately, even wildly. She thrust herself back at him with a willfulness that surprised him. Brick would have loved it. Dispatch would have loved it. Perhaps Feller would have loved it. Blondie didn't. Their lovemaking was more energetic than tender, more purposeful than spontaneous, more self-conscious than intimate. It was the last thing he would have expected. He'd fucked his dream girl and he still felt incomplete. He felt gypped.

"You don't seem happy," she said. "Isn't that what you wanted?"

What could he say? It wasn't her fault. She'd been trying to please him. She caught the look he was trying to hide. Her eyes flashed.

"I don't understand guys," she said. "They always expect something more."

"You mean there've been others?"

"Are you serious? You thought you were the first?"

She wasn't trying to be snotty, but her answer grated on him.

"Who?" He suddenly felt possessive.

"Why do you want to know?"

Blondie realized he'd put her on the defensive.

"I guess it's pretty dumb," he sighed. "I just thought you'd be a virgin."

Tammy put her arm across his chest and rubbed his side.

"Why is that so important to guys?"

It was a fair question. Was it an ego thing? Like being the first to scale a mountain? He knew that wasn't it for him. He just wanted sex to be *special*—and the only way it could be was if it were parceled out sparingly.

And, whether it was fair or not, girls were the ones who had to do the rationing. For sure, guys never would.

"There've only been two others," Tammy said after a few moments, trying to cheer him.

Blondie waited. He didn't want to ask, but he wanted to know.

"Bobby Clements..." Her chest heaved.

Of course, Bobby would have had her before him. Bobby would have always had things before Blondie. That didn't bother him. Perhaps if Bobby were still around....

"...and Merwin Fester."

So Barnwell had been telling the truth.

"How could you make love to a creep like Fester?" Blondie asked. "I'm sorry. I shouldn't have said that."

"It's okay. He is a creep."

"Then why....?"

"Because my parents detested him."

"You made love with someone to get at your parents?"

"Dumb, huh?"

Blondie didn't answer. He wanted to go. He told Tammy he needed to check in on Shakes, who'd gotten sick at the beach.

"Don't you want to split the last beer?" she asked him.

"Nah," he said, walking to the door. "You take it."

"I'm sorry it wasn't better for you," she said. "You're a nice guy."

"I'm sure we'll see each other again," Blondie said as he walked out the door. He knew it was a lie. He couldn't see her again. He had to retain some memory of the way she'd been when he'd first held her at that CYO dance—when she'd been *perfect*, the way only dreams can be.

It was dark now. Stars flickered like faraway torches. Blondie felt confused. He didn't know whether to be happy or sad. He'd gotten what he'd wanted, but it wasn't what he'd expected.

Halfway down the boardwalk, he ran into Shakes. He was the color of a tomato. His skin was peeling.

"I've b-been l-looking for you," he said.

"For *me*? Where have you guys been?"

"Tommy J-Jordan is h-having a p-party in his room."

"Who's Tommy Jordan?"

"He graduated l-last y-year. H-he's got l-lots of b-beer."

Why not get wasted? His brain was approaching meltdown anyway. Nothing that had happened since they arrived in Ocean City seemed to feel right. He felt like an alien interacting with earthlings, unable to connect.

Jordan's room turned out to be a small suite in a seedy hotel, the sitting area dimly lit by a bulb from the adjoining kitchenette. A Freddy Cannon album was blasted away on a portable phonograph, while shadow figures meandered through the murk. After his eyes adjusted Blondie was able to make out Feller, Brick, and Dispatch in one corner talking to a couple girls he'd never seen before.

Dispatch was pressing his cause with one of the girls. Blondie could tell because a look of alarm began to spread across her face. Brick sat cross-legged and shirtless on the sofa. He was shit-faced.

"Some fun," Blondie gibed when he got Feller alone.

"It's all we could find. There were some other girls here for a while, but they left."

Feller gave Blondie an inquisitive look.

"You have a strange look on your face."

"I ran into Tammy."

Feller arched his eyebrows.

"And?"

"She took me to her room."

Feller whistled.

"You must've gotten lucky," he said.

"No. Not lucky."

Blondie opened a beer. He'd just about finished it when Frank Purdy appeared. He was wearing a tattered tee shirt, ragged shorts, and a New York Yankees baseball hat.

"What's he doing here?" Blondie asked Feller.

"Oh yeah, I meant to tell you. Can you believe it? Ocean City is where he and Barnwell got their jobs."

A wave of anger washed over him. Purdy was invading his space. Blondie downed his beer and strode over to him.

"What rock did you crawl out from under?" he asked him.

"Fuck off, giraffe," Purdy retorted. "School's out. Let it rest."

Purdy wandered into the kitchen and took a beer from the fridge. Blondie followed him.

"Are you a friend of Jordan's?" Blondie challenged, as if he were a bouncer.

"What's it to you?"

Blondie straightened his back. He was three or four inches taller than Purdy. He could tell his aggressive behavior was making him nervous.

"You want some laughs?" Purdy said in an ingratiating tone.

Blondie stared at him.

"We've got Delores Clitoris down the hall naked."

"Who's we?"

"Me and Barnwell. He's making her right now. You want to see?"

Watching Buford Barnwell screw Delores was the last thing Blondie wanted to see, but something in Purdy's tone alarmed him. When Feller walked past, Blondie grabbed him.

"Purdy wants to show us something," he said. "I think we better take a look."

Purdy led them out of the suite and down the dark hallway. He knocked twice on the metal door, then turned the knob and pushed his way in.

The only light came from a flickering candle. Delores was lying naked on the bed, face down. Barnwell stood over her in his underwear, his hard, skinny body like knotted rawhide.

"Hey, no hard feelings, huh?" he said when he saw Blondie. He leaned to his left and nearly lost his balance.

"Buford drank nearly a whole fifth of brandy," Purdy boasted.

"What happened to her?" Blondie asked.

"She passed out a while ago."

"Hey, Blondie, you want to see something funny?" Buford asked.

Why was Barnwell being so friendly? Did he think he was cute? Was he trying to make peace with him?

Barnwell grabbed the brandy bottle from the floor. He lurched back toward the bed, held it over Delores and then tipped it so a small trickle of brandy ran down the small of Delore's back and into the dark cleft between her cheeks.

What was he up to? Blondie felt a worm of apprehension inch down his spine.

"Watch this..." Barnwell said. Before anyone could move, Barnwell pulled a book of matches from his pocket, struck one, and dropped it on Delores. A blue-and-orange flame flickered from the small of her back to her buttocks. An unearthly scream burst from her lips. Feller ran to her and smothered the flames with the bedspread.

Blondie flew at Barnwell. The last thing he remembered was the startled look on Buford's face. For a long time—it seemed like a long time—Blondie was aware of nothing but his intense rage and his flying fists and legs. It was a fury such as he'd never experienced before. A dam had burst inside.

Feller grabbed Blondie's arm and pulled him away.

"Stop, man, you're gonna kill him," he said.

Blondie was vaguely aware of Feller leading him back to the hotel and talking him into bed. Then, oblivion.

When he awoke, the *Georgian* was quiet and the room was dark. His face hurt, his body hurt, but his mind was still and clear, clearer than he could ever remember. More than clear—alert, *expectant*, as if awaiting some searing insight, some form of psychic surgery. But when the revelation came, it was more like a tap on the back of the head than the slice of a scalpel: *He wasn't having fun anymore.*

He wasn't having fun in spite of the fact that the Ocean City caper was already primo. Donald Duck and Gross George. Marianne and Patty. The Green Fog. The Long Run. Blondie knew the group would be regaling each other with stories about this trip for a long time to come. Yet the feeling the accompanied his thoughts about it was a tedium bordering on revulsion. He'd done it all before. He was burned out.

Looking back, it struck him that almost the entire past year had been devoted to entertaining himself—either through participating in the group's aimless escapades, or by diverting himself with romantic fantasies and heroic conceits. The conclusion was inescapable: He'd been afraid to face himself alone. Now that he felt he might be ready, he didn't know who he was. All he could say for sure was that he wasn't the same person he'd been the night before. That realization wasn't as frightening as he might have expected. After all, someone—or some *thing*—was inside his head looking out. But whatever that person or thing was, it lay beneath the personality he'd come to define as himself. It was both him and not him—a detached observer, clear-sighted, dispassionate. Was he really that free of his past? If so, perhaps he could choose who he wanted to be. But how did one go about that?

Blondie pondered the question until the first light of day unzipped the night. Then he felt a compulsion to flee the *Georgian's* confining walls. He to up and dressed without a sound.

Outside, ripples of pink gathered in the morning clouds as the sun struggled to lift itself from the sea. There was a chill in the air that raised the hairs on his legs and tickled his nose. A fine mist hung over the deserted boardwalk which, along with the lack of strollers, made it seem a long-abandoned trail through a jungle of shops, cafes and arcades. All was silent save for the slapping of his sandals against the planks and the sighing of the sea.

Blondie wandered with no destination in mind. He'd reached the end of a journey. The old lodestars—a girl, a gang, a good time—were useless. He would be going a new direction.

He began to see how completely focused he'd been upon himself. Because of it, he'd unintentionally hurt the people he cared most about—Flossie, Tammy, even Grouper. He'd treated them like cardboard cutouts from a little girl's book of dolls—dressing them and fitting them into the script of his life he was so busy creating. He'd viewed them as two-dimensional, with no depth, and when he'd finally seen them as they were, he'd abandoned them.

Blondie thought back the evening before with Tammy. Why had he found it so disappointing? Because he'd expected her to be as extraordinary in intellect and character as she was in appearance? Because he'd built her up to such mythic proportions in his mind she had no chance of satisfying him?

He hadn't been fair. She'd never read his script, "The Way I'd Like Things to Be," so how could she have played the part he'd assigned her? He had no right to be disappointed in her. If he were going to be consistent with Grouper's notion that people should operate as "free agents"—and he wanted to be—he had to accept its corollary: *other people would follow their agendas, not his.* And he had to learn to accept them for doing so, no one more than the Grouper. The sting of self-reproach and a commitment to tell him as soon as he returned accompanied the thought.

On the positive side, Blondie credited himself with drawing a line with Buford. He would not participate in, nor passively stand by and tolerate, the abuse of another human being. Knowing that pointed toward a new definition of himself. From now on, he would be a person who *stood for things*...like kindness and decency toward others. It wasn't a complete definition. Blondie was sure he could add a lot to it, would add a lot to it, but it was a start.

And no more fantasies! What else had Grouper said? You had to destroy the myths, be a *free agent*. It sounded kinda scary, but it had the gritty feel of truth.

Blondie stopped at a gap between two fast-food joints and looked out to sea. Wave after white-capped wave stretched away to the horizon. He raised his eyes to the sky. It was a parfait of cream, pink, salmon, ivory.

Was there a God in heaven? He couldn't care less.

Chapter Forty

Framed by the boundaries of the P-mobile's rear-view mirror, the ramshackle clutter of Ocean City receded from Blondie's view until it was no more than a whitish mound—like an accumulation of bird droppings. Blondie found the comparison particularly apt insofar as the last sign of the town was a mosquito-like cloud of gulls wheeling on the horizon, about to begin their day's work of cleansing the boardwalk of discarded taffy wrappers, mishandled French fries and half-eaten hot dog buns.

The gang was abuzz, galvanized by Blondie's late-night fisticuffs.

"You cl-cleaned B-buford's cl-clock," Shakes said admiringly.

"Surprised the shit out of me," Brick allowed, in an attempt at praise.

"Yeah, that was something," Feller added. "I think you broke his nose."

"I b-bet h-he won't f-fuck with the B-b and F Club anymore."

Blondie appreciated their praise, but it almost seemed as if they were viewing his triumph, if that's what it was, as a *group* victory. What had *they* done? None of them had joined the fray. Nursing a face of scattered bruises, minor cuts, and periodic throbs and pulses, Blondie didn't feel like according them any credit.

Claudine Clark was wailing on the radio about "Party Lights" of various colors. Yeah, well, he'd seen the party lights last night. In fact, he'd been chasing those lights all year. But he suspected he wouldn't be looking for any soon.

"Why so quiet, Blondie?" Feller asked.

"My head hurts."

Well, that was true, wasn't it? But that wasn't what was bothering him most. He felt as if he has just broken up with someone. But whom? He'd already called it off with Flossie. And he'd never gone with Tammy in the first place. What was going on?

The P-mobile sped ever westward as the landscape slid away. He felt a reluctance to return to Fenton. It wasn't his town. It never would be. At the same time, he felt a need to talk to the Grouper. He needed to patch things up with him. He was the only one who would understand what was going on with him. He needed his friend back.

When the guys dropped him off in front of his house, Blondie felt relieved. He hadn't had anything to say to them for a hundred miles. He just wanted a place to be quiet and relax. To lick his wounds. And think. Blondie saw right away that both his parents' cars were beneath the carport. Everyone would be home.

Blondie eased the front door open. His mom stood before him, dusting the downstairs banister. She turned as he stepped inside. When she saw him, she clapped her hand to her mouth.

"It's all right, mom. I just had a little accident. It's nothing to worry about. I just need to rest a while."

Please, please, please, he prayed, don't make me explain.

As if she'd heard him, her quizzical expression turned to one of concern.

"You go up and lie down until you feel better," she said. "Dinner will be in about an hour."

Even the pillow hurt his face, so Blondie lay on his back. He must have dozed off. The next thing he knew, his mom was calling him to dinner. When he entered the kitchen, his mom and dad were already seated.

Neither of them asked about his face. Blondie considered it a sign of newfound respect, though he didn't know why anything would have changed. Because he'd turned eighteen? Because he was off to college soon?

The atmosphere in the kitchen felt freer and easier to Blondie than it had for quite a while. Several times, his dad made comments that led to brief flurries of conversation between him and his mom. Their truce seemed to be holding. He was glad to see it. If his parents couldn't get it together after eighteen-plus years, what hope was there for any relationship? Besides, he wanted his family to stay together.

After they'd finished eating, his dad picked up a copy of *The Mayhew Courier* and riffled through the pages. When he reached the back, he furrowed his brow and glanced over at Blondie.

"That large boy you hang around with...."

He didn't finish the sentence.

"Grouper?"

Blondie didn't like the look on his dad's face.

"Isn't his last name Whipple?"

An alarm went off inside Blondie's mind. He asked his dad to show him what he was reading. It was an obituary notice: "Walter Clarence Whipple Jr., 18, son of Mr. and Mrs. Walter Clarence Whipple Sr. of Rock Creek Road, died unexpectedly yesterday evening. A funeral service, open to all who knew Walter, will be held Saturday, Sept. 8, at 3:00 p.m. at Simpson's Mortuary."

Last night. The same night he'd been making love with Tammy. "Died unexpectedly"? Blondie had no doubt what that meant. His biggest surprise was that he wasn't really surprised.

Like the tumblers of a lock falling into place, the clues came together in his mind. Grouper's speech at graduation. His lack of concern about where he was going to college. His confession to him. Why he hadn't accompanied them to Ocean City. It was obvious now. Grouper had known he was going to check out. But why? Just because of his *difference*. Hadn't Blondie tried to be understanding? Hadn't he?

"I'm sorry, son. It must be quite a shock."

For a moment, Blondie felt as if the air had been sucked from his chest, the hope drained from his heart. He realized that Grouper had represented all that Blondie found right with the world. Then he felt a surge of anger. What had become of Grouper's rhetoric about the importance of living life true? What truth was there in giving up? What was the value of being a "free agent" if one checked out of the game?

He went upstairs to his room and tried to sort through his emotions. Finally, he quit trying to make sense of them and, one by one, they faded away until nothing remained but a sorrow the size of the ocean. Blondie sobbed until his chest ached.

After a long time, his mom knocked on his door and told him he had a call. It was Feller.

"Have you heard?" Paul asked.

Blondie said he'd seen the article.

"Any idea what it was?" Feller asked.

"What's that?"

"What he died of," Feller said.

"Loss of faith."

"What?"

"No, I don't know."

Blondie wasn't going to betray Grouper's confidence. The rest of the guys could think what they wanted.

"You going to his funeral?" Feller asked.

"Sure. Are you?"

"Yeah. I'll let everyone else know."

Blondie was glad Feller had volunteered. He didn't think he could talk about Grouper's death with anyone else.

The next few days were torture. He couldn't stop thinking about the Grouper and blaming himself for what happened.

Thursday morning, Feller called and asked Blondie if wanted to shoot some pool that evening. Blondie didn't feel like it, but he needed to do something to get his mind off the Grouper.

Feller picked him up in a new Oldsmobile Cutlass.

"Surprise," he said. "It's a belated graduation present from my folks."

Blondie whistled.

The poolroom was empty. The new school year at Fenton High had begun. He and Feller shot a few games, but Blondie's heart wasn't in it and he lost almost every one.

"Boy, it's getting you down, isn't it?" Feller said.

Blondie noted that Feller seemed about the same as he always did. But then, he'd always been better at "maintaining an even keel," as he put it.

"Let's grab a six and go up to the Overlook," Feller suggested after a while.

Blondie hesitated. That had been Grouper's place. He decided Grouper wouldn't mind.

A faint mist blurred the lights of town from the Overlook. It seemed as if they were parked at the edge of a broad shallow lake and Fenton lay just below the surface.

Feller chitchatted about the Orioles and the Colts as they downed a couple beers. Blondie felt he had something else on his mind, but he didn't press him.

"Look, Blondie," Feller finally said. "I've decided not to go to Smith-Reid after all. I don't think it's fair to ask my parents to put up so much money."

"They just bought you a new car," Blondie pointed out.

"That's what I mean. They can't afford a new car *and* a high-priced college."

"So you took the car."

Blondie regretted his comment. But he couldn't help feeling he'd been sold out.

"So where will you go?" he asked.

"To Maryland, with the rest of the guys. It's a lot closer to home."

"What about your photography? You said Smith-Reid had a much stronger photography department."

"Well, yeah, but how much do you learn from school anyway? So much of it is hands-on once you get a job."

Why was he arguing with Feller? He'd made up his mind. He wanted to be with his high-school friends. He wanted to be close to Fenton. In spite of all Feller's big-time talk, Blondie realized, at heart, he was a small-town guy.

"But hey, you were accepted at Maryland, too." Feller grabbed Blondie's arm. "There's still time to change your mind. Why don't you come with us? It would be great. Just like old times."

Blondie was tempted. Feller's decision not to go put a whole new face on Smith-Reid. Could he cut it alone? What fun would it be? And the thought of recapturing "old times" had a certain appeal.

"I'll think about it."

That cheered Feller. He began to reminisce about high school as if it were already years away. The night at the submarine races with Susan Conner and Jump-em Johnson. The visit to the burlesque house in Baltimore. The time the Bear suspended them from school. Facing down old man Caldane. The big fight at the quarry. Prom night. The trip to Ocean City. The night Grouper died and came back to life.

"I guess he won't be coming back this time, huh?" Feller asked when he realized what he'd said.

No, Blondie thought, the big fellow won't be coming back. His throat felt too tight to say anything for a long while. And then, all he could think to say was, "I guess summer's over, huh?"

Saturday dawned with the threat of rain. High clouds gathered and folded into a gray massif. The wind began to howl.

Blondie dressed in one of his father's dark suits. It was big enough in the shoulders, but his sleeves stuck out and the pants, even after his mom let them down, stopped a couple inches above his shoes. But he couldn't see buying a suit he'd never wear again. He knew Grouper would understand. It wasn't from a lack of respect.

When he left the house, Potter was planting a new shrub in his front lawn. He looked up and, for a moment, his eyes met Blondie's. Blondie was surprised to find in them a trace of empathy, as if he knew where Blondie were going. Was that possible? Then, almost imperceptibly, Potter nodded. Blondie was so surprised he could think of no response until he was well on his way to the funeral. But he promised himself the next time he saw Potter, he would nod back. Maybe his dad was right. Maybe there was a human being inside. One thing was certain. You never could tell about people.

Simpson's Mortuary was on the road north toward Philadelphia. It was a two-story brick building with white columns and a white cupola, and it was protected from the world of the living by a fence of iron spikes. A smattering of cars sprinkled the lot when Blondie arrived. The P-mobile was one of them. Rain began to fall as Blondie dashed inside.

The service was in a chapel in the east wing of the building. One wall was stained glass that, even on this dark day, tinted all inside with swatches of gold, rose and aquamarine. Dominating the front was an enormous casket of black-lacquered wood trimmed in pewter and surrounded by vases of gladioli. The lid was propped open, revealing a pink satin lining.

Looming above the first row of pews, Blondie saw the broad shoulders and fleshy head of Mr. Whipple. A large woman sat beside him, her head covered by a dark hat and veil. Blondie presumed it was Grouper's mom. Feller and the rest of the guys sat in a pew several rows behind. They all were dressed as somberly as he and seemed uniformly nervous and uncomfortable.

Blondie walked slowly toward the casket. As he drew closer, the awesome body of the Grouper appeared. He was dressed almost as if for a wedding in a dark three-piece pinstriped suit with a forest green ascot at his throat. Blondie was amazed at how lifelike he looked. There was no mark, no discoloration, to indicate any misfortune had befallen him. His face seemed serene, with none of its former pinkish-purple coloring. He could have been sleeping.

When Blondie reached the side of the casket, he looked down at the boy-man he'd come to love. He was glad his eyes were shut. He wasn't sure he could have faced those deep dark eyes.

He whispered to him, "Was your life so hopeless? Couldn't you have held out?" Then, "What about me?"

How could Grouper consider suicide a right? It was too selfish to be a right. How about those left behind? How about their rights? Their right not to be left friendless. Their right not to be left burdened with guilt and remorse.

After a few moment, Blondie walked back and joined the rest of the Club.

Shortly, a cherub-faced man with white hair and a white collar entered the room from a small door in the rear. He seemed pleased to be there.

"My dear fellow Christians," he intoned, annoying Blondie with his presumption. "We are here to bid farewell to a young man God has called before his time."

Who called whom? Hadn't Grouper made the call?

The minister praised Grouper as a "good God-fearing lad." Blondie wished Grouper could hear him. He could imagine Grouper, even now, scoffing at such malarkey.

After several minutes of eulogy, the preacher asked the assembly to join in the Lord's Prayer. Blondie surprised himself by repeating the minister's words.

"Consistency was never one of my strong points," he silently apologized to Grouper.

After the minister finished his remarks, Mr. Whipple rose from a seat in the front row. He was wearing a suit similar to his son's. When he began, he seemed stern and in control, but, as he began to speak, a perplexed look overtook his face.

"Mrs. Whipple and I want to thank all of you for coming," he said. "As you may know, Walter was our only child." His voice cracked. "Everyone who knew him loved him. We loved him. I'm not sure he knew that."

He paused and took several deep breaths.

"We were very proud of Walter. He was quite bright and extremely gentle."

Mr. Whipple looked out at the crowd, as if seeking absolution.

"We only wanted what was best for him."

His voice broke and he sat down. Mrs. Whipple put her hand on his sleeve and patted his arm.

Grouper had been wrong about his folks. They *had* loved him.

After a while, people began to look around. The minister rose from his seat and said, "The service is over. Please feel free to pay your last respects to Walter."

Feller and the rest of the gang shuffled toward the casket. Blondie looked for some sign of emotion from them, but each seemed as stiff as a robot. He realized they had no idea what to do. The death of someone close was a new concept. For him, too.

When Mr. Whipple passed his seat, he gave him a lingering glance. Blondie took it as an invitation. He rose and followed him into the foyer.

"You're the one they call Blondie, aren't you?" He seemed ill at ease. "I mean you must be, with your coloring." He laughed awkwardly. "Can I speak with you a second?"

Mr. Whipple led him to a corner of the hallway.

"Walter left a note," he said, looking around as if he were afraid someone might overhear.

Blondie stared into Mr. Whipple's eyes—the ones Grouper had once referred to as "cold lawyer's eyes"—and saw only grief.

"There were just two words: 'Ask Blondie.' Do you know what Walter meant by that?"

The words cut him like a dagger. Was Grouper accusing him? Blondie couldn't believe that. Grouper would never have been so cruel. Or was Grouper asking him to try and explain to his parents why he'd done it? He wasn't sure they'd understand no matter what he said. More likely, anything he said would add to their grief. Blondie resented the note. He refused to be Grouper's apologist for an act he considered unwarranted.

Blondie felt Whipple's eyes upon him like the grasp of a drowning man.

"I'm sorry, Mr. Whipple," Blondie said. "I don't know what Walter meant."

Whipple seemed both disappointed and relieved. Blondie knew he'd been hopeful Blondie could shed some light on his son's tragic decision, but, even more, fearful Blondie would deliver a devastating judgment from his dead son.

"Thank you," he said and walked away.

Feller appeared at his side, accompanied by the others.

"What was that about?" Feller asked him.

"He thought I might know something."

"It wasn't a heart attack or anything like that, was it?" Feller asked.

"No."

"At first, it never occurred to me that he would.... well, you know."

Feller struggled to say more. He couldn't seem to find the next word.

"Why should it have?" Blondie asked.

"I never thought he was *that* unhappy." Feller said. The rest of the gang was listening intently. "We thought we'd go somewhere and talk."

"Where?"

"How about the bowling alley?"

The bowling alley? Blondie said okay, though he knew he had no intention of going there.

"See you later," Blondie said. "I want to get out of these clothes."

"Yeah. That's what we all thought. These aren't what you'd wear up there," Feller said, pointing to his suit.

Sheets of rain washed over the lot as Blondie fought his way to the Pontiac. He was drenched and shivering by the time he got inside. He turned on the heat as soon as the motor was warm, fogging all the windows.

What the hell, he thought, he might as well wait until the rain eased. He leaned back against the seat and tried to relax.

September again. One year since he'd started Fenton High. One year since he'd met Feller, Shakes, Brick, Dispatch—and the Grouper. He'd needed them so much. He'd given the Club his heart and soul. Now, he had a choice to make. Stay with them and go to the University of Maryland, or cut the cord and go to school out of state.

The idea of attending Smith-Reid alone was scary. He wouldn't know anyone. But Blondie knew if he went to the university, it would be taking the easy way out. It would be doing what everyone else did. It would be just the same as staying in Fenton. Grouper would never approve. Blondie wanted something different, something bigger, and he knew he'd never find it with the B & F Club.

He remembered Grouper's words that last night at the Overlook: *"You can't be a kid forever."*

Smith-Reid was it.

Blondie started the car.

Epilogue

An August night, 1974.

Blondie looked across the hood at Feller. He felt an emotion akin to love for the one who, seemingly millions of memory-years ago, had been the Club Poet and official Namer of Names. He wondered what Feller was thinking as he gazed up at the night sky.

Blondie wanted to speak to Feller, to say something that would join them together in the kind of conspiratorial brotherhood they'd shared. But he hadn't spent any time with Feller for twelve years now. Not since the last big sortie to Ocean City.

All Feller had said was, "Let's drive out to Grouper's Overlook tonight." When Blondie had asked him why, he'd just said, "for old times' sake." But there wasn't any overlook from the familiar dirt road. Someone had bought the open pasture and planted corn on it. Until it was harvested, it would not be possible to look down at the lights of Fenton as they once had.

It seemed absurd as Blondie thought about it—two grown men hanging out beside a 1962 Cutlass in the middle of some farmer's crop. What was Feller trying to do? Bring back old memories of the B and F Club parked in some lonely lane, drinking beer, regaling each other with preposterous stories?

They were too old for that—both thirty. Too old to be trusted by the Woodstock generation. What they were doing was kid stuff, a shameless hanging on to the past.

The sun had gone down hours ago. Feller was no more than a faint silhouette against the starlit sky. Still, Blondie could trace with his eyes the sharp lines of Feller's profile...his high straight forehead, sharply etched cheekbones, perfect nose and chin.

Feller had been silent for a long time. His face remained turned to the sky and into the net of stars night had cast upon it. Blondie followed his gaze to the Big Dipper and ran his eyes along its handle, then outward into the Milky Way's dusty congestion.

A burst of light illumined Feller's face and Blondie saw on it a sad look. What *was* he thinking?

Feller extinguished the match and took a long drag from the joint he'd just lit. Marijuana. Blondie had never considered pot legit. How could it be when flower children used it? The Grouper, if he were still around, would have scoffed at them, if not lashed them with a long-winded dissertation on the merits of Pabst's Blue Ribbon beer.

Still, when Feller passed him the glowing cylinder, Blondie took it and inhaled.

Blondie didn't expect anything to come of smoking it. He'd never been able to get off on the stuff before. Nonetheless, from politeness, he took a drag each time Feller passed the joint his way.

"You finish it," Feller finally said in a voice choked by smoke.

Blondie took two more drags and threw the roach onto the dirt road. There was a brief glow, then only darkness.

A breeze whipped up and began scurrying through the stalks of corn, making a sound like the blended murmurs of a cocktail party. Blondie began to feel lightheaded. He flashed on the thought that he was getting high after all and, then, that there were voices in the cornfield calling to him. He felt a chill in the upper part of his back, between his shoulder blades.

"Do you remember...?" Feller asked. Blondie didn't even know if Feller finished the question because suddenly he began to remember it all—the B and F Club, the Pussymobile, the sorties, Miss Darlington, *her*.

"You mean..." he began to Feller, and Feller said, "Yeah" and that's the way the conversation went for a long time. Later, Blondie wondered if they'd been so closely attuned or just whacked out of their gourds—but not then. Blondie was sure Feller was thinking the same things he was. It was eerie.

Eventually, Blondie realized the moon had risen from behind the trees at the end of the field, a silver sliver. Some of Fenton's lights had gone out. Blondie couldn't remember how long he and Feller had been there. He couldn't remember the last time either of them had spoken. He couldn't remember why they'd come. He felt entranced by the darkness. The quiet. The cannabis.

"Have you kept up your photography?" he asked Feller, to break the spell.

"Not really."

To Blondie's surprise, there was trace of regret in his voice. He'd seemed so pleased to present Barbara to him when he'd picked him up at the airport. She was a bright, cheerleader type Feller had met at Social Security headquarters in Baltimore where he worked as a program analyst or policy analyst or something like that. They had two girls—seven and three.

Blondie was a bit envious. He was still unmarried with no prospects in sight.

"You've got a good situation," he said to Feller. "I think a family would be nice."

"Yeah. Mary and Shelly are peaches, too." Feller's voice ignited in a burst of enthusiasm. "Still, it's not what I expected."

"What did you expect?"

"More adventure, I guess."

"You can't have everything."

"No."

Again, Feller was quiet for a while.

"That's what's such a bitch about life," Feller said. "The tradeoffs."

"You have to choose."

"I never felt like I did. Everything seems to have just happened."

Blondie sensed his friend's distress. He stepped closer to Feller and put his arm around him.

"You've got your freedom," Feller said. "You stuck with your dream."

That was true. He'd become a writer—of sorts. He'd studied journalism at Smith-Reid, spending the summers as a cub reporter at the local weekly. When he'd graduated he'd been offered a job as a reporter with a larger newspaper in the western part of the state. He was still there, now editor of the editorial page. No money in it, and he was hardly Woodward or Bernstein, but he was a writer.

Flat feet had kept him out of the war. A family had done the trick for Feller.

"It was good for a while though, wasn't it?" Feller asked.

Blondie nodded. As stupid as that whole year at Fenton High often seemed in retrospect, it had been the most meaningful of his life.

After a while, Feller relaxed. "I feel dumb."

"Don't worry about it."

Blondie dropped his arm. Again they fell silent.

"Someday, you should write it all down," Feller said after a while.

"What?" Blondie hadn't been paying attention.

"About the B and F Club. About what happened."

Had it been that remarkable, Blondie wondered. Or had they merely repeated the frantic and senseless antics of millions of other adolescents?

But Feller's question again pushed him back in time. He could sense the ghosts in the air around him—the B & F Club. He tried to remember what had become of them all. Well, he had a fair idea.

Shakes had married Janine Raznosky after all and now prepared blueprints for an engineering firm in Baltimore. Dispatch had disappeared, leaving Meryl to play the role of abandoned wife. According to Feller, she did it well. Brick had remained single and become the football coach at Percy Junior High—after a tour of Vietnam and some souvenir shrapnel. Then, as always, there was Grouper....

After the funeral, Mrs. Whipple sent him a note thanking him for attending. She enclosed a photograph she'd found on Grouper's dresser. It was a picture of him and Grouper at graduation, arms around each other, beaming at the camera as if they'd just won the Reader's Digest Sweepstakes.

Remorse stabbed him then and periodically ever since. Why had he moved his hand that night at the Overlook? How much had that small, unthinking gesture played in Grouper's fateful decision? Blondie hated to think about it. He wanted to tell Grouper "his aberration" didn't matter to him anymore. He wasn't even sure it had mattered much then. *Why did you have to be so damned sensitive?*

And Tammy. Feller told him she'd married a guy who'd graduated from Fenton several years before them, a lawyer and a member of the Fenton City Council. He said he saw her once in a while when he came to visit his parents and that she still looked good, but acted "kind of subdued."

When he thought about his own life, Blondie wasn't too disappointed. He enjoyed what he was doing at the paper. He went out with women now and then and had a good time. Sometimes, a combustible mixture of alcohol, lust and hope would ignite and he'd imagine himself in love. But it never lasted. His mother told him he was too particular.

Blondie conceded there was some truth in her words, although he wasn't sure why it was so. He sometimes wondered if it had anything to do with Grouper. Perhaps the closeness he and Grouper had developed—the *simpatico*—had been so unique as to preclude finding it again with anyone. He even considered that Grouper had sensed something about him that kept him from completely connecting with a woman—some fatal disenchantment—and mistaken it for something else.

If he had such a flaw, Blondie found it more plausible that it had originated with Tammy and the dream he'd woven around her. A dream that even now shaded his female relationships and ultimately turned them gray.

"Anyway, it's not like it's all over," Feller remarked, breaking into Blondie's thoughts. "I mean, most of our lives are still ahead."

Feller was right. Why were they wallowing in times past? Why were they acting as if they'd missed the last train to happiness? It was pointless, self-indulgent, defeatist.

He was hardly devoid of hope. At times, he still felt the powerful emotions of youth. Every once in a while, one of the old songs would come on the radio and Blondie would reexperience that frightening, giddy feeling that any minute something unexpected and wonderful might happen.

He looked down at the faint glare of Fenton again, then back up at the stars, and, when he shut his eyes, a shower of lights cascaded over his closed eyelids. He could see the sparks fall from that mirrored ball at his first CYO dance and hear the Lettermen's voices soft but clear in his mind:

> *Someday, when I'm awfully low and the world is cold,*
> *I will feel a glow just thinking of you*
> *and the way you look tonight.*

Tammy was looking up at him the way she had that night...her dark, surprised eyes, her smooth alabaster skin, her crimson lips. Then, the dance was over. The Lettermen's last harmony faded into the night, and, again Blondie heard the echo of Grouper's voice: *Nothing hooks the romantic soul like the unattainable.* And he knew he was forever lost.

Afterword

Grouper's Laws

1. Only an asshole takes advice from an asshole.
2. A beer is a man's best friend.
3. A woman's virtue is often a matter of circumstance.
4. Only assholes fall in love.
5. Nothing hooks the romantic soul like the unattainable.
6. Never go calling with mouse in hand.
7. Life is a shocking proposition.
8. Never, ever, conduct business with a billy.
9. One man's dog is another man's queen.
10. Never assume the road ahead is straight.
11. Everyone is desperate for love.
12. Life is consequences.
13. It's easy to be noble in advance.
14. People die.
15. With ugly girls, you always have to lie.
16. Most of us will never recover from high school.
17. Hell hath no fury like a wimp's fears.
18. You can't be a kid forever.

ABOUT THE AUTHOR

D. Philip Miller is a speechwriter for a major Northwest corporation and lives with his wife in Issaquah, Washington.